"It won't work."

"What won't?" Thalia asked. She had the nerve to look innocent.

"Trying to convince me to take the part. It won't work."

He had her full attention—and that was becoming a problem. Her eyes were wide-open, her lips were barely parted. All he'd have to do was lower his head.

Against his every wish, his head began to dip.

He could *not* kiss her; he could *not* be turned on by her; he could *not* be interested in her—but he was. She was going to ruin the life he'd made, and he almost didn't care. It was almost worth the way she looked at him, soft and innocent and waiting to be kissed.

Almost.

Dear Reader,

Welcome to the Bar-B Ranch, home of one of the hottest heroes I've written, J.R. Bradley. J.R. has a secret, you see—he used to be James Robert Bradley, the hottest actor to come out of Hollywood since Brad Pitt. But he gave up the fame and money—along with the constant scrutiny and pressure—when he bought his own ranch and a whole bunch of cows.

Since then, J.R. has been—well, he wouldn't call it hiding, but you get the idea. He's got peace, quiet, cows and a surrogate family he trusts with his life. Yup, he's got everything he ever wanted. Or so he thinks.

Into this carefully constructed life rolls Thalia Thorne, a producer looking for James Robert Bradley to star in a new Western movie. J.R. says *no* in no uncertain terms—but then a blizzard forces both of them to reconsider their positions. While the temperatures plummet outside, things inside get very hot. Suddenly J.R. finds himself questioning his entire existence. When the ground thaws, will he let Thalia leave? Or will he go with her?

A Real Cowboy is a hot story of accepting the past and redefining the future. I hope you enjoy reading it as much as I enjoyed writing it! Be sure to stop by www.sarahmanderson.com and join me when I say long live cowboys!

Sarah

At least it wasn't snowing right now, she told herself in a forcibly cheerful tone as she glanced at the car's thermometer. It was twenty-two degrees outside. Not that cold, really. She had that going for her. Of course, that didn't include the wind chill, but still. It wasn't like it was subzero out there. She could handle it.

Finally, she passed under a signpost that proclaimed Bar B Ranch, which also announced trespassers would be shot. The Camry's wheels bounced over a metal grate a part of her brain remembered was called a cattle guard. She checked the address she'd entered into her phone's GPS, and a sense of relief bum-rushed her. She was actually in the right place.

This realization buoyed her spirits. James Robert Bradley's agent, a small, nervous man named Bernie Lipchitz, dn't wanted to give up the address on his most famous— most private—Oscar-winning client. Thalia had been ed to promise Bernie she'd give his latest would-be starlet e in the new movie she was producing, *Blood for Roses*. f course, it was her movie only as long as she could get s Robert Bradley signed for the part of Sean. If she n't do that…

time to dwell on the worst-case scenario. She was excellent progress. She'd tracked down Bradley's bouts, which was no easy task. She'd gotten onto his —so far, without anyone shooting at her. Few people im to have gotten this close to Bradley since he'd ed from Hollywood after winning his Oscar almost rs ago. Now she had to sign him to the comeback fetime. Easy, right?

ck on the dash said four o'clock, but the sun was ing, shooting brilliant oranges and purples across sky. *Beautiful,* Thalia thought as the colors lit up dscape. Off to what she thought was the north of low hills that merged with taller mountains he south and east were as flat as a pancake.

A REAL COWBOY

BY
SARAH M. ANDERSON

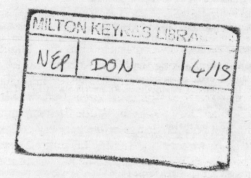

MILLS & BOON

Published in Great Britain 2013
by Mills & Boon, an imprint of Harlequin (UK) Limited,
Eton House, 18-24 Paradise Road, Richmond, Surrey TW9 1SR

© Sarah M. Anderson 2013

ISBN: 978 0 263 90470 3
ebook ISBN: 978 1 472 00594 6

51-0413

Harlequin (UK) policy is to use papers that are natural, renewable and recyclable products and made from wood grown in sustainable forests. The logging and manufacturing processes conform to the legal environmental regulations of the country of origin.

Printed and bound in Spain
by Blackprint CPI, Barcelona

To Robert and Nan...
a woman could ask for. Yo...
your family, but even if I...
I would have cho...

She could almost see it in the full bloom of spring. The land was beautiful.

Maybe we could do some of the filming here, she thought as she rounded a bend and saw a massive structure that would have been called a log cabin, except *cabin* didn't do it justice. She couldn't tell if the huge, rough-hewn logs rose up two stories or three, and she also couldn't tell how far back the building went. Behind it were a number of barns—some with an old, weathered look, others made of gleaming metal. Except for the shiny metal buildings, everything looked like it had been on this patch of land for decades. If not centuries.

She didn't see a single living thing. Not even a dog ran up to greet her as she pulled in front of the house. A wide covered porch offered some protection from the wind.

Well, she wasn't going to get anyone signed to anything by sitting in a car. Gathering up all of her positive energy, she opened the door.

The icy wind nearly slammed the door shut on her leg and cut right through her patterned tights. *Dang,* she thought as she pushed against the door. Sure, it had been cold when she'd left the small airport terminal in Billings, Montana, to get into the car—but it hadn't been this cold. Suddenly, the knee-high boots and tights under the wool dress didn't seem like a smart business outfit making a concession to winter. They seemed like the definition of foolishness.

Bracing herself against the wind, she pulled the fur-lined collar of her wool trench coat up around her neck and trudged up the porch steps. *Please be home,* she thought as she looked for the doorbell. Her coat was not rated for this kind of weather.

Another blast of winter rushed up the back of her skirt, making her teeth chatter. Where was the doorbell? *Screw it,* she thought, pounding on the door in a most unprofessional way. Manners didn't matter when she was freezing to death.

No one answered.

Freezing to death—in Montana, of all places—wasn't on her to-do list today. Thalia couldn't remember being this cold, not even when she was a kid and spent all day playing in the rare snowstorm in Oklahoma. She'd lived in L.A. for the last ten years, for crying out loud. People there complained of the cold when it got below sixty.

Thalia banged on the door again, this time with both hands. Maybe someone was in there, she reasoned. The house was huge. Maybe they were in a room way in the back. "Hello?" She shouted, but the wind wasn't done with her yet.

No one came.

Okay, time to regroup. What were her choices? She could stand here on the porch until someone showed up, at the risk of freezing. She could try one of the barns. Maybe someone was feeding the animals, and if not, well, at least she'd be sheltered from the wind. The thin stiletto heels on her expensive boots made that a risky proposition. Still, better boots than her body. Or she could get back in the car, crank the heat and wonder what she'd done to deserve this.

Her foot was on the first step down when she saw them—two cowboys on horseback cresting one of the low hills. Thalia gasped at the image before her—it was perfect. The sunset backlit the riders, giving them a halo of gold. Clouds of fog billowed from each of the horse's noses, which made them look otherworldly. Powerful, with a hint of danger. The whole thing looked like something right out of a movie—and she would know. This is exactly how she wanted to introduce the character of Sean Bridger in *Blood for Roses*. She'd been right to push for signing James Robert Bradley. This was perfect. He was going to be *perfect*. She could see the Oscar nominations rolling in.

Plus, someone was here. She could go inside and warm up.

The riders slowed as one of them pointed in her general direction. She'd been spotted. Thank heavens. Much longer, and she wouldn't be able to feel her legs anymore. She gave a hopeful wave, one that said, "Hi. I'm cold." It must have worked, because one rider broke off and came charging toward the house at full speed.

Her optimism flipped over to fear in a heartbeat. This guy didn't look like he was coming to greet her—he rode like he was going to run her down. Sure, Bradley didn't want to be found—but he or whoever that was wouldn't *hurt* her, would he? This wasn't about to become a shoot-first-ask-later situation, was it? As quickly as she could without betraying her terror, she stepped back onto the porch and out of the line of those hooves.

Still, the rider came on at full speed, pulling up only when he was parallel with her rental. The horse, a shining palomino, reared back, hooves flailing as the steam from his mouth almost enveloped the two of them. The rider's long coat fanned out behind him, giving her a glimpse of fringed chaps. If she hadn't been so afraid, Thalia would have appreciated the artistry and sheer skill of the moment. As it was, she half expected to find herself looking down the barrel of a gun.

When the horse had settled down, the rider pulled the bandanna down. "Help you?" he said in the kind of voice that was anything but helpful.

Then she saw his eyes—the liquid amber that had been one of the defining characteristics of James Robert Bradley. She'd found him. The part of her brain that was still nineteen and watching him on the big screen in the movie *Hell for Leather* swooned, and swooned hard. God, she'd had the biggest crush on this man a decade ago. And now she was here, actually talking to *People* magazine's Sexiest Man Alive. Sure, that had been thirteen years ago, but those eyes were still just as dreamy. She fought the urge to ask him for his autograph. The man was intimidating the hell out of her.

Not that she'd let him know that. The first rule of negotiating with actors was not to show weakness. Never let the other party know they held all the cards. So she sucked up what frozen courage she could and said, "James Robert Bradley?"

A look of weariness flashed over those beautiful eyes, then he said, "Miss, I'm not interested."

"That's only because you haven't heard—"

He cut her off with a wave of his hand. "I appreciate the offer, but you can be on your way now." He turned his mount toward one of the larger, newer barns.

"You didn't even listen to what I have to say!" She took off after him, her thin heels wobbling on the uneven terrain. "Your agent told me you'd—"

"I'm going to fire him for this," was the last thing she heard before Bradley disappeared into the barn.

Thalia pulled up. The wind was stronger in the middle of the drive, but she didn't think following Bradley into the barn was in her best interests. He hadn't even listened to the offer. How was she supposed to sign him to the movie when she couldn't even get a civil reply out of him? And if she couldn't sign him, how was she supposed to go into the office and tell her boss without losing her job?

She heard hoofbeats behind her, and turned to see the other rider approaching at a slow walk. "Howdy," the cowboy said, tipping his hat. "Said no, didn't he?"

Maybe it was the cold, or the blown plan, or the prospect of being unemployed in less than twenty-four hours. Whatever it was, Thalia felt her throat close up. *Don't cry,* she thought, because nothing was less professional than crying over a rejection. Plus, the tears would freeze to her face. "He didn't even listen to the offer."

The cowboy gave her a once-over. "I'd be happy to take the part, miss, providing there's a casting couch involved." Then he winked.

Was he...laughing at her? She shook her head. Maybe he was joking. She couldn't tell. "Thanks, but I was looking for—"

"An Oscar winner, yeah, I know. Wish I could help you, but…he's pretty set in his ways."

"Hoss," came a shout from inside the barn.

"Boss man's calling." The cowboy named Hoss seemed to feel sorry for her.

"Could I at least leave my card? In case he changes his mind?"

"You could try, but…"

"Hoss!" The shout was more insistent this time. Hoss tipped his hat again and headed toward the barn.

So much for making progress. Yes, she'd found Bradley, and yes, seeing those eyes of his was probably worth the trip. Everything else? The wind was blowing away her body heat, her career and her crush. If she got in that car and drove away, she'd have nothing left. Levinson would fire her butt for failing to deliver the goods, and she'd be blacklisted. Like last time, when her affair with Levinson had blown up in her face. She couldn't face having every professional door shut in her face a second time.

She needed Bradley in a way that had nothing to do with his eyes and everything to do with gainful employment.

At least the anger she currently felt was warm in nature. She'd lost contact with her toes, but she could still feel her fingers.

The barn door through which both men had disappeared slid shut.

This was her own fault, she realized. She was the one who had suggested Bradley for the role of Sean. She was the one who had convinced Levinson that even a recluse like Bradley wouldn't be able to turn down the comeback role of a lifetime. She was the one who had staked her career on something that seemed so simple—getting a man to say yes.

She was the one who had bet wrong. And now she had to pay the price.

She marched back up to the front door, her head held high

That was the second rule of negotiations—never let them know they've won. Her hands were shaking, but she managed to get a business card out of her coat pocket and wedge it in the screen door. The whole time, she mentally tried to come up with some contingency plans. Maybe she'd caught Bradley at a bad time; she knew where he lived now, and she had his number. She could try again and again—as long as it took until he at least heard her out.

Thalia remained convinced that, if he would just listen to her pitch, he'd be interested in the role. Actors, as a rule, craved public adoration, and what could be better than an Oscar-worthy movie?

No, this wasn't over. Not by a long shot. Still, hypothermia was becoming a risk. She wished she could go inside and warm up her hands and feet before she tried to drive, but it didn't look like an invitation would be forthcoming. As she turned back to the Camry, she saw the headlights of another vehicle coming down the road. Someone else meant another opportunity to plead her case, so she put on her friendliest smile and waited.

A mud-splattered SUV rolled up, window down. Before the vehicle had even come to a stop, a woman with graying hair stuck her head out. "What are you doing outside?" she demanded.

"I was hoping to talk to Mr. Bradley." Thalia kept her voice positive.

The woman gazed out at the barn. When her attention snapped back to Thalia, she looked mad enough to skin a cat. "And he left you out here? That man…" She shook her head in disgust. "Poor dear, you must be frozen. Can you wait long enough for me to pull around back and get the door open, or do you need to get in the car?"

Thalia loved this woman more than any other person in the whole world right now, because she was going to let Thalia inside. But she didn't want this stranger to know how cold she was—or how long she'd been stuck in this frozen purgatory. "I can wait." Her teeth chattered.

Without another word, the woman drove off. Thalia tried stamping her feet to keep the blood going, but it didn't do much except send pain shooting up her legs. *Just a few more seconds,* she told herself.

However, it felt like several minutes passed with no movement from either inside the house or from the barn. *Should have gotten in the car,* she thought. Then the front door swung open, and the older woman pulled her inside.

"You're frozen stiff!" she said in a clucking voice as she wrapped Thalia in what felt like a bearskin and pulled her deeper into the house. Thalia didn't have time to take in her surroundings before she found herself plunked down in a plush leather chair. Before her was a fire burning brightly in a massive stone fireplace that took up most of a wall.

Rubbing her hands together, she scooted forward to soak up the heat.

"I'm Minnie Red Horse, by the way. Let's get those boots off you. Nice boots, but not the best for winter out here."

"Thalia. Thorne." That was all she could get out as her blood began to pump through her frozen extremities. When Minnie pulled the boots off, Thalia couldn't keep the cry of pain out of her voice.

"Poor dear. You sit there and warm up. I'll make you some tea." Minnie stood and pulled the mesh covers off the fireplace before she stoked the logs. The flames jumped up, and Thalia felt closer to human.

"Thank you. So much." She managed to look at what she was wearing. Definitely an animal skin, which kind of creeped her out, but it was warm, so she ignored whatever PETA would say about it.

She heard Minnie shuffling around behind her. Thalia managed to sit up enough to look around. She was at one end of a long room. Behind her was a plank table, big enough to

seat six. Beyond that was an open kitchen with rustic cabi-
nets and a lot of marble. The whole effect was like something
out of *Architectural Digest*—and far beyond the small ranch
house her grandpa had spent his whole life in.

As big as the place seemed, it had looked much larger
from the outside. Minnie had a kettle on. "Where are you
from, Thalia?"

"Los Angeles." She tried wiggling her toes, but it still
hurt, so she quit.

"You're a long way from home, sweetie. How long you
been traveling?"

Thalia decided she liked Minnie, above and beyond the
warm fire and the tea. It'd been a long time since anyone had
called her *sweetie*. Not since Grandpa had died. Mom was
more fond of *dear*. "My flight left LAX at 3:30 this morning."

"Goodness, you made that whole trip in one day?" Minnie walked over and handed Thalia a steaming mug. "That's
quite a journey. Where are you staying tonight?"

"Um…" She'd had a plan, but her head was fuzzy right
now. "I have a room in Billings."

Minnie gave her a look that landed somewhere between
concern and pity. "You realize that's five hours away, and it's
already near sunset, right? That's a long drive in the dark."

Thalia hadn't realized how far away Billings was from
the Bar B Ranch when she'd booked the room, and given her
current state, five hours seemed like five days. How was she
going to make it that far? The drive out had been hard enough,
and that had been during daylight hours. Fighting that wind
in the dark on strange roads was kind of a scary thought.

"Here's what you're going to do." Minnie patted her arm
after Thalia took several sips of the tea. "You're going to sit
right here until you feel better, and then you're going to have
dinner. You came through Beaverhead, right?"

Thalia nodded, trying not to snicker at the juvenile name.
Minnie's tone made it clear that dinner was nonnegotiable,

but Thalia wasn't sure she could have hopped up and bailed if she'd tried. Her toes *hurt*.

"Lloyd has rooms he rents——as close as we've got to a motel 'round these parts." Thalia didn't have a clue as to what Minnie was talking about, but she was in no position to argue. She took another sip of tea, loving the way the warmth raced down her throat and spread through her stomach.

"I'll tell him you'll be by later," Minnie went on, as if Thalia was still with her. "That's only forty minutes away. You can make that."

Thalia nodded again. Now that she was returning to normal, she seemed to have lost her words.

Minnie gave her a tender smile. "I've got to see to dinner, but you rest up." She stood and headed back to the kitchen area, muttering, "All the way from L.A. in one day!" and "That man. ," as she went.

Thalia settled back into the chair, still sipping the tea. She knew she needed to be game planning dinner with Bradley, but her brain was mushy.

She heard a door open. Men's voices filled the space. One was grumbling about the weather, but the other—Bradley's—said, "Minnie, what the hell is——"

Is she still doing here. That's what he was going to say. After all, he'd pretty much kicked her off his land, and now she was sitting in his house. He sounded none-too-happy about the whole prospect. How was she going to make it through dinner with him? She debated thanking Minnie for the tea and leaving, but then the smell of pot roast filled the air and Thalia realized that she hadn't eaten anything since she'd grabbed a sandwich in the airport. The Denver airport—eight hours ago.

"Now, now!" Thalia wasn't watching the conversation—listening was bad enough—but she could imagine Minnie waggling a finger at James Robert Bradley like he was a child and she was the boss. "You boys go on and get cleaned up. Dinner will be ready by and by."

"I don't want—"

"I said, go! Shoo!"

Thalia grinned in spite of herself at the mental image that filled out that conversation. The thought of Minnie, who was on the petite side of things and probably in her late forties, scolding James Robert Bradley was nothing short of hilarious.

She was safe, for now. Minnie was going to feed her and make sure she was warm. Thalia settled back into the comfy chair, her eyelids drooping as she watched the flames dance before her. She needed to figure out how to convince Bradley to listen to her without him throwing her out of the house. She needed a plan.

But first, she needed to rest. Just a little bit.

Two

J.R. was a grown man and, as such, did not stomp and pout when he didn't get his way. Instead, he grumbled. Loudly.

"This is my house, by God," he grumbled as he went up the back stairs.

"That it is," Hoss agreed behind him.

Hoss was always quick to agree when the facts were incontrovertible. "I'm the boss around here," J.R. added, more to himself than to his best friend.

"Most days," Hoss said with a snort.

J.R. shot the man a dirty look over his shoulder. "Every day," he said with more force than he needed. He was overreacting, but damn if that woman hadn't tripped every single alarm bell in his head.

They reached the second floor. Hoss's room was at the far end, Minnie's was in the middle across from two guest rooms that never saw a guest and J.R.'s was at the other.

"She don't look dangerous." Hoss scratched at his throat in his lazy way, which J.R. knew was entirely deceptive.

"Shows what you know," J.R. replied. He knew exactly how dangerous innocent-looking people—women—from Hollywood could be. "She's not to be trusted."

Damn, but he hated when Hoss gave him that look—the look that said he was being a first-class jerk. Rather than stand here in his chaps and argue the finer points of women, J.R. turned and walked—not stomped—down to his room.

He needed a hot shower in the worst way. His face was still half-frozen from riding out to check on the cattle and buffalo. He shut his bedroom door firmly—not slamming it—and began to strip off the layers. First went the long coat, then the chaps, then the jeans and sweater, followed by the two layers of long underwear and T-shirts. Despite being bundled up like a baby, he was still cold.

And that woman—the one sitting in *his* chair, in front of *his* fire—had shown up here in nothing but a skirt. And tights. And those boots, the ones that went almost up to her knees. "Stupid," he muttered to himself as he cranked his shower on high. What was she thinking, wearing next to nothing when the wind chill was somewhere around minus forty degrees below? She wasn't thinking, that's what. Hollywood types were notoriously myopic, and there was no doubt in J.R.'s mind that she was a Hollywood type.

The hot water rushed over him. J.R. bowed his head and let the water hit his shoulders. Against his will, his mind turned back to those boots, those tights. Those *legs*. Yeah, that woman clearly underestimated the force of winter in Montana. Probably thought that little coat was enough to keep her warm.

The moment he caught himself wondering what was under that coat, J.R. slammed on the brakes. He was not some green kid, distracted by a pretty face and a great body. No matter how blue her lips had been, that didn't make up for the fact that she'd come looking for James Robert Bradley. She wanted that name—the name J.R. had buried deep in Big Sky country eleven years ago. She wasn't here for him.

No one was ever here for him.

Except Minnie and Hoss, he reminded himself. They were his friends, his family and his crew all rolled into one. They knew who he really was, and that was good enough for him.

Warm and clean, he flipped off the water and rubbed down with the towel. He was going to fire Bernie. Hell, he should have fired the man years ago, but Bernie was his one thin link to his old life. He got J.R. some nice voice-over work and had, up until now, kept J.R.'s whereabouts to himself.

What had that woman dangled in front of Bernie's greedy little eyes to make him give her directions to the ranch? She had to be good at what she did. Not good enough to dress warmly, but J.R. knew that he could expect the full-court press from her for whatever she wanted James Robert Bradley to do.

He slid into a clean pair of jeans, making sure to put all the dirty things in the hamper. If he didn't, he'd have to listen to Minnie go on and on about *men* this and *men* that. It was easier to pick up after himself. Plus—not that he'd tell Minnie this—he preferred things neat. Clean.

Simple.

J.R. went to grab a shirt and paused. His hand was on his favorite flannel, the one he'd worn so much the collar was fraying. Minnie kept threatening to make a rag of it, but so far, she'd done no such thing.

Maybe he should put on something a little nicer. A little less tattered. He could clean up well, after all. Maybe he should...

Was he serious? Was he actually standing in his closet, debating what to wear because some uninvited, unwanted *female* had barged into his house? Was he hard up or what?

His brain, ever resourceful, rushed in to remind him it had been two years and seven months since his last failed

attempt at a relationship. Pretty much the textbook definition of hard up.

Didn't matter. She wasn't welcome here. And after he hu-
mored Minnie at dinner, he'd make sure she left his property
and never, ever came back. He grabbed his favorite shirt.
Frays be damned.

His resolve set, he shoved his feet into his house mocca-
sins and threw his door open.

And almost walked right into Minnie Red Horse.

"What?" he asked, so startled by the small woman that he
actually jumped back.

He didn't jump far enough, though. Minnie reached up
and poked him in the chest. "You listen to me, young man.
You *will* be nice and polite tonight."

Immediately, he went on the defensive. "Oh, it's my fault
she doesn't know it's winter out here?"

"I am ashamed to think that you left her out there in the
wind, J.R. I thought that you knew better than to treat a guest
like that."

He felt the hackles on the back of his neck go up. Minnie
had already busted out the big, shame-based guns. He'd be
lying if he said it didn't work—he hated to disappoint Minnie
in any way. But, he was a reformed actor. Lying used to be his
entire life. So he slapped on a stern look and glared at Minnie. "She's not a guest. She's a trespasser, Minnie. And if I
recall correctly, *you're* the one who shot at the last trespasser."

That had been the nail in the coffin of his last failed relationship. He'd been trying to decide if he loved Donna or not
when he'd invited her to spend the night at the ranch. Things
had been going fine until he took her up to his room. There,
she'd taken one look at James Robert Bradley's Oscar, his
photos, his life—and everything had changed. All she had
talked about was how he was really famous, and why on
earth hadn't he told her, and this was so amazing, that she
was here with him. Except she hadn't been. She'd thought

she was with James Robert. In the space of a minute, she'd forgotten that J.R. had even existed.

He'd broken up with her a few weeks later, and then, like clockwork, a few weeks after that, a man with an expensive camera had come snooping around. J.R. had been in the barn with Hoss when they'd heard the crunch of tires. J.R. had wanted to go out and confront the stranger, but Hoss had held him back. Rifle in hand, Minnie had been the one to claim that she'd never heard of anyone named Bradley, and if she saw that man again, she'd shoot him. Then she'd put a few bullets a few feet from the man, and that had been the end of that.

"That man was a parasite," Minnie said. "This is different. She's not like that."

"How would you know? She's here for James Robert. She wants something, Minnie. She'll ruin everything we've got, everything I've worked so hard for."

Minnie rolled her eyes. "Stop being so dramatic. Call it woman's intuition, or my Indian senses, my maternal instincts—whatever floats your boat. That woman is not a threat to you or any of us." She jabbed a finger back into J.R.'s chest. "And I expect you to be a gentleman. Do I make myself clear?"

"Don't tell me what to do, Minnie. You're not my—" Before the immature retort was all the way out, J.R. bit it back. Not soon enough, though.

A pained shadow crossed over Minnie's face, which made J.R. feel like the biggest jerk in the world. The fact was, Minnie had offered to adopt him a few years after they'd settled into the ranch. Oh, not the legal, court-based adoption—J.R. was a grown man—but she'd asked him if he wanted to be adopted into her family through the Lakota tribe. The fact was, she'd always been more of a mother to him than his own flesh-and-blood mother had ever been. The Red Horse family was his family. That was all there was to it.

J.R. had said no. He'd claimed he wasn't comfortable being a white man in an American Indian tribe, which was true. He knew that if word got out that James Robert Bradley had been adopted into a Lakota tribe, the storm of gossip would hurt everyone, not just him. And he couldn't hurt Minnie or Hoss.

Any more than he had. "I'm sorry," he offered. "It's just…"

Minnie patted his arm. "It's okay. You're a little… spooked."

"Yeah." Not that he'd want Hoss to know that, but Minnie and all of her womanly, Indian-y intuition already understood, so denying it was pointless. The woman downstairs had spooked him.

"Despite that, I expect both of my boys to be nice and polite." Her gaze flicked down over his frayed collar. "Respectable, even."

That was how fights with Minnie went. J.R. was the boss, but she was the mother. Forgiveness was quick and easy, not the dance of death it had been with Norma Bradley.

"I'm not taking the part. Whatever she wants, I'm not doing it."

"Did I say anything about that? No, I did not. All I said was that you were going to be a gentleman to our guest."

"Not my guest."

"Our visitor, then." Minnie looked like she wanted to poke him again, but she didn't. "Do it for me, J.R. Do you know how long it's been since we had a visitor out here? Months, that's how long. I want to talk to someone besides you two knuckleheads, and if it's a woman who's got the latest gossip? All the better."

J.R. sighed. Minnie had a huge weak spot for gossip. She subscribed to all the tabloids, read TMZ every day and probably knew more about the goings-on in the entertainment industry than he did. "One meal. Humor me. And don't worry, I wasn't going to ask her to stay, *despite* the fact that it's late and the winds are terrible."

He ignored the unveiled attempt at guilt. She was right. He owed her, and if that meant pretending they were having a girls-night-in for dinner, well, he'd suck it up. "That's good."

"I got her a room at Lloyd's." With that semidefiant statement, Minnie turned on her heel and headed back to her kitchen domain. "Dinner's in fifteen," she called back, loud enough that Hoss could hear her in his room.

Great, just great, J.R. thought as he hung his favorite shirt back up and pulled the green flannel Minnie had gotten him for Christmas off the hanger. Somehow, he knew that forty miles wasn't enough space between him and the woman from Hollywood.

A few minutes later, he headed down to the kitchen. Minnie was checking on something in the oven. "Tell her dinner's ready," she said without looking at him.

She was punishing him, pure and simple. Bad enough that he deserved it, but still.

J.R. headed down to his chair at the far end of the room. All he could see of the stranger was her golden hair peeking out from above the chair's back. The color was the kind of blond that spoke of sun-swept days at the beach, but he'd put money on it being fake.

Aw, hell. She was asleep. Slouched way down in the chair, Minnie's buffalo robe falling off her shoulders—her mouth open enough to make her look completely kissable. J.R. swallowed that observation back, but it wasn't easy. Her now-bootless legs were stretched out before her, and the patterned tights seemed to go on forever. Lord. Despite a second attempt at swallowing, his mouth had gone bone-dry. "Miss?"

She didn't move. Her head was resting on one hand; the other hand was wrapped around her waist. Minnie was right. The woman didn't look like she was capable of destroying his life.

Looks weren't everything, he reminded himself. He couldn't let his guard down. That thought, however, didn't stop him from sitting on his heels in front of her. Her hair had been slicked back into some fancy twist, but now parts of it had come loose, falling around her face in a way that was messy and beautiful at the same time. Some parts of him hadn't gotten the message, it seemed, because he wanted to do nothing more than brush that hair away from her face.

He didn't. Instead, he gave her shoulder a gentle shake before he jerked his hand back. As if a sleeping woman could bite him. "Miss, wake up."

She jolted, her eyelids fluttering open. J.R. braced himself for the reaction when she realized he was close enough to trap. Would she immediately launch into her pitch or go for cloying flattery?

When her eyes focused on him, a small smile curved the corners of her mouth. *Here it comes,* J.R. thought.

"It's *you*," she breathed. The warm glow in her eyes didn't seem connected to the fire behind him, and the soft adoration in her voice should have grated on his every nerve. But it didn't.

"Yup. It's me." Which felt weirdly personal, because he knew she wasn't here for him, but for the man he used to be.

Then time froze—absolutely froze—as he watched her stretch out a hand and trace the tips of her fingers down his cheek and over his ten-day-old beard. The touch was way more than weirdly personal—it was downright, damnably erotic. The sudden shift of blood from his brain to other parts made him almost dizzy. Hell, yeah, she'd look this good waking up in his bed, and if he had her there, he would be damn sure it wouldn't stop with a little pat on the cheek.

What the hell was he thinking?

That was the problem. He wasn't.

He must have pulled back without realizing it, because she dropped her hand and blinked a whole bunch more. "Oh. *Oh*," she said, and he could see the consciousness dawning. "Um…"

Desperate to put a little more space between him and this woman who had spooked him in more ways than one, J.R. stood up and back. "Dinner's ready," he added, because that was the safest thing to say. Also, the most honest.

The woman dropped her eyes, warmth racing across her cheeks. Did she feel the same confusion he did? *Don't flatter yourself,* he thought. Of course she was confused. He'd woken her up from a dead sleep. She had a good excuse to feel a little lost right now.

He didn't.

She smoothed her hair back, but several of the locks refused to stay. "I had some boots," she said. All the softness was gone from her voice now, and she sounded more like the woman who had barged into his life.

"Right here." He picked up her boots from where Minnie had propped them by the fire and handed them to her.

She made sure not to touch him when she took them. And he should not have been disappointed by that. "Is there... I need to wash up..."

Women in general—and this woman in particular— should not look quite so innocent when they blushed. "Sure." He pointed to the bathroom that was behind her.

She turned, but then stopped. "Should I leave *this* here?" She motioned to the robe.

The way she said *this* made it clear that she wasn't sure she trusted it. "Minnie's buffalo robe? Yeah, that's fine."

"Oh. A buffalo robe." Some of her blush disappeared as she paled. What did she think it was? Maybe she was one of those strident vegetarians. Instead of launching into an animal-rights lecture, she put on a weak smile and said, "Okay, thanks," before she went to the bathroom.

Well, if that didn't beat all. Where was the full-court press? Where were the obnoxious compliments designed to sway his ego? Nowhere. All he got was someone who, for a sleepy second, looked happy to see him.

Dinner was a huge mistake. He debated hiding in his room until the woman—whose name he still did not know—left. Then he caught Minnie giving him a wallop of a glare from the other side of the room as she tapped a wooden spoon on the counter. Right, right. He'd promised to be nice and polite, which probably didn't include hiding.

So he set the table instead. Hoss finally clumped down the stairs, just as J.R. was finishing. For a man who wasn't afraid of putting in a hard day's work on the range, Hoss had the unique ability to never be present when a small household chore needed to be done. "Well?"

Minnie flashed her wooden spoon like it was a weapon. "She's staying for dinner, and you will behave or else."

"When am I not a perfect angel?" Hoss gave her his best puppy eyes, but it didn't work. "Can I at least sit by her?"

"No." J.R. didn't mean to sound so possessive; it burst out of him.

Minnie shot him a funny look. "No, I'm going to sit by her. You two are going to sit in your normal spots and keep your hands, feet and all other objects to yourself. Clear?"

Hoss met J.R.'s gaze and lifted one eyebrow, as if to say, *game on.* Jeez, if Hoss was acting this much the cad now, how much of a pain would he become when he saw her all warmed up? "Yes, ma'am."

Then a noise at the other end of the room drew their attention. The woman was standing by the chair now, her hair fixed, her boots on and her coat off. Whoa. The gray wool dress she had on was cut close, revealing a knockout figure that went with her knockout legs. Either she was stunning—hell, she *was* stunning—or she'd had a good plastic surgeon. One never could be sure when it came to Hollywood types.

Then her gaze locked on to his, and he swore he felt the same dizzy charge that he'd felt when she'd touched him, only this time, there was a clear thirty feet of space between them.

She's not here for you, J.R. practically shouted at himself. *She's here for James Robert.*

Damn shame she wasn't there for him, though.

"Whoa," Hoss muttered next to him, and Minnie promptly smacked his butt with the spoon. "Ow!"

"Feeling better?" Minnie pushed past J.R. and went to greet her visitor.

"Much, thanks." The woman gave Minnie a friendly smile. "Where should I put my coat?"

"Lay it on the chair. I'll make the introductions." Minnie took her by the arm and led her to where J.R. and Hoss were gaping like horny seventh graders. "This is Hoss Red Horse, and J. R. Bradley."

J.R. rolled his eyes—obviously the woman knew who he was. Otherwise, she wouldn't be here.

"Boys," Minnie went on, giving them both the warning stink eye, "this is Thalia Thorne."

Hoss stuck out his hand. "A pleasure, Ms. Thorne." Miracle of miracles, that was all he said.

"Nice to meet you…Hoss." She looked from him to Minnie. "Are you two related?"

Hoss's polite grin dialed right over into trouble. "Yeah, but she don't like people to know I'm her son. Makes her feel old or something."

Minnie hit him with the spoon again, which caused Thalia to stifle a giggle. Her eyes still laughed, though.

Not that J.R. was staring or anything.

Then those eyes—a clear, deep blue—shifted to him, and she held out her hand. "It's nice to meet you, J.R."

He couldn't do anything but stare at her. She wasn't going to insist on calling him James Robert? Just like that?

Minnie cleared her throat and shot him a dangerous glare. Right. Acknowledging that she'd spoken to him was probably the nice, polite thing to do. "Likewise, Thalia." Against his better judgment, he took her hand in his and gave it a gentle squeeze. Heat flowed between them. Probably because she'd warmed up in front of the fire. Yeah, that was it.

That small, curved smile danced over her nice lips and was then gone. "Dinner smells wonderful, Minnie. I can't remember the last time I had a home-cooked meal."

There was the flattery, and boy, was it working on Minnie. She blushed and grinned and shooed all of them to the table, saying, "Sit by me, dear, so we can talk."

Of course, sitting by Minnie also turned out to be sitting by J.R., as Thalia was on the corner between him and Minnie. His thoughts immediately turned to the patterned tights under the table—and their close proximity to his own legs—way more than they should have. Man, he was hard up.

How the hell was he going to make it through dinner?

Three

"So, tell us about yourself," Minnie said to Thalia as she passed a basket of piping hot corn muffins around the table.

J.R. waited. Everyone waited, including Hoss, which was saying something. Hoss wasn't seriously trying to make a move on this woman, was he? In front of his own mother? Ugh. This whole thing couldn't be more awkward, J.R. decided.

"I'm an associate producer." J.R. couldn't help but notice she looked at Hoss and Minnie—but not at him. "I work for Bob Levinson at Halcyon Pictures."

"He's an ass." The moment the words left his mouth, Minnie looked like she would smack him upside the head with the spoon—if only their "visitor" wasn't sitting in between the two of them. "Pardon my language."

One of those quick, nervous smiles darted over Thalia's face. But she still didn't quite meet his eyes. The closest she got was more in the region of his shoulder. What the hell kind of new negotiating tactic was this—ignore the person you were trying to ensnare? "It's true he has a certain reputation."

A certain reputation? J.R. had had the intense displeasure of working on two Levinson movies—*Colors That Run* and *The Cherry Trees*—and both had been sheer torture tests. On his good days, Levinson had been demeaning and derogatory. On his worst days, he had inspired J.R. to envision creative ways to off the man. He couldn't imagine Levinson had mellowed with age. His kind never did. They just got more and more caustic, leaving nothing but scorched earth behind them.

And, in Levinson's case, a growing list of Oscar winners. He was an ass, all right, but because he delivered the box office returns and the shiny little gold men, everyone in Hollywood gave him a free pass. Except J.R., who wasn't in Hollywood anymore.

And this Thalia—who looked soft and could pull off innocent—worked directly for him. In so many ways, she was not trustworthy.

"Are you famous?" Hoss asked.

J.R. shot Hoss a dirty look, which earned him a grin that bordered on predatory. Did Hoss think he had a shot? Hell, no.

Thalia's laugh was small but polite. "Only to my mother. Every time one of my movies comes to Norman, Oklahoma, she rounds up a bunch of friends." Hints of color graced her cheeks, but she showed no other sign of being embarrassed by this. "They sit through the credits and when my name rolls by, they all stand and cheer. And I'm famous for a whole three minutes."

"So you're not originally from California?" Minnie's eyes were bright and her smile was huge. She was having fun, J.R. realized. That made him feel better. Not much, but a little.

"No, I've only been there for about ten years."

"What does an associate producer do?" Hoss was nailing nice and polite right out of the gate, which only made J.R. look worse. When Hoss was rewarded with a nice smile, J.R.

had to fight the urge to kick him under the table. Hoss was not her type. True, J.R. didn't know exactly what her type was, but Hoss was a decent, honest, hardworking fellow, even if he was a bit of a joker. In other words, he was the kind of man that women like Thalia Thorne probably ate for breakfast.

"A little bit of everything. I scout locations, arrange funding and hire talent." She managed to say that entire line without looking at J.R. The amount of effort she put into *not* looking at him broadcast that she knew he was here, loud and clear.

"I was in a movie once." J.R. fought the urge to roll his eyes. "Me and Minnie, we were extra Native Americans in *Hell for Leather.*" Hoss shook his head in mock sadness. "First, I got killed, then they cut my part. That's why I gave up Hollywood and stuck to ranching, you know."

What a load of crap. Mostly true crap—everything except that last line, which J.R. took as a personal attack. He was about to punch Hoss in the arm when Thalia giggled. "Is that so? Fame can be fickle like that."

"Sure can." Hoss shot him a look that said one thing, and one thing only—*I'm winning.* "Were you always a producer?"

"Not originally. I wanted to be an actress." Thalia's voice got that soft quality again. "I came close—I had a three-episode arc on *Alias*—that girl-next-door-superspy show." Then her eyes brightened and she gave Hoss a grin that said she was in on the joke. "I got killed, too. It's murder on one's career to be dying all the time."

A former actress? Another strike against her—or it should have been. The way she'd said it felt like she'd plucked a single string somewhere inside J.R. and that string hummed in recognition.

So what? Hollywood was the land of broken dreams. He would not be swayed by a calculated play on his sympathies.

"Do you know that Jennifer Garner?" When Thalia nodded, Minnie's eyes lit up. "I always wondered if she was a nice person or if she'd kill you."

"She's normal—but the baby showers! You should have seen the gifts!" As Thalia revealed all sorts of firsthand details and Minnie ate it up, J.R. noticed that everything she said was warm and friendly. Nothing malicious passed her lips.

Not that he was thinking about her lips. That wasn't it at all.

No, he was thinking Minnie's sixth sense might be right— Thalia Thorne didn't act like someone who'd come digging for dirt. But she'd come for something. *What* was the question. He knew it was only a matter of time before she got around to it.

She didn't seem in a hurry, though. Instead, she ate and talked like they were all the oldest of friends while Minnie passed around the pot roast and the potatoes. They were J.R.'s favorite kind, smashed red potatoes with rosemary and garlic, but tonight, nothing tasted good. To him, anyway. Thalia sat there oohing and aahing over everything, and Minnie looked like she'd hit the jackpot. Lord, it was irritating. It was almost as if he wasn't even sitting at the table.

"So, what brings you out our way?" Minnie kept her tone light and friendly, but there was no mistaking that this was *the* question on everyone's mind. Including J.R.'s.

Her gaze cast down, Thalia wiped her mouth with her napkin. For a second, J.R. almost felt sorry for her. So far, she hadn't done a single thing he'd expected of her, and he got the sense that she knew exactly how far she'd overreached.

Then she squared her shoulders. "I'm working on a movie tentatively titled *Blood for Roses*. It's slated to be released next December."

Just in time to be considered for Levinson's required slew of Oscars, no doubt. "What's it about?" Hoss was now leaning forward, eyes on Thalia as if every word that fell from her mouth was a ruby.

"It's a Western set in Kansas after the Civil War. A family of freed slaves tries to start a new life, but some of the locals aren't too keen on the idea." She cleared her throat. This was the pitch, no doubt, but she came off as hesitant to make it. Like she knew that J.R. was going to throw her out, and she didn't want to go yet. "Eastwood is attached to direct, Freeman has signed on and we're in talks with Denzel."

It was an impressive roster. No doubt Levinson was hoping to break nomination records.

"Oh, I love Denzel, especially when he's playing the bad guy." Thalia had Minnie already, that much was clear. "Have you met him? Is he as sexy in real life as he is in the movies?"

"It's not quite the same," Thalia admitted, "although he is quite good-looking." She shrugged. "When you're around famous people long enough, you stop worrying so much about who's the most famous or who's the hottest. Sooner or later, it has to come down to whether or not they're someone you can work with." This blanket statement that could only be described as reasonable hung out there before she added, "Having said that, Denzel is someone that almost everyone enjoys working with, and his wife is lovely."

Then she looked at him. Not the kind of look that asked if he'd bought what she was selling, but the kind of look that seemed to be asking for understanding.

What the hell was this?

"So what part did you have in mind for him?" Hoss jerked his chin toward J.R. with all the subtlety of a dead skunk in the middle of the road.

She favored J.R. with another look that was lost in the no-man's-land of apologetic and sympathetic. It made her look vulnerable, honest even—which was completely disarming. He didn't like that look or how it plucked at those strings inside him, not one bit. "I thought James Robert Bradley would be perfect for the role of Sean Bridger, the grizzled Confederate Civil War vet who unexpectedly finds himself helping defend the freedmen's land." Her face was almost unread-able, but he could see the pulse at the base of her neck pounding. "I wanted to see if you'd be interested in the part, J.R."

Getting him signed on was her idea, not Levinson's? Wait. There was something more to what she'd said. He scrambled to replay it while keeping his own face blank. She'd thought James Robert was perfect—but she'd asked *him,* J.R., if he was interested. Her gaze held tight to his, and he felt that flow of energy between them again. She'd been right to avoid looking at him before—he could get all kinds of lost in her ice-blue eyes. Because now she was not just looking at him, but into him, through all the walls he'd thrown up between James Robert Bradley and J.R. That's why she wasn't doing the full-court press. She understood the difference between his two lives. Understood it, and possibly even respected it.

She was more dangerous than he'd thought possible.

Eastwood to direct. Freeman and Washington to star. The who's who of people who could pull off a Western—and she'd thought of him. He'd be lying if he said he wasn't flattered, but that didn't change things. "I'm not interested."

Not in the part, anyway. He managed to break eye contact, which snapped the tension between them.

"Any Indians in this movie?" For once, J.R. didn't want Hoss to shut up. It'd be better for everyone if Hoss did all the talking.

She was silent for two beats too long. He shouldn't care that he'd disappointed her, so he ignored the inconvenient emotion.

"Sadly, no. I believe they were all pushed off the land before our story begins. If something opens up, I'll be sure to keep you in mind."

Conversation seemed to die after that, as if no one knew what was supposed to be said next. J.R. wanted her to leave and take this discomfort with her. He didn't want her to look at him—through him—anymore. He didn't want to think about her pretty eyes or long legs, and he sure as hell didn't want her to give him another just-woke-up, so-glad-to-see-you look of longing. And if she wouldn't leave, he had a good mind to bail.

But he'd promised Minnie to be polite. So he focused on eating the food that was tasteless. After a few moments, Minnie asked another question about some actor, and Thalia responded with what felt like a little too much forced enthusiasm.

"Now, I've got a chocolate cake or there's blondies," Minnie said, which meant J.R. was almost free.

"Oh, thank you so much, but I need to get on the road." Thalia glanced at him and added, "This has been wonderful, and you've been more than kind, but I couldn't possibly take up any more of your time."

"At least take some of the blondies. I insist." Minnie was up and moving. She never let anyone leave without an extra meal.

"I'll get the dishes." Hoss started clearing the table, which wasn't like him at all.

Before J.R. could process Hoss's sudden reversal of his no-housework policy, he found himself sitting alone with Thalia. It's not that he was afraid to look at her, afraid to feel the way her presence pulled on parts of him he pretended he'd forgotten existed. Wasn't that at all. He didn't want to give her another chance to make her case. He didn't want to tell her no again. He'd already done it twice. Once should have been enough.

Nice. Polite. He could feel Minnie's eyes boring a hole in the back of his head. What the hell? He'd never see her again anyway. "What are you going to tell Levinson?"

"I'm not sure." Out of the corner of his eye, he could see her eyebrows knot together. She looked worried. For some reason, that bothered him.

"You seem like..." Aw, hell. Was he about to pay her a

compliment? "You seem like a nice person. What are you doing working for *him?*"

Her gaze locked on to his, and that connection he didn't want to feel was right there, pulling on him more and more. "I've found that life often takes you places you'd never thought you'd go."

She was doing it again, looking right into him. So what if what she said made all kinds of sense? So what if she came off as decent? So what if she was completely at ease with Minnie and Hoss?

She didn't belong here. She might well go back and tell Levinson all sorts of fabricated crap. He might find himself on the cover of next week's *Star,* and he might find more people freezing to death on his property, trying to snap a picture of the elusive James Robert Bradley.

"Here we are." *Saved by dessert,* J.R. thought as Minnie bustled up to the table. "Now don't try to get to Billings tonight. Here's directions to Lloyd's place. I'll call him and let him know you're on your way. And our number's here—" she tapped on the paper "—so call me when you get there."

J.R. cleared his throat in the most menacing way possible. Minnie was giving out their number? When did that become a good idea? Never, that's when.

"I want to make sure you get there, safe and sound." Minnie said the words to Thalia, but she shot the look of death at J.R.

Thalia didn't acknowledge his rudeness. Instead, she thanked Minnie and Hoss with such warmth that it felt like they were all old friends. Hoss got her coat and, doing his best impersonation of a gentleman, held it for her.

After Thalia buttoned up, she turned to face him. J.R. was torn between not looking at her so she'd leave faster and looking at her good and long. He wasn't going to see her again, and he certainly didn't want to, but he knew that the memory of her strange visit would haunt him for a long time after she left. He wanted to make sure he remembered her as she was.

"J.R." That was all she said as she extended her hand.

He shouldn't shake—for his own sanity if nothing else—but if he didn't, Minnie might stop feeding him. *Suck it up,* he thought. So what if she was maybe the only other woman on the planet—besides Minnie—to call him J.R. after she knew about James Robert? Didn't matter. She was leaving and that was that. "Thalia."

Her skin was soft and much warmer now. A look crossed her face, almost the same as the one she'd given him when he woke her up earlier—except she was wide awake now. That look was going to stay with him. He wanted to be annoyed with it, and with her, but he couldn't be.

"It's been such a pleasure meeting you." When Minnie started talking, Thalia let go of his hand. "You're welcome back anytime, Thalia."

Everyone paused, like they were waiting for him to say something gruff or rude, but J.R. held his tongue. Part of him wanted to see her again, to see if she was really like this, or if the whole evening had been an elaborate act designed to lull him into complacency.

He wanted to see if she'd still look at him like that. *Into* him, like that.

Minnie walked her to her car. Hoss watched them from the front window. But J.R. stood rooted to the spot.

He wanted to see her again.

He hoped like hell he never did.

Four

Billings hadn't gotten any closer overnight, Thalia realized as she drove to the airport the next morning. Five hours was a lot of time to think. Maybe too much time.

"What are you going to tell Levinson?" J.R. had asked and she still didn't have an answer. The night of dreamless sleep in a room that hadn't been touched since the days of *The Brady Bunch* and a breakfast of bacon, eggs and extra-strong black coffee with Lloyd hadn't gotten her any closer to a plan.

What were her options? She could quit before Levinson had a chance to fire her. That might help her reputation in the short-term, but sooner or later the rumor mill would start grinding again. People would dig up the old news and the old photos of her and Levinson and start asking if maybe another affair had led to her sudden departure. It wouldn't matter that there was no affair this time. Just the suggestion of one would be damaging enough—for her. For the second time, Levinson would come out unscathed and Thalia's career would be ground into a pulp. And like the last time, when no one had hired her as an actress, this time no one would hire her as a producer. And if you weren't an actor and you weren't a producer, then you weren't anybody in Hollywood.

She needed to avoid any action that had a hint of juicy gossip. So quitting was out. What could she do to keep her job? She could present Levinson with a list of reasons why Bradley had been a bad idea—*her* bad idea. Except that any reasons she came up with would pretty much have to be bold-faced lies. The man had been everything she'd hoped to find. He was less gorgeous than he'd been fifteen years ago—less polished, less perfect. He was less the pretty boy now.

No, he wasn't pretty. *Handsome.* His hair had deepened from golden-boy blond to the kind of brown that only reflected hints of gold in the firelight. His ten-day-old beard made it clear he wasn't a boy anymore. He'd put on weight, maybe thirty pounds, but instead of going right to his gut, as often happened when actors let themselves go, it seemed like he'd added an all-over layer of muscle. And not the kind that came from hours spent at a gym. No, the way his body had moved, from the way he rode his horse to the way he had sat on his heels in front of her spoke of nothing but hard-earned strength.

All of those things were swoon-worthy, but his amber eyes—those were what held Thalia's attention. They were the only things that hadn't changed. No, that wasn't true, either. They looked the same, but to Thalia, it seemed like there'd been more going on beyond the lovely color. And for one sweet, confused moment, she thought she'd been privy to what he was thinking.

She mentally slapped her head again. Had she touched that beard? Had she acted like a lovesick schoolgirl, swooning over the biggest hunk in the world? Yes, she had. And why? Because when she'd opened her eyes, she'd thought she'd still been dreaming. How else to explain the small smile he'd given her—*her,* of all people. She'd been dreaming, all right.

Neither part of him—James Robert the superstar or J.R. the reclusive rancher—would be the least bit welcoming to the likes of her. She felt like a fool. She'd embarrassed herself and, based on his behavior during the meal, she'd embarrassed him, too.

At least she thought she had. The exchange—the touch, the smile—between them couldn't have taken more than twenty seconds. J. R. Bradley was hard to read. She could see so much churning behind his eyes, but she couldn't make sense of it. She had no good idea if he'd been embarrassed, flattered or offended. Or all three. All she knew was that her little slipup had had some sort of effect on him. The other thing she knew was that J.R.'s eyes were dangerous. Looking into those liquid pools of amber was a surefire way to make another mistake.

Thalia shook her head, trying to forget the way his stubble had pricked at her fingers. She could relive that moment again when she had the time—all the time in the world, if she was going to be unemployed. Quitting wasn't the best option. Lying about J.R. was out. Anything she said would take on a life of its own, and she had the awful feeling that if she started the rumor mill churning about him, he might trample her the next time. What could she do to save her job?

She was walking into Billings Airport when she realized that she only had two options. One was to present Levinson with a list of better-suited actors to take the role and hope that he wouldn't ask questions about what had happened with Bradley. Which was asking a lot of hope. It had taken a great deal of negotiating to convince Levinson that Bradley was perfect for the role. It would take a heck of a lot more to convince him Bradley wasn't.

The other choice was to go back and get Bradley.

"May I help you?"

Thalia realized she was standing in front of the check-in desk, her return ticket in one hand.

She *had* to get Bradley. She couldn't give up on him. He wouldn't be happy to see her again—at least, she didn't think he would be—but Minnie Red Horse was another matter entirely. Thalia did have an open invitation to come back to the Bar B Ranch, after all. If she didn't take advantage of that, did she deserve to keep her job?

"Ma'am? May I help you?" The clerk at the check-in desk was beginning to get worried.

Thalia couldn't leave. But she wasn't prepared to stay. She'd planned for a quick overnight trip. She had her makeup and meds, her laptop and a change of underwear. Her dress and coat had already proven to be woefully inadequate. If she was going back out to the Bar B, she needed to be ready this time.

"Yes," she finally said as she advanced to the desk. The clerk looked relieved that Thalia wasn't some weirdo flaking out. "I need to buy some clothes. Where's a good place to shop here?"

The clerk went right back over to worried. "The Rimrock mall has a J.C. Penney."

It had been ages since she'd been in the kind of mall that had a J.C. Penney—not since she had been back in Oklahoma. It seemed fitting—and would probably cost her a fourth of what stuff in Hollywood would. She could absorb a little wardrobe adjustment, especially if it kept her employed. "Perfect."

Thalia got directions, made sure her open-end ticket was still open and then re-rented the car. She called Lloyd to tell him that she'd be back tonight, and if it was okay with him, she'd probably be staying a few nights more.

Then she went shopping.

J.R. was getting sick of winter. Another day of riding out on the range to make sure that the cattle and buffalo had open water, and another day of trucking hay out to the far

reaches of the ranch for wild mustangs they pastured. The
chores didn't bother him—it was the bone-chilling cold that
hurt more every day, and they hadn't even had a big winter
storm yet. Which was another source of worry. If it didn't
start snowing a little more, the ranch would be low on water
for the coming summer. If it snowed too much, he'd lose
some cattle.

"Getting too old for this," Hoss muttered off to his side.

"You're only thirty," J.R. reminded him. "Many happy
years of winter ranching ahead of you."

"Hell," Hoss said as a gust of wind smacked them in the
face. "At least you have options. I'm stuck out here."

"Options? What are you talking about?"

Hoss turned in the saddle, holding his hat to shield his
face from the wind. "You could have gone to California, you
know. You didn't have to stay out here with me and Minnie."

"Didn't want to." He was surprised at how much that statement felt like a lie.

"Man, why not? Pretty woman like that offers to give you
money for nothing to go where the sun is shining? Shoot. I'd
have gone."

J.R. chose not to respond to this. It had been two days
since Thalia Thorne had shown up. On the surface, nothing
had changed. He was still the boss, cattle still had to be wa-
tered and it was still cold. But something felt different. Minnie had been quiet after their visitor had left—not happy, like
J.R. had hoped she'd be. But she hadn't scolded him on his
lousy behavior. She hadn't said anything, which wasn't like
her. And now Hoss was laying into him.

He saw the something that was different as soon as they
crested the last hill between them and the ranch house J.R.
had built a year after he'd bought the place. There, in the
drive, was a too-familiar car.

"Would you look at that," Hoss mused, suddenly sounding anything but grumpy. "Looks like we got ourselves a pretty guest again."

"What is she doing here?"

Hoss shot him a look full of humor. "If you ain't figured that one out yet, I'm not gonna be the one to break it to you." Then he kicked his horse into a slow canter down to the barn.

Damn. And damn again. If he weren't so cold, he'd turn his horse around and disappear into the backcountry. Thalia Thorne might be able to find the ranch house, but she wouldn't survive the open range, not in her sexy little boots and tight dress.

The fact of the matter was, he was frozen. "She better not be in my chair again," he grumbled to himself as he rode toward the barn.

Hoss whistled as he unsaddled his horse. The sound grated on J.R.'s nerves something fierce. "Knock it off. She's not here for you."

"And you know that for sure, huh?" Hoss snorted. "She came for the shiny gold man in your lair up there—but that don't mean she won't stay for a little piece of Hoss."

J.R. felt his hands clench into fists. One of the things that had always made him and Hoss such fast friends had been that they didn't argue over women. Hoss went for the kind of bubbly, good-time gal that always struck J.R. as flighty, while he preferred women who could string together more than two coherent, grammatically correct sentences at a time. In the eleven years he'd been out here, he and Hoss had never once sparred over a woman.

There was a first for everything, apparently.

"She's off-limits." The words came out as more of a growl than a statement.

"Yeah?" Hoss puffed out his chest and met J.R.'s mean stare head-on. "I don't see you doing a bang-up job of getting her into your bed. If you aren't up to the task, maybe you should stand aside, *old* man."

J.R. bristled. He was only six years older than Hoss. The idiot was intentionally trying to yank his chain, and he was doing a damn fine job of it. J.R. did his best to keep his voice calm. As much as Thalia's reappearance pissed him off, he still didn't want to walk into the kitchen with a black eye or a busted nose. "I don't want her in my bed." Hoss snorted in disbelief, but J.R. chose to ignore him. "I don't want her in my house. And the more you make googly eyes at her, the more Minnie gushes at her, the more she'll keep coming back. She doesn't belong here."

Hoss didn't back down. But he didn't push it, either. Instead, he turned and headed for the house at a leisurely mosey, still whistling. Still planning on making a move on Thalia Thorne.

Cursing under his breath, J.R. groomed his horse at double-time speed. He did *not* want Thalia in his bed, no matter what Hoss said. She represented too big a threat to his life out here, the life he'd chosen. The fact that she was here again should be a big, honking sign to everyone that she was not to be taken lightly.

So why was he the only one alarmed? And why, for the love of everything holy, was his brain now imagining what she'd look like in his bed?

He tried to block out the images that filed through his mind in rapid succession—Thalia wrapped in the sheets, her hair tousled and loose, her shoulders bare, her *everything* bare. Waking her up with a kiss, seeing the way she gazed at him, feeling the way her body warmed to his touch…

J.R. groaned in frustration and kicked a hay bale as he headed toward the house. When had this become a problem? When had he let a woman get under his skin like this—a woman he didn't even *like?* When had his body started overruling his common sense, his self-preservation?

And when had Hoss decided a woman was more important than their friendship?

His mood did not improve when he walked into *his* kitchen to find Thalia, sitting on *his* stool, leaning into a hug with Hoss. That did it. J.R. was going to have to kill his best friend.

He must have growled, because Hoss shot him a look that said *I got here first* and Thalia sat up straight. The way her cheeks blushed a pale pink did not improve J.R.'s situation one bit.

"J.R., look who's back!" Hoss's tone of voice made it plenty clear that he was going to keep pushing J.R.'s buttons. His arm was still slung around her shoulders. "I was telling Thalia how good it was to see her pretty face again." The SOB then gave her another big squeeze. "You found a casting couch for me yet?"

Thalia laughed nervously as she pulled away from Hoss's embrace. "Sadly, I haven't found the couch that can handle you, Hoss. But I'll keep looking."

Then she turned her bright eyes to him. "Hello, J.R." She made no move to get up, no move to shake his hand—much less hug him. He wouldn't have trusted her if she had, but damned if it didn't piss him off all over again that she didn't.

Behind the Thalia and Hoss tableau, Minnie tapped her big wooden spoon on the counter as she looked daggers at him. *Be nice,* her eyes told him. Why was it his job to make nice when everyone else was flaunting his rules in his house? Screw it. Without a word, he turned away from the interloper and the two traitors and walked—not stomped—upstairs. He heard Hoss coming up behind him, but he didn't wait.

The shower did little to improve his mood, mostly because he couldn't stop thinking about that woman. At least this time, she was dressed appropriately. A cowl-neck sweater in an ice-blue color that matched her eyes had clung to her curves, revealing as much—if not more—than the short dress. Instead of those teasing tights, she was wearing jeans that hugged every inch of her long legs. And instead of delicate stilettos, she had on a pair of real cowboy boots. Her hair had been freed of the severe twist so that now it fell in loose waves around her face and shoulders.

She looked like someone who did, in fact, fit out here. Worse than that? She looked like she *belonged* out here.

It's a costume, he reminded himself as he rubbed dry with more force than normal. That wasn't the real her. He didn't know what the real her looked like, but it couldn't be that cowboy's dream come true down there.

If Hoss touched her again, J.R. would have to kill him.

He almost put on his favorite frayed shirt in protest of this whole ridiculous situation, but he couldn't pull the trigger. He went with the sweater Minnie had knit him two years ago for Christmas. It usually made her happy when he wore it. Clearly, it was his only hope of keeping her on his side right now.

He could do this. He wouldn't lose his temper, and he wouldn't add fuel to the fire. If need be, he wouldn't say anything. If he didn't engage, sooner or later Thalia Thorne would get tired of asking. It was that simple.

The glint of sunlight off gold slowed him up, and he found himself staring at his Oscar. He didn't know why he kept the damn thing out—after all, his Golden Globe and all his other awards were in a box in the back of his closet. Oscar had brought him nothing but heartache, today included. He hefted it off the mantle, feeling the cold metal. He'd been terrified the night he'd won, hoping and praying someone else—anyone else—would win, but knowing that the race was his to lose. And when they called his name, the terror had spiked right on over to panic. If he hadn't figured it out before that moment, he knew then that he'd lost any semblance of control he'd had over his life. People had always expected things of him—his mother, his agent, film people—but he'd known when he'd won that the life he'd barely managed to keep a grip on was going to be wrenched from his control.

And he'd been right. He'd stopped being a person and become nothing but a commodity.

He'd hated feeling powerless then, and he hated it now. That was the problem with Thalia Thorne. Her unwelcome intrusion left him feeling like he wasn't in control anymore.

He looked Oscar in the face. "I'm the boss around here," he said, more to himself than the inanimate object. So that woman had him a little spooked. So she'd won over Minnie and Hoss. He was not about to cede control of his life to the likes of her and, by extension, Levinson. No pretty face, no sweet touch and no amount of money would change his mind.

His resolve set, he headed downstairs. Nice? Sure. Polite? Barely. But he wasn't taking the part. He wasn't taking anything from Thalia Thorne.

At least he'd gotten back down to the kitchen before Hoss. Thalia was still on the stool with Minnie standing next to her. From the look of it, they were poring over Minnie's latest *People* magazine.

"I love this dress on Charlize," Minnie was saying in a wistful tone that was far more girlish than normal.

"Really? I thought the one she wore at last year's BAFTAs was better." Thalia glanced up at him, and damned if her face didn't light up almost exactly like it had when he'd woken her up two days ago.

He was *not* being swayed by her face. So he crossed his arms and glared at her. It didn't have the desired impact. Instead of paling or shrinking away, she favored him with a small grin. Damn.

"The BAFTAs?" Minnie was thankfully too engrossed in her fashion daydreams to notice his lack of manners.

"The British equivalent of the Oscars."

"Oh." It was hard to begrudge Minnie this little bit of fun, because she was clearly in seventh heaven. "Would pictures of that be online? We could look them up!"

"Sure." Although Thalia was talking to Minnie, she was

still looking at him like she was happy to see him again. For completely stupid reasons, J.R. was happy to note that she didn't look at Hoss like that. Just him.

"I'll go get my laptop." Minnie looked up, registering his presence for the first time. "Oh, J.R., keep an eye on the casserole, okay?"

"I'll do it," Thalia volunteered as Minnie all but ran up the back stairs to get her computer.

He was alone with Thalia. That realization left him with an uncomfortable pit in his stomach. This was his chance—maybe his only chance—to tell her off. He was tired of feeling out of place in his own home. It was time to return the favor.

When she swung those long legs off the stool to head toward the oven, he made his move. He grabbed her arm so hard that she spun into his chest with a squeak. And just like that, they were face-to-face, chest-to-chest.

Big, huge mistake. Her breasts pressed against his chest with little regard to the two layers of sweaters that stood between them. With her boots on, her face was only a few inches below his, and when she looked up into his eyes, he realized how little space separated his mouth from hers.

"What are you doing here?" Besides driving him to distraction, that was. His body strained to respond to the light scent of strawberries that hung around her. She smelled good enough to eat.

Down, boy.

"I came back to see Minnie." Her voice trembled a little as she pushed on his chest with her hands. Not hard—not enough to drive them apart—but enough to make him loosen his grip.

"It won't work."

"What won't?" She had the nerve to look innocent. That made him mad again, which distracted him from the pressure building behind his jeans' zipper.

"You're trying to get Minnie to convince me to take the part. It won't work."

He had her full attention—and that was becoming a problem. Her eyes were wide open, her lips were barely parted. All he'd have to do would be to lower his head without letting go of her. Did she taste as sweet as she smelled?

She angled her head to one side a little. Her hair tipped off her shoulders, exposing the curve of her neck. Her hands, which had been flat on his chest, curved at the fingers, as if she was trying to hold on to him, trying to pull him in closer.

Against his every wish, his head began to dip. He could not kiss her; he could not be turned on by her; he could *not* be interested in her—but he was. She was going to ruin the life he'd made, and he almost didn't care. It was almost worth the way she looked at him, soft and innocent and waiting to be kissed.

Almost.

"Did Levinson tell you to seduce me? Is that it?"

Indignant color flooded her cheeks as everything inviting about her burned up in the heat of her glare. J.R. wasn't all that surprised when she pushed him back and slapped his face all at once. "I'm not his whore." Her voice was level, cold— as if she were in complete control of the situation.

The way she hissed the words made it pretty clear that J.R. had finally, *finally* gotten under her skin. And it was still possible that her fury was an act, a cover for a seduction gone wrong.

So why did he feel like crap? "Sorry," he mumbled. "I wouldn't put it past Levinson."

"I'm not Levinson."

That fact was abundantly clear. He wished Minnie would come back so he could return to safely sulking instead of insulting Thalia's honor. But as there weren't any footsteps on the stairs, he might as well go for broke. "Why do you need me so bad? Actors are a dime a dozen."

It was only after he said it that he realized his words could be taken at least two different ways. He felt his face get hot. Luckily, she looked down at the floor, so she didn't see it.

She almost said something, he realized—but stopped short. Finally, she said, "People are curious about you. They'd pay money to find out what happened to you," in the same cold tone of voice.

And just like that, J.R. was again a commodity to be bought and sold. That unavoidable fact took what interest he had in this woman and buried it six feet under. "I'm not going to take the part, not now, not ever." Part of her face shut down, but not before he caught a glimpse of her disappointment. "And I don't care what Minnie says—you aren't welcome here."

A gasp from behind him didn't do much to break the tension. "J.R.! What did you say?"

This entire situation was spinning out of control, and fast. Her laptop clutched to her chest, Minnie skirted around him and rushed to Thalia saying, "Are you okay?" When Thalia nodded, Minnie fixed him with a glare that could melt glass. "Apologize to our guest, J.R."

Thalia's lower lip quivered—not much, but enough to make him feel like a first-class heel. He should have stuck by his original plan of not talking, but he wasn't backing down.

"I will do no such thing. This is my home, my land and trespassers *will* be shot."

Minnie's eyes narrowed, and suddenly J.R. recalled the time when, more than half-drunk, Hoss had confided that his mother once overpowered him as a teen to keep him from going out with some gang members. Right now, she looked like she was going to take him down and it was going to *hurt*.

"Fine. *Fine*." He knew he was way overreacting, but he couldn't stop himself. He was the boss around here, for God's sake, and no one seemed to be able to remember that. "She can stay for dinner. I'll leave. But when I get back, she better be gone—for good this time. Do I make myself clear?"

He didn't wait for an answer. He grabbed his coat and hat and made damn sure to slam the door behind him.

He'd almost kissed her.

What a mess.

Five

"I should go." That was the only thing Thalia could do. She'd gambled on coming back here and lost big-time. Any hope she had of signing James Robert Bradley was gone for good now. She'd slapped him, for crying out loud. That wasn't exactly a proven negotiating tactic.

Minnie and Hoss shared a look before Minnie said, "Now, don't you worry about J.R. He's just throwing a little...temper tantrum."

Thalia had seen plenty of big egos throw plenty of fits, but those were usually over petty things like trailer size or catering. This "temper tantrum" was much more intense. Much more personal.

"We're used to it," Hoss added, peeking into the oven. The smells of homemade food filled the room, making another argument for why Thalia should at least stay for dinner.

"Really?" She perched on the edge of the stool, not sure if she could relax enough to actually sit on it. "Does he do this often?" He didn't seem like the kind who had hissy fits.

"Oh, my." Minnie chuckled, and Thalia felt some of the tension leave her shoulders. "When we first moved out here, he was so melodramatic." She sighed, brushing her brow in a fake faint. "Every time someone in town called him out, he'd sulk for days."

"Can't tell you how many fights he got into," Hoss added. "Got to the point where Denny wouldn't let him in the bar for a while." He chuckled. "You can take the diva out of Hollywood, but you can't take Hollywood out of the diva."

Thalia mulled over that information as Minnie set plates around the island. "Does that happen a lot—those tantrums?"

"It's been a couple of years since he threw a good one." Hoss looked like he was going to say something else, but Minnie cleared her throat.

"Thalia, be a dear and get the salt and pepper. When it's just us, we eat at the island."

She knew the compliment was partially misdirection, but she was flattered nonetheless. At least someone in this house liked her. Too bad it wasn't the man she was here for. She wondered what had happened a couple of years ago that had provoked his last fit, but Minnie and Hoss were exchanging meaningful glances again, and she knew that she wasn't going to find out.

Still, they seemed to be in a chatty mood. Maybe they were trying to overcompensate for J.R. She decided to skip the tantrums and start at the beginning. "So you met him on the set of *Hell for Leather?*"

Hoss snorted as he dug out a huge helping of spicy chicken casserole. "Not so much *on* the set. I found him in a bar one night, a few towns over. He had on this huge hat, glasses and a fake mustache. Sitting in the corner, drinking a beer like he didn't know how." Hoss chuckled again. "Trying hard to be invisible and doing a damn lousy job at it."

Something about that statement struck Thalia. A wave of guilt washed over her. J.R. was right. She'd been trying to mount a side attack, using Minnie as cover—because she was desperate. She hadn't considered why he was so adamantly opposed to her offer. Perhaps she'd been in Hollywood for so long that she'd forgotten that people did things for reasons that had nothing to do with money or fame.

"Now, don't you fret," Minnie said, patting her arm. "He'll calm down. You know, he skipped his teenaged years. He was already famous, and his mother…she didn't allow for much deviation." The way the older woman said "mother" reminded Thalia that many people believed that J.R. had had something to do with his mother's unexpected death at forty-two, which was why he'd disappeared so quickly after the funeral. "So when he got out here, he—what's the word?"

"Regressed. Had to look that one up," Hoss said with his mouth full.

"Yes, he regressed. We had our hands full for a few years." She smiled at the memory. "But he settled. He'll settle again."

"What I don't understand is, why is he here? I mean, no one knows where he is. He just disappeared."

"I told you—invisible." Hoss made a swirling circle with his hand and added, "Poof!" for emphasis.

"I think the bigger question is why you're here." Minnie had Thalia locked under the same no-nonsense gaze that she'd been giving J.R. "As much as I enjoy talking about the gowns, I know you're not here for me. Why are you pursuing him?"

Thalia swallowed carefully, afraid that she might choke on her chicken. "It'd be good PR for the movie," she said, almost reflexively. "People want to know what happened to him."

Minnie smiled, but Thalia could tell she wasn't off the hook. Suddenly, she didn't feel as comfortable anymore. But what could she do? Minnie had stuck up for her on multiple occasions and kept her from turning into a Popsicle. At the least, she owed the older woman the truth.

Thalia felt unexpected tears crowding at the corner of her eyes. "If I don't sign him, I don't have a job. Levinson will fire me, and he'll make sure no one else will hire me." She left out the part about her past affair with Levinson, and especially the part about how his wife had destroyed her acting career because of that affair. One humiliation at a time was all she could handle right now while maintaining her composure.

"I see." An uncomfortable silence settled over the table. Thalia was miserable. The worst of it was, she liked Minnie and Hoss, and now she'd used the sincere friendship they'd offered her as a wedge between them and J.R.

No, that wasn't the worst of it. The worst of it was that she had let her feelings get in the way. If she hadn't let her decade-old crush on James Robert Bradley color her motivations, then she could have done a better job negotiating as a professional, not a love-struck teenybopper. She'd tried so hard to justify touching J.R. the first time as something she'd done only because she'd been half-asleep.

This afternoon had showed her how wrong she was. The moment he'd grabbed her, she should have pulled away. The moment he'd looked down into her eyes, she should have thrown up some sort of wall. The moment he'd looked like he'd wanted to kiss her as much as she wanted him to, she should have done…something. Anything that wouldn't have left her wide open to his insults.

"He won't do it, will he?"

Hoss was the one who answered. "I doubt it."

"He doesn't want the notoriety, and he doesn't need the money," Minnie added.

"What *does* he want?" It was some kind of pathetic to have to ask, but she was running out of ideas.

"Well…" Before Hoss could expound on that thought, he grunted. "Oof!" Thalia suspected that Minnie had kicked him.

Right. There was that whole sex thing. He had wanted to kiss her, after all. She could track him down, throw herself at him and seduce him until he was willing to agree to anything, like he'd accused her of doing. Some people operated like that.

The problem was, she knew, deep down, that J.R. wasn't one of those people. And neither was she.

"I don't know if even J.R. knows the answer to that question." It was nice of Minnie to dance around the obvious, but it didn't change things.

Thalia had hit a big, J.R.-shaped brick wall. Clearly, attempting this on his turf was a nonstarter. He'd dug in his heels, big-time. But it wasn't like she could get him to Hollywood, or some other neutral territory, to start over. Hell, she doubted she could do that even to apologize.

The moment the thought crossed her mind, she latched on. She needed to apologize. That might not buy her much goodwill, but it was obvious that there could be no professional discussions while he felt himself the wronged party.

The more this idea bounced around her head, the better she liked it. He'd gone somewhere, after all—somewhere that wasn't his home. Somewhere neutral—or more neutral than here, anyway.

She needed to head toward Beaverhead. It was a small town, to be sure, but she remembered seeing the blinking Budweiser sign in a window. She'd be willing to bet that J. R. Bradley's truck would be parked out front right about now.

She thanked Minnie and Hoss for dinner. Minnie repeated that she was welcome to stop by anytime she was in the neighborhood, but no one made any final-sounding goodbyes.

This wasn't over yet. Not by a long shot.

Denny's was hopping for the middle of the week. Not that J.R. was talking with anyone in the crowd, but as he sat in his usual spot at the end of the bar, he kept an ear open. Maybe it was the weather. The lack of snow made it easy to get out. Whatever it was, it was crowded. The noise of drunken two-stepping, bragging and pool games tried hard to distract J.R. from his little pity party.

Man, he was in so much trouble. Minnie was going to skin him alive—that was, if she didn't kill him outright. He rubbed his face, wondering when things had gone so wrong. He was mad at himself on top of things. He'd been out here for eleven years. He thought he'd gotten real good at dealing with the shadows of his past, but all it took was one woman—one single, beautiful woman—to blow up his world again. Why did he let her get to him?

And why, for the love of all things holy, was he still thinking about her?

As he nursed his third beer, J.R. felt the blast of cold air as the door opened and closed again. That wasn't so unusual. What was different this time was the way the rowdy crowd quieted down for a beat too long, as if they were all collectively staring at the new arrival. J.R. felt the hairs on the back of his neck stand up in a way that had nothing to do with the drop in temperature.

Damn it.

The bar was quiet enough that he heard the clack of Thalia Thorne's boots making straight for him. She slid onto the bar stool next to him, but she didn't say anything until Denny came down. "What'll it be?"

"I'll take a Natural Light," she said, as if that were an everyday thing.

J.R. snorted. "You drink beer?" And not just any beer. Natty Light. That was pretty low-brow for a woman like her.

"I used to," she admitted without looking at him. "When I was in college at OSU, I drank a lot of beer."

"But not in L.A." OSU—he struggled to think which *O* that was. Oklahoma? Yeah, she'd said something about her mom in Oklahoma.

"Not my scene." When Denny slid her the bottle, she thanked him and took a pull.

They sat there. J.R. didn't know what to do. Every time he'd tried to talk to this woman, some sort of social disaster had occurred. On the bright side, Minnie wasn't here to get all offended at his loutish behavior.

He could talk to this woman without losing his temper. He could try, anyway. "How much longer are you gonna keep following me?"

"Beg pardon?" She choked on her swig, and J.R. realized he was going to have to work on his timing.

"You show up at my house despite posted trespassing signs and my explicit wishes. When I finally leave, you barge into my favorite bar." He was proud that he managed to keep his voice level. "What's next, huh?" He almost added, you gonna follow me into the shower? He was stopped by the image that sprang up in his head of her, wet and naked in his bathroom, water streaming down her back, between her breasts—maybe he'd had too much beer. He cleared his throat and tried to shift on his seat without giving anything away.

She didn't say anything for a second, which again struck him as odd. Aside from her inability to respect his wishes to be left alone, she didn't negotiate like anyone else he'd ever known. Hell, even Hoss would have barged into the gap, pressing his case with a nearly religious fervor. Not her. It was almost as if she were here against her will.

Either that, or she was thinking about showers, too.

Crap. He either needed more beer or less beer. And since less was hard to pull off, he said, "Denny, one more."

The old man set the bottle down in front of J.R. "That's your fourth one, bud. You know the rule."

"The rule?" Of course Thalia would barge into *that* gap.

Denny gave her something that might have been a smile on someone less crusty. "I cut him off at four."

"Why?" She was leaning forward, as if Denny were spilling deep, personal secrets instead of company policy.

"Because," J.R. answered for the older man. "More than four and I usually wind up punching someone."

"Or something," Denny added, lifting up the corner of a poster that covered a fist-sized hole in the wall.

"Aw, man, I paid you to get that fixed." And he hadn't been allowed back in the bar for six months. "That was five years ago."

"You paid me, all right." Chuckling, Denny moved back down the counter, leaving J.R. staring at his fourth beer. As much as he wanted to drain the sucker dry, he wasn't ready to go home to face the Minnie-music, so he had to nurse it.

He waited for Thalia to make some sort of comment on his propensity for bar-based violence, but she didn't. Suddenly, J.R. got nervous. What did she know? More specifically, what had Hoss told her?

As if she was reading his mind, she said, "Hoss said he found you in a bar, trying to be invisible."

Damn. She finally looked at him, pivoting her stool around so he got the full view of her sweater-clad chest again. "You don't look so invisible now."

"I don't have to hide anymore." Which was a bold-faced lie, and they both knew it. It was so bold-faced that he heard himself lie some more. "I'm not hiding from you."

"That's why I'm here." She looked at her bottle, her fingernails peeling the label. "I wanted to apologize."

J.R. shot a look around the bar, trying to figure out if the volume had distorted her words. "You wanna *what?*"

"Apologize." She still didn't meet his eyes, but her fingers were doing interesting things with her beer bottle.

Nope, he'd heard her right the first time. "For trespassing?"

When she shook her head, her hair caught the dim light of the bar. For a second, she glowed. Why did she have to be so pretty? He managed not to say that. Score one for his big, fat mouth.

"No." She swung away from him, back to the bar. He

turned his gaze forward, too. Even though they were still sitting next to each other, it put a wall between them. He wasn't sure if he liked that illusion of distance or not. It was good because it gave him a little thinking room, but all the same, he liked looking at her.

Someone on the other side of the bar catcalled, which set his teeth on edge. Other idiots in this bar apparently liked looking at her, too.

She didn't seem to notice. "I'm sorry that I didn't realize what I was asking you to do. What I was asking you to give up."

J.R. forgot all about the catcall, the four-beer limit and how Minnie was going to kill him. He forgot everything but the woman sitting next to him. "What?" Deep inside, past the buzz he was working on, something in him hummed in recognition—the same pull he'd felt when they'd had dinner together.

She drained the last of her beer—for courage, he wondered? "I should have realized that the thing that made you—"

Whatever she was going to say—and man, did he want to hear it—was cut off by the huge arm dividing the space between them. The hand slammed into the bar top as a voice said, "Well, well, lookit what the big star drug in!"

Just when things had started to look up. J.R. didn't have to see who the voice belonged to. He recognized Jeff "Big Dog" Dorsey. *As if this evening couldn't get any worse,* he thought. He hired Dorsey on in the summer to work cattle. The man was a damn fine cowboy, but a slimy excuse for a man. "Back off, Dog."

"I ain't talkin' to you, *Hollywood.* I'm talkin' to the purty lady." He leered down into Thalia's face. "Hi, purty lady." Thalia shrank back in confusion and not a little bit of fear.

J.R. grabbed Dog's arm and shoved. "I said *back off.* You're drunk."

"Oooh, I'm scared. Shaking."

"You should be scared." When J.R. stood, fists already clenched, his stool tipped over. In the time before it hit the ground, Dorsey grabbed Thalia's arm. She shot J.R. a look of stark panic.

The next thing J.R. knew, he had Dorsey by the throat and the two of them were flying backward, crashing through tables and chairs until they hit a wall. "You touch her again," he growled, not sure where the threat was going. Instead, he leaned his forearm against Dorsey's windpipe a little harder. The big man's eyes bulged. Good. Everyone would know how dead serious J.R. was.

Dorsey took an off balance swing at J.R.'s midsection, knocking most of the wind out of him. But the blow wasn't enough to push J.R. off entirely.

The rest of the crowd was mostly yelling for Dorsey to knock J.R. to the ground, although in the background, he could hear Denny bellowing for everyone to knock it off or he was gonna call Stan, the local law. J.R. held firm, using his thigh to block Dorsey's last-ditch attempt to rack him.

As Dorsey's eyes started to roll back in his head, J.R. realized he'd lost track of Thalia. He let go of Dorsey and stepped back. The big man dropped to his knees with a *whump,* coughing hard. The crowd quieted as J.R. spun to look at them. Yeah, everyone was at least half-drunk, and yeah, it was a little scuffle, but everyone in here had been rooting for him to take a good punch or three.

He used to like this bar.

Finally, he saw Thalia at the back, cutting her way through the silent crowd. The good news was that she didn't look scared anymore. The bad news was that she seemed a little pissed.

"You like to strangle me!" Dorsey'd gotten most of his voice back. Too bad.

"You treat a woman like that again, and I'll see to it that you never find work around these parts again."

The crowd murmured, half in approval and half in dis-
agreement. J.R. didn't care. He recognized ten or so faces
from his summer crew. They knew he fed them well and paid
them better. A summer spot at the Bar B Ranch left a man
enough to live on for the long winter. Most of the eyes he met
nodded in silent agreement. No one wanted to risk their spot.

The crowd parted as he headed back to where Thalia was,
her hands on her hips. "Come on," he said, shooting a look
back to Denny. The old man shook his head in disappointment. "Let me know if I owe you anything for the chairs."

Denny waved him off.

Thalia grabbed her purse and coat and went outside with
him. "What was that?" she demanded once the door of the
bar was shut.

"That was me defending you?" Her sudden burst of anger
caught him off guard.

"Okay, yes, and I appreciate being defended. But—" she
jammed her arms in her coat and then crossed them, giving
him a highly critical once-over. He was getting mighty tired
of people looking at him like that "—that's how you handle
hecklers? No wonder you're busy *not* hiding out here."

When had he become the bad guy here? "Why are you
mad at me? Dorsey's the one being a jackass. I was putting
him in his place. It's not a big deal."

"It could be, J.R. Maybe not in a bar in the middle of nowhere, but what happens when you pull that crap in the real
world? What happens when someone with a camera finds
you? You can't beat down just anyone. As it is, you're lucky
you're not being sued for assault—and how do you think that
would look on a tabloid headline? Because gossip has a life
of its own, you know."

No doubt about it—he was the bad guy here. And he still
didn't understand what her problem was. Why should she care
about what he did? "What is your deal? This place *is* my real
world, and things were fine before you showed up. You're

the one who turned everyone's head." His words spilled out of him faster than he could figure out what he was going to say. "If you didn't stand out so much, no one would have even noticed me."

Despite the heavy coat—a different one than she'd had on last time—he saw her visibly bristle. "I will not apologize for existing."

"Yeah? Well, you were going to apologize for something, so don't act like it's beneath you."

She threw her hands up and all but snarled at him. "I do not have time for temper tantrums, not all the way out here. If I want ego trips and sexism, I'll go back to Hollywood. There, at least, I can see it coming a mile off." She turned toward her little rental car. "And," she said, spinning on her heel, "I was going to apologize, but it's clear you don't need one and I'm not about to throw a punch to make my point."

"Oh, so it's not okay for me to keep a drunk from man-handling you, but it's fine for you to slap me? Typical," he muttered at her retreating back.

She didn't retreat for long. "Excuse me?" The next thing he knew, she was bearing down on him, and the look in her eye said that punching him was still on the table. "You're allowed to defend my honor from a drunk? You—who asked me if I was Levinson's whore?" She put her hand flat on his chest and shoved. She packed a little more wallop than he would have given her credit for—he had to take a step back to keep his balance.

He grabbed her hand, but didn't pull it away from his chest. Maybe those beers had hit him harder than he thought, because he was having trouble keeping up with her. She was mad at him, that he got. But what she was mad about seemed to change with every other breath that escaped her parted, reddened lips. "I never said *whore*. Don't put words in my mouth."

"You didn't have to. Your meaning was perfectly clear.

Well, in case it's not blisteringly obvious, I'm no one's whore. Not Levinson's, not yours. I don't sleep with people to get the job done, so if that's what you're holding out for, you can keep on holding."

What the heck was she talking about? He wasn't angling for a roll in the sack—was that what she thought? He knew he should back away, disengage. He didn't. "I'm supposed to believe that, after you all but throw a casting couch at Hoss?"

"That. Was. A. Joke." Her eyes flashed in the dim neon light of the bar signs as she gave him another shove. "Or did you abandon your sense of humor in L.A. along with your life?"

They were close now, so close that he felt the warmth of her breath fan out around his face. He still had her hand pinned to his chest. For some reason, he wanted to smile. This was an argument, no doubt about it—but something about it felt real. Honest. Thalia was furious, true, but it felt good to have things out in the open. No pussyfooting around what she wanted, or who he used to be. Their differences were front and center.

"Why are you mad at me?" If they were being honest, then he was going to have to own up to his cluelessness.

"Because you don't seem to understand how your actions—grabbing a woman and questioning her reputation, brawling in a bar—can get away from you. If you did either of those things in my world, J.R., you'd wind up on the evening news, and if you think I'm a pain in your—" she paused and swallowed. She was doing that thing again, where she blushed without seeming to acknowledge her embarrassment "—neck, then you can't imagine how hard the paparazzi will make your life, your family's life."

"You being here makes it hard on me."

Everything about her changed in the space of two heartbeats. The fire in her eyes simmered down to a warm glow. Anytime she wanted to stop looking sweet and beautiful would be great. "I know. That's what I was going to apologize for." Her voice was soft, inviting.

The space between them thinned, and he briefly thought she might be the one to start the kissing. She wanted to—he thought. Then the door of the bar opened, and noise—and a few bodies—poured out.

When she stepped away, he had no choice but to let her go.

Without another word, she turned back to her car. "Hey." He jogged after her—as much as one jogged in boots, anyway. "You're still staying at Lloyd's, right?" Being the smallest of towns, every resident of Beaverhead probably knew the sexy out-of-towner was holed up at Lloyd's. Including Dorsey.

She paused, her hand on the door handle. "J.R., I..." Her voice trailed off, taking whatever she was going to say with it. Then, she got in and drove off.

Six

The truck—J.R.'s truck—was still out there. It was dark, so Thalia wasn't one hundred percent sure that it was actually him, but something told her he'd followed her back to Lloyd's.

What the heck was she supposed to do about this? J.R. had all but accused her of stalking him—somewhat rightly—and now he was staking her out? Was this normal?

No, there was nothing normal about anything this evening. Not the part where she slapped him, not the part where he nearly strangled a guy for touching her and not the moment of blistering honesty in the parking lot. Not a normal event in the bunch.

So the better question was: Was this dangerous? She'd pushed J.R. further than she'd meant to, and every one of her attempts to negotiate with him backfired on her in one way or another. Despite how much she irritated J.R.—which she knew was a lot—and despite how much he was driving her bonkers—an almost equal amount—she didn't think he was a physical threat to her.

* * *

She wasn't going to be able to sleep, much less take a hot shower, knowing he was out there without knowing why. And she was not about to go back outside and ask him.

When her cell rang, she jumped so hard she almost tore down the drapery she was hiding behind. She didn't recognize the number, but she thought it was a Montana area code. "Hello?"

"Thalia? This is Minnie Red Horse. Have you seen J.R.?"

Thalia let out a rush of air. "Yes. I went to apologize at the local bar."

After a momentary pause, Minnie said, "Oh. Do you have any idea when he'll be home? He's not answering his phone, and Denny says he left with you."

Thalia winced. They'd left at the same time, which was entirely different than leaving together. "He's not with me now, but I could try calling him for you." That way she could figure out if he was the one watching her window or not.

"Thank you, dear." Minnie gave her the number and they hung up.

Thalia looked at her phone. This wasn't about the part or the movie anymore. This felt like the point of no return. She could go one way or the other. She could call him, or she could ignore the truck outside.

She dialed. She couldn't see any movement in the truck, but then he picked up. "Hello?"

"Are you following me?"

In response, the overhead light in the truck flipped on, and she saw J.R. in profile. "I'm not so much following you as keeping an eye on you." He cleared his throat. "Are you up there?"

She turned on the small bedside lamp. It wasn't a lot of light, but it was enough that he could at least see her in profile. Luckily, the flannel pajamas she'd bought at J.C. Penney didn't lend themselves to being see-through. "Is there a difference between following me and keeping an eye on me? Because if there is, I'm not seeing it."

"Everyone in town probably knows where you're at, and Dog isn't the kind of man to let something go—not until he's sobered up." He paused, and she wished she could see his eyes. "I'm making sure he doesn't come back to prove his point."

"Oh." That was a pretty good reason. She might have conflicting feelings about J.R., but she definitely didn't want to see that brute again. Ever.

That begged another question. "Why do you care? I mean, I've been nothing but trouble for you. You could hang me out to dry."

He snorted. "I see nothing's changed about Hollywood."

"What's that supposed to mean?"

"Just because you trespass on *my* property and flirt with *my* best friend and attract all the wrong kinds of attention at *my* bar doesn't mean I'd stand by and let anything happen to you. A real man makes sure a lady is safe."

Part of Thalia melted. Maybe it was because she'd been hung out to dry on more than one occasion. After all, Levinson had let her take all of the fall for their failed affair, and she'd once fancied that he loved her. As incredible as it seemed now, she'd once fancied that she'd loved him. Just another example of letting her emotions get in the way of business.

This was different. Knowing—and believing—that J.R. would defend her instead of throwing her to the wolves was a gift in and of itself. That he thought of her as a lady, despite how wrong things had gone? *Melt*.

But as one part of her melted, another part of her wanted to throw things at him. "What is it with you? Okay, so I wasn't invited the first time. It's not like I cut a lock and snuck into your house. Minnie invited me back the second time. And I'm not flirting with Hoss. He's a nice man and all, but I'm not interested in him. Ugh. It would be like kissing my brother. And I can't help it if this town is populated with Neanderthals."

She expected him to come back with the myriad of ways this whole thing was all her fault, but he didn't say anything. The silence stretched between them, and she found herself wondering if he was done talking or what.

"That happen a lot?" was what he finally said, startling her.

"Which part?"

"Getting hung out to dry? Or what is it they say now? Thrown in front of the bus?"

"Thrown under the bus." She smiled at him, not that he could see it. Who would have guessed that the man who was once the physical embodiment of cool couldn't even handle a catchphrase?

"Yeah. That. The Hollywood I used to know was every man—and woman—for themselves. That ever happen to you?"

She exhaled, fogging up the window. Levinson had not only thrown her under the bus, but he'd backed it up over her a few times for good measure. She didn't want to tell J.R. that. He had obviously already formed an opinion of her. He hated Levinson, and with good reason. If she told J.R. how Levinson had all but tied her to the bumper of the bus, it would destroy what little respect he had for her. "It's Hollywood. Nothing I can't handle." She heard J.R. chuckle. "What?"

"I'm going to take that as a *yes*. How long you been there?"

She didn't like this, not one bit. Despite the physical distance between them, it felt like he was not only digging into her past, but getting close to striking pay dirt. It made her nervous, like she was giving something up.

How long had it been since someone had asked her these basic questions? A long time. After the affair with Levinson had blown up in her face, she'd retreated into herself. People——men—didn't ask where she was from. Was that because they were a self-absorbed lot? Or because she never gave anyone the chance to get past that first wall?

"Must be doing some hard thinking up there," J.R. mused into the silence. "Or did you forget? Hollywood can do that, you know."

"I've been there ten years. I haven't forgotten."

"Ah, now. And you can't be much over…" She could only wonder what age he was going to say. "Well, I guess you went out when you were a teenager."

She could picture the grin on his face—small, hidden beneath the beard—but at heart, the same grin that he'd had on in all those posters she'd taped up in her room when she was a teenager. Somehow, back when she'd envisioned meeting James Robert Bradley, this particular scenario never played out in her head—him making guesses on how old she was.

He'd probably keep dancing around it until she told him. This was one of the few plusses of not being an actress. Her age wasn't an immediate disqualifier. "I turned thirty in September, if that's what you wanted to know."

"Hmm." The sound he made—closer to a purr than a thoughtful observation—sent little sparks of electricity racing up and down the skin on the back of her hand. "That's not old."

She wouldn't let that count as flattery. "Boy, you have been gone a long time. I'm all but a dinosaur these days."

"Wonder what that makes me? No, don't answer that."

Not that she was going to, because then she'd have to tell him that he was clearly one of those men who only got better with age, like Cary Grant or Gregory Peck. And then she'd get all swoony again, and every time she did that, she managed to stick her foot in her mouth. "It's different," he went on, missing her awkward silence. "You've only been there for ten years. I was there for…twenty-one years."

"Really?" It seemed like a long time—but also not quite long enough. "I always kind of thought you were born there."

"Nope. St. Louis. My mother had me doing commercials when I was a baby." His voice seemed to grow softer. She couldn't tell if he was holding the phone away from his mouth or getting all sentimental. "We moved to Hollywood when I was four."

"You were so young."

"Oh, yeah." He exhaled into the phone. "You know what I wanted to be when I grew up?"

"No." She didn't know where he was going with this trip down memory lane. If she had to describe this current exchange, she'd have to call it chitchat, the conversation of two friends. It bordered on sharing, and she was afraid she didn't want the conversation to end.

"A firefighter, an astronaut and a cowboy. Oh, and an army man." He paused, and when he spoke again, she could hear the nostalgia in his voice. "I went back to St. Louis once, after I came out here. Didn't recognize anything. Not even the house I grew up in." He cleared his throat. "That was a long time ago."

"You didn't want to be an actor?"

"It's what my mother wanted."

"You were good at it." Obviously. They didn't usually give Oscars out of pity.

"It was never my choice, Thalia."

The weight of those words tried to cave in her chest. Gone was the nostalgic tone, the sentimental-sounding sighs. Heck, he didn't even sound like he'd been drinking. He was dead serious.

She felt so, so guilty, an emotion that she'd gotten used to pretending she didn't experience. She'd asked him to take the part, and he'd said no. Instead of respecting that choice, she had kept coming at him. And what made it worse was that he'd been right about the bar fight. He hadn't been sued for loutish behavior yet. He was, relatively speaking, safe out here. She was the one who could expose him. If people came looking for him, it would be because of her. If he went viral, it would all trace back to the day she landed in Montana.

But to show guilt was to show weakness, and no matter how personal this conversation seemed, she wouldn't grovel. So she tried to deflect. "A cowboy, huh?"

"Yup."

He didn't come up with another wild tangent. For the life of her, she couldn't read his mind. The silence started to bug her. Maybe she couldn't bring herself to apologize for not honoring his choice, but she still owed him something. "I'm sorry I slapped you earlier. You were right, that was uncalled for."

"It's okay. I crossed a line I shouldn't have. My apologies for that. It's just…"

When his voice trailed off, Thalia found herself leaning into the window, hoping to hear what he had to say. A story below her, she saw J.R. shift in his seat, leaning forward until he was looking up at her. She couldn't see his eyes, darn it, but she still felt a connection with him as clearly as if she was sitting across the table from him.

"Minnie's probably worried about me." He leaned back, his whole face disappearing into the cab of his truck.

"Yeah." Right—she was supposed to tell him that exact thing. "You should probably get home."

The dome light flipped off, and she thought he'd hung up on her. Then she heard him say, "I won't let anyone bother you, Thalia."

She pressed her hand to the window again, wishing she could touch him, wishing she could feel his strong hand cover hers again. "I know, J.R."

The call ended. Thalia turned out the light, but she stood at the window for a few more moments, knowing he would keep her safe.

The odd thing was, she wanted to do the same for him—to protect him. To make sure that he didn't wind up as fodder for the paparazzi.

This was all backward. There was no such thing as bad PR, after all. J.R. making a few headlines would add a big boost to the movie's bottom line.

Standing there in the dark, watching his truck, she knew she couldn't do it. She wasn't the kind of person who let someone destroy themselves for a strong opening weekend.

She wouldn't do that to him.

"I don't like this wind." Hoss tucked his chin into his coat as they headed back to the ranch house after another grueling afternoon of breaking ice. "Nope. Don't like it at all."

"What?" J.R. tried to focus on what Hoss was saying, but it wasn't easy. He was cold—nothing new there. But the cold on top of the bone-deep exhaustion made doing much of anything hard. Hell, a few fields over, he'd lost the grip on his ax midswing and nearly decapitated his best friend.

Hoss snorted. "What time *did* you get home last night?"

J.R. groaned. Hoss already knew the answer—three-thirty. "Late enough."

"Well, I don't like this wind."

J.R. sat up in the saddle, paying a little more attention to the weather. The wind cut down out of the north with bitter speed, but the air felt heavy. "Snow?"

"Snow," Hoss agreed, burrowing deeper into his coat. "Lots of it. And soon."

"How soon?" Mentally, he slapped his head. If he'd been aware of his surroundings, he'd have started moving some cattle into the more sheltered fields. Maybe it wouldn't hit for another day or two. Maybe they'd have time.

"Weather says tomorrow night." Hoss tipped his hat back and sniffed the air. "If we're lucky."

Damn it. "Better check the generators when we get back." The ranch house was well equipped to handle a blizzard. The fireplaces in each room kept the house warmish on their own, but after the first blizzard, J.R. had invested in several superpowered generators for the house and the barn. They had snowshoes, snowmobiles and enough food to last them a month.

He had a ton of books, and Minnie was fond of Scrabble. Plus, they needed the snow to hedge their bets against a dry summer. In all reality, snow was not a bad thing.

That didn't mean J.R. had to like it.

He liked it a whole lot less when he and Hoss crested the last hill and saw Thalia's rental car in front of his house again. "Oh, no."

"What is she doing out here?" Hoss asked. The fact that Hoss hadn't grabbed this opportunity to tease J.R. showed how worried his best friend was about the weather. "Don't she know it's going to snow?"

"City folk," J.R. grumbled, pushing his horse on as much as he dared in this wind.

The weather took a lousy situation and made it downright dangerous. Bad enough that Thalia felt free to drop by any old time she felt like it; worse that her presence had led to him being banned from his favorite bar for the rest of the winter. All of that was inconvenient, annoying.

But to have someone who had been so demonstrably unaware of the weather driving in blizzard conditions—hell, even a regular heavy snow—was a recipe for disaster. People died in this kind of weather. They drove off the road or got hit by a plow. Or they got disorientated and froze to death a few feet from their house.

A golden, sunshine woman like Thalia wouldn't stand a chance against a Montana blizzard. He didn't have a doubt in his mind about that. And he knew, even though she drove him well past the point of distraction, that he'd do whatever he could to keep her safe.

He didn't know what that *whatever* would mean.

He and Hoss got the horses fed and blanketed before they hurried inside. J.R. couldn't say that he was exactly *happy* to see Thalia, not under the circumstances. When she turned her pretty face to him, and he watched her eyes light up because she was glad to see him, well, damn. He was glad to see her, too.

"Before you say anything," she began without any further ado, "I'm not here about the part."

The effect this statement had on him was unexpected. Maybe he'd gotten a little too cold out in that wind, but a weird, light-headed feeling made his scalp tingle. "Oh?"

"Everything okay?" Hoss stepped around J.R., wrapping one of his arms around Thalia's shoulder and giving her an awkward squeeze. Thalia gave J.R. a look and a half smile, and he heard her voice say, "It would be like kissing my brother." The tingly feeling got a little stronger.

"Yes, it's fine." Thalia straightened, and Hoss's arm fell away. "I came to say goodbye."

Minnie made a noise, and for the first time, J.R. noticed her. She looked like she'd been crying, or something close to it—watery eyes, red nose she kept wiping with a tissue. Thalia turned and patted Minnie on the arm, like she was trying to comfort her.

What the heck was going on?

"You sure about that?" Hoss was looking worried now, too, which only made the feeling that J.R. was missing something important get even stronger.

"It'll be okay." Thalia smiled at Hoss, but J.R. could see that it didn't reach her eyes. She was lying—about what?

"Anytime you're out this way, you stop by," Minnie said with a hug. "It's been a pleasure having you out here." Then she patted Thalia's cheek. "I know it's hard to see now, but it'll work out. I believe that."

The way Minnie—and Hoss—were talking was almost like they were trying to get Thalia to stay. And here J.R. had been trying to get rid of her for days.

He didn't know what was going on, but he wasn't entirely

sure he wanted her to leave. Only because of the weather, he quickly told himself.

Thalia's smile was more real this time. "I know. If I get any extra seats to an awards show, I'll call you and you can see all those dresses in person."

Instead of acting like a kid on Christmas morning, like J.R. would have expected, Minnie sniffled again. "That'd be wonderful, dear, but call your mother first."

"Yeah, don't let the turkeys get you down," Hoss added, throwing his arm around her shoulder again. "You'll call me if you find a good casting couch, right?"

"If something comes up, you're at the top of my list."

Then Hoss and Minnie stepped back, and it was just Thalia and J.R. "So you're going back to California."

"Yes." She was lying again. He could tell by the way her eyes didn't move. She took a step toward him, her hand extended. "J.R., it has been a true pleasure meeting you."

Something about this goodbye felt so final. He didn't like it, and he didn't like that he didn't like it. He'd wanted her to go. He'd told her so in no uncertain terms. And yet... "Likewise." He took her hand in his and held it. The heat that coursed through her warmed him down to his toes. This was less erotic than when she'd touched his face, but no less dizzying. He would have sworn the room was spinning.

Don't go, he almost said. Before he could force the words out, she pulled her hand back and said, "And you don't have to worry. I won't tell Levinson where you are."

"You won't?" It was like he understood each individual word, but strung together, they didn't make any sense.

"No." She lowered her eyes, but looked at him through her thick lashes. "I won't let anyone bother you."

The room—hell, the world—spun even faster, so much so that J.R. had to put his hand on the countertop to steady himself. No one—other than Minnie and Hoss—had ever promised to protect him. And neither of them ever looked at J.R. like Thalia did.

Then she grinned and the tension broke. "Of course, I'm not your agent, so…"

"Yeah." J.R. had to clear his throat. "I'm gonna fire that man."

"Be sure to sign him to a nondisclosure agreement first. That way, if he ever tells anyone else, you can sue him."

"Oh, okay." Actually, that was a good idea. Why hadn't he thought of that before? Probably because he'd never done anything with contracts beyond sign them. His mother had always negotiated everything. J.R. had never figured out if she'd gotten what she'd wanted.

They stood there for a moment. She needed to leave—the weather wasn't going to wait on her—but he couldn't quite bring himself to be the one to say goodbye first.

"Thalia—" he began, but the shrill siren of the emergency weather radio cut him off. Everyone jumped at the sound.

Seconds later, the nasal voice of the weather guy came on. "The following is from the National Weather Service. The following counties are under a blizzard warning as of 4:00 p.m.…"

"Is that here?" Thalia looked at the clock on the stove. Three-fifteen. "I should go. I'm supposed to catch a flight out of Billings tonight."

"You won't make it." That seemed like a simple fact, but the look Thalia shot him made it clear that she took it as a personal attack on her driving skills.

"I'm perfectly capable—" This time, she was cut off by the phone ringing.

Minnie answered it while Thalia glared at him. Maybe he should get her to sign one of those nondisclosure things—just in case.

"Yes, she's here. Yes, we heard." Minnie's forehead was so knotted up with worry that her brows were in danger of swapping places. "No, that's okay. You go on. We'll take care of her." She hung up and looked at J.R. "That was Lloyd. He wants to go stay with his daughter—she's got a generator." Her gaze pleaded with J.R. He could almost hear her saying, *Don't put that woman out in this weather. She won't make it.* "He said he'd leave the key in the mailbox if we needed it."

Minnie was right. In that moment, the path forward became crystal clear. "Thalia, you'll stay here with us."

"I'm leaving. I thought that's what you wanted."

"You will stay." Thalia's mouth opened, no doubt with a snappy comeback at the ready, but when he added, "As my guest," she closed it again, looking a little off balance. How nice that J.R. wasn't the only one who felt like that.

"All of my things are at Lloyd's. I was going to swing by on my way out of town."

Women, J.R. thought. If he were the one leaving town, he'd have that car packed up, first thing. "Minnie's got stuff you can wear."

"No." Thalia's tone was insistent. "I have things I need." He saw her swallow. "Prescriptions I have to take."

Damn.

"I'll go get my things. I'll come right back."

The weather siren went off again. J.R., Hoss and Minnie shared a look. Thalia didn't have two hours. "Fine. Get your coat. I'll drive you."

"You don't have to do that."

"Yes, I do. I have four-wheel drive." Thalia probably only saw off-road vehicles stuck in traffic, but his Jeep could handle anything below two-foot drifts. If he drove real fast, they'd make it fine. He hoped.

"But—"

"No buts. Either I drive or you don't get your things." He turned to go. "I'll bring the Jeep up."

"I'll have a bag ready for you in a second." Minnie was pulling muffins and granola bars out. "Just in case."

"You know where the rope is?" Hoss asked.

"Yeah. You see to the generators." J.R. looked at Thalia, who seemed confused. *City folk,* he thought. "Get your coat. I'll pull up in front."

At least this time, she didn't argue with him—with any of them. J.R. walked through the gale-force wind, grabbed the bundle of nylon rope and fired up the Jeep. He bought a new one every three years—life out here was hard on vehicles.

The moment he pulled around to the front, Thalia and Minnie hurried out the front door. Thalia slid into the passenger seat. Minnie shoved a full bag, no doubt packed with energy foods and bottled water, and a bundle of blankets into the backseat and flat-out ran for the house without another word.

Just in case, Minnie had said.

Just in case they got stuck in a snowdrift.

Seven

Thalia sat in the passenger seat, fuming. First, J.R. couldn't get rid of her fast enough. Now he was all but holding her hostage. Yes, the wind had been vicious—but was it that much worse than it had been the first day she'd driven out here? She didn't think so.

"This is ridiculous," she said after they'd left the gravel road behind. She'd made this trip enough to know that they were only fifteen minutes outside of Beaverhead. At least, they would have been fifteen minutes if she'd been driving. J.R. seemed to be going *fast*. "I could have done this myself. You didn't need to drive me."

He had the nerve to sit there and snort in what sounded like derision.

"I can take care of myself, you know," she shot out at him.

"Thalia, the sooner you figure out this isn't Hollywood, the better off we'll all be."

The phrase *you're not the boss of me* was on the tip of her tongue, but even she knew how immature that would sound. "I'm fully aware I'm not in California."

"Ever have a blizzard down in Oklahoma?"

"It snowed sometimes, sure." A rare enough event, but she had wonderful memories sledding out at her grandfather's farm and throwing snowballs at her mom.

"I didn't say snow. I said blizzard."

As if to punctuate his point, one, then two, then two million snowflakes suddenly appeared. One minute, the road was right there. The next, she couldn't see the center stripe, much less the pavement. Each snowflake seemed to slam into the windshield with true menace.

"Uh—wow." Snow had always been a happy, joyful thing when she was a kid—no school, lots of cocoa and cookies, fluffy snow angels.

This was another beast entirely.

She felt foolish all over again, just as she had a few days ago, when she'd stood on his porch in a dress and tights and nearly froze to death. She'd grossly misjudged the situation, and now she felt stupid for having protested as much as she had.

Another emotion tempered that feeling—gratitude. J.R. had a white-knuckle grip on the steering wheel, but as far as she could tell, he hadn't slowed down. He'd known this was coming—and had refused to let her drive off into it. Just like he'd refused to let that hick get close to her.

"Timing is everything." His voice had dropped back into the no-nonsense tone he'd used to inform her he was driving. "I'll get you close to the door. Did you see where the mailbox was?"

"Yes. Lloyd showed me, in case I was out late." The whole thing had seemed hopelessly old-fashioned at the time. She was used to hotels with doormen and key cards. But now? Old-fashioned ruled.

"We'll do this together, but we've got to be fast."

The next thing she knew, he was skidding to a stop, and Lloyd's house popped out from behind a curtain of white. He reached into the back, and when he sat back up, he had a huge bundle of rope in his hands. Silently, he leaned over her and tied the rope to the door handle. "You get out first, but I'll be right behind you. We'll do this together," he repeated. "You've got to stay with me, okay?"

"Okay." She didn't know what was scaring her more—the snow or how serious he was about it.

He touched his gloved hand to hers and gave her a crooked smile, then he opened her door and all but shoved her out.

The wind. Oh, lord, the wind. What had she thought? That this wind wasn't much different from that first day? Maybe, maybe not. This wind wasn't alone. It drove each snowflake into her face with a ruthlessness that took her breath away. Snowflakes? These were more like ice knives, each bent on world domination.

"Move!" J.R. shouted before she was pushed away from the Jeep.

Right. To stand still was to die. J.R. must have driven up onto the front lawn, because she could actually see the front door and the mailbox a few feet away. Fighting the wind with every step, she pushed her way forward until she got a hand on the doorknob.

J.R. was right behind her. As far as she could tell, he had a fistful of her coat in his hand, but she wasn't about to complain. She got the lid of the mailbox open and fished out the key to the front door. The wind almost whipped it right out of her hand, but she got her pinkie finger looped through the keychain and held on.

Finally, after what felt like four false starts, she got the door unlocked and they fell into the house. A few inches of drifted snow came in with them, but Thalia and J.R. got to their feet and got the door shut. The relief she felt was physical, except for the fact they were only halfway. "Two minutes," he said, and she was off.

Thank heavens she'd at least packed her stuff before she'd gone to say goodbye. She grabbed her suitcase—with her birth control pills in it—and the shopping bags with all her winter clothes in seconds. When she flew down the stairs, struggling to hang on to her stuff, J.R. was leaning against the door, looking beat. The door was mostly shut, but she saw he still had a hold of the rope, which was wedged in the door. The wind was pushing at the door so hard, J.R. had to dig in his heels to keep his balance.

His gaze flicked over her with cold-blooded efficiency. "Three bags?"

"Yes." She braced herself for some sort of comment on women and clothes, but he didn't say anything.

With a sigh, he held out his hand. "Give me the two shopping bags so you can hold on to the rope. Whatever you do, don't let go of the rope."

"Okay." She tried to swallow, but her fear was becoming a thing so real she had half a mind to remind it to hang on to the rope, too.

J.R. turned the knob to lock it from the inside, and Thalia set the key on the hall table. If they didn't have to fumble around the mailbox and lock, they'd make it to the truck faster. "Ready?"

She nodded, and he opened the door. The wind jumped at the chance to rush in again, but—maybe for the first time—Thalia was ready for it. Head down, shoulders set, her bag in one hand and the rope in the other, she pushed through it, keeping her eyes locked on J.R.'s back. The only time she looked away was to make sure the door shut behind her. Lloyd had been such a nice host—she'd hate to leave his house full of snow.

By the time she got turned back around, she couldn't see J.R. anymore. A spike of panic stabbed at her throat, making it hard to breathe. She couldn't see anything; she couldn't feel anything but the cold that burrowed under her skin. She couldn't do this. She wasn't sure she even remembered what *this* was.

Then the rope jerked in her hand, pulling her forward so hard she almost stumbled. He was pulling her into safety, she realized, when the rope jerked again. Two more tugs, and the outline of the Jeep came into view. "Still there?" he roared over the wind as he physically hauled her into the vehicle. She realized he must have untied the rope, because, leaning across her body, he threw it outside before pulling the door shut.

The panic was still tight around her throat, smothering her with the realization that if she'd tried to do this by herself, she'd have died. J.R. had saved her from herself. She threw her arms around his neck, any words of thanks she had stuck in the back of her throat with sobs of terror she couldn't voice.

J.R. froze for a second, then his arms wrapped around her, pulling her into his chest. "You're still here," he murmured into her hair before he pressed his lips against her forehead. The touch pushed her panic back and down into her stomach, and she was able to breathe again. "I won't let anything hurt you. But we've got to go."

"Okay," she said as she released him. Not so much because she was all better now, but because they had to keep moving.

Now was probably the time to start praying.

The going was slower this time. Every so often, the winds would relent enough that the stripes on the road would pop up in surprising relief. The snow was something else, but the wind was blowing the road somewhat clear. Every time that happened, J.R. would put the pedal to the metal. Which meant his top speed was probably close to forty miles per hour, then would drop back down into the twenties. It was like bunny hopping in slow motion.

At one point, the wind died back in time to see a post sticking out of the snowbank. J.R. cut the wheel hard to the right.

Clawing for the door handle, Thalia let out a little scream as the truck skidded.

"Easy," J.R. said—the first thing he'd said since they'd left Lloyd's.

Thalia wanted to yell at the man—what about this was easy? And how did driving like a maniac make it any easier? She bit her tongue. He hadn't killed them yet, after all, and she didn't want to distract him and risk hastening their demise.

She was pretty sure they were on the gravel road that led to the ranch, but damned if she could see anything but the snow. However, J.R. seemed to know where he was going. She had no choice but to trust him.

The world had disappeared completely. It felt like the world inside this Jeep was the only thing in existence. Maybe hell wasn't hot, she thought as she tried to see something—anything. Maybe it was unending, white cold.

Suddenly, off to their left, a sputtering burst of firework red broke through the snow. "What the…?"

"Flares," J.R. said, turning the Jeep at a saner rate of speed. He didn't sound shocked about this. "Hang on."

The vehicle jumped and shuddered, as if they were now driving over curbs. Another flare of color cut the white. This time, it was closer, and straight ahead of them. J.R. laid on the horn.

Two more flares cut through the snow, but instead of shooting up into the sky like a Roman candle, they were waving in front of the truck.

"Made it." J.R. may have acted all calm, cool and collected over there, but Thalia heard the sheer relief in his voice.

When the flares got close to the hood, J.R. swung wide and turned the Jeep. The ranch house loomed out from behind the curtain of white like a ghost, hulking and dark. "Damn. Already lost power," J.R. muttered.

That seemed bad, but Thalia remembered him telling Hoss

to get the generators. Maybe the power outage was a temporary thing.

A bundle of fur that looked more like a bear than a man came toward them. "Get your bags," J.R. said, jerking his chin toward the backseat.

Thalia handed her things through the window to Hoss, who disappeared back into the house and then reappeared. "Ready?" J.R. asked seconds before the passenger door was opened.

Without a word, Hoss scooped her up, then turned around. He paused, which didn't make any sense to Thalia—why weren't they running for the house? Then she heard J.R. shout, "Okay!" behind Hoss at the same time she realized Hoss had a rope tied around his waist.

Oh. Duh, Hoss was waiting for J.R. to grab hold. Then their little people train moved into the house. It couldn't have taken more than three minutes, but to Thalia, it felt like hours of being carried through the wilderness. Hoss appeared to be wearing the buffalo robe again, and the snowflakes stuck to the fur. He looked like a yeti.

Soon enough, though, they being pulled inside the house. Minnie was braced against the door, yanking on the rope hand-over-hand. Hoss managed to set Thalia down on her feet, but J.R. stumbled in and went down on one knee before Minnie could get the door shut behind him.

"Hot damn, now *that's* a blizzard," Hoss announced as he threw off his robe and helped J.R. to his feet. "We were starting to get a little worried about you all."

"You and me both," J.R. muttered as he pulled off his coat. He didn't look exactly steady on his feet. Thalia went to his side and looped her arm around his waist. When he leaned against her, she felt inexplicably good. This wasn't on the same level as him saving her life, but at least she was helping him a little. "Power?"

"Yeah, about that." Hoss looked down at his feet as he

kicked off his snow-covered boots. "The generator won't turn over. If it was lighter, I'd be able to figure out what the deal was, but…" He sounded uncharacteristically defeated.

J.R. sagged against her a little more. "We've got wood, right?"

"Tons."

J.R. squeezed her a little tighter and said, "We'll be fine, then."

Minnie swooped into action, gathering up the coats and shooing everyone back to the kitchen. Thalia wanted to look a little more at the house she was going to be staying in for the foreseeable future—surely there was more to it than a cozy kitchen—but it was all she could do to keep walking. She and J.R. moved slowly, still leaning on each other despite having removed their coats and boots. Maybe it was the cold, or maybe it was the near-death experience that had Thalia still shaking. Whatever it was, she felt warmer and safer tucked under J.R.'s arm than she had in a long time, blizzards notwithstanding.

Minnie plunked them down on a big couch in front of the fire—a couch Thalia was sure hadn't been there a few hours ago. Not that it mattered. The couch was only a few feet from the fire, and the other chairs had been pulled in close to bookend it. It made the otherwise large space feel small and cozy.

She and J.R. slid down onto the leather. Part of her brain realized she was, for lack of a better word, being cuddled by him, and that part tried hard to get swoony.

Another part of her was filled with such an upwelling of gratitude—both to J.R. and to Hoss and Minnie—that she felt a little teary. For as long as she'd been in Hollywood, she'd been on her own, no one to lean on, no one willing to help her handle the constant bumps along the way. The last time anyone had helped her—out of the goodness of their heart and not because they wanted her to be beholden to them—had been… Well, Mom had offered to pay her way home after Thalia had been blacklisted. The thing she'd had to learn the hard way was no one else would be there for her. She was all she had.

Out here, in the proverbial middle of nowhere? J.R. hadn't let her drive off to her doom. Instead, he'd risked his life to make sure she had her things. Minnie was fussing over them with tea and hot soup. And Hoss had taken up residence in one of the chairs and apparently was recounting each and every blizzard they'd weathered out here in great detail. These people had gone out of their way to make sure she was welcome, safe and cared for. At least, they had eventually, in J.R.'s case. And they didn't do it because they wanted a favor for later or because it'd look good on the internet. They did it because that's the way they lived—helping out a neighbor, taking care of a friend.

She'd never known anyone like J.R. And, as she nestled into his arm, she knew she'd never meet another. "Thank you," she whispered so as not to interrupt Hoss's stories.

He didn't respond.

Eight

"Thalia, honey, you must be exhausted." Minnie maneuvered through the furniture to stand in front of her. "Let me show you to your room. Hoss got the fire going while you were gone, so it's fairly warm."

"Oh. Okay." Yes. Seeing other parts of the house was probably preferable to being both snuggled and ignored by J.R. But when she went to stand, J.R.'s arm weighed heavy over her shoulder.

She turned to look at him and saw his head was tucked down on to his chest and his eyes were closed. Ah. That buoyed her spirits—he wasn't ignoring her. He was asleep. Moving slowly, she lifted his arm away and then set his hand in his lap. He didn't even stir.

That was probably her fault, too. She'd turned off her light and gone to bed fairly early—maybe ten o'clock? How long had he sat outside in that truck? Add that to the stress of driving through a blizzard. No wonder the man was exhausted. She was pretty whipped by the whole day, herself.

Minnie had gathered up Thalia's things. Hoss joined them, carrying a huge kettle of water. Thalia took the two shopping bags and they headed up the back stairs. Minnie led the way with a flashlight.

"Is it going to be a problem without power?" Because, honestly, she'd been as close to freezing to death in the last week as she ever wanted to be.

"As long as the fires are burning, you'll be fine," Minnie said at the top of the stairs. Then she turned left down a long hall. "You've got your own bathroom. Can't promise the water will be warm, but at least it'll work. We heat the water for washing on the stove."

So showers were out. "Sounds good." She wasn't about to look the gift of running water in the mouth right now. Instead, she was going to be thankful for being able to wash her face and flush a toilet. It was the little things in life.

Minnie opened the door, and Thalia stepped into exactly the kind of room she'd expected to find. A stone hearth with a blazing fire and a mantle that looked carved from an entire tree took up one wall; wood paneling covered all the others, like downstairs. The big difference was that a huge four-poster bed complete with bed curtains stood in the middle of the room. The bed, while large, looked soft and inviting, the rug appeared to be Navajo, and instead of the animal heads she might have expected, framed art of mountains and trees decorated the place. It beat the heck out of Lloyd's sixties flashback.

"Bathroom's this way," Hoss said, going through a door on the opposite side. "I'll fill the sink for you. It'll be warm for a little bit."

Minnie set the bag down on a cedar chest at the end of the bed. "Let me get those curtains for you. They'll help hold in the heat," she added as she pulled three of the four curtains, but left the side facing the fire open.

Three hours ago, Thalia had been headed home. If she'd

started for Billings instead of coming to say goodbye, she'd probably be in a ditch somewhere, wondering if anyone would find her before she ran out of gas. Now, she was being settled into a guest room half the size of her whole apartment by nice people who were going to feed her and keep her warm. Thalia must have looked a little shell-shocked. God knew she felt it. Minnie came up to her and patted her on the arm in an inherently motherly way. "There's no need to worry, sweetie. We've weathered worse out here. I'm sure the boys will be able to get the generators going tomorrow, and we've got a whole garage of wood out back. We can stay out here for a month, easy."

Thalia's throat closed up on her, pulling down the corners of her mouth and making any sort of polite response all but impossible. A month? Did that mean she would have to spend Valentine's Day with J.R.? And was that a bad thing or a good thing? How was she supposed to get back to Hollywood?

Beyond that, who would miss her? Levinson might, but only because she wasn't at his beck and call. He wouldn't be worried about her, just the work she wasn't able to do. Mom knew she'd come to Montana, but unless this was the kind of blizzard that made the evening news, Mom would assume no news was good news. That was for the best, Thalia decided. She didn't want Mom to be frantic and unable to get a hold of her.

No one else would notice she was gone. She had a few work friends she ate lunch with, that sort of thing, but no roommates, no boyfriends. No close friends. No one who cared about her. She'd been facing another lifeless Valentine's Day with nothing but a solitary card from Mom to mark the occasion.

Everything was different here. She barely knew these people, but J.R. had risked his life to keep her safe, and Minnie and Hoss had welcomed her with open arms. She mattered to them. And more and more, they mattered to her, too. That realization choked her up.

Her lack of words was drowned out by the howling of the wind that seemed to be trying to pull the house apart, piece by piece.

"I've got to check on the pork chops," Minnie said. "Dinner will be in a few."

Thalia managed to nod. Dinner. And after that? She had a nice room—right across the hall from J.R. She was here for the duration. She might as well make the most of it.

J.R. sat as still as he could, straining to hear footsteps over the wind. When he was sure everyone was upstairs, he got up and went to the bathroom. The water from the tap was one step above ice cubes, but he splashed it on his face anyway, hoping it would shock some sense back into his system.

He couldn't believe he'd faked being asleep. It was an act of cowardice, and he knew it. But, like she'd been doing since she'd first set foot on his property, Thalia had caught him off guard and he hadn't known how to react.

Yeah, he was exhausted. Driving into the yawning mouth of snow hell on four hours of sleep had taken everything he had and a whole bunch more. That was the problem. If he'd had a little in reserve, he wouldn't have been so weak with relief to see those flares that he'd had to let Hoss carry Thalia inside. He wouldn't have stumbled walking into his own house, his weakness on full display.

He sure as hell wouldn't have needed her to support him. He wouldn't have had to lean on her, or have gotten so light-headed that he'd been completely unable to pull away from her. Even if he'd wanted to, he hadn't been able to let go of her. If anything, he'd held her even tighter. He still didn't know how he'd managed to get on the couch in front of the fire. Unless she'd out-and-out carried him. At this point, he wasn't sure.

J.R. couldn't see much of his reflection in the dark interior of the bathroom, but he stared nonetheless. What the hell was wrong with him?

Thalia by his side had felt warm. Real.

Safe.

He'd felt safe with her arm around his waist, with his arm around her shoulders. So much so, he hadn't wanted that moment to end.

"Don't be an ass," he said to his faint reflection. All these unwanted feelings were the result of the late night and the dangerous afternoon. Thalia had never been someone he could trust. She could ruin his life and destroy everything he'd built. Hell, if the fight at the bar was any example, she'd already gotten a head start.

But.

Because there was a huge but, and it went back before the snow started falling. Back when she'd been in his kitchen, again. Back when she'd come to say goodbye. Back when she'd promised not to tell anyone where he was.

She was from Hollywood. She was a former actress. She worked for Levinson. There was no way he could trust her, not in this life and not in the next.

So when she'd been curled up at his side, one arm around his waist, her head resting on his shoulder, and whispered, "Thank you," in a voice he knew— felt deep in his soul— wasn't an act or a negotiating tactic…well, he'd frozen up. His brain had tried to tell him it was another trap, but the rest of him? The rest of him didn't know what it wanted.

Well, that wasn't true, either. Large parts of him wanted to hold her closer, to duck his head down and plant a gentle kiss on her lips. Then maybe another, not so gentle one.

Those kissing parts and his brain parts had canceled each other out, leaving him without a clear course of action. So he'd faked it.

He heard footsteps overhead. The bathroom was tucked

under the stairs, so that meant someone was coming back
down. He finished his business and headed out. He was going
to bed good and early, but he wasn't about to miss dinner.
Not if Thalia was there.

Hoss was throwing a few more logs on the fire; Minnie
was peeking into the oven. Weather like this was one of the
reasons they had a gas stove—if they got truly desperate,
they'd turn on the oven to heat the room. In many ways, this
was a normal night. Except for the blizzard and the woman
who was still upstairs.

"She gone to bed?" he asked, hoping she had and also
hoping she hadn't.

"No, getting her things put away," Minnie said as she got
out the plates. "We'll eat in front of the fire, if that's okay
with you."

"Sure." Normally, she wouldn't have asked. When they
lost power in the winter, they always pulled the couch and
chairs up close to the fire and took their meals there. Most
of the time, they all slept down here, too, so there'd only be
one fire going. But she was going to be upstairs, someone
had to be up there with her, just in case. In case of what, he
wasn't sure, but he didn't think it would be best for her to be
all alone upstairs in the middle of a blizzard. He should stay
in his room. He'd be down the hall.

This was what Thalia did. She made things not normal.
She made *him* not normal.

She came down a few minutes later. She'd changed—her
other clothes were probably still wet from the snow. Hell, he
should have gone up and changed his jeans. Too late now.
She was here and the food was ready.

"Help yourselves," Minnie said, scooping the baked pork
chops and wild rice onto a plate.

"You okay?" J.R. asked Thalia in a low voice. She looked
okay—actually, she looked great—but something about her
face had him worried.

She gave him a watery smile. "Just a long day. You? Have a good nap?"

He supposed he should be glad he could still pull off a little bit of acting, but it left a sour taste in his mouth. "Yup." Then he was handing her a plate and talking about how good the chops smelled and having dinner with her.

And the funny thing was, it all felt perfectly normal. Which meant it wasn't.

By the time the two of them got back to the fire, Minnie and Hoss had taken the chairs. What was this—a conspiracy? J.R. took a seat on the couch and waited. Would Thalia sit close enough to touch, or would she crowd into the far side of the couch, closest to Minnie?

She split the difference. If he wanted to, he could lean over and elbow her. Which would be rude. At least Minnie wasn't giving him the stink eye this go-round.

Instead, the whole meal was easy. Thalia asked questions about blizzards, J.R. answered, Hoss told stories that scared the hell out of her and Minnie did the reassuring.

At no point did she start talking about movies or Oscars or James Robert Bradley. She didn't treat him like he was special or anything. She treated him like, well, a friend. A friend she'd go into a bar and have a drink with. A friend she'd eat dinner with.

He was almost having fun—more fun than the first meal they'd shared. Especially when she looked at him—which she did a lot. They weren't that far apart. Just a few feet and some forks and knives separated them. The firelight threw a warm glow across her face, and her grin was deep and honest.

They were stuck here for a week, maybe two. He couldn't pretend to be asleep the whole time. What was he going to do?

By the end of the meal, Thalia was trying to politely hide her yawns behind her hand. J.R. was too tired to even make that effort.

"Can I help with the dishes?" Thalia asked Minnie.

"Heavens, no." Minnie chuckled, although she was clearly pleased with the offer. "We pile them into the sink until the water heater is heating again. You go on up to bed." She gave J.R. one of her motherly looks that spoke louder than words.

Yeah, he probably looked like hell and he was in serious danger of passing out and drooling on the coffee table. "I'm going to hit the hay, too."

"You all holler—loudly—if you need anything." Already wrapped in a buffalo robe, Hoss's Lakota accent was stronger, his eyes half-closed as he stared at the fire.

J.R. knew he and Minnie would stay up half the night, telling the old Lakota legends and long-ago family stories while they kept the fire going. He'd learned a lot the first couple of winters out here, like how Hoss's father had died in a car wreck when he was a little boy and how Minnie had been raised by her grandma, who barely spoke English.

"Good night, all." Thalia looked at him as she stood, and he had to fight the urge to take her hand in his and lead her upstairs to a bedroom. Maybe hers, maybe his. Did it matter?

Damn, but he must be tired to be thinking like that. Instead, he stood and grabbed the flashlight. That was a safer option, by far.

They climbed the stairs in silence. He knew he needed to get into his room and shut the door—the sooner the better. Bolting on her would be rude, all the more so since he had the flashlight. He should make sure she was okay in her room. That was the polite, gentlemanly thing to do.

The hall was dark, but the blowing snow cast a pallid white glow over everything. In the light, Thalia's eyes looked huge. And something else. Was she scared? "It'll be fine," he said as he stood in the hall.

She nodded, but didn't say anything, which made him feel like he had to say something else. "My room is right there, so if you need anything…"

Maybe that wasn't the right thing to say? He'd messed it

up somehow, because she dropped her gaze to the floor and managed to look embarrassed.

"J.R.—" she began, and he knew she was going to try and thank him again. And he knew if she did, he'd want to kiss her again. And that would be a problem. Although, honestly, he was so tired he was having trouble remembering why that would be a problem, but he knew it would mess things up. Everything he'd built for himself would be in danger if he did something foolhardy like pursue his attraction to Thalia Thorne.

So he interrupted her with, "Yeah, knock if you need something. I'll see you in the morning. 'Night."

He was a grown man, by God, and as such, he did not sprint down the hallway to avoid uncomfortable conversations with a woman.

But he walked quickly.

Nine

That was…odd.

Thalia changed into her flannel jammies, threw another log onto the fire and climbed underneath what felt like twenty quilts and blankets.

J.R. had just…left her standing outside her door. The man had risked his life for her, but he acted like he didn't want her to thank him. If she didn't know better, she'd think he was almost afraid of her.

Which was ridiculous. He'd taken on that cowboy in the bar at the drop of hat and driven into a blizzard. He couldn't be afraid of her. Could he?

She was the one being ridiculous. What had she expected him to do? Stand there while she gushed over him? This wasn't Hollywood, and whatever he'd once been, he wasn't the kind of man whose ego needed constant reassurance.

Ugh. She was stressed and tired and all-over confused. Overthinking right now would be as productive as chasing her tail. She'd go nowhere but in circles.

She curled into a ball under all the bedding, wishing she could feel her toes more than she could now. The fire made a huge difference. The room was easily twenty degrees warmer than the stairwell and the hall. She certainly wouldn't freeze to death. That didn't make it *warm.*

Thinking about J.R.'s arm around her shoulders, though— yeah, there was a little heat there. Her mind played over the moment when he'd kissed her forehead in the car. It hadn't been a hot 'n' bothered kind of kiss, but somehow, the tenderness of it left her with a distinctly bothered feeling. He'd come close to kissing her on three different occasions now. Was she going to have to settle for a single touch of his lips when he was right across the hall?

At least the tossing and turning she was doing helped keep her warm.

Thalia slipped in and out of sleep. The fire had a mesmerizing quality to it, and she wasn't sure if she was dreaming some of the shadows it threw or not. Time seemed to have stopped. There was no day or night, no dark or light. Just white snow and red fire, a comfy bed and cold toes, and the man across the hall that she'd always wanted.

She thought about her life, her mother and what waited for her back in Hollywood. She thought about *Blood for Roses,* the movie she wouldn't get to make. It would have been a great movie, too.

At one point, Thalia knew she was dreaming because she was watching *Hell for Leather* in the theater with her college boyfriend, the one she'd left behind when she moved to Hollywood. That date had happened a long time ago, but sitting in the dark theater felt real. James Robert's amber eyes jumped off the big screen and seared themselves on to her heart. Breathless, she watched him ride across the range, his six-shooter firing with deadly accuracy. God, how she'd loved that role, that movie. That actor. She'd seen all of his movies, but this one—with him scruffy and rugged and way more than a little dangerous—this was the one that put her past schoolgirl crush and right over into borderline obsession.

Then the scene changed, and James Robert was in a cabin in front of a roaring fire, leaning against the mantle. The firelight made his hair shine like gold in the dark room, but he seemed worried.

Wait, Thalia thought. *Was that scene in the movie?* No, she'd remember it. She'd seen *Hell for Leather* enough to have the whole thing memorized.

She pushed herself up, but the scene didn't change. He was standing in her room, wearing green-and-blue-plaid flannel pajama bottoms under a thick green bathrobe. "J.R.?"

"My fire went out." His voice—no way she was dreaming. "I wanted to be sure yours was still going."

"Oh." For some reason, this disappointed her. "Are you cold?"

He shrugged, but that was the only answer she got. He hadn't even looked at her, as if he was afraid she was sleeping in the nude and he was violating her privacy by being here.

"You're cold." It wasn't a question anymore, just a statement of fact. His fire went out—so he checked on her. He'd put her first, again.

"Used to it." His voice sounded like he'd been gargling with gravel.

Thalia swallowed. Was she sure she wasn't dreaming J.R. here, in her room, almost close enough to touch? Oh, how she wanted to touch him, to feel his work-roughened hands on her body. Then she remembered how he'd bolted in the hallway. Right. Throwing herself at his feet was out. That didn't mean he had to leave. "You can stay in here, if you want."

Even though he didn't move, everything about him tensed. She half thought he was going to break the mantle off the wall. "I'll go."

"No, stay. At least long enough to warm up." Let me warm you up, she wanted to say, but the last thing she wanted was for him to accuse her of trying to seduce him for the wrong reasons.

She thought he was going to leave, but instead he sat cross-legged on the floor. "Until I warm up."

He didn't look like he was planning on sleeping. Something about this situation felt a little like the conversation they'd had on the phone last night, except this time, the distance between them was only a few feet. With him sitting so close to her, everything about him looking rugged and scruffy, she didn't think she'd be able to sleep anytime soon. What she wouldn't give to slide her arm around his waist like she had earlier, to feel his weight against her. What she wouldn't give for that moment of connection. "Why did you leave?"

Without looking away from the fire, he said, "I hated it so much. *So* much. I couldn't buy a grapefruit without someone taking pictures of me. They made fun of my clothes, my body, my everything." She saw him grin, but it was a joyless thing.

"People made fun of you? But everything I read about you was always so glowing. You were such a golden boy—so perfect."

This time, his grin seemed more real. "You read those things, did you? Or was that for research?"

"I've seen all the James Robert Bradley movies." Revealing that felt dangerous, like when she'd called him from her room. She was crossing another line that couldn't be uncrossed.

"All of them? Even *Babydoll Smile?*"

That had been one of those teen sex romps from early in his career. "Even *Babydoll Smile*. Which was terrible, I might add."

His grin widened as he tucked his knees under his chin. He didn't seem to be as cold, but she thought she saw him shiver. His back was probably freezing. "I was fully capable of bad acting. Which begs the question, Thalia. Why do you want me for your movie?"

And just when she thought things were lightening up. This was the price she paid for crossing that small line moments ago. He knew now. She thought about trying to fudge the truth, but then he said, "And don't feed me that line about how 'people' want to know and will pay, either. I think I've earned an honest answer."

He had, darn it all. She owed him the truth. Taking a deep breath, she forced herself to look at the fire. That made confessing seem less…intimate. "It was me. *I* wanted to know what happened to you." He didn't say anything, which somehow made her jumpier, so she kept talking. "You were the reason I wanted to become an actress. It sounds crazy, but…" the words, *I had the biggest crush on you* refused to actually move past her back teeth. So she hedged, hoping to turn the conversation back to him. "You'd left by the time I hit town. I missed you by months. You didn't even come back to award the Best Supporting Actress Oscar the next year. You were *gone*."

Which was a lousy thing to say—like she was mad he hadn't waited in Hollywood for her arrival. But if he kept asking her questions and she kept answering them honestly, she had no idea if she would even be able to look him in the face in the morning.

"That's the thing I don't understand about you." Every part of Thalia tensed up at this broad statement. What on Earth was he going to say? That she was some kind of nut? That she was delusional? That she'd always be a nobody? Levinson had said all those things to her, and more.

But J.R. wouldn't, a fact he illustrated when he went on. "Anyone who's ever found out about James Robert Bradley has forgotten about me. It's like I cease to exist." She could hear the hurt in his voice, could guess that more than a few women had broken the heart of the man sitting before her.

"You're different. You already knew about all that, and you still…" He turned his head to her, meeting her gaze from across the room. Head on his knees, he was curled into an impossibly small ball. Despite the massive strength displayed by his broad shoulders, she saw the little boy who'd wanted to be a firefighter, army man, astronaut and a cowboy. But never an actor. "You still treat me like I'm a real person."

The way he was looking at her did a lot to raise her personal temperature. Her heart about stopped, although she couldn't tell if that was from the heartbreak behind his statement or from the best compliment she'd ever received. She had no idea how to reply without sounding like a doofus. "You are real. To me."

The corner of his mouth crooked up—not much, but a little. The firelight lit his face from the side, bathing him in the glow of warmth. *Oh,* she thought, *that's the real smile.* The one that could melt her in the middle of a blizzard.

Then she saw a shiver shake his body, and he began to rub his shins for warmth. "Are you still cold?"

"It's fine."

Whatever moment they'd shared felt distant already.

"It's not." She'd seen movies with blizzards in them. As far as she could tell from that limited pop-culture selection, the way people kept warm when they were freezing to death was through body heat. "Come get under the covers." She hoped that came out in a no-nonsense tone, not a swoony, seductive tone. But she couldn't tell.

His eyes squeezed shut and it looked like he was gritting his teeth, like he was undergoing new and cruel mental tortures. "I'll be fine."

She had about enough of this tough-guy thing he was working. He was probably two steps from hypothermia. She was not about to let him walk out of here. She wouldn't touch him, she promised herself. She wouldn't give him a reason to think she was trying to seduce him for ulterior motives. This was entirely innocent.

Well, maybe not entirely. To be under the covers with J.R.? Somehow, that was even more exciting than the thought of sleeping with James Robert Bradley.

She tossed off the blankets and got out of bed. Even though she had socks on, the moment her feet hit the floor, the cold jolted her fully awake. And he'd been sitting on that? Heavens. Forcing a stoic J.R. into her bed wasn't exactly a dream come true, but she wasn't going to let him turn into a Popsicle to preserve his male pride.

She managed to get hold of his arm before he got to the door. "No, you're going to warm up. Come to bed."

He met her eyes, and the temperature in the room kicked up several notches. "It would be best for *both* of us if I go back to my room."

"No, it won't." She didn't know which part would keep her up more—the thought of him freezing to death, or the memory of the way he had looked at her. Either way, she wasn't sleeping. "And this isn't about sex," she added, more to remind herself than him. She wasn't doing a single thing to make him think this was a calculated negotiating tactic. Including doing exactly what she wanted with him. "This is about warmth."

"Thalia—" he said, his voice sounding deeper now. More dangerous. And much, much warmer.

She was playing with fire, but she couldn't let him see how much he was affecting her. She shoved him toward the mountains of blankets. "You're not leaving this room until you have a regular body temperature."

He stood at the side of the bed, the firelight shining in his eyes. Her breath caught in her throat, and she managed to avoid sighing in satisfaction. "This is about warmth."

"Yes." The way it came out—as a squeak—completely contradicted the words, but she refused to look away. "Just warmth." That and long-held, deeply personal fantasies. She wasn't going to let him know that. Not now, not ever.

He stood there, his gaze blazing down on her until she was sure she was going to crack. Then kicking off his slippers, he removed the bathrobe and spread it out on top of the blankets before climbing in. He scooted over and held the blankets up for Thalia to follow. Once she'd tucked the covers back up around her chin, she couldn't help but notice he was almost hanging off the other side of the bed. "For warmth." He sounded like he was speaking through clamped jaws.

"J.R., would you shut up?" Thalia rolled over to him and slid her arm around his waist, pulling him into her. Okay, so she'd immediately broken her no-touching rule. This wasn't any different than the way they'd been touching earlier, on the couch. So it was practically the same. Except for the fact that they were alone, in bed. There was that. "You've done nothing but take care of me. You beat that jerk up for me. You drove off into a blizzard for me. You have risked your life for me more times in the last few days than anyone else has in years. Decades. So you're going to let me return the favor, okay? I'm going to take care of you."

His eyes glittered. It would be so easy to push him over the edge, to take what they both wanted. But she didn't want him to think she was trying to trap him into something—into a stupid movie role. She swallowed, forcing her desire back and trying to dredge up some reason—any reason would do—that she was not seducing him. "Do you know how bad it would look if you froze to death because of me? I want to make sure you're warm."

Because he wasn't. He radiated chill through her jammies. She didn't know if she could warm him up or if he would freeze her out first.

He exhaled, then his opposite hand reached up and rested on her forearm. She fought the urge to throw her leg over his—to warm him up a little faster. It had nothing with wanting to melt into him, or wanting him to pull her in closer. Nothing at all.

Damn, he was *cold.* "It's just…" His voice was low, and close to her ear. If she closed her eyes, she could pretend this was pillow talk. "You being here makes things hard on me."

She leaned back enough to meet his eyes. The raw honesty she saw there came close to breaking her heart. "I'm not trying to make things hard." Then she realized what she'd said and her cheeks flushed hot. Which wasn't a bad thing, but the temperature under the blankets edged up again.

"I know." He moved his hand up and brushed freezing fingertips down her cheek. She shivered, but she didn't know if that was from the cold or the touch. "But you…"

Suddenly, she was the shy one, afraid of what he was going to say. Because she didn't know and couldn't guess. "Get some sleep," she said, but she couldn't help herself. She pressed his hand against her cheek and then turned her face to kiss his palm. So she'd said she wasn't going to seduce him. No more than she already had, apparently.

No, he'd been as good as his word. She had to do the same. Never mind that she was actually in bed with the former James Robert Bradley. Never mind that she'd lusted after him for a span of years that veered toward decades. Never mind that, as soon as this blizzard was a memory, she wouldn't see him again. Never freaking *mind* that this would be her one and only chance to make a long-held wish come true.

She'd loved an act, for that's all James Robert Bradley had been. That realization made her feel silly. The man in her arms wasn't some creation. He was real.

She forced herself to roll over and face the fire. After a few seconds, J.R. rolled with her, sliding one arm under her neck and the other around her waist. He pulled her back into the hard planes of his chest. This—this feeling of his body along hers, this close contact—this was what she wanted, but it wasn't, too. It wasn't enough.

"I'm glad you're here," he whispered in her ear. Then, moments later, his grip loosened and his chest rose and fell. *Get some sleep,* she told herself. As if that were possible.

Ten

Thalia did manage to drift off. After a while, J.R. stopped sucking all her body heat away from her and started to return the favor. She fell asleep feeling warm and secure in his arms. No matter what happened after this, she'd always have this sweet memory of lying in his arms. Even if that was as good as it got, it was still pretty damn good.

Lost in a dreamless fog, though, something changed. Heat coursed through her body—the kind of heat no fire, no amount of blankets, could match. She knew she was dreaming—she had to be, right? When she shifted, the pressure against her breast grew, focusing her desire.

Her eyes snapped open. Nope, not dreaming—J.R.'s hand covered her right breast and his other hand had drifted down to her hip bone. She wouldn't have thought it possible, but he'd pulled her into an even deeper embrace, and she could feel the hard length of him pressing against her backside.

He let out a little moan, his hot breath hitting her on the side of the neck and racing its way under the covers and down her back. She thought he was awake but then his hands jerked against her body, and she realized he was completely, totally, asleep. While palming her breast.

She'd think this whole situation funny, except he was turning her on. It'd been, what? A year since her last attempt at dating someone who worked in the entertainment industry? And like most of her relationships, this one had failed when Thalia had been unable—and, honestly, unwilling—to get the wannabe screenwriter's script in front of Levinson's eyes. She hated the feeling that even intimate relationships in Hollywood were predicated on favors.

J.R. shuddered, pouring more steamy breath onto her skin while digging his fingers into her body. He wasn't pawing her, but it was close, and the primal feeling of it—that even in sleep, he couldn't keep his hands off her—made her feel wanted in a basic, feminine kind of way.

And she wanted him back. She'd thought she'd lusted after James Robert the famous actor, but that juvenile emotion seemed pitiful compared to how much she wanted J.R., the real-life cowboy.

Moving slowly, so as not to disturb him, she covered his hand with hers, pressing it against her breast. His fingers were calloused, and she let hers drift over their roughness. Not the hands of a guy who had biweekly maintenance manicures, but the hands of a man who worked for a living.

The hands of a man who knew how to use them.

The thought of those hands moving over other bare parts of her body sent a shiver through her that had nothing to do with cold. She was on thin ice, that she knew. He'd expressly stated he wasn't here for her in the physical sense. His every move had shown he was here for her in the emotional sense, which was almost as big a turn-on as the thought of his body moving against hers. This was no teenaged crush, and it wasn't sheer lust. This was something different. Something special.

Except for the obvious fact that he was still out like a light and she was burning with desire. That was something of a problem.

Well, part of him was burning with desire, even if he wasn't consciously aware of it. With each shudder, each jolt, the hard length of him pressed against her with a more demanding need.

When he jerked again, the stubble of his beard scraped against the back of her neck, and Thalia couldn't bite back the low moan. Sex in Hollywood was a matter of power and negotiation, true, but it was also a competition—who had the better body, who had the better wax job, who had the money to pay for all that upkeep. The feeling of his facial hair on her bare skin was so raw, so real, that she couldn't help but grind her hips back into him. When was the last time she'd been *this* turned on?

What she wouldn't give to have fewer layers of flannel between them. *What the hell,* she thought. She wanted him. Actually, by this point, it had gone beyond mere "want" and had skipped straight on over into "need." She didn't just need the release of a good, old-fashioned orgasm. She needed to feel desirable. She needed to feel wanted. She needed *him.*

She lifted her free hand back and rested it on his hip, pulling him against her as she shimmied against him. Another moan escaped her lips.

This time, it wasn't quiet enough. J.R. stilled behind her, and she felt tension roll off him.

All the lines she'd crossed before were small, nearly invisible ones. But when she slipped her other hand down between their bodies and felt for herself how rock hard he was, she knew she was crossing the big, blinking line. She couldn't stop herself. The thing was, she had no idea if he would stop her or not.

She didn't want him to stop her. "I want you, J.R. *So*

much." To emphasize that, she formed his fingers around her breast while she traced his generous length again.

His breaths came so quick and fast that in seconds, he was panting. She tilted her head over her shoulder and managed to catch his cheek with her lips. When she did, he shuddered. She felt his body envelop hers as his lips moved against her neck. The stubble scraped over her skin, and she had to bite back another moan as he said, "I don't have anything."

"I'm on the Pill. Clean bill of health." She let go of his hand long enough to pull her shirt up, and when he placed all those calluses back on her bare nipple, she sucked in air. "You've taken care of me, J.R. Let me take care of you. All of you," she added as she rubbed against him.

For a painful, erotic second, he didn't say anything. Then he lowered his head and kissed the spot below her ear.

The relief that coursed through Thalia's body was immediate and intense, which only amplified the desire racing roughshod over her body.

They didn't speak another word. They didn't have to. She slipped her hand beneath the waistband of his pants and wrapped her fingers around the whole of him. The groan she was rewarded with spoke louder than any sweet talk could have.

When he returned the favor, sliding his hand below her waistband and rubbing those calloused hands over her most sensitive spot, she had to fight to keep what little control she had. He must have sensed how close she already was, because he used his chin to shove the shoulder of her top away and then took a nip at the bare flesh he'd exposed while stroking her harder and harder.

Wait, she wanted to tell him. She wanted to wait for him— but he didn't give her a choice. One set of calluses slid deeper into the folds of her body, rubbing with exquisite precision, while the other pulled and tugged at her nipple. The release crashed over her so hard, so fast, that she almost fell off the bed when her back arched.

He held on to her, pulling her back into him. "Whoa," was all he said, as if she were a young filly trying to buck him off, but she heard the satisfaction in his voice.

Yeah, whoa. Not since the fumbling days of her first serious boyfriend had a man taken the time to put her first. And just when she thought J.R. couldn't turn her on any more than she already was, too.

He held her as the last of the orgasm shuddered through her body, kissing her neck the whole time. If she were with some manscaped guy in Hollywood, he'd already be looking for affirmation that only he gave her that kind of climax, that he was the best she'd ever been with.

Not J.R. Instead, he made a low sound, deep in the back of his throat that sounded like pure happiness. Well, she could make him happier. She stretched back, trying to get a hold of him again.

"Whoa," he said again as he grabbed her hand. Then he was pulling her bottoms down, then his bottoms down, and finally, *finally,* no flannel stood between them.

She twisted so she could get the one thing she'd been missing—a kiss. "J.R.," she whispered, then his mouth covered hers. Their tongues tangled as his beard abraded her lips.

Primal—that was the word. Something basic in her responded, sending heat rushing down between her legs and making her angle her backside for him. She threw her top leg over his, opening for him.

He lifted her off the bed, then he was against her, then he was sliding all of that length into her. He'd revved up her engine so much her body offered no resistance to what felt like an impressive size. With two concentrated thrusts, he was buried deep inside her.

When he paused, she cried out in protest. "J.R., *please.*"

"I want to feel you for a minute." But he shifted, lowering her upper body back down onto the bed and sliding his hand down her belly again.

Man, how she loved the feel of those rough calluses sliding over her. "Smooth," he murmured as he skimmed over the area she felt compelled to keep waxed even when she wasn't seeing anyone.

Before she could offer a comment, though, his fingers delved deeper, and suddenly he was thrusting and rubbing and tweaking her nipple and Thalia had no words. None. All she could do was hold on to his thigh, his arm, and lean back for quick, hot kisses as he drove into her again and again.

He licked at her neck and shoulder, rubbing his beard over her exposed skin. The rough sensation left scorch marks of heat on her skin. She lifted her hand behind his head and laced her fingers into his hair, holding his face against her neck.

He nipped her there, which drew a ragged gasp from her. Taking that as the sign of approval it was, he bit with more pressure.

Thalia came—hard. Her body tightened around him, *against* him, as the pleasure of being consumed ran roughshod over her body. He stopped thrusting as she rode it out, instead focusing on touching all of her spots with just the right amount of pressure. *Oh, so good* was all the conscious thought Thalia was capable of thinking. As the climax ebbed, she melted back into his body, grinning like a fool and wondering if she'd be the same again.

J.R. took his cue and ran with it. He rolled toward her, putting his hands on her hips and thrusting deeper, longer and harder. He wasn't holding back—no, he was giving her everything he had, and maybe a little something extra. She had to brace herself against the edge of the bed so she didn't fall off, but she didn't care. There was something so heated, so fierce about this act between them. She had no idea how she'd ever be happy with any of the metrosexuals back in L.A. ever again. Nothing and no one could compare to her cowboy.

With a groan that started deep in his chest and rumbled into a low roar, he thrust one final time and held. A smaller, delicious orgasm peaked in Thalia just from knowing she'd satisfied him as much as he'd satisfied her.

Wow. Even in all her fantasies of a wild night with James Robert Bradley, she didn't think that she'd gotten even close to the hottest spooning sex she'd ever had. What made it even better was that it wasn't the one-night stand she'd envisioned, where he barely remembered her name.

He fell back panting, but before she could do much of anything, he was running his fingertips over her shoulder, the part where he'd bit her. "I marked you," he said in a kind of surprised tone of voice. "I'm sorry."

She rolled over, throwing her arms around him. He fell onto his back, but he held her close. "Don't be." How could she tell him he'd marked her long before they had ever met?

What happened next? She'd had dates that ended in bed—and then ended, dates she thought had potential to be more than a one-night stand, but weren't. Would he treat her like she was a dime a dozen when they left this bed? Would things be weird down in the kitchen in the morning—weirder if Hoss and Minnie figured out what had happened?

Swallowing down her anxiety, she said, "Now what?" in a carefully moderated tone.

"Well," he replied with a hearty yawn, "I'm going back to sleep." Thalia's heart sank a little at that pronouncement. Maybe she'd deluded herself into thinking he cared about her. Then he tightened his arms around her and said, "I want to make sure I'm holding you, all the same." He yawned again. Yeah, maybe the sex had been…demanding. "'Night, Thalia. Again."

Oh. *Oh.* Thalia relaxed in the warmth of his embrace. "'Night, J.R."

She knew, without a doubt, that he knew who she was. Someone real.

Eleven

When J.R. opened his eyes, he could see it was lighter out. The tip of his nose was still cold, which meant Hoss hadn't gotten the generators going yet. Still no power. He had no idea what time it was. He'd headed upstairs probably around seven, but had been awake a lot throughout the night. It could be seven in the morning, could be ten. All he knew was he hadn't slept this late since, well, the last blizzard.

He'd been alone and cold then. Now? Excepting the tip of his nose, he was warm and happy. It felt a little unreal. The smell of femininity and sex that seemed infused into the covers around him was definitely unusual.

Sighing with contentment, he stretched as much as he could without disturbing Thalia. *Thalia.* She had his arm pinned under her head, but she'd rolled onto her back. Her mouth was open, and her hair was a wild mess. She looked exactly like a woman who'd been satisfied in bed. He didn't think she'd ever looked prettier.

He'd like to stay right here in this bed, too, but he was getting that twitchy feeling he always got when he slept much past six in the morning. Life on the ranch was early to bed, early to rise. By his second summer of getting up at 3:30 a.m. to work cattle before the heat hit, he'd gotten used to it. Which was fine, except on days like this. Sleeping in wasn't his style.

Part of him wanted to wake her with a kiss and a whole lot more, but the other part of him—the rational part—knew he couldn't delay the start to the day any longer. He had to get out to the barn, get the gas for the generator and see to his horses. If the wind had compacted the snow enough, he'd try to get out to the pastures on the snowmobile and check on the cattle. He loved that sort of thing, doing real work with his hands. It was night and day from what his life had been in Hollywood, where he worked and worked and never felt like he did anything. Nothing of value, anyway.

So this morning would have to wait. Until this evening. He just had to make it twelve hours. He could do that, right?

Yeah, right, he thought as he brushed a strand of hair off Thalia's cheek. Her eyelids fluttered as she turned her face toward him. "Hmmm," she all but purred. "Time to get up?"

"Yup." Part of him was already up, but he was going to exhibit the restraint that had abandoned him last night if it killed him. Which it might. He hadn't meant to wind up in her bed, in her arms--part of his brain still wasn't sure she wasn't using sex to get him signed to the part. But he wasn't going to listen to that part of his brain. Not today.

Eyes still closed, she smiled and touched his face, rubbing her fingertips over his facial hair. He was starting to think she liked the beard. A lot. "Five more minutes."

That was an option—nah, he decided. He didn't want to rush things with her. Tonight, he could take his time. "How about I get you some coffee?"

One eyelid popped up. "Did you just offer to bring me coffee? In bed?"

The way she said it made it pretty clear that no one had

ever made such an offer to her before. Which seemed a crying shame. Had no one ever taken care of her? "I'll be back
in five minutes," he promised, but not before giving her the
kind of kiss that made his evening plans clear.

"Mmmm." That time, she did purr. Damn, but she was
making it hard to get out of this bed.

He managed to extricate himself from her body and the
covers. The fire was down to straggling embers, so he tied
his bathrobe and threw a few logs onto the coals. His slippers
were cold, but the sheepskin lining was far warmer than the
bare floor. "Be right back," he said, as if he was afraid she
would bail in the amount of time it would take him to get
downstairs and back up. Actually, he was a little nervous,
but it wasn't like she could up and leave.

"Better be," she called out as he shut the door.

J.R. grinned the whole way down. For a long time—too
long—his relationships with women had always proved true
the famous line by Rita Hayworth—"Men go to bed with
Gilda—they wake up with me." Women went to bed with
James Robert; they didn't want to wake up with J.R.

Except for Thalia. She was different, which was something of a gross understatement. Even though she knew all
about James Robert—and, from the sound of it, had harbored
a huge crush on him—she seemed to want J.R.

She seemed to like him. Especially the beard.

Lost in this train of thought, J.R. entered the kitchen. Minnie stood at the stove, frying bacon and a mess of eggs. The
smell of biscuits had his stomach rumbling something fierce.
He glanced over to where Hoss was still wrapped up in his
buffalo robe. Didn't look like he'd moved since last night.

"Morning, Minnie," he said with another yawn. "What
time is it?"

"Nigh on to ten in the morning. Coffee's ready." She
dusted flour off her hands before pointing to two thermal
mugs with lids set on the counter.

"I'll take Thalia hers," he said, trying to keep his tone uncommitted. Suddenly, he was nervous all over again—but not because of the possibility Thalia would bail. Because he hadn't given a moment's thought to what Minnie and Hoss would say, how they would treat this new development.

Minnie came up to him and touched him on the arm. "J.R.," she said, and he saw the worry in her eyes. *Are you okay?* she seemed to ask him with a look.

After all this time, it still made him feel good that Minnie cared. He remembered the first time he met her. Hoss had dragged him home from dinner after shooting one day, telling him he couldn't live on beer and peanuts. J.R. had been braced for the gushing to start the moment Hoss's truck had stopped in front of the beat-up trailer an hour away from the movie set. That's what had always happened before. But from the moment Minnie had emerged from the trailer, a scold on her lips, he'd *felt* that she was nothing like his mother and nothing like the girls who threw themselves at him. The trouble had been, he hadn't known how to act around a woman like Minnie Red Horse.

Luckily, she hadn't made it hard on him. Before he'd even gotten his hat off his head, she'd been *tsking* him. "Good lord and butter, look at you. When was the last time you ate a meal?" had been the first words out of her mouth, followed closely by, "Come in, come in."

And that had been it. The Red Horse house had been small and run-down; the food wasn't five-star anything. But Minnie and Hoss had taken him in, made a place for him at their table, and for the first time in his life, made him feel normal. *Real.* So much so that he almost hadn't even gone back to Hollywood after filming had ended. Minnie had been the one to convince him he had to honor his obligations then, but she'd made it clear he was welcome in their home anytime.

It had taken him another year and a half, plus the death of his mother, before he'd been able to untangle himself from his acting career. He might never have done it—might have slipped further into alcoholism and drugs, might have wound up dead by the time he was thirty—if he hadn't had those moments of profound normalcy at the Red Horse table.

He owed them everything. He could only hope that, by giving them a home and jobs, by making them his family, he had come close to repaying that debt of gratitude.

J.R. grinned, touching Minnie's furrowed brow. "You worry too much, you know?" *I'm good,* he thought, squeezing her hand. *It's good.*

For only the second time in his life, it was good.

"Oh." Swear to God, it looked like Minnie's eyes were welling up with actual, sentimental tears. "That's...nice." Then she spun away from him before any of those tears could spill over. Before he knew it, she had a wooden spoon in her hand and was waving it dangerously close to him. "See? I *told* you that woman wasn't a danger."

"You and your womanly, Indian-y intuition were right." J.R. poured the coffee and capped the mugs. Then he saw the kettle on the stove. "That for us?"

"Only if you can carry it all." Minnie handed him the oven mitt.

J.R. grabbed the kettle in one hand, the mugs in the other, and headed back upstairs. By no means was the awkwardness over with, but Minnie's stamp of approval added to his feeling of lightness.

Thalia was propped up in bed, the covers up to her chin. "You brought me coffee," she said in wonderment.

"And hot water. I'll pour some in your sink before I head back to my room."

She glanced up at him through sleepy lashes, but he could tell she wasn't that sleepy anymore. "Oh?"

"Been thinking," he went on, as casual as could be, while he headed back to her bathroom. "Might be better if you stay in my room tonight. Use less firewood that way."

Which was a nice, polite way of asking her to sleep with him. And also, to sleep with him. Sure, the sex had been great, but he wanted her to wake up in his arms again. He wanted that closeness, that touch.

He wanted her. Plain and simple.

"Well," she called out to him as he filled her sink with the warm water. "I certainly wouldn't want you to have to get out of bed to check on my fire again."

"Exactly." He caught sight of himself in the mirror, grinning his fool head off. How long would the snow keep her here? How long could they pretend to play house? A week, maybe longer. Wouldn't be long enough, but he'd take what he could get.

When he went back into the bedroom, he was happy to see she had a huge, silly grin on her face, too. A real smile, one that pulled on her muscles and would one day lead to laugh lines—not one of those vapid smiles most actors perfected to keep wrinkles at bay. "Minnie's got breakfast going, then Hoss and I'll try to get to the barn. If we can get the gas into the house, we can fire up the generator."

She nodded, sipping her coffee. "Sounds like fun."

She was teasing him. "No, fun is mucking a stall in sub-zero weather."

"I can help." The offer came out of nowhere, but she seemed entirely earnest.

"Muck the stalls?" She nodded, her eyes huge. "Really?"

"My grandpa made me clean the barn in exchange for going riding," she said. "I don't mind."

He was trying not to gape at her, but he wasn't doing a good job. She was full of surprises, no doubt. The good kind. How many women in Hollywood would offer to shovel manure—outdoors—in a blizzard? Maybe just this one. "We'll ask Minnie about getting you bundled, then."

"Great!"

J.R. was still shaking his head at this pronouncement ten

minutes later as he waited in the hall for Thalia to emerge from her room. He'd washed up, put on the layers of long underwear and sweaters, and was sipping the rest of his coffee. He could handle a cold house—more so if he had Thalia to help keep his bed warm—but he'd sure like to shower before nightfall, maybe trim the edges of his beard.

After several chilly minutes, she came out, bundled in what looked like two sweaters, mug in hand. "Ready?" she asked, holding out her other hand for him to take. Like it was the most normal thing in the world.

"Ready." Ready to face Hoss. Ready for the snow. Ready for anything with her by his side.

When they got downstairs, Hoss had moved. Now he was standing before the fire, stretching. "Morning, you two," he said without even looking at them. Maybe Minnie had already told him to play it cool—or risk the wrath of her spoon.

"Morning." Thalia looked confident, but he heard the waver in her voice.

"Thalia's going to be moving into my room tonight." She shot him a less-than-pleased look. So that probably wasn't the most eloquent way of phrasing things. If there was one thing he'd learned in the last decade, it was that getting things out in the open made it better on everyone.

Minnie and Hoss both paused, and Thalia's hand clamped down on his. Then Minnie said, "That's nice," in the same tone she'd used earlier, and Hoss added, "Use less firewood, eh?" and it was just that easy.

"Yup. She's going to help out in the barn this morning, so Minnie, if you could get her set up after breakfast, that'd be great."

Minnie and Hoss shared a look that, for the life of him, he couldn't read. Which was odd, as he'd lived with them for a long, long time. He let it ride. It was time for breakfast, after all, and he was hungry.

Without much more ado, Minnie set out breakfast and they

all dug in. Minnie and Thalia talked about the gear she'd need to borrow—snowshoes, coveralls, gloves and the like—while he and Hoss discussed the plan of attack. "If you can get to the gas tanks, Thalia will help me with the barn."

If Hoss doubted the wisdom of this plan, he didn't show it. Instead, chewing his way around another piece of bacon, he said, "If I get the generator going and you two take care of the barn, then you and I can get the snowmobiles out and see if there's anything to be done about the cattle."

"Deal." Getting the generator running—with the accompanying heat and hot water—was a top priority.

After breakfast, Minnie took Thalia upstairs while Hoss and J.R. suited up in the mudroom. The whole time, J.R. waited for Hoss to say something. No smart-ass comments, no waggling eyebrows came his way. "Think she can make it out to the barn?" was all he said.

J.R. thought back to the serious way she'd offered to help. Honestly, he didn't know if she could handle the snow, much less the barn. "I ain't gonna be the one to tell her she *can't* do it."

"That's probably the smart move," Hoss said. "Don't strike me as the kind of woman who listens to what other people tell her she can't do."

Even J.R. had to chuckle. "When you're right," he said as he clapped Hoss on the shoulder, "you're right."

Thalia stood in the garage, which was about the size of a barn and had half a forest of firewood stacked in it. Minnie hadn't been lying—they could heat the house for a month, easy.

"Steady," J.R. said as he kneeled before her.

Thalia balanced herself against the back of Minnie's SUV as J.R. buckled her boot-clad foot into a snowshoe. She felt like the little brother in that movie *A Christmas Story*. Between her regular clothes and the sweatshirts, sweatpants, coveralls, hat, gloves, goggles and four pairs of socks Minnie had swaddled her in—plus the huge boots J.R. was working around—she didn't think she could put her arms down.

"There's a rope that goes from the house to the barn," Hoss was saying as J.R.'s hands worked. She wished she could feel his touch, but there were too many damn layers between them. "Don't let go of the rope."

"Hold on to rope. Got it."

"There." J.R. stood up, which was a pretty impressive series of moves for a man who was also wearing snowshoes. "Ready?"

Thalia nodded, but she wasn't so sure anymore. Offering to help in the barn had seemed like a fun idea at the time, but that was before she'd been trussed up as if she were going to climb Mont Blanc.

"Here we go." From her perch back by the door that led to the kitchen, Minnie opened the garage door. The whole thing groaned, and Hoss and J.R. rushed to help shove it up.

The wall of snow on the other side was impressive. As in, terrifying. "How much did we get?" she heard herself say.

"Probably only a couple of feet," J.R. replied as he assessed the pile that was much closer to her head than her knees. "This is just a drift. Once we get to the other side..."

Hoss already had a shovel and was pushing the snow away. After a few minutes, Thalia could see the crystal-white world on the other side. Everything looked both softer—the corners of buildings were cushioned and rounded, the world blanketed in comfortable white—and harsher. The wind had blown the snow into severe, sculpted drifts more fitting for a modern art museum than the Montana wilderness.

J.R. gave Hoss a leg up to get over the snow. Then he motioned to Thalia. "Your turn." She swore she heard something close to a tease in his voice.

What, did he think she'd chicken out? Hell to the no. She squared her shoulders and clomped over to where he waited for her. She couldn't see much of anything about him—he had on a full ski mask and goggles—but she would bet money he was smiling at her. "Ready," she said, hoping she sounded more confident than she felt.

J.R. nodded his head, then picked her up and more or less hefted her through the opening Hoss had shoveled. One of her snowshoes caught on the edge and she lost any semblance of balance.

"Watch it." From beneath his mask, Hoss's easy drawl reached her ears as he caught her by the arm and got her upright on the snowshoes. "We've got to stop meeting like this, you know."

"Agreed."

Hoss guided her over to the rope and waited until she'd looped her arm around it before he went back and helped haul J.R. up.

The nice thing was, for the first time since she'd arrived in this state, she wasn't freezing her butt off outside. The many layers she had on made moving a new and interesting experience, but she only felt the wind on her face. Her toes were, for the time being, safe.

J.R. took the place in front of her, and Hoss brought up the rear. Slowly, the three of them made their way out to the largest of the three barns. For her first time in snowshoes, she did pretty well. She hoped, anyway. At least she didn't fall into either of the men and she didn't let go of the rope.

Getting into the barn was an exercise in falling with style—at least, Thalia hoped she fell off the drift and into J.R.'s waiting arms with style. He unbuckled her snowshoes for her and she stepped clear. "Wait here while we get the gas," he said.

Nodding, she looked around. The barn was massive. From where she stood, she could see a full-sized, covered arena behind a gate on her left. Straight ahead was a row of stalls—maybe twenty in all. Did he keep that many horses? Wow. To her right was a big room with a desk and a bunch of saddles on the wall—the tack room and office.

The whole place was clean and bright, with paint that looked relatively fresh on the walls and the smell of alfalfa hanging in the air. Thalia took a deep breath, smelling the scent of a childhood summer spent at Grandpa's farm.

She was hit with an unexpected burst of homesickness—not for Hollywood, but for Oklahoma. She'd been so busy with work that it had been hard to find the time to get home to see Mom and pay a visit to Grandpa's and Dad's graves. She'd been trying to tell herself she was going back when she had this project done, or that award—that Oscar—won, but maybe that hadn't been what had kept her away. Maybe it had been that she hadn't wanted to go home until she was as famous as her mother thought she was.

Thalia walked to the first stall. She hadn't lied to J.R.—she'd always loved horses and had mucked plenty of stalls in her day to earn an afternoon riding around Grandpa's land. She was less than thrilled to see it was empty.

So were the next four stalls on either side of the sawdust-covered aisle, which left her with a vague sense of unease. There were horses somewhere in here, right?

Then, in the fifth stall, she found one and, from the sound of it, the next several stalls were also filled. The horse in the stall—a dirty white gelding with a long mane that flopped every which way—nickered at her through the bars. She saw he had a quilted blue blanket over him. That was good. She didn't want to think the horses were out here freezing.

"Hello, baby," she murmured, pushing her goggles back and holding her hand out for the horse to sniff. "What's your name?"

"Coot," came a voice from behind her. "As in, Old Coot." Thalia turned to see J.R. standing, his legs spread wide as if he were master of everything in his domain.

She'd be lying if she said she didn't feel a little thrill of excitement at seeing him. He'd removed his mask and pushed his hood back, revealing his rugged face. "He's retired," J.R. added, coming up next to her and patting Coot on the neck. "We rode together for a long time, didn't we, Coot?"

Thalia once had known a lot about how horses worked. She would have thought she'd forgotten almost all that knowledge, but she was surprised by what kept bubbling up from deep in her memory. "And you keep him?" When Grandpa had retired horses, he'd sent them off to some other farm. Any animal on his farm had to earn his keep—like his granddaughter.

"We've been through a lot." J.R.'s voice was low as he scratched the old horse behind the ear. "He was the first horse I bought—taught me a lot about riding on the range. I feel better knowing he's here and taken care of." He turned a goofy grin to her, but his eyes weren't telling the same tale. "Sounds dumb, huh?"

"No." She didn't want to embarrass him—or herself—by telling him it was noble, sweet, thoughtful and touching. Instead, she rubbed Coot's nose and changed the subject. "You have a lot of empty stalls here. Where are all the horses?"

"We only keep the seven here. The rest of the stalls are for the hired help to use in the summer months." He slid open Coot's door and haltered him. "I usually let them out into the arena to run off some energy after a big storm. Get the gate?"

"Sure." She walked on the opposite side of Coot and swung the gate in for them.

J.R. led Coot into the center of the arena before he released his halter. The old horse didn't bolt, though. He stood there, sniffing J.R.'s face while J.R. rubbed his neck.

This, in a nutshell, was what made J.R. a good man—and a better man than James Robert probably ever was. He took care of his horse. Something about that said old-school cowboy, loyal and true. Thalia's heart swelled watching them. He could play the gruff cowboy, but this—a big smile on his face as he cooed to his favorite horse—was who he really was. And he trusted her enough to be that man in front of her.

J.R. sent Coot off at a leisurely trot, then went out a different door at the top of the arena. He reappeared carrying two bales of hay, one in each hand. Wow, Thalia thought, imagining all those muscles flexing underneath his coveralls. Strong, yet gentle. Tough, yet vulnerable.

She was forgetting all about her crush on James Robert. J.R. was so much better than her fantasy had ever been. *So much.*

"We'll put the grain in their stalls in a bit," he said by way of explanation after Thalia shut the gate behind him, even though she doubted Coot was a flight risk. The old guy had his nose buried in the first bale of hay, munching happily.

J.R. let her lead the next horse, a paint mare named Whipper. Whipper was only a few years old, and wasn't interested in communing with a strange woman while perfectly good hay was being eaten by Coot right over there. Thalia turned her loose and then had to step back to avoid the parting high kick Whipper threw at her on her way to the hay.

J.R. grinned at her from the gate. "Like I said, they've got a little energy to burn." It should have sounded like he was mocking her, but she thought she heard a compliment—which he confirmed when he added, "Nice move. A true greenhorn would have gotten kicked in the head."

"It's been a long time since I've gotten kicked." They were walking down the aisle toward the next horses to be turned loose. "I think I was riding Cinnamon, a little pony my grandfather kept for me. That stinker decided to jump a branch about a foot off the ground. I went down hard, and her back hoof clipped my calf on the way down."

"Aw, that don't hardly count. I took a horseshoe to the shoulder once, trying to get a rock out of Coot's hoof." He pointed to his right shoulder. "Hurt like a son of a…gun." Then he winked at her.

Next came Hoss's horse, Rabbit—"Because he hops when he trots," J.R. said—Mac, Gater and Yoda, a draft horse with massive ears and a wrinkled nose. "Hoss's doing," J.R. said by way of explanation as Thalia giggled at the name.

Then they were down to the last horse. J.R. hesitated before a stall, and as soon as she saw the horse, she knew why. The animal was a brilliant palomino, the warm color making his mane shimmer like spun silk. Thalia had seen him before, riding across the frozen land like he owned it. "This is…Oscar." The way he said it made it clear he was embarrassed. "This is my horse."

He'd named his horse Oscar. All this talk of not being an actor anymore, but he hadn't put it as far from him as he pretended he had. Thalia could only hope this Oscar loved him back. "Quite the golden boy, aren't you?" Oscar whinnied as he sniffed her hand, then moved his head back to J.R.

A ruddy blush was turning J.R. an unusual shade of red. He *was* embarrassed. "Hey." She grabbed him and pulled his head down to hers. "You don't have to be ashamed of that—of any of that. Not with me."

She brushed her lips over his, but he didn't kiss her back. His eyes were closed, and he looked like he was concentrating. She didn't know if that was a good sign or not.

"Thalia." As he said her name, he touched his forehead to hers. His arms went around her waist, pulling her in close. "About what I said earlier."

"Yeah?" He'd already apologized for asking if Levinson had assigned her to seduce him. What now?

"You…" He cleared his throat, his eyes still jammed shut. "You being here *does* make it hard on me. But you make it easy on me, too. And that's hard for a man like me to get used to."

Oh. *Oh.* She exhaled, struggling to keep her knees under her. That had to be the sweetest, most heartfelt thing a man had ever said to her. And she had no doubt he meant it, too. Every single word.

She kissed him. At first, the daylight kiss—with an equine audience—was stiff and awkward, but then she felt him relax into her as his tongue brushed her lips. The heat was there, but the barn wasn't exactly warm, and there was no way anything could be maneuvered through these layers. She broke the kiss and hugged him. The nice thing was, he hugged her back.

"Tonight?" Going to bed with him in his room, knowing he'd be there when she woke up in the morning—yeah, this could be easy. Nice and easy.

"Tonight," he agreed, the wide smile erasing any of his embarrassment. They got the last horse into the arena and then he got out the pitchforks.

They worked in silence, but she could see him watching her. Maybe he was waiting for some sort of reaction of disgust or horror? "You know, it's funny," she told him as she dumped another scoop into a wheelbarrow. "I'm pretty sure I've dealt with less crap here than in an average day in Hollywood."

He snorted in appreciation. "That, I don't doubt. Get back to me in a few more days."

"How long do you think we'll be here?"

"We've got a bulldozer—Hoss's baby. It'll take a week or two to plow out to the main road, and then it all depends on the roads." He paused, giving her a serious look. "We'll get you home one way or another."

Which was going to be a crying shame when it happened. Home, back to where Levinson would fire her, she'd be hard-pressed to find another job and she'd lose her apartment. Maybe it was wishful thinking, but she'd rather stay here, where horses played and fires—the wood kind and the personal kind—burned hot.

Thalia got lost in her thoughts as they cleaned the barn. He didn't know everything about her. He'd made his feelings about her boss, Levinson, crystal clear. How would he react to the fact that she'd had an affair with the man he detested so openly?

Badly, that's how. She hoped it wouldn't come to that, though. They'd have this brief time together, and then she'd be on her way and he'd never look at her with shock or disappointment. It wasn't lying, not exactly. Neither of them had brought up old lovers.

No, there was no room for Levinson in this…well, *relationship* was a strong word. This temporary weather situation. Whatever it was, Levinson had no place in J.R.'s bedroom or his barn.

As J.R. dumped the last wheelbarrowful, Thalia hung on the gate and watched the horses trot around. Yoda was playful for a horse as big as he was. He'd take a running start at Whipper and Rabbit, his plate-sized hooves taking huge divots out of the arena floor. Whipper and Rabbit would rear and whinny and bolt out of Yoda's reach, heels kicking the whole way. Then Yoda would stand there and nicker at them, clearly laughing at their melodramatic reactions.

Mac and Gater stood off to one side, scratching each other's back through the blankets every horse wore. Oscar trotted around the edge of the arena, keeping clear of the antics of the other horses. A creature apart, Thalia thought as he gave her a wide berth. Just like his rider.

Coot ambled up to her and blew snot on her outstretched hand. "Hey, you," she said as she scratched his head. The old boy's eyes fluttered shut as he leaned into her hand. "You like that?"

It had been years since she'd been on a horse, but she'd loved riding as a kid. Too bad she was stuck on a ranch in the middle of a blizzard. That sort of ruled out trail rides, and she couldn't say if she'd ever be out here again. And thinking that left her feeling morose.

"He likes you," J.R. said as he walked down the aisle pulling a bin of grain behind him.

"I was thinking how long it's been since I've ridden." She stood on her tiptoes to give Coot a behind-the-ear scratch.

"Yeah? How long?" He was farther down the aisle, dumping grain into buckets.

"Grandpa died during my ninth-grade year. Mom tried to hold on to the family farm, but…" It had been the hardest thing she'd ever seen her mother do. That farm had been in her family since the days of the Sooners. The day of the auction, when Thalia was a junior in high school, Mom had cried herself to sleep. "After we lost it, I felt like…I didn't have anything holding me to the state. Like I'd lost a piece of my family."

Coot sighed. *Yeah,* she thought as she smiled at the old guy. *That.*

"Your mom is still down there?" J.R. had come out of the stalls, his bin mostly empty.

"She is. Dad died a long time ago, but she's made a good life for herself. She was so mad at me when I dropped out of college to go to Hollywood because I was supposed to be the first one in the family to get a college degree. So she went back and got one instead. She works at the library, has a group of ladies she lunches with and seems happy." She still worried about her daughter and the subtle hints for grandchildren were less subtle every day. All in all, at the age of fifty-five, Thalia thought her mom had made peace with the hand Fate had dealt her.

"She loves you." Thalia could hear the wonder in J.R.'s voice.

"She does." Did that bother him, to know that other mothers loved their children and his mother hadn't—at least, not in the traditional way?

"The thing that's always been difficult for me to figure out is if my mother was more normal and Minnie is the crazy one, or if Minnie's normal and my mother...well, she *was* crazy." He shrugged, but didn't seem to be as anxious about such a blanket statement this time.

"I'd go with Minnie being the more normal of the two." She wanted to say her mother would be thrilled to meet him, but she knew that would imply that this whatever they had going right now would outlast the snow on the ground, and that would be a mistake. No matter how easy it was to spend the day petting horses and the night in his bed, she couldn't lose sight of the fact that everything about this was temporary, and sooner or later, the snow would melt.

So instead, she patted Coot on the neck and got the lead rope and started putting the horses back in the stalls, where they snarfed their grain down with great relish. She and J.R. put their goggles and snowshoes back on, and then he hefted her up the snowbank. She did better walking back to the house than she had before. *See?* She thought to herself as she slid back into the garage. *I'm not totally hopeless.* She hoped J.R. felt the same way.

When they got their snowshoes off, J.R. paused. "Listen," he said, a grin peeking out from his mask.

Thalia cocked her head to one side. At first, she didn't hear anything—but then she realized it wasn't silent. She could hear the faint sound of an engine running.

"Hoss got the generator fixed?"

"Yup." He took her hand and led her into the mudroom. The sound of a radio filled the kitchen, and Minnie was singing along.

"Oh, thank heavens." She certainly wasn't frozen stiff, but a hot shower was high on her to-do list. Especially if she was going to be spending the night with J.R. She grinned up at J.R., who gave her a squeeze. It was a small move, but—

given that Minnie was only feet away—it felt like this huge, almost-public declaration of togetherness.

Sheesh, she felt like she was in junior high again. What would happen if they got caught kissing?

Twelve

They got the snowmobiles up and running, and talking was impossible once they were streaking across an almost unrecognizable range. The snow had drifted over their heads in some spots. The going was cold and treacherous, and it required J.R.'s full attention. They couldn't even make it to the far north pasture. Might be a few more days before they could get hay out to the animals.

When they made it back to the barn, Hoss didn't say anything that wasn't directly related to cows, horses or food. Even then, he was uncharacteristically restrained. He was making J.R. nervous, plain and simple.

"She really help muck the barn?" was Hoss's big question.

"Yup." Which had been as much of a shock to J.R. as it was now to Hoss. He'd entertained the thought that her offer to shovel manure was one of those things some women did to convince a man they loved everything he did, but, when faced with actual crap, she'd try to talk her way out of it. Or at least pale and complain about the smell. But no, she'd shoveled like it was second nature. And, somehow, looked good doing it, snowsuit and all.

"Huh." Hoss scratched his nose, and J.R. braced himself for something inappropriate. "Wouldn't have figured she was the type."

"Nope," J.R. agreed, even thought it wasn't wholly clear which type Hoss was referring to—the type that mucked barns, or the type that J.R. fell into bed with.

Maybe both, as it had been a long time since he'd fallen into bed with anyone. In the past, he'd spend a lot of time trying to gauge how much his lady friend knew and how she'd react when she found out about James Robert Bradley. Dating had felt like a negotiation, as intense and demanding as any contract negotiation he'd ever been a part of. Every step had to be calculated for risk and damage control—an exhaustive process that left little for the actual courting of a beautiful woman.

For the last decade, dating had been hard. But Thalia knew all about James Robert, and she honestly didn't seem to care. Well, maybe she did care. But that wasn't the only thing she cared about. That's what made her different. He didn't have to hide that part of his life from her, and she wasn't going to hold it against him. She made it easy on him. He didn't have to do any of that negotiation stuff this time, which freed up his brain to think of a whole bunch of other fun stuff. Stuff that involved a crackling fire, a warm bed and a very naked Thalia.

Claiming he was cold, he pushed Hoss out of the barn. Low clouds scuttled across the gray sky, which meant they might have another couple of inches of snow on top of this fine mess in the morning. Normally, J.R. would be cursing the weather gods right about now.

He wasn't. All he knew was another few inches of snow meant another few days with Thalia. He couldn't remember looking forward to something so much in a long, long time.

When he and Hoss got into the house, Thalia had changed. She looked like she'd taken advantage of the hot water, and her hair was loose and long. Had she showered in his room? Without him? Man, it was warm in the house. Or maybe that was his personal temperature.

When she saw him, her eyes lit up so bright that he got hot just looking at her. "How was it?"

"Bad," he said, but he thought, *good.* Good, deep snow. The Department of Transportation didn't plow the twenty miles from the main road to his house. Hoss could dig them out, but that took time. The last time it had snowed this much, it had taken two weeks to get the drive plowed. The fact of the matter was that Thalia was his, all his. Odds were good she wouldn't be able to leave before Valentine's Day, which was a few weeks away.

He made his way over to her. Hoss and Minnie were doing their best to watch him without actually looking at him as he pulled Thalia into his chest and kissed her...forehead. *Damn,* he thought, feeling his face flush. Couldn't pull the trigger and seal the deal. But kissing Thalia in front of Minnie was too much like making out in front of a mom. It felt awkward.

"Have a good afternoon?" he said, more to cover his embarrassment than anything else.

Thalia's cheeks were pinking up, which made her glow. "Minnie managed to get the satellite up." The way she said it made it pretty clear she was used to 4G-broadband-whatever, and not the satellite connection they had to depend on way out here in the country. "And I was able to email my mom."

"Good." He was almost afraid to look at Minnie, but he'd be hard-pressed to say why. It wasn't like she would send him to his room without supper—or, like his mother would have done, threaten to kill herself if he ever left her. "And work?" What had she told Levinson?

Her grin turned sly. "I told them I was stranded in Billings."

He wanted to hug her, which might have led to something embarrassing, like him blushing, but like she'd done many times, Minnie saved him from himself. "You boys need to get cleaned up before you sit on my furniture. Go on, shoo."

Thalia barely hid her giggle behind her hand before she pushed him toward the stairs. "She's right, you know," she called out behind them.

"That seemed to go well," Hoss said as they took the stairs.

J.R. knew he should not engage, should *not* run the risk of provoking Hoss's smart mouth, but he couldn't help himself. The man was more than his best friend, he was his brother. "You think?"

"Yup." They reached the top of the stairs, and Hoss turned to look at him. "It's odd, you know."

J.R. swallowed, refusing to be nervous as his friend passed judgment on this thing with Thalia. "What is?"

"Seeing you smile." Hoss was completely, totally serious, with nary a wisecrack in sight. The sentiment was so real, so unexpected, J.R. didn't know what to do.

The moment didn't last. "I forgot you had so many teeth." Hoss threw his hands up in front of his eyes and staggered back. "Damn, man. Put those things away before you blind me." Chuckling, he didn't even wait for whatever snappy comeback J.R. didn't have. He headed down to his room, peeling off layers as he went.

J.R. took his time getting cleaned up. Thalia's bag sat on the end of his bed, the promise of another night in her arms making him want to rush. However, rushing was the last thing he wanted to do. He spent a few extra minutes taking his beard down a layer and cleaning up the edges. His first instinct was to shave the whole thing off—he'd never had a beard and a lady friend at the same time—but something told him that was the wrong move, and that something was the memory of all the little noises Thalia made in the dark.

Down, boy, he thought as he wrangled his button fly. He

still had to make it through dinner, and it would probably be bad form to throw Thalia over his shoulder and carry her away the moment the plates were in the dishwasher. Which meant he had to keep his cool for another couple of hours. He could do that.

He hoped.

It turned out the time moved at a comfortable pace. Thalia and Minnie had, if possible, become even better friends over the course of the afternoon, and were now talking about movie stars who did TV shows. That wasn't so unusual, he guessed, but the way they kept drawing him, and even Hoss, into the conversation was, well, odd. It should have felt like he was being cornered for all his insider info—after all, he had known several of the actors they were talking about—but no one plumbed him for dirt, or expected him to have the right answer. Thalia asked him what he thought, he stated his piece and they talked about it. If anything, she had way more insider info than he did. All of his knowledge was sorely out of date.

After dinner was over, Minnie said, "J.R., why don't you show Thalia the rest of the house? She's going to think we live in the kitchen."

"What about me?" Hoss asked. He had the nerve to look hopeful. J.R. wanted to smack that puppy-dog face right off him.

"You can help with the dishes," Minnie replied in her no-nonsense tone before she motioned for J.R. to go on.

"Come on," J.R. said, taking Thalia's hand as he led her into the hallway that divided the house in two. They left a winking Minnie and a grumbling Hoss in the kitchen. "This is the dining room."

She took in the table built to seat fourteen. "My, what a big table you have."

He couldn't help but grin at her. "We only use it during the summer, when we've got hired hands to feed."

"That's a lot of hired help." She was impressed, he could tell.

"I've got about six guys who stay the whole summer out in the bunkhouse, and some other local fellows who come out for the day. I pay them, but I think they stay for Minnie's cooking." He leaned down, getting close enough to her that he could smell the scent of strawberries. "More than one of the older guys has proposed to her, you know."

Thalia gave him a sly smile. "The way to a cowboy's heart is his stomach?" Then she leaned up on her tiptoes and placed an innocent-feeling kiss on his lips.

Yeah, the stomach was one way—but not the only one. He tried to pull her in closer, but she pushed back on his chest and shot him a look that managed to walk the line between scolding and teasing. "You're supposed to be showing me around."

"And you're supposed to be looking." Man, he liked that smile on her. He liked being the one who brought it out even more. Somewhat begrudgingly, he moved her across the entry hallway. He didn't let go of her waist this time. He wanted to keep a hold of her as much as he could.

He led her past the front stairs and into the open room on the other side of the house. "This is the living room." She shot him a sideways glance, as if she didn't believe him. "Well, it is." The massive TV took up the wall opposite of the hearth. A pool table was in one corner, and Minnie had leather armchairs everywhere. The architect had wanted to make this two separate rooms—a parlor, he'd said, and a family room. J.R. had nixed that idea straight out. At the time, he'd assumed he'd never have a family. And the kitchen did double duty, anyway.

Thalia leaned back into him, rubbing her hand over his beard before snaking it up into his hair and pulling his head down to her neck. "I see. You use this more in the summer, too?" It was a perfectly polite question, but the way she shimmied her hips against his button fly was anything but polite. In fact, it bordered on cruel.

"Yeah," was all he got out as he scraped his facial hair over her earlobe. *That's right,* he thought, *two could play at this game.*

With great reluctance, she released him. "What's through there?"

Hell, yes, he was excited to hear how much of an impact he was having on her—her voice was strained. "The office."

Moving slowly, they maneuvered their way around all the chairs and through the doorway, all without taking their hands off each other. J.R. couldn't remember feeling this hot for a woman, and he couldn't remember a time when a woman had seemed this hot for him. James Robert, sure. Lots of women wanted to sleep with him for the record books. Even his few nights with lady friends since then hadn't had this urgency, this *need* behind them.

He spun her around and backed her up against his desk. Or maybe it was Hoss's desk—hell, he didn't know. It was a desk, and she was against it. Against him.

The full weight of her breasts pressed against him, high and heavy and begging for him to touch, so he did. He cupped them both, feeling her nipples peaking through all of her clothes beneath his thumbs. "J.R." His name came out as a low moan, like it had last night. She tilted her hips up, brushing her center against the front of his jeans as she dragged his mouth to hers.

Whoa. The kiss was one of those no-holds-barred kinds that obliterated anything else but *this* woman. He was straining so hard behind his fly that he was in danger of breaking his jeans. The ache ran deeper than that, though—it went all the way through him. She made him *hurt* in the best possible way. She was his pain and his salvation at the same time.

He was in over his head. Luckily, his head wasn't wasting too much time thinking about that. "Yeah. This is the office."

"Nice," she agreed, sliding her hands down his waist and over his backside.

What little control he had left—and he was damnably impressed he had any—helped him to realize that sex in the office would be crossing a line that even Minnie wouldn't let slide. "That's the downstairs."

Her eyes shined in a co-conspiratorial way. "I haven't seen everything upstairs. Haven't seen your room. Minnie moved my things," she added before he could ask.

"I should show you." It was almost impossible to let go of her enough that they could get the hell out of this room, but he forced himself to take a step back.

She was better at this than he was. He could tell because, even though she pushed him back, her chest was heaving and her eyes blazed with the same kind of barely contained desire that held a tight grip on him.

"Front," was all he could say, but she understood. No need to cut through the kitchen and get bogged down in chitchat with Minnie about how well Thalia liked the house. A distraction like that would kill him.

With long strides, she almost pulled him to the front stairway. He let her go up in front of him for selfish reasons—so he could watch her bottom move at eye level. As much as he was trying to be a mature, responsible lover, he couldn't resist skimming his hands over the back of her jeans. She giggled, which he took as a good sign.

All the way down the hall, he touched her. He squeezed her bottom, ran his hands over her hips, slipped his fingertips below her waistband. Anything to get closer to the skin he'd barely gotten to touch last night. Anything to get closer to her.

They ran into his door with a thud. He was still behind her, and he took this moment to slip his hand down the front of her jeans. One hand on her warm center, the other stroking her breast, his mouth on her neck, her ear—if he didn't need to get rid of all these clothes, he'd hold her here and make her come.

When she said, *"Please,"* in a low, whimpering voice, he knew he couldn't wait. He needed her too much.

He fumbled the doorknob open, and they all but fell into his room. It wasn't warm—the fire was far too low in the hearth to add much heat to the room—but it wasn't as cold as last night had been. He managed to kick the door shut at the same time he grabbed the hem of her sweater and peeled it over her head.

Disappointment came in the form of a white tank top. But the black straps of her bra peeked out at her shoulders, so that kept him going. He lifted the top over her head and was immediately rewarded with the full view of her breasts, barely contained by the black lace.

"Wow," he said, unable to keep his hands to himself. He let their luscious weight fill his hands again.

Another low moan escaped her lips. He covered her mouth with his, feeling the sound of her pleasure rocket through him. Then they were moving again. He was pushing her back toward the bed, she was working each agonizing button on his fly, and he was trying to undo her bra strap. He was out of practice. Took three times to get the whole thing undone.

They hit the bed, a tangle of arms and legs and clothing flying off every which way. Man, how he wanted to slow down and appreciate her body, to let her know how special she was, how she made him feel—but he couldn't. It wasn't physically possible to take it nice and easy with her pushing his jeans and his boxers down, with her wrapping her long fingers around his shaft, with her arching her back as he sucked on her breast. Hell, it wasn't even possible to get all the way *on* the bed. He couldn't wait. He had to have her right now.

With one foot tangled in his jeans and still on the floor, he lifted her legs until she had them wrapped around his waist.

"Yes," she hissed, running her fingers over his chest hair as he positioned himself. Then, with two hard thrusts, he was lodged deep in her welcoming body, feeling her shiver and shake as she cried out.

Oh, yeah, he thought, but he didn't have the voice to say it. Her body was tight and wet around him as he drove into her. Her hands moved over him without rhyme or reason—stroking his face, rubbing over his nipples, running her nails down his back with enough pressure to make him groan. It was the only noise he was capable of making.

"Yes, *yes,*" she kept saying, and he knew he was doing that to her, for her. He was the one she wanted—not James Robert, not Hoss—not anyone. Just him. When she said, "J.R.!" as she grabbed hold of his hip bones and pulled him even deeper into her, well, he lost it. He couldn't control himself.

With a final thrust, he came as her shock waves rolled through her. The feeling was so *much* that he lost his balance and fell on top of her with a muffled *whump.* He was worried he'd hurt her, but she giggled again and wrapped her arms around him.

She held him. It shouldn't have felt like a big deal—especially not compared with the amazing sex—but it was, and J.R. wasn't sure why. She hugged him tight to her chest. He felt her heartbeat steady and her chest rise and fall more regularly.

He managed to prop himself up on one arm. He didn't want to crush her, after all. This would be the time to come up with some smooth line, some tender pillow talk—all things he'd done in the past and was perfectly capable of doing again.

But when he looked into her eyes, he had nothing—nothing except the feeling of being both lost and found at the same time. He was lost—to her.

She smiled, a small, special thing that made him ache again. "So," she said, her voice still smiling for her. "This is the bedroom."

"Yup." *Keep it together,* he yelled at himself. He managed to pat the bed next to her head. "This is the bed."

"Nice." She leaned up and kissed him—not the fevered thing from before, but a touch of honesty.

He pulled out and managed to get back on his feet. He wasn't as young as he once was, back when a wild night of drunken partying was a standard Saturday, but he hoped he had enough gas in the tank to make one more go of it tonight. Later, he promised himself, he'd take his time. "Be right back."

He got cleaned up in a hurry. When he got back to the bedroom, she had a sheet wrapped around her. "Cold?"

"A little." She grinned at him in all his naked glory, which was basically cheating. He needed this room to be a lot warmer so she wouldn't hide behind a sheet.

"I'll get the fire going." When the bathroom door shut, he slipped his boxers back on and got to work on the fire. By the time she came out a few minutes later, he'd built a respectable blaze.

Still wrapped in that damn sheet, she came up next to him and rested her head against his arm. Wrapping her up in a hug, he pulled her in close. They stood like that for a few minutes. He knew she was looking at his Oscar and all the photos on the wall, but it didn't feel like a dangerous act, not like it had with Donna.

"Do you miss him?"

Thalia's question caught him off guard. "Who?" he asked, trying to figure out which of the celebrities in the photos she was referring to. All of them had been professional acquaintances, at best.

"Him." She stepped forward and touched a photo of James Robert posing with a young Brad Pitt. J.R knew he'd been about twenty in that photo. It felt like a lifetime ago.

She wasn't touching Brad's face in the photo.

"Do you ever miss being James Robert?"

J.R. felt himself breathe. She didn't ask like she couldn't believe he'd given up all that fame and money. She didn't weigh down her words with expectations of what he should be, should do. She just asked—and waited for the answer.

If it had been anyone else, he'd have gone on the defensive, loudly protesting how much he'd hated that life, how much he loved this new one he'd made for himself. But he didn't have to lie to her. He didn't have to lie to himself anymore.

"Sometimes. I get up at 3:30 a.m. in the summer to work cattle. I get stepped on, kicked, crapped on—you name it. Everyone has bad days, and when I have a bad day, it's my own damn fault, and no one else is going to come along and clean up my mess." Like the mess he'd made in Denny's bar the other night. J.R. had screwed up, and he had to deal with the consequences. "And I do miss the warm weather some days."

She shot him a silly smile. "And to think—I'm enjoying my first blizzard."

"Anytime you want to come back out here and be snowed in, you let me know." It was supposed to sound flippant, supposed to be this funny little joke he told, but it didn't come out that way. Not even close. All he heard himself say was, *Come back to me.* He didn't want this feeling, this, well, happiness to end when the snow melted. Honestly, he didn't think he wanted it to end at all.

The silliness of her grin faded a little bit, and she looked sad. He wasn't sure why, and he was afraid to find out. Maybe she didn't feel the same way about him? Then she said, "That goes for you, too. Anytime you want to hit a beach, you come see me. Just you," she added, curling into his arms. "No movie stars allowed."

Oh, yeah. He was lost to her, but it was okay.

She'd found him.

Thirteen

The next five days were some of the best ones J.R. could remember. He woke up with Thalia's arms around him. They made sweet love in the morning and then, after breakfast, bundled up and went out to the barn together. He even saddled up Old Coot and let her walk him around the arena. The way her face almost cracked in two from her smile was more than enough reward.

After that, he'd take her back into the house, pick up Hoss and do his best to get hay out to his herds. He'd come home to happy women and a hot meal. A couple of nights after dinner, they lit the fire in the living room and watched a movie while eating popcorn. Then back to bed, back to her arms. Back to loving on her.

Thalia shouldn't have fit in his house—his life—so well, but she did. Minnie was thrilled to have someone to talk to and help out with the meals. Hoss settled into a nice place of gentle teasing without being over the top, and J.R. was, well...

He was in danger of falling for Thalia.

That was a problem because, sooner or later, the snow would melt, and she'd go back to Hollywood and he'd still be out here. And that would take everything easy about being with Thalia and make the rest of his life hard to swallow.

She was the best thing to ever happen to him. How the hell was he going to let her drive away?

He tried not to think about it, reasoning the snow would keep her out here.

Except it didn't. On the fifth day after the blizzard, the temperatures spiked up to thirty-nine, which didn't make much of a dent in the depth of the snow. The next day, it was forty-four, and the day after that, it hit fifty-two. Fifty-two damn degrees on January 29. In Montana.

Hoss kept plowing the drive, making more progress every day. J.R. entertained notions of sabotaging the bulldozer, but he knew that would come back to bite him on the butt, so he didn't. On the third straight day of mid-fifties weather, Hoss made it to the road.

"It's clear enough," he reported at dinner, his eyebrows notched in worry. "Road's probably good to Billings."

"I don't know if I can drive that far on clear enough," Thalia said. "I haven't driven on snow in a long time."

"J.R. will take you, and we'll get the rental back to Billings for you," Minnie offered in what was supposed to be a helpful tone. It made J.R. want to yell at her. What were the two of them trying to do, push Thalia out of here?

"You can stay as long as you want." He told her that at dinner, and he told her that in bed that night, the scent of sex still hanging over them. He wanted to tell her she could stay forever, but it sounded crazy, even to him.

"I have to get back." He hugged her tight, wishing she wasn't right but knowing she was. "But not tomorrow."

"Yeah. One more day," he said. One more day of happiness.

How was he going to let her go?

There had to be a way. He just didn't know what it was.

That last day together was hard on Thalia. She knew she needed to be enjoying every last second of her time with J.R., but reality was too insistent. She was heading home tomorrow morning—where she'd have to face Levinson without the actor she'd promised to deliver. She had no doubt he'd fire her on the spot, and she had little doubt he'd make sure she didn't get another job.

Inevitable unemployment wasn't what she found the most depressing. No, the most depressing thing was that she was going to have to say goodbye to J.R. True, they'd get a few extra hours together on the drive to Billings, but then she'd get on her plane and he'd get back in his truck, and that would be that.

Maybe not, she found herself hoping. He'd said she could come back; she'd invited him out to California. Maybe she'd see him again. Maybe this wasn't *The End.* Maybe it was *To Be Continued...*

Of course, the last time she'd attempted a long-distance relationship had been when she left her college boyfriend behind to go to Hollywood in the first place, and that hadn't made it a month before the relationship fell to bits.

The whole thing sucked. She couldn't give up the life she had—the career she'd made—to take up with a rancher, even if that rancher was J.R. This wasn't the movies, after all. This was real life.

So, on February 2, she packed up her things and carried her bags down to the kitchen. J.R. was outside with Hoss, which was just as well. He'd been quiet the whole night and morning, and Thalia wanted to say goodbye to Minnie without any men around. She was pretty sure there would be tears.

"You'll let me know how it goes?" Minnie said while hugging Thalia.

"Of course." How could she not let Minnie know how the firing went? "You'll take care of J.R. for me, won't you?"

"Oh," Minnie said, sniffling a little as she waved the question away. "I predict a few months of temper tantrums after this." Thalia guessed it was supposed to be a little joke, but it almost broke her heart.

J.R. and Hoss came back in, and J.R. went upstairs to get his bag. He'd told Thalia he was packing a change of clothes, in case the roads were bad enough that he couldn't make it home in the dark. That left Thalia with a sniffling Minnie and Hoss, who looked as uncomfortable as a man of his size could. "Thalia," he said, sticking out a hand for what was bound to be an awkward handshake.

"Hoss." She couldn't leave it at a shake. These people had become too important to her. She gave him one of those awkward hugs with their clasped hands in between their bodies.

"Don't forget, I'm still looking for a casting couch."

"I'll do my darnedest to find you a good one." Thalia had to blink a couple of times to keep the tears from spilling over.

Then she heard J.R. thumping back down the stairs. Putting on the happiest face she could muster, she turned to him.

He stood there, taking in the scene. He had a duffel bag in his hand, a hat on his head—and a suiter slung over his shoulder. "J.R.?"

He locked his gaze on her. "I'm going with you."

She couldn't tell if this was a dream come true—he wanted to come with her—or a nightmare of epic proportions. "What? No—you can't!"

A look crossed his face—the same look he'd given her on that first day, when he'd left her out in the cold. It sent a chill through her. "I'm not saying I'll take the part. But I'll meet with Levinson."

"But—but—but you hate him! And if word gets out about you, the press will come after you—you have no idea what it's like these days, J.R.!" The irony of her words struck her.

Was she actively trying to keep him from coming with her? Really?

"I'm not afraid of him or anyone." He squared his shoulders. "I can take it. I'm coming with you."

He was doing this for her. She knew that with unwavering certainty. He wasn't protecting himself. He wasn't throwing her under the bus—or, as he said it, in front of the bus. He was putting himself at risk for *her*

No one had ever laid it on the line for her before. He'd said it himself—a real man made sure a lady was safe. If he came, if he took the part, if he made a big return to the screen, she'd get to keep her job. She might even get to see him on a semiregular basis, especially while they were filming. It could work.

But he wouldn't be happy being famous again. She knew it—and so did he.

"No."

That was the hell of it. He wanted to come with her, she wanted him to come with her—but she had to protect him. From himself, it seemed. She couldn't let him throw away everything he'd worked for, just for her.

The tension in the room felt like a rubber band about to snap. J.R. leveled those beautiful amber eyes at her. God, he would be her undoing. "I'm coming with you, and that's final."

"I'll make Hoss take me."

This threat proved empty before the words had dissipated out of the air. Hoss coughed behind her. "Sorry, Thalia. I got work to do."

The desperation that gripped Thalia was sadly familiar. She wasn't going to be able to talk herself out of this. She couldn't control the situation—instead, the situation was controlling her. Still, she heard herself say, "Minnie?"

"I don't drive on snow if I can help it," Minnie said, her voice small. "Black ice," she added.

One corner of J.R.'s mouth curled up, a smile in victory. He looked like a mercenary. "I'm going."

"It'll change everything."

That wasn't some half-baked attempt to stall. That was the truth. Everything would be different for him. For her, too.

His face softened. He looked less deadly, more thoughtful. "Maybe it should." Then he picked up her bag and walked out the door.

"Take care of him," Minnie said, and Thalia heard the catch in her voice.

"I will." It felt like an empty promise, though. Taking care of him would be making sure his secret was safe—that he was safe. Letting him come to Hollywood? How was she supposed to take care of him there?

The path Hoss had plowed was passable, at best, and she was extra glad she didn't have to drive. J.R. was silent, both hands gripping the wheel. She wanted to try and talk him out of making the journey with her, but she also didn't want to make him drive into a snowbank.

Hoss had been right—the road was pretty good, once they reached it. J.R. loosened his grip on the wheel and relaxed back into his seat a little. They still had a long way to go, though.

Again, she found herself knowing she had to plead her case to J.R. and not knowing how to go about it. At least this time, she wasn't in danger of freezing to death.

She'd spent a week and a half in this man's bed. Trying to talk to him shouldn't seem like such a treacherous mountain to climb.

"Listen," she started, because she didn't have any better ideas but also because that's what she wanted him to do.

"No, I understand how it is. Beautiful, intelligent woman like you—you probably have someone else."

He thought she'd lied to him. "That's what you think?"

His only response was a curt nod of his head.

"J.R., you listen to me. The only thing I want more than for you to come with me is for me to stay with you. But I can't—and not because I've got some other lover stashed somewhere. The only reason I'm trying—*trying*—to talk you out of getting on that plane with me is because I know it won't work."

"It could," was his gruff reply.

"It won't—and not because we don't want it to. It won't work because sooner or later, you'll be James Robert Bradley again, and the moment that happens, the *moment* you lose J.R., you'll hate it all over again. And since I'm the reason you gave it up, you'll…" *Hate me.* She couldn't say the words. She hated having to say these things, hated having to break her own heart. Most of all, she hated being right.

Because she was. When she'd shown up on his porch that first day, she hadn't cared about J.R. All she had cared about was the great press James Robert Bradley would bring to the role, the tickets his comeback performance would sell.

All that had changed. Now, money was the last thing on her mind. The man was more important. The man, she realized, was everything.

Unable to keep her tears back, she turned to look out the passenger side window. It was better this way, she tried to tell herself. Better to end it now, when they could just be unhappy with each other, before both of their lives got turned upside down and inside out. She'd seen that happen too many times. People on a set—away from their real lives—fell madly in love, only to watch the whole thing disintegrate on them when they had to go back to the real world.

She didn't want that to happen to them.

The silence in the cab of the truck weighed down on her. *Breathe,* she told herself.

J.R. cleared his throat. Thalia tensed, but he didn't say anything for a few more agonizing seconds. "You aren't seeing anyone else?"

"No. Dating within the industry is a death trap on the best

of days." Why did she have to defend herself here? She'd been honest with him. She hadn't slept with anyone in a year. She'd dumped her last boyfriend before Valentine's Day as a matter of self-preservation.

Of course, the moment she thought that, guilt rushed in. She hadn't been completely honest. She hadn't told him about her disastrous affair with Levinson. When she'd been leaving and he'd been staying, it hadn't seemed relevant. But now?

The silence stretched for another painful minute. Thalia couldn't decide if she should keep her mouth shut or tell J.R. about her messy history with Levinson.

Was it any of his business who she had or had not slept with in the past? They were lovers now—obviously. That didn't necessarily entitle her to the list—and she knew it was long—of his previous paramours, both of the famous and not-so-famous variety. Why would it be any different for him?

The past was just that—the past, she decided.

"I'm, uh, not real good with apologizing." J.R.'s hesitant statement should have been awkward, but instead it only made Thalia want to smile. She looked at him. His eyes were still glued to the road, but his face had relaxed. He was in danger of smiling.

No, he wasn't good at apologies. But he was willing to attempt it. For her. "Practice makes perfect."

He reached over and squeezed her leg. Then they hit a slick spot and he had to put both hands back on the wheel. "Look, I know it's going to be hard. But you're..." He cleared his throat again. Thalia felt like she should look away from him, so he could get what he was about to say off his chest. He was incapable of talking with eye contact. At least, out of bed.

So she moved her gaze to the windshield and waited.

"You're important to me and I'll fight to be with you." The words came out in a rush, like air escaping a balloon.

Now how was she supposed to argue with that? Was she supposed to say that she wasn't that important? Tell him he didn't mean as much to her as she did to him? Was she supposed to lie to his face and tell him that wasn't one of the more romantic things anyone had ever said to her? That he didn't make her melt?

No. There wasn't any way to argue with the fact that she was important to him, and he was willing to take a huge risk for her.

"It's my choice. Even if it isn't the best one, I want to be the one who makes it. And I choose to hold on to you right now. If you don't feel the same way, I'll understand." This time, he didn't talk like he was mad at the world. His voice was tender again, more questioning than demanding.

Thalia couldn't remember if she was supposed to breathe in or out and wound up coughing. "You okay?" he asked, giving her leg another quick squeeze.

Nothing ventured, nothing gained. Things could still go a thousand ways wrong, but she had to take a chance—*this* chance—that things would go right. She had to trust him, and she had to trust herself.

She leaned over and touched his cheek. "I don't think I've ever been better, J.R."

Fourteen

One thing was for sure. J.R. wasn't used to traveling anymore. The drive to Billings wasn't so bad, but the puddle jumper to Denver about did him in, and the 737 to LAX wasn't much better. Even from first class.

Another thing he learned real quick was that, even though he could handle a Montana summer, he wasn't ready for the warm air that hit him in the face the moment they stepped outside the airport in sunny California. Despite having to deal with manure on a daily basis, the smell of L.A. made his head hurt. Was that a new odor, or had he just not noticed it before?

The throng of people was the third thing that set him back on his heels. Yeah, he had a lot of cowboys on the ranch in the summer, and yeah, he did fine in the bar in Beaverhead, even when it was crowded.

But he'd forgotten about the sheer volume of humanity that walked around L.A., often in outfits that barely qualified as clothing. Thalia had offered to put him up at the Chateau Marmont, but he had too many memories of the hotel where

Hollywood went to party. When she had then suggested he stay at her place, he jumped all over it. After all, it didn't matter so much about the noise or the people or the smell as long as he was with her. It felt strange to sleep in a different bed, but she was in it with him, so it wasn't that strange at all.

The next day, instead of hiding from people who might or might not recognize him, he'd spent part of the afternoon sitting in a coffee shop a block away from Thalia's apartment, reading *Variety* and drinking cups of coffee with six-word names while she was at work. He'd watched the people, too. Everyone was so skinny here, with the women all looking eerily similar to plastic dolls and the men appearing to be waxed within an inch of their lives. J.R. had found himself stroking his chin. Very few beards around here. He stuck out like a sore thumb, which didn't jibe well with the whole trying-to-be-invisible angle he was working on.

Thalia had called a couple of hours ago, after she got out of her meeting with Levinson. Yes, he was excited to hear J.R. was interested in the part, but he didn't want to wait until tomorrow, she'd said. There was a party happening tonight at some club that hadn't existed eleven years ago. If she'd told him what the party was for, he didn't remember. Everything but the fact that he was going to have to go to a social event with God only knew how many celebrities—and accompanying paparazzi—washed over him.

"You don't have to go," Thalia had said when he hadn't come back with a response.

On the one hand, he liked that she wanted to protect him. He knew his trust in her wasn't misplaced, that she cared for him. It made him want to spend another night making love to her—to hell with parties.

On the other hand, it was a direct blow to his male pride. He would not cower in this apartment, by God. He *didn't* cower. "It's fine."

The pause had been long, and he could see her trying to

decide if she should argue with him or let it ride. "I'll be home in an hour. We'll eat dinner and go. We won't stay long, not if you don't want to."

"It's fine," was all he had been capable of saying.

Which is how he found himself standing in Thalia's bathroom, wearing nothing but a towel and a beard. The options weighed heavy on him.

No one else in this town seemed to have a beard, not a full one like his. It wasn't like he was married to the beard. He shaved in the summer, when extra insulation wasn't required. Plus, he cleaned up well. If he shaved, he'd look more like his old self, the celebrity people would recognize.

But he didn't want to be what people expected, not anymore. He lived his life on his terms now. Maybe he should keep it. Thalia loved it, after all. It'd be a quick 'n' easy way to announce to these people that he didn't play by their rules. He didn't have to conform to their expectations. He was his own man, for crying out loud, and he could wear a beard if he wanted.

Jeez, it was like the beard was his life. Did he want to look like James Robert or J.R.?

Who the hell was he?

"Screw it," he muttered to himself. Ten minutes later, he rinsed off his face and looked at his reflection. God, he hoped Thalia liked it.

He'd never worn a goatee, but sometimes, a man had to split the difference.

"Ms. Thorne," a beefy, bald bouncer said, nodding his head in greeting. He lifted the velvet rope—they still had velvet ropes, so that hadn't changed—and motioned her up the staircase in the middle of the club. The thing seemed to be made of solid glass, and J.R. saw a go-go dancer, or whatever they were called now, gyrating on the landing halfway up.

Thalia led the way, which gave J.R. a chance to appreciate the fine view of her backside in a skintight red cocktail dress that was backless. As far as he could tell, the dress didn't make any allowances for underthings of any sort, and his imagination was running rampant. Raw desire was the only thing that kept him from panicking at this point.

The club pulsed with a bass beat timed to strobe lights. Men and women made out with women and men everywhere, which was unnerving enough, but plenty of them were breaking their embraces to stare at him. Once, this had been his life. Hit a club, get smashed, pick up a chick, have forgettable sex. He looked back at the people staring at him. Once, he'd been one of them. Not anymore.

"Whoa, cowboy. Name?" The beefy bouncer held him back with a hand on his chest. Already on edge, it took a lot of work to keep from snapping the man's fingers.

"He's on the list, Trevor." Thalia turned back and scrolled down the man's tablet—clipboards had gone out of fashion, apparently. "There. Bradley."

At least the bouncer uniform hadn't changed much—black pants, black T-shirt. Trevor gave J.R. the once-over, clearly amused by the crocodile-skin boots, the Stetson and the bolo tie. "Enjoy the party, Mr. Bradley."

Fat chance that would happen, but Thalia gave him an encouraging smile before she began to climb the stairs again.

He wished he could hold her hand, but even he had seen the folly of public displays of affection in front of Levinson and associates. For all intents and purposes, he and Thalia were business acquaintances and nothing more.

That became a problem, at least for him, as they reached the private party on the second floor. Women—and men—greeted Thalia with kisses on the cheeks, and J.R. felt himself getting the kind of jealous that only led to trouble. He knew the rituals but it still bugged him to watch other men touch her. She was his, as much as he was hers.

It got worse. Everyone knew he was here, but no one knew

who he was. He swore he heard whispers over the grinding
music. Maybe he should have worn all black and shaved the
beard. He wouldn't have looked like himself, but he would
have been almost invisible here.

"Who's this tall drink of water?" a woman J.R. didn't recognize said. She was all but licking her chops as her gaze
swept over him like a hungry cat.

"Kathryn, this is James Robert Bradley."

J.R. knew she was going to do that—they'd game-planned
out how to handle the party and the people. But it still felt almost like a physical blow below the solar plexus. Damn near
knocked the wind out of him.

"*The* James Robert Bradley?"

That was part of the script he and Thalia had discussed.
At this point, he was loving the script. "One and the same,
ma'am." And he tipped his hat, mostly to keep her from kissing him.

Kathryn whoever's hand flew to her mouth. "Oh, my God,
the James Robert Bradley? I thought you were dead!"

"Nope. Just ranching." He wasn't going to mention the
state. Thalia had agreed that the less identifying information
he gave out, the better everything would be.

"You," this Kathryn said, her eyes narrowing as a mani-
cured nail flicked in his direction, "were supposed to give
me my Oscar, and you bailed. They had to get Tom to give
it to me. I've never forgiven you for that."

Oh, hell. He should know who this Kathryn was. Luckily,
Thalia came to his rescue. "Excuse us, I see Bob," she said
with a gracious smile before she took him by the elbow and
led him away. "Great job," she added in a low voice. "Only
another two hundred to go."

He tried to laugh, but it got stuck in his throat. "I could
go for a beer right now."

"They might have one at the bar." She angled him in a
different direction.

"Might?" He glanced around. Everyone else had martini glasses with fruity drinks. No one was drinking a simple beer. Man, he was out of his league here.

Getting to the bar took some time. Word of his continual living spread like wildfire and a crowd started to form. Young guys started telling him how he had been such an inspiration, older women looked at him like hungry dogs staring at a bone, and a few men—men he'd known and partied with—slapped him on the back and told him he had on "a hell of a hat for Hollywood."

"Where *have* you been?" That question came from Eli Granger, who J.R. remembered as a young punk actor bent on self-destruction but now, according to Thalia, was a respectable agent.

"Not here."

Eli snorted as he sipped his Cristal. "Was 'not here' good, man?"

"'Not here' was great," he admitted, casting a glance at Thalia. He couldn't tell in this crappy light, but she might have blushed. J.R. wondered how far down that blush went if she didn't have on anything underneath the dress.

Eli slapped him on the back. "I'm almost jealous." His self-confident mask fell away, and J.R. saw a guy who was tired of running a race he was never going to win. J.R. recognized that look. He'd been tired once. It had almost killed him.

"You should come visit 'not here' sometime. It's normal there, if you like cows." He couldn't believe he was extending the offer to a man who was more or less a complete stranger, but once, he and Eli had been whatever passed as friends in this place.

"Thanks, but I don't eat red meat." As quick as his mask had fallen off, Eli was back to sipping his expensive champagne and looking cynical.

And so it went. Thalia got J.R. some brand of beer he'd never heard of from the bar, but hey, it was a beer and he drank it. Slowly. The four-beer limit was in effect here, too. She stayed close to him, guiding introductions and extracting him from conversations that started to spiral out of control, which happened a lot. Half the people in the room were either drunk or high. Or both.

J.R. was able to relax enough to appreciate her skills. She knew every single person by name and had a compliment at the ready at all times without giving anything away. She flattered egos and said the right thing about projects finished or coming soon. She was good at what she did, he saw. A realization that was followed by a tinge of disappointment. She fit well here. She wouldn't want to give this up to come live with an occasionally cranky rancher in the middle of nowhere.

He shoved those thoughts aside and focused on surviving the evening. After what felt like several hours of meeting and greeting, they made their way back to where Bob Levinson was holding court.

He was shorter than J.R. remembered, with a barrel chest contained by a three-piece suit. Once, J.R. remembered Levinson had been passably handsome. No more. One too many face-lifts or Botox or whatever people did to themselves here had left Levinson looking like a clownish version of himself. His hair hadn't changed, though—shoe-polish black and slicked into an embarrassment of a ponytail. A watch chain hung out of his vest pocket, and his cuff links appeared to be gemstones. As if he needed further accessorizing, he sat in a booth with four different women wearing blond hair and spandex dresses. He looked like a pimp for the mutual fund set.

Thalia started to introduce J.R., but Levinson cut her off. "Well, well. Look who's back." Levinson's voice hadn't aged well. He'd always had a weak spot for cigars and cocaine, which meant he both sounded and smelled old.

"Bob," Thalia said, apparently determined to press on. "You remember James."

The ladies around Levinson shifted as they appraised him. He didn't tip his hat, but he nodded in greeting. One of them waggled her fingers at him.

Levinson sat there, looking at him with a greedy little smile on his face. J.R. knew that look. That was the look that said J.R. wasn't a man standing here. He was a commodity to be bought and sold.

Damn, but he hated that feeling.

"Ladies." Levinson shooed them all out of the booth, then he looked at Thalia. "You, too."

J.R. looked at Thalia, who was about to crack that smile right off her face. She didn't like this; he didn't like it. But Levinson was the one calling the shots. "I'll get you another beer," she said before she stiffly turned and walked away.

This wasn't part of the script.

"Sit down." Levinson clearly hadn't gotten any more into the habit of social graces in the interim.

"I'll stand." That was the nice thing about not caring about the part or his career or what anyone else—besides Thalia— thought of him. He could do whatever he wanted, and more than anything, he didn't want to take orders from this slimy man.

Levinson's oily smile faded a little. He looked like a barracuda ready to strike. "Damn shame about your mother. She was a wonderful woman."

They both knew that was a bald-faced lie. J.R. knew he hadn't forgotten what condescending compliments were like, but he hadn't exactly remembered how freaking irritating it was. "You let me know when you're done with the B.S."

Levinson didn't miss a beat. "This is going to be a big winner, James. Another Oscar for your collection." He looked J.R. up and down with a calculating eye. "Hell, think of the money we'll save on wardrobe alone." He leaned forward and snorted a line of coke off the tabletop.

Ugh, J.R. thought. Once upon a time, he might have done

the same to feel like he belonged. Not anymore. He stood his ground, waiting for the B.S. to be over.

It wasn't. "She's something, isn't she?" The way he said it set the hackles up on J.R.'s neck.

"Who?" He knew who, but he was praying that Levinson was talking about one of the bimbos.

Levinson leaned back, clearly lost in the rush of his high. "She said she'd find you, and she said she'd bring you back—signed, sealed and delivered. What did it take?" He grinned, an ugly, leering thing that seemed three sizes too big for his small head. "Did she make it worth your while?"

The suggestion was anything but subtle. J.R. felt his temper beginning to flare, but he fought to keep it cool. "I don't know what you're talking about." Except he did. Once, he'd accused Thalia of doing just that, and she'd properly slapped him for it. Now that he knew her, he knew she wouldn't use sex to trap him.

"Oh, she's amazing." Even though J.R. could tell by the look on Levinson's face that he was intentionally trying to get a reaction out of him, it was still working. It was all J.R. could do to keep his fist clenched as Levinson went on, "Damn shame her acting career died on the vine. She had potential. Of course, after my wife found out about us, well…" He shrugged, looking anything but apologetic. "You know Miranda and her unique talent to make things difficult."

Something in J.R.'s brain misfired, so he tried to turn his mental engine over what Levinson had said a second time. Had he said that he and Thalia had been an "us"? Had she seriously had an affair with this *slimebag?* Why hadn't Thalia told him—at least to warn him? They'd scripted out the entire evening—and she hadn't bothered to mention this as a conversational death trap? And if she hadn't told him something important, like the fact that she'd been intimate with this—this—*man,* what else wasn't she telling him? What else was a lie?

"How is your wife?" This last gasp at civility was all he had to hold on to before he broke something. Or someone.

Levinson waved off the comment. "Left me for a younger man. Good riddance." His eyes narrowed as he wiped a thin trail of cocaine-snot off his nose. "Or did you not have her? She told me she'd do whatever it took to get you here, and," he said, sweeping his hands across the booth, "here you are."

If J.R. were in Montana instead of California, he'd have already broken Levinson's nose. And maybe a few other bones. "I haven't signed anything yet." Then, because he was losing the last of his self-control, he added, "I was waiting to see if I could stomach working with you again. You couldn't pay me enough money in the world to have another conversation with you, much less do a movie. You can take your Oscars and shove them where the sun don't shine."

Three things happened in quick succession. One, a hush fell over the club. Even the DJ paused the pounding beat, and J.R. got the sense that everyone—*everyone*—was listening to him do the unprecedented and say *no* to Bob Levinson. The second thing was that anything jovial or, heaven forbid, cheerful about Levinson stopped cold, and J.R. found himself looking at an ugly old man.

The third thing was that Thalia chose that moment to re-enter the conversation. The room was so quiet that he heard the click of her impressive heels as she walked up to him, a beer in one hand and a cocktail in the other.

J.R. didn't want to look at her. He didn't want to see the face of the woman he thought he could trust and know that he'd been wrong. She'd slept with Levinson—he couldn't get his head around that, and he couldn't get past Levinson's claim that Thalia would do anything—everything—to sign him.

Did that include making him fall in love with her?

Had he ever been a bigger idiot? Had he thought that she'd

been different, that she'd actually cared about him? Or had it all been about the movie, the money?

Had it all been an act?

"You said you had him signed, sealed and delivered," Levinson said to Thalia. He could have cut glass with his voice.

This was the true soul of the man, the one who killed careers and destroyed people because it was easy and fun. This man was the living embodiment of why J.R. had left Hollywood in the first place. He never should have come back. Not even for a woman.

Not even for Thalia.

"I said that—"

Levinson cut her off. "There are no excuses. This is what I get for taking pity on a brainless whore like you. You make promises you can't keep." He snorted, his eyes glittering with the kill. "Mark my words, you couldn't screw enough people to get another job in this town. No one wants to work with a failure."

J.R. wasn't sure what happened next. Either he flipped over the table and then Thalia dropped both of the drinks, or she dropped the drinks as he flipped over the table. Didn't matter so much in the long run. The drinks were dropped and the table flipped, catching Levinson in the chin.

J.R. was so mad he couldn't think straight. He grabbed at Levinson with nothing but blood on his mind. Someone screamed. He got Levinson by the prissy tie, but before any satisfying punching could take place, hands were on him and he was being hauled backward.

"Damn, man," someone said, and J.R. realized it was Eli. "Knock it off!"

J.R. ignored him and focused on getting his arms free. He could still land a good blow, if he could just get back to that tapeworm of a man.

The next thing he knew, he was picked up and was bodily

hauled down the stairs. When he realized that each appendage had at least one guy holding on to it, he knew his chance to kill Levinson with his bare hands had passed. The club was now entirely silent, and as he was dragged out the door, he saw a whole bunch of people holding up phones.

He was in big-time trouble, and he knew it. The anger bailed on him as fast as it had rushed in, and was replaced by a sinking pit in his stomach. This was way worse than being kicked out of Denny's bar for a few months. This was probably going to screw up the rest of his life.

His vision cleared enough to see that a beautiful woman in a striking red dress was following him at a distance. She wasn't crying, nor was she screaming or even shouting. She looked like someone had gut-shot her.

"Put me down," he demanded, although he couldn't tell if he wanted to comfort Thalia or lash out at her.

"Not happening, cowboy." In the next moment, they were out the doors, and J.R. felt himself breathe in air that only reeked a little. Then he was unceremoniously dumped on the sidewalk.

A crowd had gathered by this point. More phones, plus some old-fashioned flashbulbs, were now going off. Eli was still by him, and Thalia wasn't far away.

She told you not to come, the one rational brain cell left in his head whispered to him. But J.R. was in no mood for rational. He shoved that thought aside. Hard.

Eli was talking. "I don't think I've ever seen that old fart look as scared, man!" He thwacked J.R. on the back. "Half of this town has dreamed of getting the old man on the chin, but no one else has had the balls!"

"Move." Thalia made it to them. "Walk."

"I'm not going anywhere with you. You lied to me."

"Not here," she whispered, but it was too late. People were crowding in on them, and the name James Robert Bradley rode lead on the wind.

The situation kept getting worse. J.R. knew he was spiraling out of control, but he was powerless to stop it. He hated the feeling of being unable to control himself, his life. But that was where he was at. Out of control. "You slept with *him?*"

"Not *here,*" she said again. He heard the plea in her voice, but he couldn't do a damn thing about it.

"Yo, man, we gotta get you off the street." Eli had him under the arm and was hauling him somewhere. "Everyone's watching."

"His stuff is at my place," Thalia said, her voice breaking.

He heard the hurt, but he didn't want to care. Caring about her had recently become a painful thing. Too painful. He couldn't take it. He didn't want to feel anymore. "I'm not going anywhere with you. You lied to me," he said again.

"J.R., please—can we talk about this anywhere else but here?" A tear spilled over, but he had no way of knowing if it was real or just another act.

"I'll follow you to your place," Eli said, shoving J.R. toward an expensive-looking car.

"No." He stood up and shook Eli off. *"No."*

Another tear raced down her cheek. It wasn't working. He wasn't letting her make him feel guilty. He wasn't going to feel a damn thing for her, even if it killed him.

"Please, J.R. All your things."

He stood up straight and glared at her. He'd let himself get used, and for what? He'd destroyed everything he'd worked for, everything he'd built, because he thought he'd fallen for a woman.

He looked her in the eyes, trying so hard not to feel anything. "There's nothing there that I can't replace."

He didn't feel like crap when she choked and buried her face in her hands. He didn't feel like the world's biggest ass when he slid into Eli's car. He didn't feel like he was as bad as Levinson, or worse.

As Eli put the pedal to the metal for parts unknown, J.R. only knew one thing.

He didn't want to feel anything.

Fifteen

"Can I get you a snack, sweetie?"

Thalia did her best not to roll her eyes at her mother. As if another bowl of potato chips would make everything all better. "No thanks, Mom."

She'd been visiting, as Mom insisted on calling it, for a week now, and Mom was doing everything but coddling her. Mostly, it was driving her nuts. She'd lived by herself for so long that having to share a bathroom with a woman who had a shaky definition of privacy and having to sleep in a twin daybed with a ruffled duvet seemed like insult on top of injury. However, homemade meals, a shoulder to cry on and the kind of unconditional love that didn't exist in Hollywood went a long way. Thalia could use a little coddling after her collapse, so she worked on overlooking the irritating parts.

Only two weeks had passed since life as she knew it had ended on the sidewalk outside a club. She'd tried to stick it out in Hollywood, but with each day that passed, it had become that much clearer that there was no fixing the mess she'd found herself in. Even the baristas at her favorite coffee shop had looked at her funny. No one took her calls. The only person who responded to her emails was Levinson's personal assistant, Marla, and that was mostly out of fear that she was next on the chopping block.

Levinson was so enraged that he'd had a mild heart attack, which was another thing he was going to sue J.R. for. Apparently, the list of legal claims he had against J.R. was quite long. Not that Thalia knew firsthand, but Marla had taken to sending her private emails with hour-by-hour updates. The movie had fallen apart after her public character assassination. Clint and Morgan had both backed out as word of the fight spread around town, and once that news hit, Denzel wasn't far behind. She was taking more than her fair share of the blame, but, according to Levinson's assistant, other deals were in danger. The untouchable producer was suddenly vulnerable.

Not that the thought gave Thalia much comfort. At this point, not even Mom's homemade chocolate chip waffles did much to improve her outlook. She'd messed up in every possible way. She knew—and Mom kept reminding her—that she'd get past this. She had once before. But she was almost thirty, for God's sake. She felt a little too old to be starting over. At the age where most of the girls she'd gone to high school with were going to soccer games and school parties, Thalia was living with her mother again, unemployed and broke. The only assets she had were her high-end clothes, which she was auctioning off on eBay to the highest bidder. She tried to use the money to help buy groceries, but Mom wouldn't hear of it. Thalia had left almost everything else behind. Like J.R. had said, there wasn't much there that she couldn't replace.

The question she couldn't bring herself to answer was whether or not he intended to replace her.

So she was approaching middle age, single, unemployed,

living with her mom and had $429.34 in her bank account. This was going to go down in history as the most miserable Valentine's Day ever. "Getting past this" seemed as easy as climbing Mount Everest in flip-flops. She couldn't see how she was going to do it.

Not to mention that her heart was broken. Why hadn't she planned on the contingency of Levinson using the affair against her—against J.R.? She knew the answer. She'd let her feelings for J.R. blind her to the real danger Levinson posed to both of them.

She'd tried to keep J.R. from going to Hollywood. She knew she had, but she still couldn't shake the feeling that she should have done something more. She shouldn't have let him get on that plane, but she couldn't see how she would have kept him off it. When J.R. made up his mind, there was no unmaking it. And then he'd decided that he hated her, just like *that*. She knew she wouldn't be able to change his mind, but again she had that nagging feeling that she should have tried a little harder.

He hadn't listened to her when she told him not to come, and he hadn't listened to her outside the club. At some point, a girl had to cut her losses. And sometimes, there was nothing left to cut.

Thalia had lost everything. That was the sort of realization that made getting up in the morning hard to face, no matter how great the bacon smelled.

The doorbell rang. Thalia cringed, wishing she could be more invisible. Some resourceful reporters had tracked her down to her mother's house outside of Norman, Oklahoma, and were persistent—bordering on stalking—about getting details for resale.

"I'll get it," Mom said, casting a motherly eye over Thalia's yoga pants and sweatshirt outfit.

Hey, Thalia thought at her mother's back, *at least they're clean.* Why, she'd even showered today. She felt almost human.

She was headed back to the kitchen, to make sure that no one was trying to sneak in the back door while Mom was distracted at the front one, when Mom hissed, "It's *him!*"

That tripped Thalia up so fast she stumbled. "Him who?" Because it couldn't be the one *him* she wanted to see. It couldn't be J.R. He'd made up his mind about her.

"Him!" Mom was panicking, her hands flapping like a goose failing at takeoff. "That man!"

"I'm not here." Even as she said it, she hurried to the front door, peeking through the sheer curtains that covered the side window.

J. R. Bradley—complete with hat—stood on her mother's front porch, looking as stoic as she'd ever seen him. He was studying the tips of his boots, his expression unreadable. His face looked odd. He was growing his beard out again, and he hadn't quite got it matched up to the goatee. She looked around. No truck, just a car that was probably a rental.

Part of her ached at the sight of him. He was dressed well, in nice jeans and a heathered blazer that matched his hat. No bolo tie today, but he'd clearly put some thought into his outfit. She knew she'd missed him, but seeing him there crystallized the loneliness into a pain so sharp that she didn't think she could breathe.

"What do I do?" Mom whispered. How nice that Thalia wasn't the only one panicking.

"Tell him I'm not here. I'm out." She had on sweats and no makeup. That alone would make her hesitant to go face-to-face with the person who had been, until a few weeks ago, the man of her dreams.

But him showing up, with no other communication since he'd roared off with Eli Granger? What else could he say to her?

Unless he'd come to apologize. Although she couldn't say

why, that scared the heck out of her. What would he say? What would she say back? No. She wasn't ready for him. Not now, maybe not ever.

Mom cracked the door open. "May I help you?" Thalia had to hand it to her—she was doing a fine job acting not-panicked.

"Mrs. Thorne? You don't know me, but my name is J. R. Bradley, and I'm trying to find your daughter, Thalia." Even though he was fuzzy through the fabric, Thalia thought she saw his eyes cut to where she was watching him. She jumped back, terrified he had seen her. "Is she home?"

"No, I'm sorry. Thalia's not here right now." Mom even managed to sound a little sympathetic. Maybe that acting thing ran in the family.

"Do you know when she'll be back? I've got some things to say to her, and I'd like to say them in person."

Thalia's mouth ran dry as she waited to hear what her mother would come up with. Was he here to apologize? He'd said so himself—he wasn't real good at apologizing. It didn't seem likely that he'd come all this way to tell her off again. The J.R. she knew had a short temper, but he wasn't intentionally cruel. He wouldn't have come a few extra thousand miles to break her heart a second time.

She hoped, anyway.

"She's at a job interview at the local television station. I'm not sure when she'll be back."

Not shabby, thought Thalia. Probably better than anything she would have come up with.

A moment of silence followed, and Thalia realized she was holding her breath. What if he wouldn't leave? Or worse, what if he did?

J.R. cleared his throat. "Will you tell her I stopped by, please? Tell her to call me? My number hasn't changed. She should still have it."

"I'll pass the message along." Mom shut the door, then sagged against it. "Was that okay?" she whispered.

Thalia nodded, but she was paying attention to what was going on outside. J.R. stood there for a moment before he glanced back to where Thalia hoped the curtains were hiding her. Then he turned around, took two steps down the stairs—and stopped. There, on the sidewalk, stood a man with a camera. The flash was going at top speed.

Paparazzi. In Oklahoma. Snagging photos of a cowboy. Everything about this seemed wrong.

The words were muffled, but she could piece together what was happening. J.R. was telling the photographer to stop, the photographer was ignoring him and J.R. was getting mad.

"Damn it," she muttered, shoving her feet into the closest pair of shoes she had, a ratty pair of sandals that perfectly complimented her look. She knew where this would end up. J.R. would wind up breaking the man's camera, and there'd be another lawsuit. "When will he realize the whole world is not a honky-tonk?"

"Honey?" Mom hadn't moved from the door. "What are you doing?"

"Trying to keep the cops from getting involved." With a final reproachful look, Mom stepped to the side.

Thalia was out the door, trying to ignore her vanity. It wasn't hard, given that J.R. was actively attempting to grab the man's camera. Was physical violence far behind? "Hey!" At the sound of her voice, both men froze in mid-lunge-and-dodge. "What's your name?"

"George," the man said, taking a cautionary step away from J.R.

For his part, J.R. was dumbstruck. His mouth hung open as he watched her close the distance between them. She wanted to think that he was happy to see her, but she wasn't sure.

"You got a buyer for this photo?" she asked George the paparazzo.

"TMZ," he replied, looking nervous. *Must be new at this, despite the expensive camera,* she thought.

"Here's the deal, George. You get one photo of the both of us, and then you get off my mother's lawn. If I see your face around here again, well, I can't be responsible for what happens next." She pointedly looked at J.R., whose hand still hung midgrab. "Deal?"

George shifted from one foot to the next, not sure if this was something that was done or not. "Are you serious?"

"Do I look serious? Here." She stood next to J.R., lowering his hand and placing it around her waist. "One shot, George. Make it count, because he's a card-carrying member of the NRA."

George lost a little of his color, and Thalia noted with satisfaction that his camera shook as he focused the shot. "Is smiling part of the deal?" he asked, the terror in his voice obvious.

"No," J.R. said.

"Thought you used to be this great actor," she muttered under her breath while she tried to strike a pose that would hide everything about her appearance. Which was a colossal waste of time—nothing about the way she looked right now was salvageable. But this was the deal.

J.R.'s hand pressed against her side, and she swore she felt the heat through her sweatshirt. "You're home," he said through clenched teeth while George focused his camera.

"You're here," she replied.

Then George said, "Smile?" and took his one shot. "Thanks."

J.R. half lunged at George. "Get," he growled, and George got. Fast.

Which left Thalia and J.R. standing on her mother's lawn, arm in arm. For a second, neither of them moved. Moving would mean dealing with what had brought him here, and she still didn't think she could handle it. Whatever it was.

J.R.'s chest rose with an extra-deep breath. "You're good at that."

"Good at what?" She refused to look at him, even though she was touching him.

"Handling those kinds of situations."

What the hell. If this was an apology, it was a piss-poor one. Suddenly, she realized why she wasn't ready to talk to him. She was freaking *furious* with the man. "You mean the kinds of situations where people treat you like a commodity instead of a person? Yes. I'm familiar with the protocol. Unlike some people I know."

She felt, more than saw, his shoulders slump. Fine. He'd attempted to apologize, and she'd, well, she'd heard him out. They could be done now.

She disengaged herself from his arm and headed back into the house. She wasn't surprised in the least to hear his footfalls behind her, but she was too mad to care.

"Ma'am," J.R. said behind her, and she swore she heard him tip his hat to her mother.

"Hello again. Thalia, I'll...get some coffee?"

Right. A grown woman probably didn't want her mother in the room while she hashed out her last failed affair. "Thanks, Mom."

For lack of anything better to do, she sat down at one end of the dining-room table. She was so mad at J.R. that she was having trouble not yelling at him. But she was familiar with the protocol, so she waited until he took a seat. Of course he took the one closest to her. "What brings you down to Norman?"

"You."

At that moment, Mom bustled into the dining room with coffee and fresh cookies on a silver tray. "There you two go. Is there anything else I can get you?"

"Mom," Thalia said, feeling like a fifteen year old again.

"Mrs. Thorne, thank you. This is wonderful." J.R. looked

to her for approval. Well, what did she know—he could pull off some social graces when he put his mind to it. "You have a lovely home."

Hand to God, Mom blushed like a schoolgirl. Thalia was seconds away from rolling her eyes. "Oh, you're welcome, Mr. Bradley. I'll just…be in the kitchen if you need any more coffee."

Neither of them said anything until Mom was out of sight. Thalia knew she was still listening, but at least she wasn't hovering over them.

They sat in silence, neither of them apparently knowing how to start. Thalia was still reeling from the realization that she was mad at J.R. She'd spent the last two weeks being upset with herself for not doing a better job of controlling the situation, and she hated Levinson. She hadn't allowed herself to put some of the blame on J.R.

Until now, that was.

"I got a box of my things." J.R. took one of the cups of coffee off the tray, but he didn't drink it. "No return address, no note."

She'd mailed his stuff to him on her second-to-last day in California. She'd almost thrown it all in the trash, but she couldn't get rid of him that easily. "You were expecting a note?" He nodded, and that made her mad all over again. "If you think I'm going to apologize, well, think again."

"Wasn't expecting an apology." Then he got up and stood in front of the large picture window. Not looking at her, she noted. Maybe now they were getting somewhere. "I was kind of hoping for an explanation."

"What was I supposed to do, J.R.? If I told you that I'd had an affair with Levinson, you would have thought less of me—which you did when you found out. If I didn't tell you, you'd think I was lying to you when you did find out—which also happened. There was no way for me to win in this situation. Either way, I come off looking like Levinson's whore, when what happened nine-plus years ago was none of your business anyway."

When he didn't say anything, she kept going, if only so she didn't have to hear the painful silence. "I had an agent who was getting me into parties. I met Levinson. Of course I knew who he was, but you've got to remember—there were no smartphones back then, and if I wanted to get on the internet, I had to go to an internet café. I couldn't even afford dial-up. I had no way of knowing he was married. Yes, I slept with him, of my own accord." She couldn't believe her own ears. Despite the fact that she didn't owe him an explanation, here she was, explaining anyway. "I had no idea that was what he did—take advantage of eager, innocent women like me. Then his wife showed up and got me blackballed. No one would hire me. Even my agent dropped me like a rock. I was broke and clueless because I believed him when he told me he loved me and promised he could jump-start my career. If you want to hold my naivety against me, so be it. But I will *not* apologize for it."

He stood there, staring out the window so hard that Thalia began to wonder if George the paparazzo had come back, if J.R. was even listening to her. Then he said, "You don't owe me an apology. I'd like to know how you wound up working for the man who ruined your career. Can I ask that?" It could have come off as snotty or snarky, a cut meant to draw blood from someone who had seen her naked, but it didn't. It came across as an honest question.

So she gave him an honest answer. "I was about to be evicted. Days away from having to come home to Oklahoma, tail tucked between my legs. I used my last ten bucks to bribe the security guard to let me into his office, and I told him that he had to give me a job or I'd make him pay." She thought she saw J.R.'s mouth curve up in a smile, but he wasn't exactly facing her, so she couldn't be sure. "He called security on me, but by the time they got there, he'd taken pity on me, which may have been the only time he ever took pity on another living being in his entire, miserable life. Gave me a job as a gofer. I didn't sleep with him again after that, and I earned my place at the table." Had he taken pity on her, or had he seen another innocent, vulnerable young woman he could control—except instead of through sex, this time through a paycheck? Had her life ever been her own since the day Bob Levinson walked into it? "I lost my career because I made a mistake. And you know what happened to Levinson?"

"Nothing."

"*Nothing.* Just another day at the office. J.R., I never cared who you'd slept with when you were James Robert. Never wanted to know, not even a rough estimate. Why is it different for me?" She knew the answer. The infamous double standard in action.

J.R. appeared to think on that for a few seconds. "Was he always going to fire you if I didn't take the part?"

"Yes."

He held his posture—strong, stoic—for another beat, then dropped his head in something that looked like shame. "And you were willing to lose your job for me."

"Unlike Levinson, I don't enjoy destroying people." She was not going to cry, thank you very much. She was keeping her voice level, her face neutral. She was perfectly in control of herself. Too bad her tear ducts hadn't gotten the message, and blinking wasn't helping. "I didn't want to be the reason why what happened, happened."

He scrubbed a hand over his face. For the first time, she noticed how tired he looked—worn down. She wanted to ask if people had found his home, if he'd shot any trespassers. She wanted to know if he regretted the time they'd had together. She wanted to know if he regretted *her*.

"I'm...I'm no good with apologies, Thalia. Never have been."

The way his voice shook was something new, something

vulnerable. It made her want to protect him again, shield him from the dangers of her reality.

This time, she didn't. "Then why are you here?"

"I wanted to make things right."

She honestly didn't know if she should be worried or scared. He stood up straight again, his eyes focused on the world right outside her mother's house. Make things right? What sort of things? "And how are you going to do that?"

Taking a deep breath, J.R. said, "I don't know how to handle myself in public."

"I'm aware of that."

Again, she thought she saw the corner of his mouth hitch up into a smile. "And because I did such a lousy job of handling myself in public, I'm now more public than ever."

Where was he going with this? How was this making things right? How was this even close to sort of apologizing? "To the point where the Georges of the world follow you across state lines."

"Pretty much. I'm getting all sorts of offers—indie movies, TV shows, commercials even. So, I got to thinking. Minnie's not talking to me right now, and Hoss hasn't been in the mood to shoot the breeze. So I've had a lot of time to think. And I've come to the conclusion that I need a manager."

The more he talked, the more confused she got. "I thought you had an agent."

"I did. Do. I'm going to fire him, but someone really smart told me I needed to get him to sign some sort of agreement first, and I'm not sure what that'd look like."

She'd told him to sign the agent to a nondisclosure agreement. Suddenly, she felt the ground shift under her seat. She had to clutch the table to keep from falling out of her chair.

"I need someone who knows her way around Hollywood, who knows how to negotiate with those people and how to keep them happy. Someone who understands how the media works these days. Someone who knows how I get in high-pressure situations and knows how to keep me from blowing my top and doing something stupid." He turned to her then, his eyes, his beautiful amber eyes, staring at her. "I need someone more than an agent. I need someone who cares about me, who understands what I want and what I can't stand, someone who won't throw me in front of the bus."

"Under the bus," she managed to say. She had to keep holding on to the table, though. The ground kept shifting underneath her.

"Yeah, that." God, those eyes—they would be her undoing. Always. "It'd be best if that someone understood what ranching is, understood that I get up real early. It'd be best if that someone got along with my crew—my family. If that someone didn't mind a blizzard every now and then."

Wait—the conversation had taken a heck of a turn there at the end. "Are you offering me a job or—"

Before she could finish the thought, he reached into his pocket and pulled out a small, black velvet box. The kind of box that often contained jewelry. Like a ring. He stepped forward and placed it in the middle of the table. She stared at it, half expecting some man to pop up from the other side of the couch and shout, "Surprise! You're on camera!" No one did.

This was real.

"I want to make things right," he said again, taking a step back. "You are, hands down, the best thing that has ever happened to me, and I did wrong by you. You showed me that I didn't have to hide from my past, didn't have to be ashamed of the things I'd done a long time ago. You showed me it didn't change the man I am now."

Thalia wanted so badly to have a smart-aleck comeback, something that would put him in his place, but she didn't. "That's what I wanted, too." Someone who wouldn't hold her mistakes against her.

He nodded. Or at least, she thought he did. She couldn't rip her gaze away from that small black box. "I should have

trusted you, listened to you, stood by you and *protected* you
from Levinson. That I didn't…" His voice broke, and it took
him a second to get himself back under control. "It's killing
me, Thalia. That's what the old me would have done—tuck
tail and run. That's not who I am anymore. I'm a man who
takes responsibility for his actions. I screwed up. I let myself
get sucked into that world and I didn't give you the benefit of
the doubt. I failed you when you needed me. I won't let that
happen ever again. I'm asking for another chance to prove
to you that I'll take care of you."

She sat there, stunned. For a man who wasn't so good
at apologizing, he'd made one of the better ones she'd ever
heard, either in real life or on film. When had any man ever
been so honest and taken his share of the blame? She couldn't
recall anyone, short of her grandfather, who manned up like
this. Who manned up for her.

She reached for the little box, but before she touched it, she
pulled her hand back. He was right—he'd screwed up, big-
time. All the heartfelt apologies in the world didn't mean he
automatically got another chance to break her heart.

"What if I say no?"

J.R. stood there, his expression almost unreadable. Then
he took his hat off and ran a hand through his hair. "Then I
will take responsibility for that, too. But the offer stands."

She knew she was pushing her luck, but what the hell. She
was in the negotiation of her life. "Which offer? The job or
the marriage?"

He held his hat in front of his chest like a shield. "The job
offer stands. I need a manager." That statement sent a wave
of disappointment through her, but then he said, "I'm not so
much offering you a marriage as I am asking you to marry
me, Thalia."

She didn't know what she expected when he moved—
maybe he was going to retract the ring?—but before she knew
it, he was on both knees in front of her. "You make me real,

Thalia. I don't know how you do it, but when you're around me, I'm a real person, the man I always wanted to be. These past two weeks without you…I haven't felt real. I haven't been right because you're not with me and I'm not with you and it was all my fault. Even if you say no, the offer stands. There'll never be another woman like you. Not for me." He shut his eyes and swallowed, a single tear escaping to run a trail down his cheek. Thalia wiped it away before it got lost in his beard. At her touch, he opened his eyes. He held her hand to his face, where his facial hair pricked at her skin. It made her feel alive again. The sensation drove away the fog she'd been lost in for the past fourteen days.

"Will you marry me, Thalia? Will you give me another chance to be the man you deserve?"

Now how was she supposed to negotiate with that? She couldn't. It was that simple.

"What if I say yes?"

He smiled then, the real one that melted her heart in the middle of a blizzard, as he scooted closer to her, still on his knees. He looped his arms around her waist, making it the most awkward hug ever, but she didn't care. He would always be her undoing, but that wasn't a bad thing. In fact, it might be the best thing to ever happen to her. "Then we can be on a plane by tonight. We can go home, you and me."

She looked around her mother's small house. She didn't have much here, but she still needed to get her things in order. "I might need a day or two."

"Then I'll wait." He reached up and cupped her cheek in his hand, pulling her down to his lips. "There's someone here I can't replace."

* * * * *

"You might very well be the hottest male on the planet, but I am not willing to be your latest conquest."

Her hands clenched into fists and socked against his chest. For emphasis. And maybe to unleash some frustration. He didn't move an iota.

For who knew what ill-advised reason, he reached out, but then wisely stopped shy of her face. "Is it so difficult to believe you intrigue me and I simply want to unwrap the rest of you?"

"Yeah. It is." She crossed her arms to prevent any more unloading of frustration. His chest was as hard as his head. And other places. "You're feeling deprived. Go find one of the women who text messaged you earlier in the car, and scratch your itch with her, because I'm not sleeping with you."

A smile curved his mouth, but the opposite of humor flashed through his steely gaze. "In case it's slipped your mind, I'm married. The only person I'll be sleeping with for the next six months is my wife."

Dear Reader,

Once upon a time there was a reader who believed so strongly in the magic of romance novels, she dreamed of creating one of her own. She put pen to paper and, later, fingers to the keyboard, and like the very best of spells, words wove together and became people, settings, conflict, emotion and finally, a story complete with a happily-ever-after. One day, after many missed carriages and a distinct lack of awesome shoes, her (very young and beautiful) fairy godmother called. She waved her wand and said the magic words: "We'd like to publish your book."

As I'm sure you guessed, I'm that reader, and because you're holding this book in your hands, I'm also now a published author. Mills & Boon chose this story as the winner of the 2011 So You Think You Can Write competition, which has indeed been the most magical of journeys, and I'm so excited to be a part of the Mills & Boon® family.

I adore this story about a laid-back Southern hero who lacks only a spitfire heroine to keep him on his toes. Lucas and Cia are two of my favorite fictional people and I hope you enjoy them as much as I enjoyed writing them.

I love to hear from readers—after all, I wrote this book for you! Please visit me at www.katcantrell.com.

Kat Cantrell

MARRIAGE WITH BENEFITS

BY
KAT CANTRELL

Published in Great Britain 2013
by Mills & Boon, an imprint of Harlequin (UK) Limited,
Eton House, 18-24 Paradise Road, Richmond, Surrey TW9 1SR

© Katrina Williams 2013

ISBN: 978 0 263 90470 3
ebook ISBN: 978 1 472 00595 3

51-0413

Harlequin (UK) policy is to use papers that are natural, renewable and recyclable products and made from wood grown in sustainable forests. The logging and manufacturing processes conform to the legal environmental regulations of the country of origin.

Printed and bound in Spain
by Blackprint CPI, Barcelona

Kat Cantrell read her first Mills & Boon® novel in third grade and has been scribbling in notebooks since she learned to spell. What else would she write but romance? She majored in literature, officially with the intent to teach, but somehow ended up buried in middle management at Corporate America, until she became a stay-at-home mom and full-time writer.

Kat, her husband and their two boys live in north Texas. When she's not writing about characters on the journey to happily-ever-after, she can be found at a soccer game, watching the TV show *Friends* or listening to 80s music.

Kat was the 2011 So You Think You Can Write winner and a 2012 RWA Golden Heart finalist for best unpublished series contemporary manuscript.

This one is for you, Mom.
Thanks for sharing your love of books with me.

One

Other single, twenty-five-year-old women dreamed of marriageable men and fairy-tale weddings, but Dulciana Allende dreamed of a divorce.

And Lucas Wheeler was exactly the man to give it to her.

Cia eyed her very male, very blond and very broad-shouldered target across the crowded reception hall. The display of wealth adorning the crush between her and Lucas bordered on garish. A doddering matron on her left wore a ring expensive enough to buy a year's worth of groceries for the women's shelter where Cia volunteered.

But then, if Cia had the natural ability to coax that kind of cash out of donors, she wouldn't be here in the middle of a Dallas society party, where she clearly did not belong, about to put plan B into action.

There was no plan C.

She knocked back the last swallow of the froufrou drink some clueless waiter had shoved into her hand. After she'd put considerable effort into securing a last-minute invitation to Mrs. Wheeler's birthday party, the least she could do was play along and drink whatever lame beverage the Black Gold Club pretended had alcohol in it. If she pulled off this negotiation, Mrs. Wheeler would be her future mother-in-law, and Cia did want to make a favorable impression.

Well, Mrs. Wheeler was also her future ex-mother-in-law, so perhaps the impression didn't matter overly much.

A guy near the bar tried to catch her eye, but she kept walking. Tonight, she cared about only one man and, conveniently, he stood next to his mother greeting guests. Cia's unfamiliar heels and knee-binding slim dress slowed her trek across the room. Frustrating but fortunate, since a giraffe on roller blades had her beat in the grace department.

"Happy birthday, Mrs. Wheeler." Cia shook the hand of the stylish, fifty-something woman and smiled. "This is a lovely party. Dulciana Allende. Pleased to meet you."

Mrs. Wheeler returned the smile. "Cia Allende. My, where has the time gone? I knew your parents socially. Such a tragedy to lose them at the same time." She clucked maternally.

Cia's smile faltered before she could catch it. Of course Mrs. Wheeler had known her parents. She just didn't know Cia's stomach lurched every time someone mentioned them in passing.

"Lucas, have you met Cia?" Mrs. Wheeler drew him forward. "Her grandfather owns Manzanares Communications."

Cia made eye contact with the man she planned to marry and fell headfirst into the riptide of Lucas Wheeler in the flesh. He was so…everything. Beautiful. Dynamic. Legendary. Qualities the internet couldn't possibly convey via fiber-optic lines.

"Miz Allende." Lucas raised her hand to his lips in an old-fashioned—and effective—gesture. And set off a whole different sort of lurch, this time someplace lower. *No, no, no.* Attraction was not acceptable. Attraction unsettled her, and when she was unsettled, she came out with swords drawn.

"Wheeler." She snatched her hand from his in a hurry. "I don't believe I've ever met anyone who so closely resembles a Ken doll."

His mother, bless her, chatted with someone else and thankfully didn't hear Cia's mouth working faster than her brain. Social niceties weren't her forte, especially when it came to men. How had she fooled herself into believing she could do this?

Lucas didn't blink. Instead, he swept her from head to toe with a slow, searching glance that teased a hot flush along her skin. With an amused arch to one brow, he said, "Lucky for me I've got one up on Ken. I bend all sorts of ways."

Her breath gushed out in a flustered half laugh. She did not want to like him. Or to find him even remotely attractive. She'd picked him precisely because she assumed she wouldn't. As best as she could tell from the articles she'd read, he was like the Casanovas she'd dated in college, pretty and shallow.

Lucas was nothing but a good-time guy who happened to be the answer to saving hundreds of women's lives. This marriage would help so many people, and just in case that wasn't enough of a reason for him to agree to her deal, she'd come armed with extra incentives.

That reassuring thought smoothed out the ragged hitch to her exhale. Refocusing, she pasted on a smile. His return smile bolstered her confidence. Her business with Lucas Wheeler was exactly that—business. And if she knew anything, it was business. If only her hands would stop shaking. "To be fair, you do look better in a suit than Ken."

"Now, I'd swear that sounded like a compliment." He leaned in a little and cocked his head. "If our parents knew each other, how is it we've never met?"

His whiskey-drenched voice stroked every word with a lazy Texas drawl that brought to mind cowboys, long, hard rides in the saddle and heat. She met his smoky blue eyes squarely and locked her knees. "I don't get out much."

"Do you dance?" He nodded to the crowded square of teak hardwood, where guests swayed and flowed to the beat of the jazz ensemble playing on a raised stage.

"Not in public."

Something flittered across his face, and she had the impression he'd spun a private-dance scenario through his head. Lips pursed, he asked, "Are you sure we haven't met before?"

"Positive."

And Cia wished circumstances had conspired differently to continue their mutual lack of acquaintance. Men like Lucas—expert at getting under a woman's skin right before they called it quits—were hazardous to someone who couldn't keep her heart out of it, no matter what she promised herself.

But she'd make any sacrifice necessary to open a new women's shelter and see her mother's vision realized. Even marrying this man who radiated sensuality like a vodka commercial laced with an aphrodisiac. "We're only meeting now because I have a proposition for you."

A slow, lethal smile spilled across his face. "I like propositions."

Her spine tingled, and that smile instantly became the thing she liked least about Lucas Wheeler. It was too dangerous, and he didn't hesitate to wield it. *Dios,* did she detest being disconcerted. Especially by a man she hoped to marry platonically. "It's not that kind of proposition. Not even close. I cannot stress enough how far removed it is from what that look in your eye says you assume."

"Now I'm either really interested or really not interested." Smoothly, he tapped his lips with a square-cut nail and sidled closer, invading her space and enveloping her with his woodsy, masculine scent. "I can't decide which."

The man had the full package, no question. Women didn't throw themselves at his feet on a regular basis because he played a mean hand of Texas hold 'em.

"You're interested," she told him and stepped back a healthy foot. He couldn't afford not to be, according to her meticulous research. She'd sifted through dozens of potential marriage candidates and vetted them all through her best friend, Courtney, before settling on this one.

Of course, she hadn't counted on him somehow hitting spin cycle on her brain.

"So," she continued, "I'll get right to it. Hundreds of women suffer daily from domestic abuse, and my goal is to help them escape to a place where they can build new lives apart from the men using them for punching bags. The shelters in this area are packed to the brim, and we need another one. A big one. An expensive one. That's where you come in."

They'd already taken in more bodies than the existing shelter could hold, and it was only a matter of time before the occupancy violation became known. Lucas Wheeler was going to change the future.

A shutter dropped over Lucas's expression, and he shook his head. "My money is not subject to discussion. You're barking up the wrong sugar daddy."

"I don't want your money. I have my own. I just have to get my hands on it so I can build the shelter my way, without any benefactors, investors or loans."

She flinched a little at her tone. *What* about this man brought out her claws?

"Well, darlin'. Sounds like I'm unnecessary, then. If you decide to go in the other direction with your proposition, feel free to look me up." Lucas edged away, right into the sights of a svelte socialite in a glittery, painted-on dress, who'd clearly been waiting for the most eligible male in the place to reject her competition.

"I'm not finished." Cia crossed her arms and followed him, shooting a well-placed glare at Ms. Socialite. She wisely retreated to the bar. "The money is tied up in my trust fund. In order to untie it, I have to turn thirty-five, which is nearly a decade away. Or get married. If my husband files for divorce, as long as the marriage lasts at least six months, the money's mine. You're necessary since I'd like you to be that husband."

Lucas chuckled darkly and, to his credit, didn't flinch. "Why is every woman obsessed with money and marriage? I'm actually disappointed you're exactly like everyone else."

"I'm nothing like everyone else." Other women tried to keep husbands. She wanted to get rid of one as soon as possible, guaranteeing she controlled the situation, not the other way around. Getting rid of things before they sank barbs into her heart was the only way to fly. "The difference here is you need me as much as I need you. The question is can you admit it?"

He rolled his eyes, turning them a hundred different shades of blue. "That's a new angle. I'm dying to hear this one."

"Sold any big-ticket properties lately, Wheeler?"

Instantly, he stiffened underneath his custom-made suit, stretching it across his shoulders, and she hated that she noticed. He was well built. So what? She had absolute control of her hormones, unlike his usual female companions. His full package wasn't going to work on her.

"What's real estate got to do with your trust fund?"

She shrugged. "You're in a bit of a fix. You need to shore up your reputation. I need a divorce. We can help each other, and I'll make it well worth your while."

No other single male in the entire state fit her qualifications, and, honestly, she didn't have the nerve to approach another stranger. She scared off men pretty quickly, which saved her a lot of heartache, but left her with zero experience in working her feminine wiles. That meant she had to offer something her future husband couldn't refuse.

"Hold up, sweetheart." Lucas signaled a waiter, snagged two drinks from the gilded tray and jerked his head. "You've got my attention. For about another minute. Let's take this outside. I have a sudden desire for fresh air. And double-plated armor for that shotgun you just stuck between my ribs."

Lucas could almost feel the bite of that shotgun as he turned and deftly sidestepped through the crowd.

His brother, Matthew, worked a couple of local business-men, no doubt on the lookout for a possible new client, and glanced up as Lucas passed. The smarmy grin on Matthew's face said volumes about Lucas's direction and the woman with him.

Lucas grinned back. Had to keep up appearances, after all. A hard and fast quickie on the shadowed balcony did smack of his usual style, but it was the furthest thing from his mind.

The gorgeous—and nutty—crusader with the intriguing curtain of dark hair followed him to the terrace at the back of the club. By the time he'd set down the pair of drinks, she'd already sailed through the door without waiting for him to open it.

Lucas sighed and retrieved the glasses, seriously consid-ering downing both before joining the Spanish curveball on the balcony. But his mama had raised him better than that.

"Drink?" He offered one to Cia, and surprise, surprise, she took it.

Twenty-five stories below, a siren cut through the muted sounds of downtown Dallas, and cool March air kissed the back of his hot neck. If nothing else, he'd escaped the stuffy ballroom. But he had a hunch he'd left behind the piranhas in favor of something with much sharper teeth.

"Thanks. Much better than the frilly concoction I got last round." She sipped the bourbon and earned a couple of points with him. "So. Now that I have your attention, listen carefully. This is strictly a business deal I'm offering. We get married in name only, and in six months, you file for divorce. That's it. Six months is plenty of time to rebuild your reputation, and I get access to my trust fund afterward."

Reputation. If only he could laugh and say he didn't care what other people thought of him.

But he was a Wheeler. His great-great-grandfather had founded Wheeler Family Partners over a century ago and almost single-handedly shaped the early north Texas landscape. Tradition, family and commerce were synonymous with the Wheeler name. Nothing else mattered.

"You're joking, right?" He snorted as a bead of sweat slid between his shoulder blades. "My reputation is fine. I'm not hard up for a magic wand, thanks."

The little bundle of contradictions in the unrevealing, yet oddly compelling, dress peered up steadily through sooty lashes. "Really, Wheeler? You're gonna play that card? If this fake marriage is going to work, know this. I don't kowtow to the Y chromosome. I won't hesitate to tell you how it is or how it's going to be. Last, and not least, I do my research. You lost the contract on the Rose building yesterday, so don't pretend your clients aren't quietly choosing to do business with another firm where the partners keep their pants zipped. Pick a different card."

"I didn't know she was married."

Brilliant, Wheeler. Astound her with some more excuses. Better yet, tell her how great Lana had been because she only called occasionally, suggested low-key, out-of-the-way places to eat and never angled to stay overnight. In hindsight, he'd been a class A idiot to miss the signs.

"But she was. I'm offering you some breathing room. A chance to put distance and time between you and the scandal, with a nice, stable wife who will go away in six months. I insist on a prenup. I'm not asking you to sleep with me. I'm not even asking you to like me. Just sign a piece of paper and sign another one in six months."

Breathing room. Funny. He'd never been less able to breathe than right now. His temple started throbbing to the muted beat of the music playing on the other side of the glass.

Even a fake marriage would have ripples, and no way could it be as easy as a couple of signatures. Mama would have a coronary if he so much as breathed the word *divorce* after giving her a daughter-in-law. She'd dang near landed in the hospital after her first daughter-in-law died, even though Amber and Matthew had barely been married a year.

A divorce would set his gray-sheep status in stone, and he'd been killing himself to reverse the effects of his monumental lapse in judgment with Lana. Why eliminate what little progress he'd achieved so far?

The other temple throbbed. "Darlin', you're not my type. Conquistador Barbie just doesn't do it for me."

The withering scowl she leveled at him almost pared back his skin. "That's the beauty of this deal. There's no chance of being tempted to turn this physical. No messy ties. It's a business agreement between respected associates with a finite term. I can't believe you're balking at this opportunity."

Because it was *marriage*. Marriage was a "someday" thing, a commitment he'd make way, way, way in the future, once he found the right woman. He'd be giving this stranger his name, sharing his daily life with her.

And of course, he'd be married, the opposite of single. "For the record, I'm wounded to learn my temptation factor is zero. It can't be as simple as you're making it out to be. What if someone finds out it's not real? Will you still get the money?"

"No one will find out. I'm not going to tell anyone. You're not going to tell anyone. We only have to fake being madly in love once or twice around other people so my grandfather buys it. Behind closed doors, we can do our own thing."

Madly in love. Faking that would be a seriously tall order when he'd never been so much as a tiny bit in love. "Why can't you have the money unless you get divorced? That's the weirdest trust clause I've ever heard."

"Nosy, aren't you?"

He raised a brow. "Well, now, darlin', you just proposed to me. I'm entitled to a few questions."

"My grandfather is old-fashioned. When my parents died…" Her lips firmed into a flat line. "He wants me to be taken care of, and in his mind, that means a husband. I'm supposed to fall in love and get married and have babies, not get a divorce. The money is a safety net in case the husband bails, one I put considerable effort into convincing my grandfather to include."

"Your grandfather has met you, right?" He grinned. "Five minutes into our acquaintance, and I would never make the mistake of thinking you can't look after yourself. Why thirty-five? You don't strike me as one to blow your trust fund on cocaine and roulette."

"I donated all the money I inherited from my parents to the shelter where I work," she snapped, as if daring him to say something—anything—about it. "And don't go thinking I'm looking for handouts. My grandfather set up the trust and deposits the considerable interest directly into my bank account. I have more than enough to live on, but not enough to build a shelter. He's hoping I'll lose enthusiasm for battered women by thirty-five."

"Well, that's obviously not going to happen."

"No. And I don't enjoy being manipulated into marriage." She tightened the lock of her crossed arms. "Look, it's not like I'm asking you to hurt puppies or put your money into a pyramid scheme. This is going to save lives. Women who suffer domestic abuse have nowhere to go. Most of them don't have much education and have to work to feed their kids. Consider it charity. Or are you too selfish?"

"Hey now. I'm on the Habitat for Humanity board. I tithe my ten percent. Give me a break."

Good button to push, though, because against his will, wheels started turning.

Six months wasn't too much of a sacrifice for the greater good, was it? Abuse was a terrible evil, and a charity that helped abuse victims was well worth supporting. He took in Cia's fierce little form and couldn't help but wonder what had sparked all that passion. Did she reserve it for crusading or did she burn this brightly in other one-on-one situations, too?

Through the glass separating the balcony from the ballroom, he watched his grandparents slow dance in the midst of his parents' friends. Could he make this fake marriage work and protect his family from divorce fallout at the same time? He couldn't deny how far a nice, stable wife might go toward combating his problems with Lana's husband. Probably not a bad idea to swear off women for a while anyway. Maybe if he kept Cia away from his family as much as possible, Mama would eventually forget about the absentee daughter-in-law.

No. No way. This whole setup gave him hives.

Mama would never let him keep a wife squirreled away, no matter what he intended. Cia could find someone else to marry, and together he and Matthew would straighten out the kinks in Wheeler Family Partners' client list. "As…interesting as all this sounds, afraid I'll have to pass."

"Not so fast." Her gaze pierced him with a prickly, no-nonsense librarian thing. "I'm trusting you with this information. Don't disappoint me or you'll spend the next six months tied up in court. My grandfather is selling the cell phone division of Manzanares and moving the remainder of the business to a smaller facility. I'm sure you're familiar with his current location?"

Four buildings surrounding a treed park, centrally located and less than ten years old. Designed by Brown & Worthington in an innovative, award-winning Mediterranean/modern architectural mix. Approximately three million square feet with access to the DART light-rail.

"Slightly."

"My grandfather would be thrilled to give the exclusive sales contract for the complex to my husband."

She waited, but calculations had already scrolled through his head.

The commission on Manzanares beat the Rose building by quadruple. And the prestige—it could lead to other clients for Wheeler Family Partners, and instead of being the Wheeler who'd screwed up, he'd be the family's savior.

Out of nowhere, the fifty-pound weight sitting on his chest

rolled off. "If I went so far as to entertain this insane idea, can I call you Dulciana?"

"Not if you expect me to answer. My name is Cia, which, incidentally, sounds nothing like *darling,* so take note. Are you in or out?"

He had to tell her *now?* Evidently Cia did not subscribe to the Lucas Wheeler Philosophy of Life—anything worth doing was worth taking the time to do right. "Why me?"

"You may play the field well and often, but research shows you treat women with respect. That's important to me. Also, everything I've read says you'll keep your word, a rare commodity. I can't be the one to file for divorce so I have to trust you will."

Oddly, her faith touched him. But the feeling didn't sit well. "Don't you have a boyfriend or some other hapless male in your life you can railroad into this?"

"There's no one else. In my experience, men have one primary use." She let her gaze rove over him suggestively, and the atmosphere shifted from tense to provocative. Hidden terrace lighting played over her features, softening them, and that unrevealing dress dangled the promise of what she'd hidden under it.

Then she finished the sentiment. "To move furniture."

That's why this exotically beautiful woman didn't have a boyfriend stashed somewhere. Any guy sniffing around Miz Allende had to want it bad enough to work for it. Nobody was worth that much effort, not even this ferocious little crusader with the mismatched earrings who'd waltzed into the Black Gold Club and walked across the room with a deliberate, slow gait he'd thoroughly enjoyed watching. "You win. I'll call you Cia."

Her brows snapped together. "Throw down your hand, Wheeler. You've got nothing to lose and everything to gain by marrying me. Yes or no?"

She was all fire and passion, and it was a dirty shame she seemed hell-bent on keeping their liaison on paper. But he usually liked his women uncomplicated and easygoing, so treating this deal as business might be the better way to go.

He groaned. At what point had he started to buy into this lunatic idea of a fake-but-pretend-it's-real marriage to a woman he'd just met? Call him crazy, but he'd always imagined having lots of sex with the woman he eventually married…way, way, way in the future.

If he pursued her, he'd have to work hard to get Miz Allende into bed, which didn't sound appealing in the least, and the deal would be difficult enough.

Business only, then, in exchange for a heap of benefits.

The Manzanares contract lay within his grasp. He couldn't pass up the chance to revitalize his family's business. Yeah, Matthew would be right there, fighting alongside Lucas no matter what, but he shouldn't have to be. The mess belonged to Lucas alone, and a way to fix it had miraculously appeared.

"No," he said.

"No?" Cia did a fair impression of a big-mouth bass. "As in you're turning me down?"

"As in I don't kowtow to the X chromosome. You want to do business, we'll do it in my office tomorrow morning. Nine sharp." Giving him plenty of time to do a little reconnaissance so he could meet his future wife-slash-business-partner toe-to-toe. Wheelers knew how to broker a deal. "With lawyers, without alcohol, and darlin', don't be late."

Her face went blank, and the temperature dropped at least five degrees. She nodded once. "Done."

Hurricane Cia swept toward the door, and he had no doubt the reprieve meant he stood in the eye of the storm. No problem. He'd load up on storm-proof, double-plated armor in a heartbeat if it meant solving all his problems in one shot.

Looked like he was going to make an effort after all.

Two

Cia had been cooling her heels a full twenty minutes when Lucas strolled into the offices of Wheeler Family Partners LLC at 9:08 a.m. the next morning. Renewed anger ate through another layer of her stomach lining. She'd had to ask Courtney to cover her responsibilities at the shelter to attend this meeting, and the man didn't have the courtesy to be on time. He'd pay for that. Especially after he'd ordered her not to be late in that high-handed, deceptively lazy drawl.

"Miz Allende." Lucas nodded as if he often found women perched on the edge of the leather couch in the waiting area. He leaned on the granite slab covering the receptionist's desk. "Helena, can you please reschedule the nine-thirty appraisal and send Kramer the revised offer I emailed you? Give me five minutes to find some coffee, and then show Miz Allende to my office."

The receptionist smiled and murmured her agreement. Her eyes widened as Cia stalked up behind Lucas. The other women often found on Lucas's couch must bow to the master's bidding.

Cia cleared her throat, loudly, until he faced her. "I've got other activities on my agenda today, Wheeler. Skip the coffee, and I'll follow *you* to your office."

Inwardly, she cringed. Not only were her feminine wiles out of practice, she'd let Lucas get to her. She couldn't keep being so witchy or he'd run screaming in the other direction long before realizing the benefits of marrying her.

If only he'd stop being so…Lucas for five minutes, maybe she'd be able to bite her tongue.

Lucas didn't call her on it, though. He just stared at her, evaluating. Shadows under his lower lashes deepened the blue of his irises, and fatigue pulled at the sculpted lines of his face. Her chin came up. Carousing till all hours, likely. He probably always looked like that after rolling out of some socialite's bed, where he'd done everything but sleep.

Not her problem. Not yet anyway.

Without a blink, he said, "Sure thing, darlin'. Helena, would you mind?"

He smiled gratefully at the receptionist's nod and ushered Cia down a hall lined with a lush Turkish rug over espresso hardwood. Pricey artwork hung on the sage walls and lent to the moneyed ambience of the office. Wheeler Family Partners had prestige and stature among the elite property companies in Texas, and she prayed Lucas cared as much as she assumed he did about preserving his heritage, or her divorce deal would be dead on arrival.

She had to convince him to say yes. Her mother's tireless efforts on behalf of abused women must reach fruition.

They passed two closed doors, each with name plaques reading Robert Wheeler and Andrew Wheeler, respectively. The next door was open. Lucas's office reflected the style of the exterior. Except he filled his space with a raw, masculine vibe the second he crossed the threshold behind her, crowding her and forcing her to retreat.

Flustered, she dropped into the wingback chair closest to

the desk. She had to find her footing here. But how did one go about bloodlessly discussing marriage with a man who collected beautiful women the way the shore amassed seashells?

Like it's a business arrangement, she reminded herself. Nothing to get worked up over. "My lawyer wasn't able to clear her morning schedule. I trust we can involve her once we come to a suitable understanding."

Actually, she hadn't called her lawyer, who was neck-deep in a custody case for one of the women at the shelter. There was no way she could've bothered Gretchen with a proposal Lucas hadn't even agreed to yet.

"Lawyers are busy people," Lucas acknowledged and slid into the matching chair next to Cia instead of manning the larger, more imposing one behind the desk.

She set her back teeth together. What kind of reverse power tactic was that supposed to be?

He fished a leather bag from the floor and pulled a sheaf of papers from the center pocket, which he then handed to her. The receptionist silently entered with steaming coffee, filling the room with its rich, roasted smell. She passed it off and exited.

With a look of pure rapture stealing over his face, Lucas cupped the mug and inhaled, then drank deeply with a small moan. "Perfect. Do you think I could pay her to come live with me and make my coffee every morning?"

Cia snorted to clear the weird little tremor in her throat. Did he do everything with abandon, as if the simplest things could evoke such pleasure? "She'd probably do it for free. You know, if there were other benefits."

Shut up. Why did the mere presence of this man turn her stupid?

"You think?" Lucas swept Cia with a once-over. "Would you?"

"Ha. The other benefits couldn't possibly be good enough

to warrant making coffee. You're on your own." Her eyes trailed over the sheaf of papers in her hand. "What's all this?"

"A draft of a prenuptial agreement. Also, a contract laying out the terms of our marriage and divorce agreement." Lucas scrutinized her over the rim of his mug as he took a sip. He swallowed, clearly savoring the sensation of coffee sliding down his throat. "And one for the sale of Manzanares."

Taken aback, she laughed and thumbed through the papers. "No, really. What is it?"

He sat back in his chair without a word as she skimmed through the documents. He wasn't kidding—legalese covered page after page.

Now completely off balance, she cocked a brow. "Are you sleeping with your lawyer? Is that how you got all this put together so fast?"

"Sure enough," he said, easily. "Can't put nothing past you."

Great. So he'd no doubt ensured all the terms favored him. Why hadn't she had her own documents drawn up last week? She'd had plenty of time, and it threw her for a loop to be so unprepared. Business was supposed to be her niche. It was the only real skill she brought to the equation when continuing her mother's work. If passion was all it took, her mother would have single-handedly saved every woman in danger.

"Run down the highlights for me, Wheeler. What sort of lovely surprises do you have buried in here?"

It dawned on her then. He was on board. She'd talked Lucas Wheeler into marrying her. Elation flooded her stomach so hard, it cramped. *Take that, Abuelo*. Her grandfather thought he was so smart, locking up the money, and she'd figured out a way to get it after all.

"No surprises. We each retain ownership of our assets. It's all there in black and white." His phone beeped, but he ignored it in favor of giving her his full attention. "You were up front with me, and I appreciate that. No better way to start a partnership than with honesty. So I'll direct your attention to page fifteen."

He waited until she found the page, which took longer than it should have, but she had this spiky, keen awareness of him watching her, and it stiffened her fingers. "Fifteen. Got it."

"I want you to change your name to Wheeler. It's my only stipulation. And it's nonnegotiable."

"No." She spit out the word, eyes still stumbling over the lines of his unreasonable demand. "That's ridiculous. We're going to be married for a short time, in name only."

"Exactly. That means you have to do the name part."

The logic settled into her gut and needled. Hard. She couldn't do it, couldn't give up the link with her parents and declare herself tied to this man every time she gave her name. It was completely irrational. Completely old-fashioned. *Cia Wheeler.* And appalling. "I can't even hyphenate? No deal. You have to take out that stipulation."

Instead of arguing, he unfolded his long frame from the chair and held out his hand. "Come with me. I'd like to show you something."

Nothing short of a masked man with an Uzi could make her touch him. She stood without the offered hand and scouted around his pristine, well-organized office for something worth noting. "Show me what?"

"It's not here. I have to drive you."

"I don't have all day to cruise around with you, Wheeler." If his overwhelming masculinity disturbed her this much in a spacious office, how much more potent would it be in a tiny car?

"Then we should go."

Without waiting for further argument, he led her out a back entrance to a sleek, winter-white, four-door Mercedes and opened the passenger door before she could do it. To make a point, obviously, that he called the shots.

She sank into the creamy leather and fumed. Lucas Wheeler

was proving surprisingly difficult to maneuver, and a husband she couldn't run rings around had not been part of the plan. According to all the society articles she'd read, he only cared about the next gorgeous, sophisticated woman and the next party, presumably because he wasn't overly ambitious or even very bright.

Okay, the articles hadn't said that. *She'd* made presumptions, perhaps without all the facts.

He started the car and pulled out of the lot. Once on the street, he gradually sped up to a snail's pace. She sat on her hands so she couldn't fiddle with a hem. When that failed, she bit alternate cheeks and breathed in new-car smell mixed with leather conditioner and whatever Lucas wore that evoked a sharp, clean pine forest.

She couldn't stand it a second longer. "*Madre de Dios,* Wheeler. You drive like my grandfather. Are we going to get there before midnight?"

That drawn-out, dangerous smile flashed into place. "Well, now, darlin', what's your hurry? Half the fun is getting there and the pleasures to be had along the way, don't you think?"

The vibe spilling off him said they weren't talking about driving at all. The car shrank, and it had already been too small for both her and the sex machine in the driver's seat.

Slouching down, she crossed her arms over the slow burn kicking up in her abdomen. Totally against her will, she pictured Lucas doing all sorts of things excruciatingly slowly.

How did he do that? She'd have sworn her man repellant was foolproof. It had worked often enough in the past to keep her out of trouble. "No. I don't think. The fun is all in the end goal. Can't get to the next step unless you complete the one before. Taking your time holds that up."

Lucas shook his head. "No wonder you're so uptight. You don't relax enough."

"I relax, women suffer. Where are we going? And what does all this have to do with me changing my name? Which

I am not going to do, by the way, regardless of whatever it is we're going to see."

He fell quiet for a long moment, and she suspected it wasn't the last time she'd squirm with impatience until he made his move. Their whole relationship was going to be an unending chess match, and she'd left her pawns at home.

"Why don't we listen to the radio?" he said out of nowhere. "Pick a station."

"I don't want to listen to the radio." And if she kept snapping at him, he'd know exactly how far under her skin he'd gotten. She had to do better than this.

"I'll pick one, then," he said in that amiable tone designed to fool everyone into thinking he couldn't pour water out of a boot with instructions printed on the heel. Not her, though. She was catching on quick.

George Strait wailed from the high-end speakers and smothered her with a big ol' down-home layer of twangy guitars. "Are you trying to put me to sleep?"

With a fingertip, she hit the button on the radio until she found a station playing Christina Aguilera.

"Oh, much better," Lucas said sarcastically and flipped off the music to drop them into blessed silence. Then he ruined it by talking. "Forget I mentioned the radio. So we'll have a quiet household. We're here."

"We are?" Cia glanced out the window. Lucas had parked in the long, curving driveway of an impressive house on a more impressive plot of painstakingly landscaped property. The French design of the house fit the exclusive neighborhood but managed to be unique, as well. "Where is here?"

"Highland Park. More specifically, our house in Highland Park," he said.

"You picked out a house? Already? Why do we need a house? What's wrong with you moving in with me?" A house was too real, too…homey.

Worse, the two-story brick house was beautiful, with elegant stone accents and gas coach lights flanking the arched entryway. Not only did Lucas have more than a couple of working brain cells, he also had amazing taste.

"This place is available now, it's close to the office and I like it. If this fake marriage is going to work, we can't act like it's fake. Everyone would wonder why we didn't want to start our lives together someplace new."

"No one is going to wonder that." Is that what normal married people did? Why hadn't she thought longer and harder about what it might take to make everyone believe she and Lucas were in love? Maybe because she knew nothing about love, except that when it went away, it took unrecoverable pieces with it. "You're not planning on sharing a bedroom, are you?"

"You tell me. This is all for your grandfather's benefit. Is he going to come over and inspect the house to be sure this is real?"

Oh, God. He wouldn't. Would he? "No, he trusts me."

And she intended to lie right to his face. Her stomach twisted.

"Then we'll do separate bedrooms." Lucas shrugged and crinkled up the corners of his eyes with a totally different sort of dangerous smile, and this one, she had no defenses against. "Check out the house. If you hate it, we'll find another one."

Mollified, she heaved a deep breath. Lucas could be reasonable. Good to know. She'd need a huge dollop of reasonable to talk him out of the Cia Wheeler madness. *Dios,* it didn't even sound right. The syllables clacked together like a hundred cymbals flung against concrete.

She almost got the car door open before Lucas materialized at her side to open it the rest of the way. At least he had the wisdom not to try to help her out. With a steel-straight spine, she swung out of the car and followed him to the front door, which he opened with a flourish, then pocketed the key.

With its soaring ceilings and open floor plan, the house

was breathtaking. No other word would do. Her brain wasn't quick on the draw anyway with a solid mass of Lucas hot at her back as she stopped short in the marble, glass and dark wood foyer.

He skirted around her and walked into the main living area off the foyer.

Heavy dustcovers were draped over furniture, and heavier silence added to the empty atmosphere. People had lived here once and fled, leaving behind fragments of themselves in their haste. Why? And why did she want to fling off the covers and recapture some of the happiness someone had surely experienced here once upon a time?

"Well?" Lucas asked, his voice low in the stillness. "Do you want to keep looking? Or will it do?"

The quirk of his mouth said he already knew the answer. She didn't like being predictable. Especially not to him. "How did you find this place?"

He studied her, and, inexplicably, she wished he'd flash that predatory smile she hated. At least then his thoughts would be obvious and she'd easily deflect his charm. This seriousness freaked her out a little.

"Vacant properties are my specialty," he said. "Hazard of the job. The owner was willing to rent for six months, so it's a no-brainer. Would you like to see the kitchen? It's this way."

He gestured to the back of the house, but she didn't budge.

"I don't have to see the kitchen to recognize a setup. You're in commercial real estate, not residential. Why did you bring me here?"

"I'm throwing down my hand." He lifted his chin. In the dim light, his eyes glinted, opening up a whole other dimension to his appeal, and it stalled her breath. What was wrong with her? Maybe she needed to eat.

"Great," she squeaked and sucked in a lungful of air. "What's in it?"

In a move worthy of a professional magician, he twirled

his hand and produced a small black box. "Your engagement ring."

Her heart fluttered.

Romance didn't play a part in her life. Reality did. Before this moment, marrying Lucas had only been an idea, a nebulous concept invented to help them reach their individual goals. Now it was a fact.

And the sight of a man like Lucas with a ring box gripped in his strong fingers shouldn't make her throat ache because this was the one and only proposal she'd ever get.

"We haven't talked about any of this." She hadn't been expecting a ring. Or a house. She hadn't thought that far ahead. "Do you want me to pay half?"

"Nah." He waved away several thousand dollars with a flick of his hand. "Consider the ring a gift. Give it back at the end if it makes you feel better."

"It's not even noon, Wheeler. So far, you've presented me with contracts, a house and a ring. Either you already planned to ask someone else to marry you or you have a heck of a personal assistant." She crossed her arms as she again took in the fatigue around his eyes.

Oh. That's why he was tired. He'd spent the hours since she'd sprung this divorce deal on him getting all this arranged, yet he still managed to look delicious in a freshly pressed suit.

She refused to be impressed. Refused to reorganize her assumptions about the slick pretty boy standing in the middle of the house he'd picked out for them.

So he hadn't been tearing up the sheets with his lawyer all night. So he'd rearranged his appointments to bring her here. So what?

"Last night, you proposed a partnership," he said. "That means we both bring our strengths to the table, and that's what I'm doing. Fact of the matter is you need me and for more than a signature on a piece of paper. You want everyone to believe this marriage is real, but you don't seem to have any concept of how to go about it."

"Oh, and you do?" she shot back and cursed the quaver in her voice.

Of course she didn't know how to be married, for real or otherwise. How could she? Every day, she helped women leave their husbands and boyfriends, then taught them to build new, independent lives.

Every day, she reminded herself that love was for other people, for those who could figure out how to do it without glomming on to a man, expecting him to fix all those emotionally bereft places inside, like she'd done in college right after her parents' deaths.

"Yeah. I've been around my parents for thirty years. My brother was married. My grandfather is married. The name of the company isn't Wheeler Family Partners because we like the sound of it. I work with married men every day."

Somehow he'd moved back into the foyer, where she'd remained. He was close. Too close. When he reached out to sweep hair from her cheek, she jumped.

"Whoa there, darlin'. See, that's not how married people act. They touch each other. A lot." There was that killer smile, and it communicated all the scandalous images doubtlessly swimming through his head. "And, honey, they like to touch each other. You're going to have to get used to it."

Right. She unclenched her fists.

They'd have to pretend to be lovey-dovey in public, and they'd have to practice in private. But she didn't have to start this very minute.

She stepped back, away from the electricity sparking between her and this man she'd deny to her grave being attracted to. The second she gave in, it was all over. *Feelings* would start to creep in and heartbreak would follow. "The house will do. I'll split the rent with you."

With a raised eyebrow, he said, "What about the ring? You haven't even looked at it."

"As long as it's round, it's fine, too."

"I might have to get it sized. Here, try it." He flipped open the lid and plucked out a whole lot of sparkle. When he slid it on her finger, she nearly bit her tongue to keep a stupid female noise of appreciation from slipping out. The ring fit perfectly and caught the sunlight from the open front door, igniting a blaze in the center of the marble-size diamond.

"Flashy. Exactly what I would have picked out." She tilted her hand in the other direction to set off the fiery rainbow again.

"Is that your subtle way of demonstrating yet again how much you need me?" He chuckled. "Women don't pick out their own engagement rings. Men do. This one says Lucas Wheeler in big letters."

No, it said Lucas Wheeler's Woman in big letters.

For better or worse, that's what she'd asked to be for the next six months, and the ring would serve as a hefty reminder to her and everyone else. She *had* proposed a partnership; she just hadn't expected it to be fifty-fifty. Furthermore, she'd royally screwed up by not thinking through how to present a fake marriage as real to the rest of the world.

Lucas had been right there, filling in the gaps, picking up the slack and doing his part. She should embrace what he brought to the table instead of fighting him, which meant she had to go all the way.

"I'll take the contracts to my lawyer this afternoon. As is."

Cia Wheeler. It made her skin crawl.

But she was perfectly capable of maintaining her independence, no matter what else Lucas threw at her. It was only a name, and with the trust money in her bank account, the shelter her mother never had a chance to build would become a reality. That was the true link to her parents, and she'd change her name back the second the divorce was final. "When can we move in?"

Three

Cia eased into her grandfather's study, tiptoeing in deference to his bowed head and scribbling hand, but his seventy-year-old faculties hadn't dimmed in the slightest. He glanced up from the desk, waved her in and scratched out another couple of sentences on his yellow legal pad. Paper and pen, same as he'd used for decades. Benicio Allende owned one of the premier technology companies in the world, yet remained firmly entrenched in the past.

A tiny bit of guilt over the lie she was about to tell him curled her toes.

Abuelo folded his hands and regarded her with his formidable deep-set gaze. "What brings you by today?"

Of course he cut right to the purpose of her unusual visit, and she appreciated it. A dislike of extraneous decorum was the only thing they had in common. When she'd come to live with him after her parents' accident, the adjustment had been steep on both sides. Prior to that, he'd been just as much her dad's boss as her dad's father. She'd long since stopped wishing for a grandfather with mints in his pocket and a twin-kly smile.

Instead, she'd gleaned everything she could from him about how to succeed.

"Hello, Abuelo. I have some news. I'm getting married." Better leave it at that. He'd ask questions to get the pertinent information.

Their stiff holiday dinners and occasional phone calls had taught her not to indulge in idle chatter, especially not about her personal life. Nothing made him more uncomfortable than the subject of his granddaughter dating.

"To whom?"

"Lucas Wheeler." Whose diamond glittered from her third finger, weighing down her hand. She'd almost forgotten the ring that morning and had had to dash back to slip it on. A happily engaged woman wouldn't even have taken it off. "Of Wheeler Family Partners."

"Fine family. Very good choice." He nodded once, and she let out a breath. He hadn't heard the rumors about Lucas and his affair with the married woman. Usually Abuelo didn't pay attention to gossip. But nothing about this fake marriage was usual.

"I'm glad you approve."

The antique desk clock ticked as Abuelo leaned back in his chair, his shock of white hair a stark contrast to black leather. "I'm surprised he didn't come with you for a proper introduction."

Lucas had insisted he should do exactly that, but she'd talked him out of it in case Abuelo didn't buy the story she and Lucas had concocted. Everything hinged on getting over this hurdle, and she needed to handle it on her own. She owed Lucas that much.

"I wanted to tell you myself first. We're getting married so quickly...I knew it could be viewed as impulsive, but I actually dated Lucas previously. When I started focusing on other things, we drifted apart. He never forgot me. We reunited by chance at an event last week, and it was as if we'd never been separated."

Dios. When she and Lucas had discussed the story, it hadn't sounded so ridiculously romantic. Since she'd never talked to Abuelo about her love life, hopefully he wouldn't clue in on the implausibility of his granddaughter being swept off her feet.

"Other things? You mean the shelter." Abuelo's brows drew into a hawklike line. He didn't like the way she'd buried herself in her mother's passion and never missed an opportunity to harp on it, usually by telling her what her life should look like instead. "I expect you'll now focus on your husband, as a wife should."

Yeah, that was going to happen.

Abuelo was convinced a husband would make her forget all about the shelter and help her move past the loss of her parents. He grieved for his son and daughter-in-law by banishing them from his mind and couldn't accept that she grieved by tirelessly pursuing her mother's goal—a fully funded shelter with no danger of being closed due to lack of money.

Her grandfather refused to understand that the shelter provided more lasting satisfaction than a husband ever could.

"I know what's expected of me in this marriage."

Did she ever. She had to pretend to be in love with a man who turned her brain into a sea sponge. Still, it was worth it.

"Excellent. I'm very pleased with this union. The Wheeler fortune is well established."

Translation—she'd managed to snag someone who wasn't a fortune hunter, the precise reason Abuelo hadn't tied the trust to marriage. The reminder eliminated the last trace of her guilt. If he'd shown faith in her judgment, a fake marriage could have been avoided.

"I'm pleased that you're pleased."

"Dulciana, I want you to be happy. I hope you under-stand this."

"I do." Abuelo, though fearsome at times, loved her in his way. They just had different definitions of *happy*. "I'm grate-ful for your guidance."

He evaluated her for a moment, his wrinkles deepening as he frowned. "I don't pretend to understand your avid in-terest in hands-on charity work, but perhaps after you've es-tablished your household, you may volunteer a few hours a week. If your husband is supportive."

She almost laughed. "Lucas and I have already come to an agreement about that. Thanks, though, for the suggestion. By the way, we're going to have a small civil ceremony with no guests. It's what we both want."

"You're not marrying in the church?"

The sting in his tone hit its mark with whipping force. She'd known this part couldn't be avoided but had left it for last on purpose. "Lucas is Protestant."

And divorce was not easily navigated after a Catholic cer-emony. The plan was sticky enough without adding to it.

"Sit," he commanded, and with a sigh, she settled into the creaky leather chair opposite the desk.

Now she was in for it—Abuelo would have to be con-vinced she'd made these decisions wisely. In his mind, she was clearly still a seventeen-year-old orphan in need of pro-tection from the big, bad world. She put her game face on and waded into battle with her hardheaded grandfather, de-termined to win his approval.

After all, everything she knew about holding her ground she'd learned from him.

Four days, two phone calls and one trip to notarize the con-tracts and apply for a marriage license later, Lucas leaned on the doorjamb of Matthew's old house—correction, his and

Cia's house, for now anyway—and watched Cia pull into the driveway. In a red Porsche.

What an excellent distraction from the text message his brother had just sent—We lost Schumacher Industrial. Lucas appreciated the omission of "thanks to you."

Matthew never passed around blame, which of course heightened Lucas's guilt. If Wheeler Family Partners folded, he'd have destroyed the only thing his brother had left.

As Cia leaped out of the car, he hooked a thumb in the pocket of his cargos and whistled. "That's a mighty fine point-A-to-point-B ride, darlin'. Lots of starving children in Africa could be fed with those dollars."

"Don't trip over your jaw, Wheeler," she called and slammed the door, swinging her dark ponytail in an arc. "My grandfather gave me this car when I graduated from college, and I have to drive something."

"Doesn't suck that it goes zero to sixty in four-point-two seconds, either. Right, my always-in-a-hurry fiancée?" His grin widened as she stepped up on the porch, glare firmly in place. "Come on, honey. Lighten up. The next six months are going to be long and tedious if you don't."

"The next six months are going to be long and tedious no matter what. My grandfather is giving us a villa in Mallorca as a wedding present. A *villa*, Wheeler. What do I say to that? 'No, thanks, we'd prefer china,'" she mimicked in a high voice and wobbled her head. That dark ponytail flipped over her shoulder.

The times he'd been around her previously, she'd always had her hair down. And had been wearing some nondescript outfit.

Today, in honor of moving day no doubt, she'd pulled on a hot-pink T-shirt and jeans. Both hugged her very nice curves, and the ponytail revealed an intriguing expanse of neck, which might be the only vulnerable place on Cia's body.

Every day should be moving day.

"Tell your grandfather to make a donation, like I told my parents. How come my family has to follow the rules but yours doesn't?"

"I did. You try telling my grandfather what to do. *Es imposible.*" She threw up her hands, and he bit back a two-bulldozers-one-hole comment, which she would not have appreciated and wouldn't have heard anyway because she rushed on. "He's thrilled to pieces about me marrying you, God knows why, and bought the reunion story, hook, line and sinker."

"Hey now," Lucas protested. "I'm an upstanding member of the community and come from a long line of well-respected businessmen. Why wouldn't he be thrilled?"

"Because you're—" she flipped a hand in his direction, and her engagement ring flashed "—you. Falling in and out of bimbos' beds with alarming frequency and entirely too cocky for your own good. Are we going inside? I'd like to put the house in some kind of order."

Enough was enough. He tolerated slurs—some deserved, some not—from a lot of people. Either way, his wife wasn't going to be one of them.

"Honey?" He squashed the urge to reach out and lift her chin. Determined to get her to meet him halfway, he instead waited until she looked at him. "Listen up. What you see is what you get. I'm not going to apologize for rubbing you the wrong way. I like women, and I won't apologize for that, either. But I haven't dated anyone since Lana, and you're pushing my considerable patience to the limit if you're suggesting I'd sleep with another woman while my ring is on your finger. Even if the ring is for show."

A slight breeze separated a few strands of hair from the rest of her ponytail as she stared up at him, frozen, with a hint of confusion flitting across her face. "No. I didn't mean that. It was, uh… I'm sorry. Don't be mad. I'll keep my big mouth shut from now on."

He laughed. "Darlin', I don't get mad. I get even."

With that, he swept her off her feet and carried her over the threshold. She weighed less than cotton candy, and her skin was fresh with the scent of coconut and lime. Did she smell like that all the time or only on moving day?

Her curled fist whacked him in the shoulder, but he ignored it, too entranced by the feel of previously undiscovered soft spots hidden amid all her hard edges.

"What is this?" she sputtered. "Some caveman show of dominance?"

Gently, he set down the bundle of bristling woman on the marble floor in the foyer.

"Neighbors were watching," he said, deadpan.

They hadn't been. Matthew had carried Amber over the threshold and had told the story a bunch of times about nicking the door frame when he whacked it with his new bride's heel.

Lucas had always envisioned doing that with his way, way, way in the future wife, too—minus the door frame whacking—and wasn't about to let the Queen of Contrary tell him no. Even if they weren't technically married yet. Close enough, and it was practice for the eventual real deal, where his wife would gaze at him adoringly as he carried her.

He couldn't get a clear picture of this fictitious future wife. In his imagination, Cia reappeared in his arms instead.

"We have an agreement." She jammed her hands down onto her hips. "No division of property. No messiness. And *no* physical relationship. What happened to that?"

He smirked. "That wasn't even close to physical, darlin'. Now, if I was to do this—" he snaked an arm around her waist and hauled her up against him, fitting her into the niches of his body "—I'd be getting warmer."

She wiggled a little in protest and managed to slide right into a spot that stabbed a hot poker through his groin. He sucked in a cleansing breath.

This was *Cia,* the most beautiful and least arousing female he'd ever met. Why did his skin feel as if it was about to combust? "That's right. Snuggle right in, honey. Now that's so close to physical, it's scorching hot."

"What are you doing, Wheeler?" She choked on the last syllable as he leaned in, a hairbreadth from tasting that high-speed mouth, and trailed a finger down her tight jaw.

"Practicing."

If he moved one tiny neck muscle the right way, they'd be kissing. Soon, this firecracker in his arms would be Mrs. Lucas Wheeler, and he hadn't kissed her once. Maybe he should. Might shut her up for a minute.

"Practicing for what?"

"To be a happy couple. My parents invited us over for dinner tonight. Engagement celebration." Instantly she stopped wiggling, and the light hit her upturned face and her wide, frightened eyes. "Well, I'll be hog-tied and spoon-fed to vultures for breakfast. Your eyes are blue. Not brown."

"My grandparents came from northern Spain. It's not that unusual."

"A man should know the color of his wife's eyes. Marriage 101." Disconcerted, he released her. He had to get her scent out of his nose.

He shoved a hand through his hair, but it didn't release a bit of the sudden pressure against his skull.

He'd wanted to kiss her. It had taken a whole lot of will-power not to. What had he gotten himself into?

He barely knew her, knew nothing about how to handle her, nothing about her past or even her present. He had to learn. Fast.

The Manzanares contract represented more than a vital shot in the arm for his livelihood. It was a chance to fix his problems on his own, without his big brother's help, and prove to everyone that Lucas Wheeler wasn't the screw-up womanizer people assumed.

"What else don't I know?" he asked.

"That I have to work tonight. I can't go to your parents' for dinner. You have to check with me about this kind of stuff."

Yeah. He should have. It hadn't occurred to him. Most women of his acquaintance would have stood up the president in order to have dinner with his parents. He'd just never invited any of them. "Call in. Someone else can cover it. This is important to my mother."

"The shelter is important to me. Someone else has been covering my responsibilities all week." Her hands clenched and went rigid by her sides. "It's not like I'm canceling a round of golf with a potential client, Wheeler."

Golf. Yeah. His workday consisted of eye-crossing, closed-door sessions with Matthew, poring over his brother's newest strategies to improve business. "What is it like, then? Tell me."

"The women who come to the shelter are terrified their husbands or boyfriends will find them, even though we go to extreme lengths to keep the location secret. Their kids have been uprooted, jammed into a crowded, foreign new home and have lost a father, all at the same time. They're desperate for someone they know and trust. Me."

Bright, shiny moisture gathered in the pockets of her eyes as she spoke, and that caught him in the throat as much as her heartfelt speech. No one could fake that kind of passion for a job. Or anything else. "Dinner tomorrow night, then."

Mama would have to understand. God Almighty, what a balancing act. The ripples were starting already, and it was going to be hell to undo the effects after the divorce.

He had to believe it would be worth it. He had to believe he could somehow ensure his family didn't get attached to Cia without vilifying her in the process. He needed a nice, stable wife to combat the Lana Effect nearly as much as he needed Manzanares.

She nodded, and a tear broke loose to spill down her cheek. "Thanks."

All of a sudden, he felt strangely honored to be part of something so meaningful to her. Sure, his own stake meant a lot, too, but it was nice that his investment in this fake marriage would benefit others.

"Come on." He slung an arm around her slim shoulders. Such a small frame to hold so much inside. "Better. You didn't even flinch that time."

"I'm trying." As if to prove it, she didn't shrug off his arm.

"We'll get there."

Legs bumping, he guided her toward the kitchen, where he'd left every single box intact because God forbid he accidentally put the blender in the wrong spot.

Most of Amber's touches had been removed, thrown haphazardly into the trash by a blank-faced Matthew, but a few remained, like the empty fruit bowl his sister-in-law had picked up at the farmers' market.

Must have missed that one. During those weeks following the funeral, even he had been numb over Amber's sudden death, and neither he nor Matthew had put a whole lot of effort into clearing the house.

Maybe, in some ways, his marriage to Cia would be a lot easier than one built on the promise of forever. At least he knew ahead of time it was ending and there would be no emotional investment to reconcile.

"Look how far we've come already," he told her. "You're not going to make cracks about my past relationships, and I'm not going to make plans for dinner without checking first. The rest will be a snap. You just have to pretend you love me as much as you love being a crusader. Easy, right?"

She snorted and some color returned to her cheeks.

Good. Hell's bells, was she ever a difficult woman, but without him, she'd be lost. She had no idea how to fake a relationship. Her fire and compassion could only go so far, though he liked both more than he would have thought. If she ditched that prickly pear personality, she'd be something else. Thank the good Lord she hadn't.

Otherwise, he'd be chomping at the bit to break the no-physical-relationship rule and that would be plain stupid. Like kissing her would have been stupid.

No complications. That was the best way to ensure he put Wheeler Family Partners back on the map. He and Cia were business partners, and her proposal challenged him to be something he'd never been before—the hero. She deserved his undivided attention to this deal.

But he had to admit he liked that she wasn't all that comfortable having a man's hands on her. Maybe he had some caveman in him after all.

Cia spent a few hours arranging the kitchen but had to get to the shelter before finishing. Okay, so she took off earlier than planned because there was too much Lucas in the house.

How could she sleep there tonight? Or the next night or the next?

This was it, the real thing.

She'd taken her bedroom furniture, clothes and a few other necessary items, then locked up her condo. She and Lucas now lived together. They'd attend Mr. and Mrs. Wheeler's engagement dinner tomorrow night, and a blink after making the man's acquaintance, she'd marry Lucas at the courthouse Monday afternoon.

Cia Wheeler. It wasn't as if Lucas had made forty-seven other unreasonable demands. It was petty to keep being freaked about it.

So she spent a lot of her shift trying to get used to the name, practicing it aloud and writing it out several hundred times while she manned the check-in desk.

Dios, she'd turned into a love-struck teenager, covering an entire blank page with loopy script. *Mrs. Lucas Wheeler.*

Cia Wheeler. Dulciana Alejandra de Coronado y Allende Wheeler. Like her full name hadn't already been pretentious enough. Well, she wouldn't be writing that anywhere except on the marriage certificate.

The evening vaporized, and the next set of volunteers arrived. Cia took her time saying goodbye to everyone and checked on Pamela Gonzalez twice to be sure she was getting along okay as her broken arm healed.

A couple of weeks ago, Cia had taken the E.R. nurse's call and met Pamela at the hospital to counsel her on options; then she'd driven Pamela to the shelter personally.

Victims often arrived still bloodstained and broken, but Cia considered it a win to get them to a safe place they likely wouldn't have known about without her assistance. It wasn't as if the shelter could advertise an address or every abuser would be at the door, howling for his woman to be returned.

Pamela smiled and shooed Cia out of the room, insisting she liked her three roommates and would be fine. With nothing left to do, Cia headed for the new house she shared with her soon-to-be husband, braced for whatever he tossed out this time.

She found Lucas's bedroom door shut as she passed the master suite on the way to her smaller bedroom.

She let out a rush of pent-up air. A glorious, blessed reprieve from "practicing" and that smile and those broad shoulders, which filled a T-shirt as if Lucas had those custom-made along with his suits. A reprieve by design or by default she didn't know, and she didn't care. Gratefully, she sank into bed and slept until morning.

By the time she emerged from her room, Lucas was already gone. She ate a quick breakfast in the quiet kitchen someone had lovingly appointed with warm colors, top-of-the-line appliances and rich tile.

The house came equipped with a central music hub tied to the entertainment system in the living room, and after a few minutes of poking at the touch-screen remote, she blasted an electronica number through the speakers. Then she went to work unpacking the remainder of her boxes.

Sometime later, Lucas found her sitting on the floor in the living room, straightening books. She hit the volume on the remote, painfully aware that compromise and consideration, the components of a shared life, were now her highest priority.

"You're up," he said and flopped onto the couch. His hair was damp, turning the sunny blond to a deep gold, and he wore what she assumed were his workout clothes, shorts and a Southern Methodist University football T-shirt. "I didn't know how late you'd sleep. I tried to be quiet. Did I wake you?"

"You didn't. I always sleep in when I work the evening shift at the shelter. I hope I didn't make too much noise when I came in."

"Nah." He shrugged. "We'll learn each other's schedules soon enough I guess."

"About that."

She rose, shook the cramps out of her knees—how long had she been sitting there?—and crossed to the matching leather couch at a right angle to the one cradling entirely too much of Lucas's long, tanned and well-toned legs. "I appreciate the effort you put into making all this possible. I want to do my part, so I found a questionnaire online that the immigration office uses to validate green card marriages. Here's a copy for you, to help us learn more about each other." He was staring at her as if she'd turned into a bug splattered on his windshield. "You know, so we can make everyone believe we're in love."

"That's how you plan to pretend we're a real couple? Memorize the brand of shaving cream I use?"

"It's good enough for the immigration department," she countered. "There are lots of other questions in here besides brand names. Like, which side of the bed does your spouse sleep on? Where did you meet? You're the one who pointed out I haven't got a clue how to be married. This is my contribution. How did you think we would go about it?"

His eyes roamed over the list and narrowed. "A long conversation over dinner, along with a good bottle of wine. The way people do when they're dating."

"We're not dating, Wheeler." *Dating.* Something else she had no idea how to do. If she'd had a normal high school experience, maybe that wouldn't be the case. "And we don't have that kind of time. Your parents' party is tonight."

"Yeah, but they're not going to ask questions like which side of the bed you sleep on."

"No. They'll ask questions like how we met." She stabbed the paper. "Or what made us decide to get married so quickly. Or where we plan to go on our honeymoon. Look at the questionnaire. It's all there."

"This is too much like school," he grumbled and swept a lock of hair off his forehead. "Is there going to be a written exam with an essay question? What happens if I don't pass?"

"My grandfather gets suspicious. Then I don't get my money. Women don't get a place to escape from the evil they live with. You don't get the Manzanares contract." She rattled the printed pages. "Pick a question."

"Can I at least take a shower before spilling my guts?"

"Only if you answer number eighteen."

He glanced at the paper and stood, clearly about to scram as soon as he recited the response. "'What do the two of you have in common?'" Eyebrows raised, he met her gaze. Then he sat back down. "This is going to take hours."

"I tried to tell you."

For the rest of the day, in between Lucas's shower, lunch, grocery shopping and an unfinished argument over what Cia proposed to wear to dinner, they shot questions back and forth. He even followed her to her room, refusing to give her a minute alone.

Exhausted, Cia dropped onto her bed and flung a hand over her eyes. "This is a disaster."

Lucas rooted around in her closet, looking for an un-frumpy dress. So far, he'd discarded her three best dresses from Macy's, which he refused to acknowledge were prac-tical, and was working up to insulting the more casual ones in the back.

"I agree. Your wardrobe is a cardigan away from an ep-isode of Grandmas Gone Mild." Lucas emerged from her closet, shaking his head. "We gotta fix that."

"Nowhere in our agreement did it say I was required to dress like a bimbo. You are not allowed to buy me clothes. Pe-riod." Knowing him, he'd burn her old outfits, and then what would she wear to the shelter? BCBG and Prada to work with poverty-stricken women? "That's not the disaster."

"You dressing like something other than a matronly li-brarian is for my benefit, not yours. What could possibly be more of a disaster than your closet?"

It was disconcerting to have that much Lucas in her bed-room, amid her familiar mission-style furniture, which was decorating an unfamiliar house. An unfamiliar house they would share for a long six months. "Do you realize we have nothing in common other than both being born in Texas and both holding a business degree from SMU?"

He leaned his jean-clad rear on her dresser, and *Dios en las alturas,* the things acid-washed denim did to his thighs. *Not noticing,* she chanted silently. *Not noticing at all.*

But therein lay the problem. It was impossible not to notice Lucas. He lit up the room—a golden searchlight stabbing the black sky, drawing her eye and piquing her curiosity.

"What about bourbon?" he asked. "You drink that."

"Three things in common, then. *Three.* Why didn't I look for someone who at least knows how to spell hip-hop?"

His nose wrinkled. "Because. That's not important. Marriages aren't built on what you have in common. It's about not being able to live without each other."

First clothes. Then declarations à la Romeo and Juliet. "Are you sure you're not gay?"

"Would you like to come over here and test me? Now, darlin', that's the kind of exam I can get on board with." His electric gaze traveled over her body sprawled out on the bed, and she resisted the intense urge to dive under the covers. To hide from that sexy grin.

"Save it for tonight, Wheeler. Go away so I can get dressed."

"No can do. You've maligned my orientation, and I'm not having it." He advanced on her, and a dangerous edge sprang into his expression. "There must be a suitable way to convince you. Shall I make your ears bleed with a range of baseball statistics? Rattle off a bunch of technical specs for the home theater system in the media room down the hall? Hmm. No, none of that stuff is specific to straight men. Only one way to go on this one."

In an effortless move, he tumbled onto the bed, wrapped her up in his arms and rolled, tangling their legs and binding her to his hard body. Heat engulfed her, and that unique, woodsy Lucas scent swirled through her head in a drugging vortex.

When his lips grazed the hollow beneath her ear, she gasped for air as the world ignited around her.

Lucas's fingers threaded through her hair, and his mouth burned down her throat. The impressive evidence of his orientation pressed against her thigh, and she went liquid.

The plan to ignore her feminine parts for the next six months melted faster than ice in the blazing sun.

This wasn't supposed to be happening, this flood of need for a man who did this for sport. She was smarter than that.

He hadn't even kissed her yet.

"Stop," she choked out before surrender became inevitable.

No doubt he could make her body sing like a soprano with little effort. But intimacy at that level was never going to happen for her. Not with anybody. She'd learned her lesson the hard way in college, and it still stung.

He took one look at her face and swore, then rolled away to stare at the ceiling. "I'm sorry. That was juvenile, even for me. Please, let's pretend I'm not such a jerk."

She jumped off the bed and backed away from the slightly rumpled and wholly inviting male lying in it. "It's not a big deal. I know you were only messing around."

"It is a big deal. You're skittish enough already." He glanced up at her, and darkness dawned in his eyes. "Oh, man, I'm slow, I'll admit, but I shouldn't be *that* slow. Some guy beat up on you, didn't he? That's why you're so passionate about the shelter."

"What? No way. I teach self-defense. Any creep who laid a hand on me would find his balls in his back pocket. If I was in a good enough mood to return them."

"Then why are you so scared of men touching you?"

"I'm not scared of men touching me." *Just you.* History proved she couldn't trust herself, and she didn't plan to test it.

She shrugged and prayed her expression conveyed boredom or nonchalance or anything other than what she was feeling. "I'm just not interested in you that way. And that little interlude was four exits past practicing. We'll never have a public occasion to be lying in bed together."

Her tone could have frosted glass, and he didn't overlook it. In his typical fashion, he grinned and said, "I might have missed the exit for practicing, but the one I took had some great scenery. Meet me downstairs at six?"

She tried to be irritated but couldn't. He'd apologized and put them back on even ground effortlessly. No point in sulking about it. "I'll be downstairs at six. I'll expect you about ten after."

Chuckling, he left and shut the door behind him, sucking

all the vibrancy out of the room. She took a not-so-hot shower and washed her hair twice but couldn't erase the feeling of Lucas's fingers laced through it. The towel scraped across her still-sensitized flesh, and she cursed. She couldn't give him any more openings. It was too hard to fake a nonreaction.

In deference to Lucas's parents, she spent an extra couple of minutes on her hair and makeup. Lucas would likely complain about her lack of style regardless, so it certainly wasn't for his sake. The less she encouraged the trigger on his libido, the better.

With a small sigh, she twisted Lucas's diamond ring onto her finger, the only jewelry a man had ever bought her, and pretended she hated it.

Four

After firing off at least half a dozen emails and scheduling a couple of walk-throughs for early Monday afternoon, Lucas descended the hardwood and wrought-iron stairs at six sharp. Dinner was important to Mama, which meant being on time, plus he'd already done enough to provoke Cia today. Though she should be apologizing to him for the solid fifteen minutes it had taken to scrub the coconut and lime from his skin.

Why did that combination linger, like a big, fruity, tropical tattoo etched into his brain? Couldn't she wear plain old Chanel like normal women? Then the slight hard-on he'd endured since being in Cia's bed, her luscious little body twisted around his, would be easy to dismiss. Easy, because a blatant, calculated turn-on he understood.

This, he didn't.

He shouldn't be attracted to her. Keeping his hands to himself should be easy. Besides, he scared the mess out of her every time he touched her. That was reason enough to back off, and there were plenty more reasons where that one came from. He'd have to try harder to remember them.

Cia had beaten him to the living room, where she paced around the sofa in a busy circle. The demons drove her relentlessly tonight. There must be a way to still them for a little while.

"Ready?" he asked, and caught her hand to slow her down. It was shaking. "Hey. It's just dinner with some old people. It's not like barging into a birthday party and proposing to a man you've never met."

"My hands were shaking then, too." She actually cracked a tiny smile. "It's not just dinner. It's a performance. Our first one, and we have to get it right. There's no backup parachute on this ride."

"That's where you're wrong, darlin'. I always have a backup parachute in my wallet."

"Only you could twist an innocent comment into an innuendo." Her eyes flashed deep blue with an unexpected hint of humor. How had he ever thought they were brown?

"If you don't like it, stop giving me ammo."

Her bottom lip poked out in mock annoyance, but he could see she was fighting a laugh. "You really are juvenile half the time, aren't you?"

And there she was, back in the fray. *Good.* Those shadows flitting through her eyes needed to go. Permanently. He'd enjoy helping that happen.

"Half the time? Nah. I give it my all 24/7." He winked and kissed her now-steady hand. A hand heavy with her engagement ring. Why did that flash on her finger please him so much? "But you're not nervous about dinner anymore, so mission accomplished. Before we go, can we find you some matching earrings?"

Fingers flew to her ears. "What? How did that happen?"

"Slow down once in a while maybe. Unless of course you

want my parents to think we rolled straight out of bed and got dressed in a big hurry."

She made a face and went back upstairs. The plain black dress she wore, the same one from the other night, did her figure no favors. Of course, only someone who had recently pressed up against every inch of those hidden curves would know they were there.

He groaned. All night long he'd be thinking about peeling off that dress. Which, on second thought, might not be bad. If she was his real fiancée, he'd be anticipating getting her undressed *and* the other choice activities to follow. No harm in visualizing both, to up the authenticity factor.

Imagining Cia naked was definitely not a chore.

When she returned, he tucked her against his side and herded her toward the garage before she could bolt. Once he'd settled her into the passenger seat of his car, he slid into the driver's seat and backed out.

Spring had fully sprung, stretching out the daylight, and the Bradford pears burst with white blooms, turning the trees into giant Q-tips. Likely Cia had no interest in discussing the weather, the Texas Rangers or the Dow, and he refused to sit in silence.

"You know, I've been curious." He glanced at the tight clamp of her jaw. Nerves. She needed a big-time distraction. "So you're not personally a victim of abuse, but something had to light that fire under you. What was it?"

"My aunt." She shut her eyes for a blink and bounced her knee. Repeatedly. "The time she showed up at our house with a two-inch-long split down her cheek is burned into my brain. I was six and the ghastly sight of raw flesh…"

With a shudder, she went on, "She needed stitches but refused to go to the emergency room because they have to file a report if they suspect abuse. She didn't want her husband to be arrested. So my mom fixed her up with Neosporin and

Band-Aids and tried to talk some sense into her. Leave that SOB, she says. You deserve better."

What a thing for a kid to witness. His sharpest memory from that age was scaring the maid with geckos. "She didn't listen, did she?"

"No." Cia stared out the window at the passing neighborhood.

When he looked at a house or a structure, he assessed the architectural details, evaluated the location and estimated the resale value. What did she see—the pain and cruelty the people inside its walls were capable of? "What happened?"

"He knocked her down, and she hit her head. After a two-month coma, they finally pulled the plug." Her voice cracked. "He claimed it was an accident, but fortunately the judge didn't see it that way. My mom was devastated. She poured all her grief into volunteer work at a shelter, determined to save as many other women as she could."

"So you're following in your mom's footsteps?"

"Much more than that. I went with her. For years, I watched these shattered women gain the skills and the emotional stability to break free of a monstrous cycle. That's an amazing thing, to know you helped someone get there. My mom was dedicated to it, and now she's gone." The bleak proclamation stole his attention from the road, and the staccato tap of her fingernail against the door kept it. "I have to make sure what happened to my aunt doesn't happen to anyone else. Earlier, you said marriage is about not being able to live without someone. I've seen the dark side of that, where women can't leave their abusers for all sorts of emotional reasons, and it gives me nightmares."

Oh, man. The shadows inside her solidified.

No wonder she couldn't be still, with all that going on inside. His chest pinched. She'd been surrounded by misery for far too long. No one had taken the time to teach her how to have fun. How to ditch the clouds for a while and play in the sun.

Wheeler to the rescue. "Next time you have a nightmare, you feel free to crawl in bed with me."

Her dark blue eyes fixed on him for a moment. "I'll keep that in mind. I'd prefer never to be dependent on a man in the first place, which is why I'll never get married."

"Yet that looks suspiciously like an engagement ring on your left hand, darlin'."

She rolled her eyes. "Married for real, I mean. Fake marriages are different."

"Marriage isn't about creating a dependency between two people, you know. It can be about much more."

Which meant much more to lose. Like what happened to Matthew, who'd been happy with Amber, goofy in love. They'd had all these plans. Then it was gone. Poof.

Some days, Lucas didn't know how Matthew held it together, which was reason enough to keep a relationship simple. Fun, yes. Emotional and heavy? No.

Lucas had done Matthew a favor by taking over his monument of a house, not that his brother would agree. If Matthew had his way, he'd mope around in that shrine forever. Cia had already begun dissolving Amber's ghost, exactly as Lucas had hoped.

"Looks suspiciously like a bare finger on your left hand, Wheeler. You had an affair with a married woman. Sounds like you deliberately avoid eligible women."

At what point had this conversation turned into an examination of the Lucas Wheeler Philosophy of Marriage? He hadn't realized he had one until now.

"Marrying you, aren't I?" he muttered. Lana had been an eligible woman, at least in his mind.

"Boy, *that* proves your point. I'm the woman who made you agree to divorce me before we got near an altar," she said sweetly and then jabbed the needle in further. "Gotta wonder what *your* hang-up is about marriage."

"Nagging wife with a sharp tongue would be hang-up number one," he said. "I'll get married one day. I haven't found the right woman yet."

"Not for lack of trying. What was wrong with all of your previous candidates?"

"Too needy," he said, and Cia chortled.

He should have blown off the question, or at least picked something less cliché. But cliché or not, that's what had made Lana so disappointing—she'd been the opposite of clingy and suffocating. For once, he'd envisioned a future with a woman. Instead, she'd been lying.

Had he seen the signs but chosen to ignore them?

"Exactly," she said. "Needy women depend on a man to fill holes inside."

"Who are you, Freud?"

"Business major, psych minor. I don't have any holes. Guess I must be the perfect date, then, huh, Wheeler?" She elbowed his ribs and drew a smile from him.

"Can't argue with that."

Now he understood her persistent prickliness toward men. Understood it, but didn't accept it.

Not all men were violent losers bent on dominating someone weaker. Some men appreciated a strong, independent woman. Some men might relish the challenge of a woman who went out of her way to make it clear how not interested she was five seconds after melting into a hot mess in a guy's arms.

The stronger she was, the harder she'd fall, and he could think of nothing better than rising to the challenge of catching her. Cia wasn't scared like he'd assumed, but she nursed some serious hang-ups about marriage *and* men.

Nothing about this marriage was real. None of it counted.

They had the ultimate no-strings-attached arrangement, and he knew the perfect remedy for chasing away those shadows—

not-real-doesn't-count sex with her new husband. Nothing emotional to trip over later, just lots of fun. They both knew where
their relationship was going. There was no danger of Cia becoming dependent on him since he wasn't going to be around
after six months and she presented no danger to his family's
business.

Everyone won.

Instead of only visualizing Cia out of that boring dress,
he'd seduce her out of it. And out of her hang-ups. A lot rode
on successfully scamming everyone. What better way to
make everyone think they were a real couple than to be one?

Temporarily, of course.

Lucas's parents lived at the other end of Highland Park, in
a stately colonial two-story edging a large side lot bursting
with tulips, hyacinth and sage. A silver-haired older version
of Lucas answered the door at the Wheelers' house, giving
Cia an excellent glimpse of how Lucas might age. She hadn't
met Mr. Wheeler at the birthday party.

"Hi, I'm Andy," Mr. Wheeler said and swung the door
wide.

Lucas shook his dad's hand and then ushered Cia into the
Wheelers' foyer with a palm at the small of her back. The
casual but reassuring touch warmed her spine, serving as a
reminder that they were in this together.

Through sheer providence, she'd gained a real partner,
one who didn't hesitate to solve problems she didn't know
existed. One who calmed her and who paid enough attention
to notice she wore different earrings. She'd never expected,
never dreamed, she'd need or want any of that when concoct-
ing this scheme.

Thanks to Lucas everything was on track, and soon they
could get on with their separate lives. Or as separate as possible while living under the same roof.

Lucas introduced Cia to his brother, Matthew, and Mrs.

Wheeler steered everyone into the plush living area off the main foyer.

"Cia, I'm happy to have you here. Please, call me Fran. Have a seat." Fran motioned to the cushion next to her on the beige couch, and Cia complied by easing onto it. "I must tell you, I'm quite surprised to learn you and Lucas renewed a previous relationship at my birthday party. I don't recall the two of you dating the first time."

"I don't tell you everything, Mama," Lucas interrupted, proceeding to wedge in next to Cia on the couch, thigh to thigh, his heavy arm drawing her against his torso. "You should thank me."

Fran shot her son a glance, which couldn't be interpreted as anything other than a warning, while Cia scrambled to respond.

Her entire body blipped into high alert. She stiffened and had to force each individual muscle in her back to relax, allowing her to sag against Lucas's sky-blue button-down shirt as if they snuggled on the couch five times a day. "It was a while back. A couple of years."

Matthew Wheeler, the less beautiful, less blond and less vibrant brother, cleared his throat from his position near the fireplace. "Lucas said four or five years ago."

Cia's heart fell off a cliff. Such a stupid, obvious thing to miss when they'd discussed it. Why hadn't Lucas mentioned he'd put a time frame to their fictitious previous relationship?

"Uh…well, it might have been four years," Cia mumbled. In a flash of inspiration, she told mostly the truth. "I was still pretty messed up about my parents. All through college. I barely remember dating Lucas."

His lips found her hairline and pressed against it in a simple kiss. An act of wordless sympathy but with the full force of Lucas behind those lips, it singed her skin, drawing heat into her cheeks, enflaming them. She was very aware of his fingertips trailing absently along her bare arm and very aware an engaged man had every reason to do it.

Except he'd never done it to her before and the little sparks his fingers generated panged through her abdomen.

"Oh, no, of course," Fran said. "I'm so sorry to bring up bad memories. Let's talk about something fun. Tell me about your wedding dress."

In a desperate attempt to reorient, Cia zeroed in on Fran's animated face. Lucas had not inherited his magnetism from his father, as she'd assumed, but from his mother. They shared a charisma that made it impossible to look away.

Lucas groaned, "Mama. That's not fun—that's worse than water torture. Daddy and Matthew don't want to hear about a dress. I don't even want to hear about that."

"Well, forgive me for trying to get to know my new daughter," Fran scolded and smiled at Cia conspiratorially. "I love my sons, but sometimes just because the good Lord said I have to. You I can love because I want to. The daughter of my heart instead of my blood. We'll have lunch next week and leave the party poopers at home, won't we?"

Cia nodded because her throat seized up and speaking wasn't an option.

Fran already thought of her as a daughter.

Never had she envisioned them liking each other or that Lucas's mother might want to become family by choice instead of only by law. The women at the shelter described their husbands' mothers as difficult, interfering. Quick to take their sons' sides. She'd assumed all new wives struggled to coexist. *Must have horrible mother* should have been on her criteria list.

And as long as she was redoing the list, *Zero sex appeal* was numero uno.

"Isn't it time for dinner?" Lucas said brightly, and everyone's gaze slid off her as Fran agreed.

The yeasty scent of baked bread had permeated the air a

few minutes ago and must have jump-started Lucas's appetite. She smiled at him, grateful for the diversion, and took a minute to settle her stomach.

Andy and Matthew followed Fran's lead into the dining room adjacent to the living area, where a middle-aged woman in a black-and-white uniform bustled around the twelve-seat formal dining table. A whole roasted chicken held court in the center, flanked by white serving dishes containing more wonderful food.

Lucas didn't move. He should move. Plenty of couch on the other side of his thigh.

"Be there in a minute," he called to his family and took Cia's hand in his, casually running a thumb over her knuckles. "You okay? You don't have to have lunch with my mother. She means well, but she can be overbearing."

"No." She shook her head, barely able to form words around the sudden pounding of her pulse. "Your mother is lovely. I'm...well—we're lying to her. To your whole family. Lying to my grandfather is one thing because he's the one who came up with those ridiculous trust provisions. But this..."

"Is necessary," he finished for her. "It would be weird if I never introduced you to my parents. For now it's important to play it like a real couple. I'll handle them later. Make something up."

He didn't understand. Because he'd had a mother his whole life.

"More lies. It's clear you're all close. How many other grown sons go to their mother's birthday party and then to dinner at her house in the same week?" Cia vaulted off the couch, and Lucas rose a split second later. "I'm sorry I put you in this position. How do we do this? How do I go in there and eat dinner like we're a happy, desperately in love couple?"

"Well, when I'm in an impossible situation, and I have no idea how to do it, I think to myself, 'What would Scooby do?'"

In spite of the ache behind her eyes, a shuddery laugh

slipped out. A laugh, when she could hardly breathe around the fierce longing swimming through her heart to belong to such a family unit for real.

"Scooby would eat."

"Yep." Lucas flashed an approval-laden smile. "So here's a crazy idea. Don't take this so seriously. Let's have fun tonight. Eat a good meal with some people I happen to be related to. Once it's over, you'll be one step closer to your money and I'll be one step closer to Manzanares, which will make both of us happy. Voilà. Now we're a happy couple. Okay?"

"We're still lying to them."

"I told my parents we're engaged to be married, and that's true."

"But there's an assumption there about us—"

He cut her off with a grunt. "Stop being so black-and-white. If anyone asks, don't lie. Change the subject. My parents are waiting on us to eat dinner. You've got to figure it out."

She took a deep breath. One dinner. One short ceremony. Then it would be over. "I'm working on it."

"Maybe you need something else to think about during dinner."

In a completely natural move, Lucas curved her into his arms, giving her plenty of time to see him coming. Plenty of time to anticipate. The crackle in the air and the intent in his eyes told her precisely what he'd give her to think about.

And still, when he kissed her, the contact of Lucas's mouth against hers swept shock waves down her throat, into her abdomen, spreading with long, liquid pulls.

She'd been kissed before. She had. Not like this, by a master who transformed the innocent touching of mouths into a carnal slide toward the depths of sinful pleasure.

He cupped her jaw with a feathery caress. When her knees buckled, he squeezed her tighter against him and deepened the kiss slowly, sending the burn of a thousand torches down the length of her body.

Her brain drained out through her soles to puddle on the Wheelers' handmade rug.

Then it was over. He drew his head back a bit, and she nearly lost her balance as she took in the dark hunger darting through his expression.

He murmured, "Now, darlin'. You think about how we'll finish that later on. I know I will be."

Later?

Lucas tugged at their clasped hands, and she followed him on rubbery legs into the dining room, still raw from being kissed breathless. Raw and confused.

It didn't mean anything. It couldn't mean anything. That kiss had been window dressing. It had been a diversion to get her to lay off. She wasn't stupid. Lucas had a crackerjack gift for distraction when necessary, and this had been one of those times. There was no later.

No one asked about the relationship between her and Lucas during dinner.

It might have had to do with the scorching heat in his eyes every time he looked at her. Or the way he sat two inches from her chair and whispered in her ear every so often. The comments were silly, designed to make her laugh, but every time he leaned in, with his lips close to her ear, laughing didn't happen.

She was consumed with *later* and the lingering taste of him on her lips.

Clearly, she'd underestimated his talent when it came to women. Oh, she wasn't surprised at his ability to kiss a fake fiancée senseless, or how the wickedness of his mouth caused her to forget her own name. No. The surprise lay in how genuine he'd made it feel. Like he'd enjoyed kissing her. Like the audience hadn't mattered.

He'd been doing his job—faking it around other people.

And despite the unqualified awareness that it wasn't real, that it never, ever could be, he'd made her *want* it to be real.

A man who could spin that kind of straw into gold was dangerous.

After dinner, Fran shooed everyone to the huge screened-in porch for coffee. Andy, Matthew and Lucas small talked about work a few feet away, so Cia perched on the wicker love seat overlooking the pool, sipping a cup of coffee to ward off the slight chill darkness had brought. Decaf, because she'd have a hard enough time sleeping tonight as it was. Her body still ached with the unfulfilled promise of Lucas's kiss.

After a conspicuous absence, Fran appeared and joined her.

"This is for you," Fran said, and handed Cia a long, velvet jewelry box. "Open it."

Cia set her coffee aside and sprung the lid, gasping as an eighteen-inch gray pearl and diamond necklace spilled into her hands. "Oh, Fran, I couldn't."

Fran closed Cia's hand over the smooth, cool pearls. "It belonged to my mother and my grandmother before that. My mother's wedding ring went to Ambe—" She cut herself off with a pained glance at Matthew. "My oldest son, but I saved this for Lucas's wife. I want you to have it. It's your something old."

Madre de Dios, how did she refuse?

This was way worse than a villa—it was an heirloom. A beautiful expression of lineage and family and her eyes stung as Fran clasped it around Cia's neck. It hung heavy against her skin, and she couldn't speak.

"It's stunning with your dark hair. Oh, I know it's not the height of fashion," Fran said with a half laugh. "It's old-lady jewelry. So humor me, please, and wear it at the ceremony, then put it away. I'll let Lucas buy you pretty baubles more to your taste."

Cia touched the necklace with the tips of her fingers.

"Thank you." A paltry sentiment compared to the emotion churning through her.

Fran smiled. "You're welcome. At the risk of being tactless, I was crushed you didn't want any family at the wedding. I'm more than happy to pitch in as mother of the bride, if that's part of the issue. You must be missing yours."

Before Cia's face crumpled fully, Lucas materialized at her side and pulled her to her feet. "Mama. I told you Cia doesn't want a big ceremony or any fuss. She doesn't even like jewelry."

Obviously he'd been listening to the conversation. As Fran sputtered, Cia retreated a few mortified steps and tried to be grateful for the intervention.

Her dry eyes burned. No big church wedding for her. No flower girls, chamber music or a delicate sleeveless ecru dress with a princess waist, trimmed in lace. All that signified the real deal, an ability to gift someone with her love and then trust the fates not to rip her happiness away with no warning.

Neither could she in good conscience develop any sort of relationship with Mrs. Wheeler. Better to hurt her now, rather than later.

With her heart in shredded little pieces, Cia unclasped the necklace. "Thank you, but I can't wear this. It doesn't go with a simple civil ceremony. I'm pretty busy at work for the foreseeable future, so lunch is out of the question."

Fran's expression smoothed out as she accepted the return of her box and necklace. "I overstepped. You have my apologies."

"It's fine, Mama. We should go," Lucas said and nodded to the rest of his family, who watched her coolly.

Excellent. Now they all hated her. That's what she should have been going for all night. Then when she and Lucas divorced, he could blame it all on her, and his family would welcome him back into the fold with sympathy and condolences. His mother would say she knew Cia wasn't the right girl for him the moment she'd thrown his great-grandmother's pearls back in her face.

Cia murmured her goodbyes and followed Lucas through the house and out into the starless night.

Once they were settled in their seats, he drove away, as slow as Christmas. But she didn't care so much this time and burrowed into the soft leather, oddly reassured by the scent of pine trees curling around her.

"Thanks, Lucas," she said, and her voice cracked. "For giving me the out with your mother. It was…"

"No problem," he said, jumping in to fill the silence when she couldn't go on. "It takes two to make marriage work, fake or otherwise. I'll do damage control with Mama in the morning. And, darlin', I must confess a real fondness to you calling me Lucas."

His gaze connected with hers, arcing with heat, and the current zinged through the semidark, close quarters of the car. Goose bumps erupted across her skin and her pulse skittered.

All of a sudden, it was later.

Five

Lucas spent the silent, tense ride home revamping his strategy.

Fragileness deepened Cia's shadows, and it was enough to cool his jets. Nothing would have pleased him more than to walk into the house, back her up against the door and start that kiss over again, but this time, his hands would stroke over the hot curves of her body and she'd be naked in short order.

But she wasn't like other women. She wasn't in touch with her sexuality, and he had to live with her—and himself—for the next six months. While he'd like to sink straight into a simple seduction, he had to treat her differently, with no idea what that looked like.

Once they cleared the detached garage, he slid his hand into hers. "Thanks for going to dinner."

Her fingers stiffened. She glanced at him, surprise evident. "You say that like I had a choice."

"You did. With me, you always have a choice. We're partners, not master and slave. So, I'm saying thank you for choosing to spend the evening with my family. It was difficult for you, and I appreciate it."

Her gaze flitted over him, clearly looking for the punch line. "You're welcome, then."

He let go of her hand to open the door. "Now, I don't know about you, but my parents' house always makes me want to let loose a little. I'm half-afraid to move, in case I accidentally knock over one of Mama's precious knickknacks."

Cia smiled, just a little, but it was encouraging all the same. "It is easier to breathe in our house."

Our house. She'd never called it that before, and he liked the sound of it. They were settling in with each other, finding a groove.

He followed her into the living room. "Let's do something fun."

"Like what?"

Instead of answering, he crossed to the entertainment center and punched up the music she'd been playing earlier, when he'd returned home from playing basketball. A mess of electronic noise blasted through the speakers, thumping in his chest. "Dance with me," he yelled over the pulsing music.

"To this?" Disbelief crinkled her forehead. "You haven't even been drinking, white boy."

"Come on." He held out a hand. "You won't dance in public. No one is watching except me, and I can't dance well enough to warrant making fun of you."

He almost fell over when she shrugged and joined him. "I don't like people watching me, but I never said I couldn't dance."

To prove it, she cut her torso in a zigzag and whirled in an intricate move worthy of a music video, hair flying, hands framing her head.

He grinned and crossed his arms, content to be still and watch Cia abandon herself to the beat. His hunch had been right—anyone with her energy would have to be a semicompetent dancer.

After a minute or so of the solo performance, she froze and threw him a look. "You're not dancing."

"Too hard to keep up with that, honey. I'm having a great time. Really. Keep going."

"Not if you're just going to stand there. You asked me to dance *with you*."

Only because he hadn't actually thought she'd say yes. "So I did."

He could be a good sport. But he could not, under any circumstances, dance to anything faster than Brooks & Dunn.

So, he let her make fun of him instead, as he flapped his arms and stomped his feet in what could easily be mistaken for an epileptic seizure. When she laughed so hard she had to hold her sides, nothing but pure Cia floated through her eyes.

The shadows—and the fragileness—had been banished. Score one for Wheeler.

"All right, darlin'. Unless you want to tend to me as I'm laid out flat on my back with a pulled muscle, we gotta dial it down a notch."

She snickered. "What are you, sixty? Shall I run and collect your social security check from the mailbox?"

Before she could protest, he grabbed her hand and twirled her into his arms, body to body. "No, thanks. I've got another idea."

Her arms came up around his waist and she clung to him. Progress. It was sweet.

"Slow dancing?" she asked.

"Slow something, that's for sure." He threaded fingers through her amazing hair and brushed a thumb across her cheek. Her skin was damp from dancing.

As he imagined the glow she'd take on when he got her good and sweaty between the sheets, he went hard. She noticed.

Her eyes widened, and all the color drained from her face as she let go of him faster than a hot frying pan. "It's late. I have a shift in the morning, so I'm about danced out."

All his hard work crumbled to dust under the avalanche of her hang-ups. He let her go with regret. Should have gone with slow dancing, and, as a bonus, she'd still be in his arms. "Sure thing. Big day tomorrow."

The wedding. Realization crept over her expression. "Oh. Yeah. Well, good night."

She fled.

He stalked off to bed and stared at the news for a good couple of hours, unsuccessfully attempting to will away his raging hard-on, before finally drifting off into a restless sleep laced with dreams of Cia wearing his ring and nothing else.

In the morning, he awoke bleary eyed but determined to make some progress in at least one area sorely requiring his attention—work.

The muted hum of the shower in Cia's bathroom traveled through the walls as he passed by.

Cia, wet and naked. Exactly as he'd dreamed.

He skipped breakfast, too frustrated to stay in the house any longer. An early arrival at work wasn't out of line anyway, as Mondays were usually killers. A welcome distraction from the slew of erotic images parading around in his head.

At red lights, he fired off emails to potential clients with the details of new listings. His schedule was insane this week. He had overlapping showings, appraisals and social events he'd attend to drum up new business.

An annoying buzz at the edge of his consciousness kept reminding him of all the balls he had in the air. He'd been juggling the unexpected addition of a full-time personal life and the strain was starting to wear. As long as he didn't drop any balls or clients, everything was cool.

Four o'clock arrived way too fast.

As anticipated, Cia waited for him outside the courthouse,

wearing one of her Sunday-go-to-meeting dresses a grand-mother would envy and low heels.

With her just-right curves and slender legs, put her in a pair of stilettos and a gauzy hot-pink number revealing a nice slice of cleavage…well, there'd be no use for stoplights on the street—traffic would screech to a halt spontaneously. But that wasn't her style. Shame.

Her gaze zeroed in on the bouquet of lilies in his fist. "You just come from a funeral, Wheeler?"

So they were back to *Wheeler* in that high-brow, back-off tone. One tasty kiss-slash-step-forward and forty steps back.

"For you." Lucas offered Cia the flowers. Dang it, he should not have picked them out. If he'd asked Helena to do it, like he should have, when Cia sneered at the blooms, as she surely would, he wouldn't be tempted to throw them down and forget this whole idea. Even a man with infinite patience could only take so much.

But she didn't sneer. Gently, she closed her fingers around the flowers and held them up to inhale the scent.

After a long minute of people rushing by and the two of them standing there frozen, she said, "If you'd asked, I would have said no. But it's kind of nice after all. So you get a pass."

He clutched his chest in a mock heart attack and grinned. "That's why I didn't ask. All brides should have flowers."

"This isn't a real wedding."

She tossed her head and strands of her inky hair fanned out in a shiny mass before falling back to frame her exotic features. This woman he was about to make his wife was such a weird blend of stunning beauty and barbed personality, with hidden recesses of warmth and passion.

What was wrong with him that he was so flippin' attracted to that mix? This marriage would be so much easier if he let it go and worried about stuff he could control, like scaring up new clients.

But he couldn't. He wanted her in his bed, hot and enthusiastic, hang-ups tossed out the window for good.

"Sure it is. We're going to be legally married. Just because it's not traditional doesn't make it less real."

She flipped her free hand. "You know what I mean. A church wedding, with family and friends and cake."

"Is that what you wanted? I would have suffered through a real wedding for you." His skin itched already to think of wearing a tux and memorizing vows. God Almighty…the rehearsal, the interminable ceremony, the toasts. Matthew had undergone it all with a besotted half smile, claiming it was all worth it. Maybe it was if you were in love. "But, darlin', I would have insisted on a real honeymoon."

He waggled his brows, and she laughed nervously, which almost gave him a real heart attack.

A hint of a smile still played around her lips. "A real wedding would have made both of us suffer. That's not what I wanted. I don't have a perfect wedding dress already picked out in hopes my Prince Charming will come along, like other women do. I'm okay with being single for the rest of my life."

"Hold up, honey. You're not a romantic? All my illusions about you have been thoroughly crushed."

Romantic gestures put a happy, glowy expression on a woman's face, and he liked being the one responsible. It was the only sight on this earth anywhere near as pleasurable as watching a woman in the throes of an orgasm he'd given her.

He had his work cut out for him if he wanted to get Cia there.

He put an arm around her waist to guide her inside the courthouse because it was starting to seem as if she wanted to avoid going inside.

The ceremony was quick, and when he slid the slender wedding band of diamonds channel-set in platinum onto her finger, Cia didn't curl her lip. He'd deliberately picked something low-key that she could wear without the glitzy engagement ring. The set had cost more than his car, but he viewed both as an investment. Successful real estate brokers didn't cheap out, and especially now, with Lana's husband on the warpath, every last detail of his life was for show.

With a fast and unsexy kiss, it was over. They were Mr. and Mrs. Wheeler.

The cool, hard metal encircling his finger was impossible to ignore, and he spun it with his pinkie, trying to get used to the weight. Uncomfortable silence fell as they left the courthouse and neither of them broke it. Cia had asked a friend to drop her off, so she rode home with him.

Half-surprised Mama hadn't crashed the event, he called her with the update before he pulled out of the courthouse parking lot. By the time the wheels hit the driveway of the house, Mama had apparently posted the news to Facebook, which then took on a life of its own.

Text messages started rolling in, and he glanced at them as he shifted into Park.

Pete: Dude. Are we still on for bball Sunday? Or do you have to check with the missus?

Justine: REALLY Lucas???? Married???? REALLY????

Melinda: **&^$%. Missed it by that much. Call me the second you get tired of her.

Lucas rolled his eyes. He hadn't spoken to either woman in months. Pete yanked his chain twice a day and had since college.

When Lucas went to shut off his phone, a message came in from Lana: Congrats. Nothing else. The simple half a word spoke volumes and it said, *Poor Lucas, marrying that woman on the rebound.*

"You're popular all of a sudden," Cia said after the fourth beep in a row, and her tone tried and convicted him for a crime he'd not been aware of committing.

"It's just people congratulating us."

And he was done with that. Lana's name popping up on

the screen, after all this time, had unburied disillusionment he'd rather not dwell on.

He hit the phone's off button and dropped it in his pocket, then left the car in the driveway instead of pulling into the garage so it would be easier for Cia to get out.

His efforts to untangle Cia's hang-ups last night had failed. Tonight, he'd try a different approach. "Have dinner with me. To celebrate."

Before he could move, she popped the door and got out. He followed her up the drive and plowed through Amber's fancy flowerbed to beat her to the porch.

"Celebrate what?" she asked, annoyance leaking from her pores. "I was thinking about soaking for an hour or two in a hot bath and going to bed early, actually."

Before she could storm through the entryway, Lucas stopped her with a firm hand on her prickly little shoulder. "Wait."

With an impatient sigh, she turned. "What?"

"Just because you've got your marriage license doesn't mean we're going to walk through this door and never speak again. You realize this, don't you?" He searched her face, determined to find some glimmer of agreement. "This is the beginning, not the end. We've been faking being a happily engaged couple. Now we have to fake being a happily married couple. No, we don't have to put on a performance right now, when no one's around. But to do it in public, trust me, darlin', when I say it will be miles easier if you're not at my throat in private."

Her tight face flashed through a dozen different emotions and finally picked resignation. "Yeah. I know. I owe you an apology. It's been a rough day."

For both of them. "Because you didn't want to get married?"

She shrank a little, as if she couldn't support the heavy weight settling across her shoulders. As if she might shatter into a million shards of razor-sharp glass if he touched her. So he didn't.

But he wanted to, to see if he could soften her up, like during the five seconds he'd had her pliant and breathless in his arms and so off guard she'd actually kissed him back.

"I've been prepared to be married ever since I came up with the idea." Misery pulled at her full mouth. "It's just...I didn't have any idea how hard it would be to get married without my father walking me down the aisle. Me. Who was never going to get married in the first place. Isn't that ridiculous?"

One tear burst loose, trailing down her delicate cheekbone, and he had to do something.

"Hey now," he said, and wrapped his arms around her quivering shoulders, drawing her in close. She let him, which meant she must be really upset. Prickly Cia usually made an appearance when she was uncomfortable about whatever was going on inside her. "That's okay to cry about. Cry all you want. Then I'll get you drunk and take advantage of you, so you forget all about it."

She snorted out a half laugh, and it rumbled pleasantly against his chest. There was something amazing about being able to comfort a woman so insistent on not needing it. He'd grown really fond of soothing away that prickliness.

"I could use a glass of wine," she admitted.

"I have exactly the thing. Come inside." He drew back and smiled when some snap crept back into her watery eyes. "You can drink it while you watch me cook."

"You cook?" That dried up her waterworks in a hurry. "With an oven?"

"Sure enough. I can even turn it on by myself." As he led the way into the kitchen, a squawk cut him off. "Oh, good. Your wedding present is here."

Cia raised her brows at the large cage sitting on the island in the middle of the kitchen. "That's a bird."

"Yep. An African gray parrot." He shed his suit jacket and draped it over a chair in the breakfast nook.

"You're giving me a bird? As a wedding present?"

"Not any bird. African grays live up to fifty years, so you'll have company as you live all by your lonesome the rest of your life. And they talk. I figure anyone who likes to argue as much as you do needed a pet who can argue back. I named her Fergie." He shrugged. "Because you like hip-hop."

Speechless, Cia stared at the man she had married, whom she clearly did not know at all, and tried to make some sort of sound.

"I didn't get you anything," she managed to say.

"That's okay." He unbuttoned his sleeves and rolled them deftly halfway up his tanned forearms, then started pulling covered plates out of the stainless steel refrigerator. "I wasn't expecting anything."

"Neither was I," she mumbled. "Doesn't seem like that matters either way."

She'd never owned a bird and would have to take a crash course on its recommended care. As she peered into the cage, the feathered creature blinked and peered back with intelligent eyes, unafraid and curious. She fell instantly in love.

The psychology of the gift wasn't lost on her. Instead of showering her with expensive, useless presents designed to charm her panties off, he'd opted for a well-thought-out gift. An extremely well-thought-out gift designed for…what?

Every time she thought he was done, Lucas Wheeler peeled back another one of his layers, and every time, it freaked her out a little more.

Regardless, she couldn't lie. "It's the best present I've ever gotten." And she'd remember forever not that her father hadn't been there to give her away, but that her fake husband had given her something genuine on their wedding day. "Thanks, Lucas."

The sentiment stopped him in his tracks, between the

stove and the dishwasher, pan dangling, forgotten, from his hand. That indefinable energy crackled through the air as he treated her to a scorching once-over. "Darlin', you are most welcome."

"Didn't you mention wine?" she asked, to change the subject, and slid onto a barstool edging the granite island.

There was a weird vibe going on tonight, and she couldn't put her finger on it. Alcohol probably wouldn't help.

Lucas retrieved a bottle from the refrigerator. "Sauvignon blanc okay?"

When she nodded, he pulled a corkscrew from a wall hanger, then expertly twisted and wiggled the cork out in one smooth motion. The man did everything with care and attention, and she had a feeling he meant for her to notice. She did. So what?

Yes, his amazing hands would glide over her bare body in a slow seduction and turn her into his sex-starved lover. No question about it.

The real question was why she was envisioning Lucas touching her after simply watching him open wine. Okay. It had nothing to do with wine and everything to do with being in his arms last night. With being kissed and watching him dance like a spastic chicken, draining away all her misery over hurting his mother.

Lucas skirted the barstools and handed her a glass of pale yellow wine. His fingers grazed hers for a shocky second, but it was over so fast, she didn't have time to jerk away. Good thing, or she would have sloshed her drink.

He picked up his own glass and, with his smoky blue-eyed gaze locked with hers, dinged the rims together. "To partnership," he said. "May it be a pleasurable union."

"Successful, you mean. I'll drink to a successful union." As soon as the words came out, she realized her mistake. She and Lucas did not view the world through the same lens.

He took his time swallowing a mouthful of wine, and she

was so busy watching his throat muscles ripple that when his forefinger tipped up her chin, she almost squealed in surprise. His thumb brushed her lips, catching on the lower one, and her breath stuttered when he tilted his head toward hers.

"Darlin'," he said, halting way too close. His whiskey-smooth voice flowed over her. "If you find our union as pleasurable as I intend, I'll consider that a success. Dinner will be ready in forty-five minutes."

A hot flush stole over her cheeks and flooded the places he'd touched. He went back to cooking.

As she watched him chop and sauté and whatever, she had to instruct her stomach to unknot. He'd been messing around, like always. That's all. For Lucas, flirting was a reflex so ingrained he probably didn't realize he was doing it, especially when directing it at his fake wife in whom he had no real interest.

She bristled over his insincerity until Fergie squawked. A fitting distraction from obsessing about the feel of Lucas's thumb on her mouth. She retrieved her laptop from the bedroom and researched what parrots ate while Lucas finished preparing the people food.

"The guy at the pet store said to feed her papaya. They like fruit," Lucas said and refilled her wineglass. "There's one in the refrigerator if you want to cut it up."

She sighed. He'd even bought a papaya. Did the man ever sleep? "Thanks, I will."

Silence fell as she chopped alongside her husband, and it wasn't so bad. She shouldn't be hard on him because he dripped sexiness and made her ache when he looked at her, as if he knew the taste of her and it was delicious. Might as well be ticked over his blue eyes.

The simple celebratory dinner turned into a lavish poolside spread. Lucas led her outside, where a covered flagstone patio edged the elegant infinity pool and palm trees rustled overhead in the slight breeze. Dust coated the closed grill in the top-of-the-line outdoor kitchen, but the landscaping appeared freshly maintained, absent of weeds and overgrown limbs.

Lucas set the iron bistro table with green Fiestaware and served as she took a seat.

"What kind of chicken is this?" she asked and popped a bite into her mouth. A mix of spices and a hint of lime burst onto her tongue.

He shrugged. "I don't know, I made it up. The kitchen is one of the places where I let my creativity roll."

Gee. She just bet she could guess the other place where he rolled out the creativity.

"Oh. I see." She nodded sagely. "Part of your date-night repertoire. Do women take one bite and fall into a swoon?"

"I've never made it for anyone else." His eyes glowed in the dusky light as he stared at her, daring her to draw significance from the statement.

When he stuck a forkful of couscous in his mouth and withdrew it, she pretended like she hadn't been watching his lips.

This was frighteningly close to a conversation over a good bottle of wine, the idea he'd thrown out as the way to get to know each other. But they still weren't dating. Perhaps he should be reminded. "Really? What do you normally make when you have a hot date you want to impress?"

He stopped eating. As he sat back in his chair, he cupped his wineglass and dangled it between two fingers, contemplating her with a reckless smile. "I've never cooked for anyone, either."

She dropped her fork. Now he was being ridiculous. "What, exactly, am I supposed to take from that?"

"Well, you could deduce that I cooked you dinner because I wanted to."

"Why? What's with the parrot and dinner and this—" she waved at the gas torches flaming in a circle around the patio and pool "—romantic setting? Are you trying to get lucky or something?"

"Depends." His half-lidded gaze crawled up inside her and speared her tummy. "How close am I?"

Why couldn't he answer the question instead of talking in his endless, flirty Lucas-circles?

Oh, no.

His interest in her was real. As real as the hunger in his expression after kissing her. As real as the evidence of his arousal while dancing last night. Clues she'd dismissed as… what? She didn't even know; she'd just ignored them all so she didn't have to deal with them. Now she did.

Firmly, she said, "We can't have that kind of relationship." The kind where she gave him a chunk of her heart and he took it with him when he left. The kind where she'd surrender her hard-won self-reliance, which would happen over her dead body. "We have an agreement."

"Agreements can be altered." That dangling wineglass between his fingers raked up her nerves and back down again. He couldn't even be serious about holding stemware.

"This one can't. What if I got pregnant?"

Dios. With fingers trembling so hard she could scarcely grip the glass, she drained the remainder of her wine and scouted around for the bottle. There'd be no children in her future. Life was too uncertain to bring another generation into it.

"Well, now that's just insulting. What about me suggests I might be so careless?"

"Arrogance is your preferred method of birth control?"

They were discussing *sex.* She and Lucas were talking *about having sex.* Sitting by the pool, eating dinner and talking about sex with her fake-in-name-only-going-away-soon husband.

"I'm not worried, darlin'. It's never happened before."

She stood so fast the backs of her knees screeched the chair backward until it tipped over. "Well, that's a relief. Please stand back as I become putty in your hands."

He followed her to his feet without fanfare, no more bothered than if they were discussing what color to paint the bathroom.

In one step, he was an inch away, and then he reached out and placed a fingertip on her temple. Lazily, he slid the fingertip down her face, traced the line of her throat and rested it at the base of her collarbone with a tap. "What's going on in there? You're not afraid of getting pregnant."

"Stop touching me." She cocked a brow and refused to move away from the inferno roiling between Lucas's body and hers. He was the one who should back down, not her. Last night, she'd run from this confrontation and look where that had gotten her. "Nothing is going on other than the fact that I'm not attracted to you."

Liar. The hot press of his fingertips against her skin set off an explosion way down low. But wanting someone and being willing to surrender to the feeling were poles apart.

"I don't believe you," he murmured.

He wasn't backing down. His hands eased through her hair, and unmistakable heat edged into his eye.

"What, you think you're going to prove something by kissing me?"

"Yep," he said and dipped his head before she could protest.

For a sixteenth of a second, she considered all possible options, and then his lips covered hers and she went with dissolving into his arms. It was all she could do when Lucas kissed her, his mouth hot and the taste of his tongue sudden and shocking.

His fingers trailed sparklers through her hair and down her spine, molding her against the potent hardness of his body. Clicking them together like nesting spoons, foretelling how sweetly they would fit without clothes.

He angled his head and took her deeper, yanking a long, hard pull from her abdomen. A burst of need uncoiled from a hidden place inside to burn in all the right places. It was real, and it was good. He was good.

So good, she could feel her resistance melting away under the onslaught of his wicked mouth. But she couldn't give in, and, *Dios,* it made her want to weep.

If only he'd kept a couple of those layers hidden. If only she had a way to insulate herself from someone like him. The intensity between them frightened her to the bone, because he had the unique ability to burrow under her defenses and take whatever he wanted.

Then he'd leave her empty, and she'd worked too hard to put herself back together after the last disastrous attempt at a relationship.

She broke away, wrenched out of his arms and rasped, "All that proves is you've practiced getting women naked."

His face was implacable and his shoulders rigid beneath the fabric of his slate-gray button-down. He cleared his throat. "Darlin', why are you fighting this so hard? At first I thought it was because you've been around so much misery, but there's something else going on here."

"Yeah. Something else, like I don't want to. Is your ego so inflated you can't fathom a woman not being interested in you?"

He laughed. "Hon, if that's how you kiss a guy you're not interested in, I'll lick a sardine. Pick a different card."

How dare he throw her own phrase back in her face.

"This is funny to you? How's this for a reason? You might very well be the hottest male on the planet, but I am not willing to be your latest conquest, Wheeler." Her hands clenched into fists and socked against his chest. For emphasis. And maybe to unleash some frustration. He didn't move an iota.

For who knew what ill-advised reason, he reached out, but then he wisely stopped shy of her face. "Is it so difficult to believe you intrigue me and I simply want to unwrap the rest of you?"

"Yeah. It is." She crossed her arms to prevent any more unloading of frustration. His chest was as hard as his head. And other places. "You're feeling deprived. Go find one of the women who text messaged you earlier in the car and scratch your itch with her, because I'm not sleeping with you."

A smile curved his mouth, but the opposite of humor flashed through his steely gaze. "In case it's slipped your mind, I'm married. The only person I'll be sleeping with for the next six months is my wife."

Panic spurted at the back of her throat. Upon meeting her for the first time, he'd kissed her hand—how had she not considered that his old-fashioned streak didn't end there?

Of course, he'd also flat-out told her he wouldn't sleep with another woman while she wore his ring. "Your wife just turned you down flat."

"For tonight anyway."

His supreme confidence pricked at her temper. So he thought he could seduce away her resistance?

"For forever. Honestly, I don't care if you sleep with someone else. It's not really cheating."

The sudden image sprang to mind of Lucas twined with another woman, the way he'd been with her on the bed, his mouth open and heated against the tramp's throat, then kissing her senseless and dipping a clever hand under her clothes.

Her stomach pitched. Ridiculous. She didn't care what he did. She really didn't.

"I care," he said, his silky voice low.

"Why? This isn't a real marriage. You aren't in love with me. You barely like me."

"We're legally married. That makes it really cheating, whether I've had you naked and quivering in my arms or not. Have I made my position clear enough?" Fierceness tightened his mouth and scrunched his eyes and had her faltering.

Anger. It was so foreign, so wrong on Lucas, she didn't know what to do with it.

"I think so." She swallowed against a weird catch in her throat. So, maybe he wasn't quite the horn dog she'd assumed. "Are you clear on my position?"

"Crystal."

Relieved he wasn't going to push some macho, possessive sexual agenda on her, she nodded. "Great. I'm glad we talked this out. It's incredibly important that we handle this fake marriage like rational adults. Now we can go forward as we've discussed, as pure business associates, without any additional complications. Agreed?"

Reflected torchlight danced in his eyes, obscuring his true thoughts. He leaned in and motioned her closer.

With his lips almost touching her earlobe, he said succinctly, "Sweetheart, the only thing I plan to do going forward is regroup. And then, my darlin' Mrs. Wheeler, all bets are off."

He turned on his heel and left her on the patio. She had the distinct impression he was both mad *and* plotting how to get even.

Six

Lucas waited almost a week before cornering the lioness in her den, partially because he'd been hustling his tail off eighteen hours a day to secure at least one elusive client—which had failed miserably—and partially because Cia needed the distance. Pushing her was not the right strategy. She required delicacy and finesse. And patience. God Almighty, did she ever require patience. But when her thorny barriers came tumbling down...well, experience told him she'd be something else once she felt safe enough to let loose. He'd gladly spent a good chunk of unrecoverable work hours dreaming up ways to provide that security.

He did appreciate a challenge. No woman he'd ever romanced had forced him to up his game like she did. He'd have sworn on a stack of Bibles that kind of effort would have him bowing out before sunset. Not this time.

Cia's routine hadn't varied over the past week, so she'd be home from the shelter around four. Usually, he was mired in paperwork in the study or on a conference call or stuffing food in his mouth while doing research as he prepared for a late meeting with a potential client—all activities he could have done at the office.

But he'd developed the habit of listening for her, to be sure she and her zero-to-sixty-in-four-point-two-seconds car made it home in one piece.

Today, he waited in the kitchen and talked to Fergie, who so far only said "hello," "goodbye" and imitated the microwave timer beep so perfectly he almost always turned to open it before realizing she'd duped him. He'd been trying to get her to say "Lucas," but Fergie might be more stubborn than her owner.

When Cia walked in the door, hair caught up in a sassy ponytail, he grinned but kept his hands by his sides instead of nestling her into his arms to explore that exposed neck.

A woman named Dulciana had to have a sweet, gooey center, and he itched to taste it.

"Hey," she said in wary surprise. They hadn't spoken since she'd laid down the law during his aborted celebratory poolside dinner. "What's up?"

"I have a favor to ask," he said. It was better to get to the point since she'd already figured out he wanted something. Being married to Mrs. Psych Minor kept him honest. When the woman at the heart of the challenge was onto him, it made things so much more interesting.

Guarded unease snapped her shoulders back. "Sure. What is it?"

"WFP sold a building to Walrich Enterprises a few months ago, and they're having a ribbon cutting tonight. I'd like to take you."

"Really?" Her forehead bunched in confusion. "Why?"

He swallowed a laugh. "You're my wife. That's who you take to social stuff for work. Plus, people would speculate why I attended solo after just getting married."

"Tell them I had to work." She cocked her head, swinging that ponytail in a wide pendulum, taunting him. So she wanted to play, did she?

"I used that excuse at the last thing I went to. If everyone was curious before, they're rabid now. You don't have much of a social presence as it is, and you're going to get labeled a recluse if you keep hiding out."

"You didn't ask me to go to the last thing." She smiled sweetly enough, but he suspected it was a warning for what would be an excellent comeback. "If I get a reclusive reputation, seems like we might revisit who's to blame."

Yep. She got the first point in this match. But he was getting the next one. "The last thing was boring. I did you a favor by letting you skip it, so you owe me. Come to the ribbon cutting tonight."

"Wow. That was so slick, I didn't see it coming." She crossed her arms, tightening her T-shirt—sunny yellow today—over her chest. "I'd really prefer to skip it, if it's all the same."

With a couple of drunken ballerina sidesteps, she tried to skirt him.

"Cia." He easily stepped in front of her, halting her progress and preventing her from slamming the door on the conversation.

Her irises transformed into deep pools of blue. "You called me 'Cia.' Are you feeling okay?"

His brow quirked involuntarily as he filed away how mesmerizing her eyes became when he called her Cia. It was worth a repeat. "This is important or I wouldn't have asked. You proposed this marriage as a way to rebuild my reputation. That's not going to happen by taking a picture of our marriage license and posting it on the internet. With my nice, stable wife at my side during this event tonight, people will start to forget about Lana."

With a sigh, she closed her lids for a beat. "Why did you have to go and make the one logical point I can't argue with?

Let's pretend I say yes. Are you going to complain about my outfit all night?"

Here came the really tricky part. "Not if you wear the dress I bought you."

Fire swept through her expression, and she snapped, "I specifically asked you not to buy me clothes."

"No, you ordered me not to, and I ignored you. Wear the dress. The guests are the cream of society."

"And you don't want to be ashamed to be seen with me." Hurricane force winds of fury whipped through her frame, leaving him no doubt she'd gladly impale him with a tree limb or two if her path happened to cross them.

"Darlin', come on." He shook his head. "You'd be gorgeous in pink-and-teal sofa fabric, and I'd stand next to you all night with pride. But I want you to be comfortable alongside all those well-dressed people. Appearance is everything to them."

"To them. What about you? Are you that shallow, too?" Her keen gaze flitted over him.

"Appearances aren't everything, but they are important. That's what a reputation is. Other people's view of how you appear to them, which may or may not reflect reality, and that's what makes the world go round. All you can do is present yourself in the best possible light."

Her ire drained away, and a spark of understanding softened her mouth. "That's why you got so angry when I said I didn't care if you slept with other women. Because of how it would look."

And here he thought he'd covered up that unexpected temper flare. Must need more practice. He rarely let much rile him, and it was rarer still to let it show. A temporary, in-name-only wife shouldn't have that kind of effect. He shrugged. "People talk and it hurts, no matter how you slice it. I would never allow that to happen to you because of me."

If Lana had been of the same mind, he'd never have met

this fierce little conquistador now called Mrs. Lucas Wheeler. A blessing or a curse?

"I'm sorry I suggested it. It was insensitive." With a measured exhale, she met his gaze. "I'll go. But I want to see the dress before I agree to wear it. It's probably too big."

Well, then. She'd conceded not just the point but the whole match. A strange tightness in his chest loosened. "It's hanging in your closet. Try it on. Wear it if you like it. Throw it in the trash if you hate it. We should leave around seven, and I'll take you to dinner afterward." He risked squeezing her hand, and the cool band of her wedding ring impressed his palm. "Thanks. I promise you'll have fun tonight."

She rolled her eyes. "I don't even want to know how you plan to guarantee that." She let their hands slip apart and successfully navigated around him to leave the kitchen. Over her shoulder, she shot the parting volley. "See you at seven-ten."

Later that night, Lucas hit the ground floor of their house at six fifty-five. When Cia descended the stairs at seven on the dot, his pulse stumbled. Actually *stumbled*. He'd known the floor-length red sheath would look amazing on her as soon as he'd seen it in the window.

Amazing didn't cover it. She'd swept her hair up in a sexy mess of pins and dark locks and slipped black stockings over legs that peeped through the skirt's modest slit.

"Darlin', you take my breath away," he called up with a grin contrived to hide the fact that he was dead serious. His lungs hurt. Or at least something in his chest did.

Compared to his vivacious wife, Lana was a pale, lackluster phantom flitting along the edges of his memory.

"Yeah, well, I have a feeling when I trip over this long dress, I'll take *my* breath away, too," she said as she reached the ground floor. "Did you seriously tell me to throw Versace in the trash?"

The distinctive scent of coconut and lime wafted over him.

"Not seriously." His mouth was dry. He needed a drink. Lots of drinks. "I knew you wouldn't hate it."

"Don't pat yourself on the back too hard. I'm only wearing it because the price tag is equal to the GDP of some small countries. It would be wrong to throw it away." Sincerity oozed from her mouth. But he was onto her.

He stared her down. Even in heels, she only came up to his nose. "I still have the receipt. Pretty sure the store would take it back. Run upstairs and change. I'll wait."

"All right, all right." She spit out a bunch of Spanish, and danged if it wasn't sexy to watch her mouth form the foreign words. Then she sighed, and it was long-suffering. "It's beautiful and fits like a dream. Because your ego isn't big enough already, I will also admit you have an excellent eye for style. If you undress a girl as well as you dress one, your popularity with the ladies is well deserved."

A purifying laugh burst out of him. He'd missed sparring with her this past week and the mental gymnastics required. When she engaged him brain to brain, it thoroughly turned him on.

Something was definitely wrong with him.

"Well, now. As it happens, I believe I'm pretty proficient at both. Anytime you care to form your own opinion, let me know. Ready?"

She laughed and nodded. Obviously, something was wrong with both of them, because he'd bet every last dollar that she enjoyed their heated exchanges as much as he did, though she'd likely bite off her tongue before saying so. Which would be a shame since he had a very specific use in mind for that razor-sharp tongue of his wife's.

The ribbon-cutting ceremony at Walrich's new facility was packed. People talked to Lucas, and he talked back, but he couldn't for the life of him recall the conversations because he spent the evening entranced by his wife's bare neck.

Since they were in public, he had every reason to touch

her whenever the inclination hit, which happened often. The torch-red dress encased her slim body with elegance, and the sight of her very nice curves knifed him in the groin.

Sure he'd bought women clothes before, but not for a woman who lived under his roof and shared his last name. Everything felt bigger and more significant with Cia, even buying her an age-appropriate dress. Even bringing her to a social event with the strict intent of jump-starting his reputation rebuild.

Even casually resting his hand on the back of her neck as they navigated the room. The silk of her skin against his fingers bled through him with startling warmth. Startling because the response wasn't only sexual.

And that just wasn't possible.

"Let's go," he told Cia. Matthew could work potential clients, which was his strength anyway. "We've done enough mingling."

"Already?" She did a double take at the expression on his face. "Okay. Where are we going for dinner?"

He swore. Dinner put a huge crimp in his intent to distance himself immediately from the smell of coconut and lime.

But if he bailed, whatever had just happened when he touched Cia would stick in his mind, nagging at him. Not cool. That fruity blend was messing with his head something fierce.

What was he thinking? He couldn't leave the schmoozing to Matthew like he used to. Cia hadn't balked at attending the ribbon cutting. What kind of coward let his wife do all the hard work?

The best way to handle this divorce deal, and his disturbing attraction to the woman on his arm, was obviously to remember the Lucas Wheeler Philosophy of Relationships—have a lot of sex and have a lot of fun, preferably at the same time.

This was a temporary liaison with a guaranteed outcome, and besides, he was with an inarguably beautiful woman. What other kind of response was there except sexual?

Shake it off, Wheeler.

"A place with food," he finally said.

Cia eyed her decadently beautiful husband, who should be required by law to wear black tie every waking hour, and waited a beat for the rest of the joke. It never came.

She hadn't seen Lucas in a week and had started to wonder exactly how mad she'd made him by the pool. Then he'd appeared and asked her pretty please to attend this boring adult prom, which she couldn't legitimately refuse, so she hadn't. For her trouble, he'd spent the evening on edge and not himself. "Great. Places with food are my favorite."

Matthew Wheeler materialized in front of them before they could head for the exit.

Lucas glanced at his brother. "What's the climate with Moore?"

Since Matthew was pretending she was invisible, Cia openly studied her authoritative, remote brother-in-law. A widower, Lucas had said, and often dateless, as he was tonight. Clearly by choice, since any breathing woman would find Matthew attractive—as long as he didn't stand next to Lucas. When he did, he was invisible, too.

"Better than I expected." Matthew signaled a waiter and deposited his empty champagne flute on the tray. "He's on the hook. I booked reservations in your name at the Mansion for four. Take Moore and his wife to dinner on me. Since closing the deal is your forte, I'll bow out. Bring it home."

As if they'd practiced it a dozen times, Lucas kissed Cia's temple, and she managed to lean into it like his lips weren't hotter than a cattle brand. Nothing like a spark of Lucas to liven up the prom.

Not that she'd know anything about prom. She'd missed that and the last half of senior year, thanks to the accident that had taken her parents.

"Do me a favor," Lucas said, "and hang out with Matthew

for a minute. Looks like we might have different plans for the evening."

Then he strode off through the crowd to go work his magic on some unsuspecting guy named Moore.

Matthew watched her coolly through eyes a remarkably close shade to Lucas's. "Having a good time, Cia?"

Oh, so she'd miraculously reappeared. But she didn't mistake the question as friendly. "Yes, thank you. Your clients are impressive."

"What few we have, I suppose." His shrewd gaze narrowed. "I'll be honest. I have no idea what got into Lucas by marrying you, but I see the way he looks at you and I hope there's at least a chance you're making him happy."

What way did Lucas look at her—like a spider contemplating a particularly delectable fly? His brother should find a pair of glasses. She narrowed her gaze right back. "So, you'll hunt me down if I hurt him?"

He laughed, and the derisive note reminded her again of Lucas. They didn't look so much alike but they did have a similar warped sense of humor, apparently.

"I highly doubt you have the capacity to hurt Lucas. He's pretty good at staying emotionally removed from women. For example, he didn't blink when he found out about Lana. Just moved right along to the next one."

As warnings went, it was effective—if she'd been harboring some romantic illusion about Lucas's feelings toward her. "How many of the next ones did Lucas marry?"

"Touché." Her brother-in-law eyed her and then nodded to an older couple who'd swept past them on the way to the bar. "I know you're not after Lucas's money. I checked out you and your trust fund. I'm curious, though, why didn't you stay at Manzanares?"

The loaded question—and Matthew's bold and unapologetic prying—stomped on her defenses. "I worked there for a year to appease my grandfather. I'm probably the only one he'd trust to take over." Shrugging, she wrapped it up. She didn't owe him any explanations. "It's not my passion, so he plans to live forever, I guess."

Matthew didn't smile. Thank goodness Lucas had been the one in need of a wife and not his brother. There was a brittleness to Matthew Wheeler, born of losing someone who meant everything, and she recognized it all too well.

In contrast, Lucas played at life, turning the mundane fun, and he smiled constantly in a sexy, self-assured way, which sometimes caught her with a lovely twist in the abdomen. That was the thing she liked most about him.

Dios. When had that happened?

"Family may not mean much to you, Cia. But it's everything to us." Matthew's expression hardened, and she revised her opinion. The frozen cerulean of his irises scarcely resembled the stunning smoky blue of Lucas's. "Lana punched a hole in Lucas's pride, which is easily dismissed, but in the process, she nearly destroyed a century of my family's hard work. That's not so easily overcome. Be an asset to him. That's all I'll say."

Matthew clammed up as Lucas rejoined them with a deceptively casual hand to the place where her neck and shoulder met. The dress she wore nearly covered her from head to foot and yet her husband managed to find the one bare spot on her body to brush with his electric fingertips.

She'd missed him. And no way would she ever admit it.

"Dinner's on," he told Matthew. "I'll call you later."

Matthew's advice echoed in her head as she let Lucas lead her to his car. Well, she was here, wasn't she? There was also a contract somewhere in Lucas's possession granting him the sales rights to the Manzanares complex, which Abuelo had gladly signed.

Her relationship with Lucas was as equitable as possible. How much more of an asset could she be?

Regardless, all through dinner she thought about Fergie.

And the house. She wore the Versace and the diamond rings her husband had selected. The scales in her mind unbalanced, and she was ashamed Matthew had to be the one to point out how little she'd given Lucas in return for throwing his strengths on the table.

She'd been so focused on making sure she didn't fall for his seduce-and-conquer routine, she'd forgotten they had an agreement.

Their partnership wasn't equitable at all, not with her shrewish behavior and giving him a hard time about attending a social event. She should have been glad to attend, but she wasn't because her husband was too much of a temptation to be around.

Lucas didn't try to kiss her or anything at the end of the evening, and she reminded herself four times how pleased she was the back-off messages were sinking in.

She slept fitfully that night and woke in the morning to dreary storm clouds, which she should have taken as a warning to stay in bed.

A young Hispanic woman in a crisp uniform was scrubbing the sink when Cia walked into the kitchen.

The girl smiled. *"Buenos días, señora."*

Cia looked over her shoulder automatically and then cursed. *She* was the *señora,* at least for the next few months. "Good morning," she responded in Spanish. "I'm sorry, I didn't realize Mr. Wheeler hired a maid."

Of course if he'd bothered to tell her, she would have. Men.

"I'm to come three days a week, with strict instructions you must be happy with my work." The girl bobbed her head and peeled yellow latex gloves from her hands, which she dropped into the sink. "I've already cleaned the master suite. With your permission, I'd like to show you what I've done."

"Sure." Cia was halfway to the stairs before the raucous clang of a big, fat warning bell went off in her head. "You, um, cleaned the master suite? The bathroom, too?" Where there was a noticeable lack of cosmetics, hair dryer or conditioner.

Her heart flipped into overtime.

Satanás en un palo. The maid had cleaned Lucas's bedroom while Cia slept in her room down the hall. They might as well have put out a full-page ad in the *Dallas Morning News*—Mr. and Mrs. Lucas Wheeler Don't Share a Bedroom.

While the maid politely pointed out the sparkling tile and polished granite vanity in the master bathroom, Cia listened with about a quarter of her attention and spent the other three-quarters focusing on how to fix it.

Lucas had royally screwed up. Not on purpose. But still.

"So you'll be back on Wednesday?" Cia asked when the maid finished spouting about the cleaning process.

"Tomorrow, if acceptable. This week, I have Wednesday off. And then back again on Friday."

Of course she'd be back tomorrow. "Fine. That's fine. Your work is exceptional, and I'm very pleased with it. Please let me know when you've finished for the day."

The maid nodded and went off to clean, oblivious to Cia's ruined day. Cia called the shelter to let them know she'd be unavoidably late and sent Lucas a text message: Come home before eight. I have to talk to you.

The second the maid's compact car backed out of the driveway, Cia started transferring her clothes into Lucas's bedroom. Fortunately, there was a separate, empty walk-in closet inside the bathroom. It took twelve trips, fourteen deep breaths and eight minutes against the wall in a fetal position, forehead clamped between her fingers, to get all her clothes moved.

Toiletries she moved quickly with a clamped jaw, and then had to stop as soon as she opened the first dresser drawer, which contained tank tops and drawstring shorts. Sleepwear.

She'd have to sleep in the same room with Lucas. On the floor. Because there was no way she'd sleep in the same bed.

No way she'd sleep in it even if he wasn't in it. No doubt the sheets smelled all pine-tree-like and outdoorsy and Lucas-y.

And, boy, wouldn't the floor be comfortable? Especially with Lucas breathing and rustling and throwing the covers off his hard, tanned body as he slept a few feet away.

God, he better be several feet away. What if he pounced on the opportunity to try to sweet-talk her into bed?

What if? Like there was a snowball's chance he'd pass up the opportunity. And after last night, with the dress and the warm hand on her shoulder all evening and the way he kept knocking down her preconceptions of him, there was a tiny little corner of her mind afraid she'd let herself be swept away by the man she'd married.

Her feminine parts had been ignored for far too long—but not long enough to forget how much of a mess she'd been after the last time she'd jumped into bed, sure that *this* was finally the right man to heal the pain from losing her parents, only to scare yet another one away with colossal emotional neediness.

She was pretty passionate about whatever she touched, and there weren't many men who could handle it, especially not when it was coupled with an inadvertent drive to compensate for the gaping wound in her soul. Until she figured out how to be in a relationship without exposing all the easy-to-lose parts of herself, the best policy was never to get involved— or to get out as quickly as possible.

There had to be another way to solve this problem with the maid besides sleeping in the same room with Lucas. What if she moved her stuff to Lucas's room and got ready for bed there but slept in her room? She could get up early the days the maid came and make up the bed like she'd never been there. Or maybe she could pretend the maid hadn't met her standards and dismiss her. Maybe moving her stuff was a total overreaction.

Her phone beeped. She pulled it from her back pocket. Incoming text from Lucas: What's wrong? What do you need to talk about?

She texted him back: It's an in-person conversation. BTW, how did you find the maid?

In thirty seconds, the message alert beeped again. Lucas: She just started working for my mother and came highly recommended by your grandfather. Why?

Abuelo. She moaned and sank to the floor, resting her forehead on the open drawer full of sleepwear.

Well, if anything, she'd underreacted. The maid was her grandfather's spy, commissioned to spill her guts about Cia's activities at the shelter, no doubt. Abuelo probably didn't even anticipate the coup of information coming his way about the living arrangements.

It was too late to dismiss her. Imagine the conversation where she said a maid who was good enough for Lucas's mother wasn't good enough for Cia. And was she really going to fire a maid who probably sent at least fifty percent of her take-home pay back to extended family in Mexico?

Not only did she and Lucas need to be roommates by tomorrow, she'd have to come up with a plausible reason why they hadn't been thus far and a way to tell the maid casually.

With a grimace, she weaved to her feet and started yanking tank tops out of the drawer, studiously avoiding thoughts about bedrooms, Lucas, beds and later.

Beep. Lucas: Still there? What's up?

Quickly, she tapped out a response: Yeah. No prob with the maid. Late for work. Talk 2U tonight. Have a good day.

She cringed. Wait until he found out his wife telling him to have a good day was the least of the surprises in store.

Seven

Lucas rescheduled three showings he could not afford to put off and pulled into the garage at home by five, thanks to no small effort and a white-knuckle drive at ten over the speed limit. Suspense gnawed at his gut. Something was wrong, and Cia being so closemouthed about it made it ten times worse. Most women considered it worthy of a hysterical phone call if the toilet overflowed or if they backed the car into the fence. With his wife, the problem could range from serious, like the shelter closing down, to dire, like her grandfather dying.

Cia's car wasn't in the garage or the driveway, so he waited in the kitchen. And waited. After forty-five minutes, it was clear she must be working late. More than a little irritated, he went upstairs to change. As he yanked a T-shirt over his head, he caught sight of the vanity through the open bathroom door.

The counter had been empty when he left this morning. Now it wasn't.

A mirrored tray sat between the twin sinks, loaded with

lotion and other feminine stuff. He picked up the lotion and opened it to inhale the contents. Yep. Coconut and lime.

In four seconds, he put the cryptic text messages from Cia together with the addition of this tray, a pink razor, shaving cream and at least six bottles of who knew what lining the stone shelf in the shower.

The maid had spooked Cia into moving into the master bedroom. Rightly so, if the maid had come recommended by Cia's grandfather, a detail he hadn't even considered a problem at the time.

Man, he should have thought of that angle long ago. In a few hours, Cia might very well be sleeping in his bed.

He whistled a nameless tune as he meandered back to the kitchen. No wonder Cia was avoiding home as long as possible, because she guessed—correctly—he'd be all over this new development like white on rice. Her resistance to the true benefit of marriage was weakening. Slowly. Tonight might be the push over the edge she needed.

At seven o'clock, he sent her a text message to find out what time she'd be home. And got no answer.

At eight o'clock he called, but she didn't pick up. In one of her texts, she'd mentioned being late for work. Maybe she'd stayed late to make up for it. He ate a roast beef sandwich and drank a dark beer. Every few bites, he coaxed Fergie to say his name.

But every time he said, "Lucas. Looo-kaaaas," she squawked and ruffled her feathers. Sometimes she imitated Cia's ringtone. But mostly the parrot waited for him to shove a piece of fruit through the bars, then took it immediately in her sharp claws.

At nine-thirty, Lucas realized he didn't know the names of Cia's friends and, therefore, couldn't start calling to see if they'd heard from her. There was avoidance, and then there was late.

Besides, Cia met everything head-on, especially him. Radio silence wasn't like her.

At eleven o'clock, as he stared at the TV while contemplating a call to the police to ask about accidents involving a red Porsche, the automatic garage door opener whirred.

A beat later, Cia trudged into the kitchen, shoulders hunched and messy hair falling in her face.

"Hey," he said.

"Hey," she repeated, her voice thinner than tissue paper. "Sorry. I got your messages."

"I was kind of worried."

"I know." The shadows were back in full force, and there was a deep furrow between her eyes he immediately wanted to soothe away.

"I'm sorry," she repeated. "It was unavoidable. I'm sure you saw my stuff in your room."

None of this seemed like the right lead-up to a night of blistering passion. "I did. So we're sharing a bedroom now?"

She squeezed her temples between a thumb and her middle finger, so hard the nail beds turned white. "Only because it's necessary. Give me fifteen minutes, and then you can come in."

Necessary. Like it was some big imposition to sleep in his bed. He knew a woman or two who'd be there in a heartbeat to take her place. Why couldn't he be interested in one of them instead of his no-show wife, who did everything in her power to avoid the best benefit of marriage?

Fearful of what he might say if he tried to argue, he let her go without another word and gave her twenty minutes, exactly long enough for his temper to flare.

He was married, mad and celibate, and the woman responsible for all three lay in his bed.

When he strode into the bedroom, it was dark, so he felt his way into the bathroom, got ready for bed and opted to sleep naked, like normal. This was his room and since she'd moved into it without asking, she could deal with all that entailed.

He hit the button on the TV remote. She better be a heavy sleeper, because he always watched TV in bed, and he wasn't changing his habits to suit anyone, least of all a prickly wife who couldn't follow her own mandate to be home by eight.

The soft light of the flat screen mounted on the wall spilled over the empty bed. He glanced over at it. Yep, empty. Where was she?

A pile of sheets on the floor by the bay windows answered that question. "Cia, what are you doing over there?"

"Sleeping," came the muffled reply from the mass of dark hair half-buried under the pile.

Since she still faced the wall, he turned the volume down on the TV. "You can't sleep on the floor."

"Yes, I can."

"This bed is a California king. Two people could easily sleep in it without touching the entire night." Could. But that didn't necessarily mean he'd guarantee it. Although, given his mood, he was pretty sure he'd have no problem ignoring the unwilling woman in his bed.

After a lengthy pause, she mumbled, "It's your bed. I'm imposing on you. The floor is fine."

The martyr card. Great. A strangled sigh pushed out through his clamped teeth. "Get in the bed. I'll sleep on the floor."

"No. That's not fair. Besides, I like the floor. This carpet is very soft."

"Well, then." Two could play that game. "Since it's so comfortable, I'll sleep on the floor, too."

With a hard yank, he pulled the top sheet out from under the comforter, wrapped it around his waist and threw a pillow on the floor a foot from hers. As he reclined on the scratchy carpet, she rolled over and glared at him.

"Stop being so stubborn, Wheeler. The bed is yours. Sleep in it."

Coconut and lime hit his nose, and the resulting pang to the abdomen put a spike in his temper. "Darlin', you go right ahead and blow every gasket in that pretty little head of yours. I'm not sleeping in the bed when you're on the floor. It's not right."

She made a frustrated noise in her throat. "Why do you always have to be such a gentleman about *everything?*"

"'Cause I like to irritate you," he said easily.

She flipped back to face the wall. As he was about to snap out more witticisms, her shoulders started shaking.

"Hey," he called. "Are you crying?"

"No," she hissed, followed by a wrenching sob.

"Aw, honey, please don't cry. If it'll make you feel better, you can call my mother and yell at her for teaching me manners. Either way, I'm not sleeping in the bed unless you do."

This pronouncement was greeted with a flurry of sobbing. Every ounce of temper drained away.

Obviously, his manners weren't as well practiced as he'd bragged, and he'd been too worked up to remember arguing and prickliness were Cia's way of deflecting the comfort she sorely needed but refused to ask for.

He scuttled forward and cursed the binding sheet and sandpaper carpet impeding his progress, but finally he wormed close enough to gather her in his arms. "Shh. It's okay."

She stiffened as the war going on inside her spread out to encompass her whole body. Then, all at once, she surrendered, melting into a puddle of soft, sexy woman against him, nestling her head on his shoulder and settling her very nice backside tight against his instantly firm front side.

Hell on a horse. He'd only been trying to get her to stop crying. He honestly expected her to kick him away. The sheet chafed against his bare erection, spearing his lower half with white-hot splinters. He sucked in a breath and let it out slowly. It didn't help.

Prickly Cia he could resist all day long. Vulnerable Cia got under his skin.

Her trim body was racked with sobs against his, yet he was busy trying to figure out what she had on under that pile of sheets. *Moron.*

He shut his eyes and pulled her tighter into his arms, where she could sob to her heart's content for as long as it took. His arousal ached every time he moved, but he stroked her hair and kept stroking until she fell still a million excruciating years later.

"Sorry." She sniffed into the sudden silence. "I'm just so tired."

He kept stroking her hair in case the torrent wasn't over. And because he liked the feel of its dark glossiness. "That wasn't tired. That was distraught."

"Yeah." A long sigh pushed her chest against his forearm. "But I'm tired, too. So tired I can't pretend I hate it when you calm me down. I don't know what's worse, the day I had or having to admit you've got the touch."

His hand froze, dark strands of her hair still threaded through his fingers. "What's so bad about letting me make you feel better?"

She twisted out of his arms and impaled him with the evil eye. "I hate being weak. I hate you seeing my weaknesses. I hate—"

"Not being able to do everything all by yourself," he finished and propped his head up with a hand since she was no longer curled in his arms. "You hate not being a superhero. I get it. Lie down now and take a deep breath. Tell me what tall building you weren't able to leap today, the one that made you cry."

Her constant inner battle played out over her face. She fought everything, even herself. No wonder she was tired.

With a shuddery sigh, she lay on the pillow, facing him, and light from the TV highlighted her delicate cheekbones. Such a paradox, the delicacy outside veiling the core of steel inside. Something hitched in his chest.

Oh, yeah. This strong woman hated falling. But he liked being the only one she would let catch her.

"One of the women at the shelter…" she began and then faltered. Threading their fingers together, he silently encouraged her to go on. A couple of breaths later, she did. "Pamela. She went back to her husband. That bastard broke her arm when he shoved her against a wall. And she went back to him. I tried to talk her out of it. For hours. Courtney talked to her, too. Nothing we said mattered."

He vaguely recalled Courtney was Cia's friend and also her partner in the new shelter. A psychologist. "You can't save everyone."

She pulled their fingers apart. "I'm not trying to save everyone. Just Pamela. I work with these women every day, instilling confidence. Helping them see they can be self-sufficient…" Her voice cracked.

She looked at this as failure—as her failure. Because these women, and what she hoped to accomplish with them, meant something, and she believed in both. It went way past fulfilling her mother's wishes. Her commitment was awe inspiring.

The line between her eyes reappeared. "She threw it all out to go back to a man who abused her. He might kill her next time. What could possibly be worth that?"

"Hope," he said, knowing his little psych minor couldn't see past her hang-ups. "Hope people can change. Hope it might be different this time."

"But why? She has to know it's got a one hundred percent certainty of ending badly."

"Honey, I hate to rain on your parade, but people naturally seek companionship. We aren't meant to be alone, despite all your insistence to the contrary. This Pamela needs to hope the person she chose to marry is redeemable so they can get on with their lives together. Without hope, she has nothing."

Hair spilled into her face when she shook her head. "That's not true. She has herself, the only person she can truly rely on. The only person who can make sure she's taken care of."

"Are you talking about Pamela or Cia?"

"Don't go thinking you're smart for shoving a mirror in my face. It's true for both of us, and I've never had any illusions about my beliefs, particularly in relation to men."

"Illusions, no. Blind spots, yes." He ventured a little closer. "You're so black-and-white. You saw the trust clause and assumed your grandfather intended to manipulate you into a marriage where you'd be dominated by a man. You said it yourself. He wants you to be taken care of. Allowing someone to take care of you isn't weakness."

Her mouth tightened. "I can take care of myself. I have money, I have the ability to—"

"Darlin', there's more to being cared for than money." He swept a lock of hair off her shoulder and used the proximity as an excuse to run his hand across her silky skin again. "You have physical needs, too."

"Oh, my God. You do indeed have a gift. How in the world did you manage to drop sex into this conversation?"

He grinned in spite of the somber tone of their illuminating conversation. "Hey, I didn't say anything about sex. That was you. I was talking about holding you while you cry. But if you want to talk about sex, I could find some room in my schedule. Maybe start with telling me the most sensitive place on your body. Keep in mind, I'll want to test it, so be honest."

She smacked him on the arm without any real heat. "You're unbelievable. I'm not having sex with you simply because we've been forced into sharing a room."

Touching him on purpose. Would wonders never cease? He caught her gaze. "Then do it because you want to."

Her frame bristled from crown to toe, and the sheet slipped

down a few tantalizing inches. "I don't want to, Wheeler! You think you're God's gift to women and it never occurs to you some of us are immune to all your charm and…and—" her hungry gaze skittered over his chest, which he had not hidden under a sheet mummy-style, like she had "—sexiness. Stop trying to add another notch to your bedpost."

Could she have protested any more passionately? "Okay."

"Okay?" One eye narrowed and skewered him. "Just like that, you're giving up?"

"That was not an okay of concession. It was an okay, it's time to change the subject. Roll over."

"What? Why?"

A growl rumbled through his chest. "Because I said so. You need to relax or you'll never go to sleep. If you don't go to sleep, you'll keep arguing with me, and then I won't sleep. I'm just going to massage your shoulders. So shut up and do it."

Warily, she rolled, and he peeled the sheet from her as she spun, resettling it at her waist. Tank top with spaghetti straps. Not the sexiest of nightclothes, but when he lifted the dark curtain of hair away from her neck, the wide swath of bare skin from the middle of her back up to her hairline pleaded for his touch.

So he indulged.

First, he traced the ridges of her spine with his fingertips, imprinting the textures against his skin. Once he reached her neck, he went for her collarbone, following it around to the front and back again.

She felt amazing.

He wanted more of her naked flesh under his fingers. Under his body. Shifting against his skin, surrounding him with a hot paradox of hard and soft.

The stupid floor blocked his reach, so he settled for running his fingers over her exposed arm, trying to gauge whether she'd notice if he slipped the tank top strap off her shoulder.

"What, exactly, are you doing?" She half rolled to face him. "This is the least relaxing massage I've ever had."

"Really?" he asked nonchalantly and guided her back into place. No way was he missing a second of unchecked access to Cia. "Someone who's immune to my charms should have no problem relaxing while I'm impersonally rubbing her shoulders."

"Hmpf." She flipped back to face the wall. Must not hate it too much.

He let the grin spread wide and kneaded her neck muscles. "Darlin', there's no sin in enjoying it when someone touches you."

She snorted but choked on it as his hand slid up the inside of her arm again and a stray finger stroked her breast. He needed the tank top gone and that breast cupped in his palm.

"There is the way you do it," she rasped.

"You know," he said, closing the gap between them, spooning her heated back to murmur in her ear, a millimeter from taking the smooth lobe into his mouth. "I don't for a moment believe I'm God's gift to women. Women are God's gift to man. The female form is the most wonderful sight on earth. The beautiful design of your throat, for example."

He dragged his mouth away from her ear and ran his lips down the column of her neck. "I could live here for a decade and never completely discover all the things I love about it," he said, mouthing the words against her skin.

He was so hard and so ready to sink into her, his teeth hurt.

Her head fell back onto his shoulder, her eyes closed and her lashes fluttered, fully exposing the area under discussion. Her sweet little body arched in wanton invitation, spreading against his. He wanted to dive in, find Dulciana's gorgeous, gooey center and feast on it.

This visceral attraction would be satisfied, here and now.

"Lucas," she breathed, and his erection pulsed. "Lucas, we can't. You have to stop."

"Why?" He slid a hand under her tank top, fanning his palm out on her flat stomach and working it north. Slowly. Familiarizing his fingertips with velvety skin. "And if you use that smart mouth to lie to me again about your lack of interest, I will find something better to do with it."

"I doubt even I could pull off that lie anymore," she said wryly.

The admission was so sweet, he couldn't help it.

He found her lips and consumed them, kissing her with every bit of frustrated, pent-up longing. And God Almighty, her lips parted just enough, and he pushed his tongue into her mouth, tasting her, reveling in the hot slide of flesh.

For a few magnificent seconds she tasted him back, triggering a hard coil of lust.

But then she ripped her lips away, mumbling, "No more," as his thumb brushed the underside of her breast.

She bowed up with a gasp, and his erection tingled. She was so responsive, like it had been ages since she'd... He pulled his hand free and gripped her chin to peer into her eyes. "Hold up a sec. You're not a virgin, are you?"

That would explain a few things.

He let his fingers fall away as she sat up. "My past experience is not the issue. We agreed to keep this business only."

No. No more of this endless circling. *Business only* disappeared eons ago, and she knew it as well as he did.

"Why are you here, in my bedroom? You could have easily moved your stuff and still slept in your room. But you didn't. Your signals are so mixed up, you've even confused yourself. Talk to me, honey. No more pretending. Why the roadblocks, when it's obvious we both want this?"

She crossed her arms and clamped her mouth shut. But then she said, "I don't like being some big challenge. If I give in, you win. Then off you go to your cave to beat your chest and crow over your prize."

"Give in?" He shook his head to clear it. They should both

be naked and using their mouths on each other. Not talking. "You better believe you challenge me. Something fierce, too, I'll admit. You challenge me to be better than I ever thought I could be, to rise to the occasion and go deep so I can keep up. I dig that seven ways to Sunday. Feel what you do to me, Cia."

Her eyes went liquid as he flattened her hand over his thundering heart, and when the muscle under her cool palm flexed, she curled her fingers as if trying to capture his response. She weaved closer, drawn by invisible threads into his space.

"You're so incredibly intelligent," he continued, fighting to keep from dragging her against him and sinking in like he ached to do. She had to choose this on her own. "How have you not figured out that gives you all the power? I'm just a poor, pathetic man who wants to worship at the altar of the goddess."

She hesitated, indecision and longing stamped all over her face. Whatever stopped her from jumping in—and it wasn't dislike of being a challenge—drove the battle inside of her to a fever pitch. She spent way too much energy thinking instead of feeling and way too much time buried in shadows.

And here he was trying to help her fix that, if she'd lay down that stubborn for a minute.

"You're the strongest woman I've ever met, and I like that about you," he said. "We both know strings aren't part of the deal. This is about one thing only. Sex. Fantastic, feel-good, uncomplicated sex. Nobody gets hurt. Everyone has fun. Sounds perfect for an independent woman with a divorce on the horizon, doesn't it?"

"Seducing me with logic. Devious."

"But effective."

The curve of her lips set off a tremor in his gut. "It's getting there."

Hallelujah. He threw his last-ditch inside straight on the table. "Then listen close. Let me take care of you. Physically. You give to your women till it hurts. Take for once. Let me make you feel good. Let me help you forget the rest of the world for a while. Use me, I insist. Do I benefit from it, too? Absolutely. That's what makes for a great partnership."

He'd laid the foundation for a new, mutually beneficial agreement. The next move had to be hers. She needed to be in control of her fate, and he needed to know she could never accuse him of talking her into it.

"Now, darlin', the floor sucks. I'm going to get in that nice, comfortable bed over there and if you want to spend the next few hours being thoroughly pleasured, join me. If not, don't. You make the choice."

Eight

Choice.

Instead of seducing her, Lucas had given her a choice. And with that single empowering act, Cia's uncertainty disappeared.

They were partners—equals—and he'd done nothing but respect that, and respect her, from the very beginning. He got her in ways she'd only begun to realize. Domination was not part of his makeup, and all he wanted from her was to join him in taking pleasure from sex, the way he took pleasure from every aspect of life.

She longed to indulge in the foreign concept, to seize what she wanted—Lucas.

To let his talents wash away all the doubt and frustration and disappointment about Pamela and help Cia forget everything except how he made her feel. He'd stripped the complexity from the equation and, suddenly, sex didn't mean she'd lose something.

The only way Lucas Wheeler could take a chunk of her

soul when he left was if she gave it to him. She wouldn't. Simple as making a choice. Who knew the secret to avoiding emotional evisceration was to lay out divorce terms first?

She stood and crossed the carpet with sure steps until her knees hit the side of the bed. Lucas lounged against a pillow, watching her, sheet pulled up to midtorso, bisecting the trio of intriguing tribal circles tattooed along the left edge of his ribs.

His eyes were on fire.

He was so gorgeous, and he was all hers for the night. As many nights as she chose, apparently. A shiver shimmied up her back, part anticipation and part nerves.

"You want to know what tipped the scales?" she asked, arms crossed so it wasn't obvious her hands were shaking.

"More than I want to take my next breath."

She eyed the length of his body stretched out in the bed. "Ironically, that you were willing to sleep on the floor."

He laughed, and the vibration thrummed through her abdomen. "So you're saying I had you at hello?"

"No. I'm pretty sure you had me at Versace. It's painful to admit I was so easily bought with a designer gown." She said it flippantly, so he'd know she was kidding.

Except she wasn't, exactly. It was difficult to swallow how much she liked his gifts. What did that say about her?

"I'm glad one of us thinks this was easy. I've never worked so hard to get a woman into bed in my life."

"An unrecoverable blow to your ego, no doubt." She cocked her hip and jammed a hand down on it. Had she been so exhausted less than an hour ago that she could barely stand? Adrenaline and a hefty craving for Lucas coursed through her. "And it's so funny, but I'd swear I'm not actually in bed yet. Perhaps your work isn't done after all."

With a growl, he flung off the sheet, sprang up from the mattress and crawled toward her, completely, beautifully naked. Her mouth went dry.

Wickedness flashed through his expression, and the shiver

it unleashed in her this time was all anticipation. She absolutely could not mistake how much she turned him on.

This was all for her. Not for him. He'd said so, and she intended to hold him to it.

He rose up on his knees in front of her and extended a hand. She took it and braced to be yanked onto the bed. Instead, he held each finger to his lips and kissed them individually. By the time he reached the pinkie, he'd added licking and sucking and the rough texture of his tongue burned across her flesh.

He pressed her palm to his chest and left it there. Then, he cupped her face reverently. "Beautiful. So beautiful."

Before she could squawk out a lame "Thank you," he captured her mouth with his and held the kiss, lips suspended in time, and a tornado of need whirled through her womb.

Slowly, he angled his head and parted her mouth with his lips, and heat poured into her body. His tongue found hers, gliding forward and back in a sensuous dance.

Her nails dug into his rock-hard chest, scrabbling for purchase to keep her off the carpet. The kiss went on and on and stoked the flame of desire higher and higher in her belly.

Slow. It was all about slow with Lucas, and it was exquisite torture. She needed more, needed him now.

She broke away and reached for him, but he shook his head. His hands skimmed up her arms and down her back, came around to the front again, and both thumbs hooked the hem of her tank top. Gradually, he drew it skyward as he watched her from below half-closed lids.

"You're, um, not going to make me get in the bed?" she asked hoarsely.

"Nope." He pulled her top free from her raised arms and tossed it over his shoulder, and then he encircled her waist with an arm to draw her closer, his gaze ravenous as it traveled over her bare breasts. "You chose not to get in bed. I choose to take care of you right where you're at."

Her nipples rubbed his naked torso and beaded instantly and fire erupted in her womb, drawing a moan from deep in her throat. If he kept whispering that whiskey-smooth voice across her bare skin, it wouldn't take long to rip a verbally induced climax out of her. But she hoped for a hands-on approach.

He obliged her. One hand glided to the small of her back and pushed, jutting her breasts up and allowing him to capture a nipple with his tongue in a searing, swirling lasso.

She gripped his shoulders, lost in a slow spiral toward brainlessness as he sucked and laved at her sensitive flesh.

He switched sides and treated the other nipple to his magically delicious mouth. When he skated hard teeth across the peak, her legs buckled. Why hadn't she gotten in bed?

His hand delved inside her shorts, along her bare bottom. His fingers slipped into the crevice, lifting her and crushing her to his torso, supporting her.

The shock of Lucas touching her *there* had her gasping, but a solid pang of want swallowed the shock. *"Madre de Dios."*

Lucas groaned against her breast. With it still in his mouth, he mumbled, "I love it when you talk dirty."

A throaty laugh burst out of her. "It means mother of God, dingbat."

"I don't care. Anything you say in Spanish sounds dirty. Say something else." He licked his way down her stomach and bit the tie on her shorts, pulling the strings loose with his mouth.

"Quiero que ahora—"

And then her brain shut off when he yanked down her shorts and panties. He turned her and pressed her spine to his torso, settling her rear against his hard length. His firm arm snaked between her breasts, locking her in place, and his clever fingers slid down her stomach to find her center.

He mouthed her throat and rubbed the hard button between

her folds until she squirmed against the restraining band of steel disguised as his arm.

One finger slid inside and then two, in and out, and her head rolled against his shoulder in a mindless thrash. So good, so hot. So everything.

His heavy arousal burned into the soft flesh of her bottom, thrilling her. His thumb worked her nub in a circle and the sensuous onslaught swirled into one bright gathering point against his fingers. She came so hard she cried out.

The ripples tightened her inner walls around his fingers, and he plunged his fingers in again and again to draw out the climax to impossible lengths until, finally, it ended in a spectacular burst.

Lucas had just ruined her for any other man.

Too spent to stand on her own, she slumped in his arms and her knees gave out. The additional weight must have caught him off guard, and she pulled him down with her. In a tangle of limbs, they hit the carpet, and Lucas laughed as he rolled her back into his arms.

"There you have it," he said into her hair. "Now we don't have to lie. Next time someone asks why we got married, you can truthfully say we fell for each other."

A giggle slipped out and cleared the fog in her head, along with any lingering tension from being with Lucas, naked and exposed. His ability to bring the fun was unparalleled.

He picked her up and laid her gently on the bed.

"The first one is for you," he said, eyes crystal clear blue and dazzling. "The next one is for me."

"That's fair." She cleared her throat. He deserved more than she knew how to give him. "Lucas? I'm nowhere near as um…practiced at this as you are. However, I promise to give it my best shot."

She dragged an elbow under her to sit up but he knocked it away. She flopped back on the tangle of sheets and watched as he straddled her, powerful thighs preventing his gorgeous body from crushing her.

All of him was beautiful, but in this position, the really good stuff lay at eye level. She didn't hesitate to look her fill and reached out to run her palms along his legs. So hard and so delectable.

"No." He shook his head. "*Your* next orgasm is for me. The first one doesn't count. It's only to take the edge off, and, honey, you were wound tight. I barely touched you and you went off like a Roman candle."

She moaned. "That was a demonstration of 'barely'?"

With a wicked smile, he laced their fingers together and drew her arms up above her head, manacled her wrists together with one hand and slid the other hand down the length of her side from shoulder to hip. "Oh, yeah. There's much, much more. But this time, I get to pick where you'll be, and it'll be right here, where I can watch you."

He began to touch her, watching her as he did, and his heavy-lidded stare unnerved her, even as it heightened the sensations of his hands and mouth on her bare skin. He did something sinful to every inch of her body until she couldn't breathe with the need for him to fill her.

Why had she resisted a man with Lucas's skill for so long? There wasn't a whole lot of taking pleasure necessary when he gave it so freely. How selfish was she that she stingily upped it up?

After what felt like hours of lovely agony, he settled between her legs and his talented mouth dipped to the place he'd pleasured with his fingers. With his lips and teeth and, oh, yes, his tongue working her flesh, he drove her into the heavens a second time.

His eyes never left her, and her shuddering release intensified with the knowledge that he was watching her, taking his own pleasure in hers. The manifestation of the power he spoke of, the power she held, was exhilarating.

"Enough," she gasped. "I admit it. You were right. I could have slept in my room, but I guess part of me wanted you to force the issue. So I could keep pretending I'm not attracted to you. No more pretending. I want you. Now."

"That might be the sweetest confession I've ever heard." He rose up over her and captured her mouth in way-too-short, musky kiss. "But we have all night. And tomorrow night. So, slow down, darlin'. Half the fun is getting there."

"How is it not making you insane to keep waiting your turn?"

He laughed and threaded his hands through her hair in a long caress. "Good things come to those who wait. Besides, I'm dead center in the middle of my turn. Every nuance of desire flashing through your eyes turns me on. Every moan from your mouth is like music. I could watch you shatter for hours."

Hours? *Dios.* She should have read between the lines a little better when he blew off the pregnancy issue back by the pool. "You, um, do plan to eventually get around to a more traditional version of sex. Right?"

"Oh, you better believe it, honey. Later."

Later. She loved later.

Sacrifice and selflessness had ruled her for so long, it felt incredible to let go. To let Lucas take care of her. To be greedy for once and wallow in pure sensation and pleasure instead of shoving aside her needs for fear everything she depended on would be taken away in an instant.

How freeing to have it all on the table and be given permission to just have fun.

For all his talk, Lucas almost lost it—again—during Cia's third climax.

She was beautiful, like Mozart at sunrise, and she was so sensitive, he set off the third one accidentally by blowing on her. She cried out his name and exploded, bowing up with that awesome arch to her back, and an answering pulse grew stronger in his gut.

He clamped his teeth down hard to keep his own release under control. His muscles strained, aching with the effort it took not to plow into her sweet, sweet center right then and there, no condom, just her and unbelievable satisfaction.

The battle stretched out for an eternity and, for a moment, he feared he'd do it. He rolled away and fixated on the oscillating ceiling fan above the bed, willing back the crush of lust.

This little fireball he'd married was not going to break his self-control. Never mind that he'd invented this game of multiple orgasms to demonstrate this was nothing but sex between two people who were hot for each other. To confirm that this insane attraction wasn't as strong as he'd imagined and that there was nothing special about this particular woman.

Somewhere along the way, the scent of Cia's arousal and the total surrender in her responses eliminated his intentions.

She fell back onto the pillow with a sexy sigh, lifting her breasts and making his mouth water. "You melted my bones that time. As soon as I can walk, I'm going to make you the best cup of coffee you've ever had in your life."

That pulled a chuckle out of him, though it hurt clear to his knees to laugh. "The benefits are good enough to reverse your stance on making a man coffee, huh?"

"I cannot believe there wasn't a picket line of your ex-lovers at the courthouse the day we got married."

Yeah, he knew a trick or two about pleasuring a woman, and his genuine enjoyment of it helped, but this was a far cry from how he normally went about it. Nothing about this affair with Cia remotely resembled how he normally interacted with a woman.

How did he explain that to her when he didn't get it, either?

"You're funny. There are more women who would be happy to read my obituary notice than would be upset I married you."

She snorted. "I doubt that. But as your wife, I believe I have the right to claim a few privileges."

If he breathed through his mouth, he couldn't smell her lotion anymore, and the lack eased the pain a tiny bit. "Yeah? Like what?"

"Like the right to say it's later."

Without another word, she flipped and crawled on top of him, sliding up the length of his body, hot as a lava flow, and whipping his crushing need into a frenetic firestorm.

Her eyes were so dark, they were almost black. They met his with thirst in their depths. The evidence of her desire lanced through his gut.

Her mouth fit to his, pulling on his lips and sucking his tongue forward. A guttural moan wrenched free from his throat, and she absorbed it into the heat of her kiss. He flung his arms around her and bound her to his chest, desperate to keep her in place.

The things this woman did to him. It defied description. Thankfully, she'd agreed to exorcise this wicked draw between them by acting on it instead of pretending it didn't exist.

Long dark hair fell into his face, trailing along his fevered skin, sensitizing it and begging for attention. He wound it up in a fist and guided her head to the side, lips following the line of her neck with fierce suction, laving her skin with his tongue, crazy with the craving to taste her.

Lime and coconut invaded his senses, both curse and cure, snaking through his head like a narcotic, heightening the wild lust.

Her body covered his, scalding breasts flat against his chest, her hands shoved in his hair, fingers sparking where she touched his scalp. One leg straddled him, opening her up. Her hips gyrated and tilted her center against his throbbing tip. Damp heat flared out, enveloping him, and his eyes glazed

Now. The keening scream exploded in his head as she dragged her slick center up the length of his erection.

"Wait," he bit out, with no idea whether he was talking to her or his questing hips, which had a mind of their own.

He stretched out a hand to fumble with the drawer knob on the bedside table, shifting her center. Should have already had a foil packet under the pillow, top torn off. Fingers closed over the box and an eternity later, he unrolled the condom.

The second he was sheathed, Cia wiggled back into place atop him, nudged him once and impaled herself to the hilt with a feminine gasp.

His eyelids snapped shut as he filled her. His body shrieked to start pumping, but he forced himself to give her a minute to adjust.

Amazing. So tight. He pulsed as she stretched to accommodate him. Stretched perfectly, just enough, just right. Experimentally, she slid up and back down, rolling her pelvis, driving him home.

Home. A place for him. Only him.

He echoed her hip thrusts and heaviness built upon itself, spiraling higher and energizing him to move faster and faster.

"Lucas," she breathed. "I... Will you, um, look at me? I like it when you watch me."

He worked his lids open and greedily soaked in the visual perfection of the female form astride him. Why had his eyes been closed this whole time? The empowerment, the sheer magnificence, plastered across her face forced all the air from his lungs in a hard whoosh.

He'd done that for her. Unleashed her desire from its boundaries and allowed her free rein to take pleasure from his body, exactly as he'd insisted.

And she was taking it. Acknowledging it. Returning it unfold. It was unbelievably hot.

Her torso undulated in a primal dance, nipples peaked and

firm atop alabaster breasts. She threw her head back, plunging him deeper, and long hair brushed his thighs.

Sparkling pressure radiated from his groin. Willing it back, he clamped a hand on her thigh, trying to slow her wanton thrusts, but she bucked against him and the tightness shoved him to the very edge.

He couldn't stop. He couldn't wait for her.

But then she came apart and the shock waves blasted down his length, triggering his release. Their simultaneous climaxes fed each other, like oxygen to a flame, dragging out the sensations and flooding his whole body with warmth.

Flooding his body with something else, something nameless and heavy and powerful.

With a sated moan, she collapsed against him, nestling into the hollow of his shoulder, and he gripped her close, absorbing every last bit of warmth, too lost in the lush, thick haze of Cia to move. They were still joined, and he basked in a thrilling sense of triumph.

Only with him could Cia be like this.

Now would be an excellent time to put distance between them. But he couldn't find the energy. Couldn't figure out why he wasn't all that interested in distance when he knew he should be. Never had sex been like that, a frantic and mindless rush toward completion.

Completion, not release. Even this—*especially* this—was bigger, stronger and more meaningful with Cia.

He'd proven something to himself, all right. Something earthshaking. Something fearsome. This wasn't casual sex between two people. He'd been making love to his wife.

Nine

In the morning, Cia woke half-buried under Lucas, and it made her smile. One heavy arm pinned her to his chest and his legs tangled with hers, trapping her bottom against his abdomen. His heat at predawn was delicious, warming her sore and stretched body.

It had been a while. Since college, back when she'd still been convinced the right man's love would heal her. All she'd done was prove sex didn't equal love, and both were ingredients in the recipe to misery.

If her high school days had resembled most red-blooded Americans', she might have figured out how to handle relationships then, instead of lumbering into her mid-twenties without a clue. Now she finally got it.

As long as she divorced sex from emotion and commitment, no problem. Divorce rocked.

She unscrambled their limbs without waking him and slipped out of bed to head for a much-needed hot shower. It probably wouldn't have taken any effort at all to nudge

Lucas into semiawareness and then take shameless advantage of him, but she was anxious to get to the shelter. A part of her hoped Pamela would still be there, but in her heart, she knew better. Regardless, the other women would need someone to talk to.

In no time, she dressed and tiptoed out of the bedroom she now shared with the sexy, slumbering man sprawled out across the bed. *Later,* she promised. No-strings-attached sex was the most awesome thing ever invented.

Pamela was indeed gone for good when Cia arrived at the shelter. The other women seemed dejected and upset. How self-centered was she for being in such a good mood, for shutting her eyes and savoring memories of the previous night? But she couldn't help it and had to force herself to stop humming three times while handling the most unexciting tasks.

Since she'd stayed so late the night before and arrived at seven that morning, Cia elected to leave at three.

She should be wiped out, but as she drove home, her mind got busy with one topic only—seeing Lucas again as soon as possible. She couldn't stop fantasizing about him. About the beyond-sexy trio of tattoos down the length of his torso and how she'd like to experiment on him a little to see how many times she could make him explode in a night.

Was it cool to call him and ask about his schedule? She'd almost sent him a text at least once every ten minutes, just to check in. Or say thanks for an awesome time last night. Or something else not so lame, but she had no idea about the rules when the person she was sleeping with was also her fake husband.

They'd done a lot of talking last night. But not once had Lucas mentioned what their relationship would look like going forward.

So frustrating. And ridiculous. It wasn't as if she could casually ask Courtney the requisite number of days to wait before calling when the guy involved was Cia's husband. As far as her friend knew, the marriage was still business only, and Cia wanted to get used to the change before admitting anything to anyone.

Besides, she and Lucas *still* weren't dating. Maybe it was okay to let her spouse know she was into him. In a strictly hot for his body kind of way.

Once at home, she stopped in the kitchen to get a glass of water and drank it while standing at the sink. Before she could swallow the second mouthful, said spouse blew through the door, startling her into dropping the glass into the sink.

"What are you doing home?" she asked.

Lucas strode toward her in a dark suit, which encased his shoulders with perfection, and a dark, impossible-to-misread expression on his face. Raw masculinity whipped through the kitchen to engulf her a moment before the man did.

He caught her in his arms and kissed her, openmouthed, hungrily, working her backward until her butt hit the countertop's edge.

She was trapped between hard granite and hard Lucas, and he was devouring her whole with his mouth. A whirlwind of desire kicked up in her center.

Dull thunks registered, and Lucas's hands delved inside her shirt, yanking down her bra and palming her breasts. Buttons. He'd popped all the buttons on her shirt and they'd thunked to the floor.

Four seconds later, he stripped her. Then he tore off his jacket, ripped the rest of his clothes half off and boosted her onto the counter. Cold stone cooled her bare bottom and sizzled against her fevered core.

Less than five minutes after he'd walked in the door, he spread her legs wide and plunged in with a heavy groan.

She dropped into the spiral of need and hooked her legs behind him, urging him on. His mouth was everywhere, hot and insatiable. His thrusts were hard, fast. She met him each time, already eager for the next one. Pinpoints of sensation swirled and then burst as she came, milking his climax.

What happened to *slow down?*

They slumped together, chests heaving, her head on his shoulder and his head on hers. She put her arms around him for support since her spine had been replaced with Jell-O.

"Um, hi," she said, without a trace of irony. If this was what their relationship would look like going forward, the view agreed with her quite well.

"Hi," he repeated, and she heard the smile in his voice. "How was your day?"

He laughed and it rumbled against her abdomen. "Unproductive except for the last ten minutes. You distracted me all day. Don't disappear tomorrow morning. I'd like to wake up with you."

The explosive countertop sex had been hot, but the simplicity, the normalcy, of his request warmed her. "It's not my fault you're such a heavy sleeper. Set an alarm."

"Maybe I will." Carefully, he separated from her and trashed the condom. He helped her to the floor and gathered up her clothes, which he handed off, then began pulling on his own clothes with casual nonchalance. "I have another favor. I swear I was going to ask first but, darlin', you have to stop looking at me like that when I come in."

When his muscled, inked torso disappeared behind his ruined shirt, she sighed. Those tribal tattoos symbolized Lucas to a T—untamed, unexpected and thoroughly hidden beneath the surface. One of his many layers few people were aware existed, let alone privileged enough to experience. How lucky was she?

"You looked at me first." Of course, he always looked at her like a chocoholic with unlimited credit at the door of a sweetshop. "What's the favor? Do I get another dress out of the deal?"

He grinned and kissed her hand. "Of course. Except this time, I intend to take it off of you afterward."

"Or during." She shrugged and opted to toss her irreparable blouse in the trash. Lucas might end up buying her a new wardrobe after all, by default. "You know, if it's boring and you happen to spy a coat closet or whatever."

His irises flared with heat and zinged her right in the abdomen. "Why, Mrs. Wheeler, that is indeed a fine offer. I will surely keep it under advisement. Come with me and let's see about your dress."

Mrs. Wheeler. He'd called her that before, and it was her official title, so it shouldn't lodge in her windpipe, cutting off her air supply.

But it did. Maybe because she'd just been the recipient of a mind-blowing climax courtesy of Mr. Wheeler.

He took her hand and led her upstairs, where the couture fairies had left a garment bag hanging over her closet door. Her fake husband was a man of many, many talents, and she appreciated every last one.

"By the way," Lucas said. "When I ran into the maid earlier, I told her we'd had a little misunderstanding about a former girlfriend, but you were noble enough to get past it. I hope that's okay. Any excuse for why we weren't sharing a bedroom is better than nothing, right?"

"More than okay. Perfect." And not just the excuse. While she still basked in the afterglow of amazing sex, everything about Lucas was perfect.

The deep blue dress matched her eyes and eclipsed the red one in style and fit. Lucas leaned against the doorjamb of the bathroom, watching her dress with a crystalline focus and making complimentary noises. His attention made her feel beautiful and desired, two things she'd never expected to like.

Lucas Wheeler was a master of filling gaps, not creating them. Of giving, not taking. Ironic how she'd accused him of being selfish when trying to convince him to marry her.

As they entered the Calliope Foundation Charity Ball, a cluster of Wheelers surrounded them. Lucas's parents, she already knew, but she met his grandparents for the first time and couldn't help but contrast the open, smiling couple to Abuelo's tendency to be remote.

Matthew joined them amid the hellos, and his cool smile reminded her she owed Lucas one asset of a wife. It was the very least she could do in return for his selflessness over the entire course of their acquaintance.

A room full of society folk and money and lots of opportunities to put her foot in her mouth were nearly last on her list of fun activities, right after cleaning toilets and oral surgery. But she kept her hand in Lucas's as they worked the room; she laughed at his jokes, smiled at the men he spoke to and complimented their wives' jewelry or dress.

There had to be more, a way to do something more tangible than tittering over lame golf stories and smiling through a fifteen-minute discourse on the Rangers' bull pen.

"Are these clients or potential clients?" she asked Lucas after several rounds of social niceties and a very short dance with Grandfather Wheeler because she couldn't say *no* when he asked so nicely.

"Mostly potential. As I'm sure you're aware, our client list is rather sparse at the moment."

"Is there someone you're targeting?"

"Moore. He still hasn't signed. Matthew invited another potential, who's up here from Houston. George Walsh. He's looking to expand, and if I'm not mistaken, he just walked in."

If Walsh lived elsewhere, the Lana fiasco probably factored little in his decision process. "Industry?"

"Concrete. Pipes, foundations, that sort of thing. He's looking for an existing facility with the potential to convert but wouldn't be opposed to build-to-suit." He laughed and shook his head. "You can't be interested in all this."

"But I am. Or I wouldn't have asked. Introduce me to this Walsh."

With an assessing once-over, he nodded, then led her to where Matthew conversed with a fortyish man in an ill-fitting suit.

Matthew performed the introductions, and Cia automatically evaluated George Walsh. A working man with calluses, who ran his company personally and preferred to get his hands dirty in the day to day. Now what?

Schmoozing felt so fake, and she'd never been good at it. Lucas managed to be genuine, so maybe her attitude was the problem. How could she get better?

Though it sliced through her with a serrated edge, she shut her eyes for a brief second and channeled her mother in a social setting. What would she have done? Drinks. Graciousness. Smiles. Then business.

Cia asked Walsh his drink preference and signaled a waiter as she chatted about his family, his hobbies and his last vacation. Smiling brightly, she called up every shred of business acumen in her brain. "So, Mr. Walsh, talk to me about the concrete business. This is certainly a booming area. Every new building needs a concrete foundation, right?"

He lit up and talked for a solid ten minutes about the weather, the economy and a hundred other reasons to set up shop in north Texas. Periodically, she threw in comments about Lucas and his commitment to clients— which in no way counted as fabrication since she had firsthand experience with his thoughtful consideration and careful attention to details.

Somehow, the conversation became more than acting as an asset to Lucas and enhancing his reputation, more than reciprocation for upholding his end of the bargain. She'd failed at drumming up donations for the shelter, despite believing in it so deeply. Here, she was a part of a partnership, one half of Mr. and Mrs. Wheeler, and that profoundly changed her ability to succeed.

It reiterated that this marriage was her best shot at fulfilling her mother's wishes.

"Did I do okay?" she whispered to Lucas after Matthew took Walsh off to meet some other people.

Instead of answering, he backed her into a secluded corner, behind a potted palm, and pulled her into his arms. Then he kissed her with shameless heat.

Helplessly, she clung to his strong shoulders as he explored every corner of her mouth. His strength and solid build gave him the means to do the only thing he claimed to want—to take care of her. It wasn't as horrible or overbearing as she might have anticipated.

It was…nice. He understood her, what she wanted. Her dreams. Her fears. And they were partners. Who had amazing sex.

When he pulled back, the smile on his face took her breath.

"More than okay," he said. "Are you angling to join the firm?"

"Well, my name *is* Wheeler," she said in jest, but it didn't seem as funny out loud. That was a whole different kind of partnership. Permanent. Real. Not part of the plan.

"Yes. It is." He lifted her chin to pierce her with a charged look. The ballroom's lighting refracted inside his eyes, brightening them. He leaned in, and the world shrank down to encompass only the two of them as he laid his lips on hers in a tender kiss. A kiss with none of the heat and none of the carnal passion sizzling between them like the first time.

It was a lover's kiss. Her limp hands hung at her sides as her heart squeezed.

Oh, no. No, no, no.

"We have to find that coat closet. Now," she hissed against his mouth. Sex. That's all there was between them, all she'd allow. No tenderness, no affection, no stupid, girlie heart quivers.

His eyebrows flew up. "Now? We just got he— Why am I arguing about this?"

Linking hands, he pulled her along at a brisk trot, and she almost laughed at the intensity of his search for a private room. Around a corner of the hotel's long hallway, they found an empty storage room.

Lucas held the door and shooed her in, slammed it shut and backed her against the wood, his ravenous mouth on hers.

The world righted itself as the hard press of his body heated hers through the deep blue dress. This, she accepted. Two people slaking a mutual wild thirst and nothing more.

"Condom," she whispered.

He had about four seconds to produce it. An accidental pregnancy would tie her to this man for life, and, besides, she didn't want children. Well, she didn't want to cause herself heartache, which was practically the same thing.

"Right here. I was warned I'd need it."

Fabric bunched around her waist an instant later, and her panties hit the ground. He lifted her effortlessly, squashing her against the door and spreading her legs, wrapping them around him.

The second he entered her—buried so deep, every pulse of his hard length nudging her womb—she threw her head back and rode the wave to a mind-draining climax.

Yes. Brainless and blistering. Perfect.

When she came down and met the glowing eyes of her husband, a charged, momentous crackle passed between them.

She'd keep right on pretending she hadn't noticed.

Warm sunlight poured through the window of Lucas's office. He swiveled his chair away from it and forced his attention back to the sales contract on his laptop screen. Property—dirt, buildings, concrete or any combination—lived in his DNA and he'd dedicated his entire adulthood to it. It shouldn't be so difficult to concentrate on his lifeblood.

It was.

His imagination seemed bent on inventing ways to get out of the office and go home. In the past few weeks, he'd met a sprinkler repairman, an attic radiant barrier consultant and a decorator. A *decorator*. Flimsy, he had to admit.

A couple of times after showings, he'd swung by the house, which was mostly on the way back to the office. Through absolutely no fault of his own, Cia had been home all those times, as well, and it would have been a crime against nature not to take advantage of the totally coincidental timing.

Ironic how a marriage created to rescue his business was the very thing stealing his attention from business.

Moore had signed. Walsh had signed. Both men were enthusiastic about the purchases they'd committed to, and Lucas intended to ensure they stayed that way. Cia's interactions with them had been the clincher; he was convinced.

His dad had gone out of his way to tell Lucas how good this marriage was for him, how happy he seemed. And why wouldn't he be? Cia was amazing, and he got to wake up with her long hair tangled in his fingers every morning.

The past few weeks had been the best of his life. The next few could be even better as long as he kept ignoring how Cia had bled into his everyday existence. Every time they made love, the hooks dug in a little deeper. Her shadows rarely appeared now, and he enjoyed keeping them away for her. He liked that she needed him.

If he ignored it all, it wasn't really happening.

Matthew knocked on the open door, his frame taut and face blank. "Dad called. Grandpa's in the hospital," he said. "Heart attack. It's not good. Dad wants us to come and sit with Mama."

Heart attack? Not Grandpa. That heavy weight settled back into place on his chest, a weight that hadn't been there since the night he met Cia.

Lucas rose on unsteady legs. "What? No way. Grandpa's

healthier than you and me put together. He beat me at golf a month ago."

Protesting. Like it would change facts. His grandfather was a vibrant man. Seventy-five years old, sure, but he kept his finger on the pulse of Texas real estate and still acted as a full partner in the firm.

When Lucas had graduated from college, Grandpa had handed him an envelope with the papers granting Lucas a quarter ownership in Wheeler Family Partners. A careworn copy lined the inner pocket of his workbag and always would.

"I'll drive." Matthew turned and stalked away without waiting for Lucas.

Lucas threw his laptop in his bag and shouldered it, then texted Helena to reschedule his appointments for the day as he walked out. Once seated in Matthew's SUV, he texted Cia. His wife would be expected at the hospital.

The Cityplace building loomed on the right as Matthew drove north out of downtown. They didn't talk. They never talked anymore except about work or baseball. But nothing of substance, by Matthew's choice.

They'd been indivisible before Amber. She'd come along, and Matthew had happily become half of a couple. Lucas observed from a distance with respect and maybe a small amount of envy. Of course his relationship with Matthew had shifted, as it should, but then Amber died and his brother disappeared entirely.

Lucas sat with his family in the waiting room, tapped out a few emails on his phone and exchanged strained small talk with Mama. His dad paced and barked at hospital personnel until a dour doctor appeared with the bad news.

Lucas watched his dad embrace Mama, and she sobbed on his shirt. In that moment, they were not his parents, but two people who turned to each other, for richer or poorer, in sickness and in health.

Apart from everyone, Matthew haunted the window, stoic

and unyielding as always, refusing to engage or share his misery with anyone. Not even Lucas.

The scene unfolded in surreal, grinding slow motion. He couldn't process the idea of his grandfather, the Wheeler patriarch, being gone.

Cia, her long, shiny hair flying, barreled into the waiting room and straight into Lucas. He flung his arms around her small body in a fierce clinch.

The premise that she'd come solely for the sake of appearances vanished. She was here. His wife was in his arms, right where she should be. The world settled. He clutched her tight, and coconut and lime wafted into his senses, breaking open the weight on his chest.

Now it was real. Now it was final. Grandpa was gone, and he hadn't gotten to say goodbye.

"I'm glad you came," Lucas said, and his voice hitched. "He didn't make it."

"I'm sorry, so sorry. He was a great man," she murmured into his shirt, warm hands sliding along his back, and they stood there for forever while he fought for control over the devastating grief.

When he tilted his head to rest a cheek on top of Cia's hair he caught Matthew watching them, arms crossed, with an odd expression on his face. Missing his own wife most likely

Finally, Lucas let Cia slip from his embrace. She gripped his hand and followed silently as he spoke to his dad, then she drove him to his parents' house with careful attention to the speed limit.

Mama talked about funeral arrangements with his father and grandmother, and through it all Cia never left his side, offering quiet support and an occasional comforting squeeze. Surely she had other commitments, other things she'd rather be doing than hanging out in a place where everyone spoke in hushed tones about death.

Her keys remained in her purse, untouched, and she didn't leave.

It meant a lot that she cared enough to stay. It said a lot, too—they'd become friends as well as lovers. He hadn't expected that. He'd never had that.

For the first time, he considered what might happen after the divorce. Would they still have contact? Could they maintain some kind of relationship, maybe a friends-with-benefits deal?

He pondered the sudden idea until Matthew motioned him outside. Cia buzzed around the kitchen fixing Mama a drink, so he followed his brother out to the screened-in porch.

Matthew retrieved a longneck from a small refrigerator tucked into the corner, popped the top with the tail of his button-down in a practiced twist and flopped into a wicker chair, swigging heartily from the bottle.

Lucas started to comment about the hour, but a beer with his brother on the afternoon of his grandfather's death didn't sound half-bad. Might cure his dry throat.

Bottle in hand, Lucas took the opposite chair and swung one leg over the arm. "Long day."

Matthew swallowed. "Long life. Gets longer every day."

"That's depressing." His life got better every day, and considering the disaster it had been, that was saying something. Lucas hesitated but plunged ahead. "Do you want to talk about it?"

"No. But I have to." He sighed. "First Amber. Now Grandpa. I'm done. It's the last straw. I can't take it anymore."

That sounded serious. Suicidal even. Lucas looked at his normally solid and secure brother. "Do you need a vacation?"

"Yeah." Matthew laughed sarcastically. "From myself. Problem is they don't offer that with an all-inclusive resort package. I don't know what it's going to take to get me back on track, but whatever it is, it's not here."

"Where is it?"

Shrugging, Matthew drained his beer in record time. "I

have no idea. But I have to look for it. So I'm leaving. Not just for a few days. Permanently."

"Permanently?" Lucas shook his head. Matthew was a Wheeler. Wheelers didn't take off and let the chips fall. Everything Lucas knew about being a Wheeler he'd learned from watching his brother succeed at whatever he attempted. Obviously Matthew was overtired. "You can't leave. Take some time away. You've been working too much, which is my fault. Let me handle clients for a week or two. Backpack through the Himalayas or drink margaritas in Belize. But you have to come back."

"No, I don't. I can't." Stubborn to the core. That was one Wheeler trait they shared.

"Wheeler Family Partners isn't a one-man show. We just lost Grandpa. Dad's been taking a backseat for a couple of years, and now he's going to be the executor for Grandpa's estate. We're it."

And Matthew was more it than Lucas-the-gray-sheep could ever be.

Matthew's sharp gaze roved over Lucas in assessment. "You can do it without me. You've changed in the past year. Maybe Lana snapped some sense into you, or maybe it started happening long before and I didn't see it. Regardless, you've turned into me."

"Turned into you? What does that mean?"

"Responsible. Married. Committed. I always thought I'd be the one to settle down, have a family. Raise the next generation of Wheelers to carry on WFP. But lo and behold, it's not going to be me. It's going to be you."

The beer bottle slipped out of Lucas's hand and broke in two against the concrete patterned patio. The sharp yeasty scent of the last third of a beer split the air. "What are you talking about? I'm not settling down. There's no family in my future."

"Right." His brother snorted. "If Cia's not pregnant within a month, I'll fall over in a dead shock."

Oh, man. They'd done a spectacular job of fooling everyone into believing this was the real thing, and now Matthew felt safe leaving the firm in Lucas's hands. "Uh, we're being careful. She's not interested in having children."

"Yeah, well, accidents happen. Especially as many times as I'd bet you're doing it. You're not quite as subtle as you must think when you dash off during an event and sneak back in later, without giving Cia a chance to comb her hair. You two are so smoking hot for each other, I can't believe you haven't set something on fire."

So now he was supposed to apologize for enjoying sex with his wife? "Sorry if that bothers you," Lucas retorted. "We have a normal, healthy relationship. What's the problem?"

Matthew raised his brows. "No problem. Why so defensive? I'm pointing out that you landed on your feet. That's great. I'm happy for you. I admit, I thought you rushed into this marriage because of Lana or, at the very least, because you'd screwed up and gotten a one-night stand pregnant. Clearly, I was wrong. Cia's good for you. You obviously love each other very much."

He and Cia surely deserved Oscars if Matthew, who missed nothing, believed that. "Thanks."

"Although," Matthew continued in his big-brother tone, "you probably should have thought twice about marrying someone who doesn't want kids. Isn't family important to you?"

If the marriage had been intended to last, he definitely would have thought more about it back on that terrace. Now Matthew's words crowded his mind, shoving everything else out. "Isn't it important to *you?* You're the one talking about abandoning everyone."

"Only because you can take my place. You can be me and

I can be you. I'll go find fun and meaningless experiences, without worrying about anything other than myself."

"Hey now." Was that how his brother saw him? "Lay off the cheap shots."

"Sorry." Matthew gave him an assessing once-over. "Six months ago, you wouldn't have blinked at such a comment. It's an interesting transposition we have going on. You have no idea how hard it is for me to think about marrying again. Having a baby with someone who isn't Amber. Something is busted inside, which can't be repaired. Ever."

Quiet desperation filled Matthew's voice, the kind Lucas would never have associated with his older brother, who had always looked out for him. Whom Lucas had always looked up to, ever since the first time Matthew had stood shoulder to shoulder with his little brother against bullies. As Matthew took full responsibility for a broken flowerpot because he hadn't taught Lucas the proper way to hold a bat. As Matthew passed off the first client to his newly graduated brother and whispered the steps to Lucas behind the scenes.

A long surge unsettled Lucas's stomach. His brother had never been so open, so broken.

Matthew needed him. The firm, his family, his heritage all needed him. Lucas had to step up and prove his brother's faith in him wasn't misplaced. To show everyone Lucas knew what it meant to be a Wheeler, once and for all.

It would be hard, and parts of it would suck. But he had to.

Of course, he lacked a wife who wanted all the ties of a permanent marriage or who looked forward to filling a nursery with blankets and diapers. Where in the world would he find someone he liked as much as Cia, who excited him like she did even when they were nowhere near a bed? It would take a miracle to tick off all the points on his future-wife mental checklist. A miracle to find a wife as good as Cia.

Matthew clamped his mouth into a thin line and shifted his attention as Cia's hand slid across Lucas's shoulder.

"I didn't mean to interrupt," she said. "I just wanted to check on you. Doing okay?"

Concern carved a furrow between her brows, and he didn't like being the cause of that line. "Fine, darlin'. Thanks."

"Okay. I'm going to sit with your mom for a little while longer. She's pretty upset." She smiled and bent to kiss the top of his head, as if they were a real married couple in the middle of for better or worse.

His vision tunneled as future and present collided, and a radical idea popped fully formed into his head. An idea as provocative and intriguing as it was dangerous. One that would pose the greatest challenge thus far in his relationship with Cia.

What if they didn't get divorced?

Ten

A noise woke Cia in the middle of the night. No, not a noise, but a sixth sense of the atmosphere changing. Lucas. He'd finally pried himself loose from his laptop and paperwork. His study might be in the same house, but it might as well have been in Timbuktu for all she'd seen of him lately.

She glanced at the clock—1:00 a.m.—as he slid into bed and gathered her up against his warm, scrumptious body, spooning them together.

"Sorry," he whispered. "Time got away from me."

"It's okay. You're earlier than last night." And the night before that and the night before that. In the weeks since his grandfather's death and Matthew's disappearance, he'd been tense and preoccupied, but closemouthed about it other than to say he'd been working a lot.

She rolled in his arms and glued her body to his, silently offering whatever he wanted to take, because he'd done the same when she'd needed it. Sometimes he held her close and dropped into a dead sleep. Sometimes he was keyed up and wanted to talk. Sometimes he watched TV, which she always left on for him despite her hatred of the pulsing lights.

Tonight, he flipped off the TV and covered her mouth in a searing kiss. His hands skimmed down her back to cup her bottom, sliding into the places craving his careful attention.

Oh, yes. Her favorite of the late-night options—slow, achingly sensual and delicious. The kind of night where they whispered to each other in the dark and pleasured by touch, lost inside a world where nothing else existed.

In the dark, she didn't have to worry about what hidden depths of the heart might spring into her eyes. No agonizing over whether something similar crept through his eyes, as well. Or didn't. It was better to leave certain aspects of their relationship unexamined.

Of course, ignoring the facts didn't magically rearrange them into a new version of truth.

The truth was still the truth.

This was more than just sex.

Sex could be fun, but it didn't erase the significance of doing it with Lucas. Not some random, fun guy. *Lucas,* who got out of the way and let her make her own choices. Lucas, who'd proven over and over he was more than enough man to handle whatever she threw at him.

When the earth stopped quaking, Lucas bound her to him in a tight tangle of limbs. He murmured, *"Mi amante,"* and fell asleep with his lips against her temple.

When had he managed to squeeze in a Spanish lesson? His layers were endless and each one weighed a little more, sinking a little deeper into her soul.

This thing with Lucas was spiraling out of control. They were still getting a divorce, and all this *significance*—and now much she wanted it—freaked her out. It would be smart to back off now, so it wouldn't be so hard later.

In the morning, she woke sinfully late, still nestled in Lucas's arms for the first time in a long time, and she didn't hesitate to test how heavily he slept. The exact opposite of backing off. *Stupid* was her middle name lately.

"Mmm. Darlin', that is indeed a nice way to wake up," he murmured, after she'd sated them both.

"Stay in bed tomorrow morning, and you might get a repeat." She flipped on the TV and settled in to watch the weather while contemplating breakfast. "Can you eat or are you going to go drown yourself in listings right away?"

"I'm taking a little personal time this morning. I deserve it, don't you think?"

"Yeah. Does that mean I'm breakfast?"

He laughed. "Yep. Then I want to take you somewhere."

But he wouldn't tell her where until after they'd eaten, showered and dressed, and he'd driven to a run-down building miles off the freeway in an older part of town full of senior centers and assisted-living facilities.

"This just came up for sale," he told her as he helped her out of the car and led her to the edge of the parking lot. "It's an old hotel."

She glanced at him and back at the building. "I'm sorry. I'm not following why we're here or what the implication of this is."

"For the shelter," Lucas said quietly. "It can be retrofitted, and I checked on the zoning. No problems."

"The shelter." It took another thirty seconds for his meaning to sink in. "You mean my shelter? I'm planning to have it built."

"I know. This is another option. A less expensive option. Thirty-five percent down and I know a few people we can talk to about the financing."

"Financing?" If he'd started speaking Swahili, she'd have been equally as challenged to keep up. "I'm not getting a loan. That's the whole point of accessing my trust fund, so I can pay cash and the shelter will never be threatened with closure. We went over this. Without the trust money, I don't have thirty-five percent, let alone enough to purchase."

He clasped her hand with painstaking care. "I'll give you the money for the down payment."

The air grew heavy and ominous, tightening her chest. Their agreement specifically called for their assets to remain separate, and that might prove to be a touchier subject than sex. "You didn't get a terminal cancer diagnosis or something, did you? What's this all about?"

"You inspire me. Your commitment to victims of abuse is amazing. If I help you do this, you could start the shelter now instead of waiting until you get your money when the divorce is final. Save a few more women in the meantime."

"Oh, Lucas."

And that was it. Her heart did a pirouette and splattered somewhere in the vicinity of her stomach.

She rushed on, determined not to dwell on how many king's horses and how many king's men it would take to put everything back together again. "I appreciate what you're saying—I really do. But I can't get a loan, not for the kind of money we're talking about. I told you, Courtney and I tried. Our business plan wasn't viable, and venture capitalists want profits. Asking you to marry me was the absolute last resort, but it turned out for the best. If we have a loan, there's always a possibility of foreclosure if donations dry up, and I can't have that hanging over our heads."

No bank would ever own her shelter. Nothing would have the power to rip it from her fingers. It was far, far better to do it all on her own and never depend on anyone else. Much less painful that way.

"Okay. So, no loan." A strange light appeared in his eyes. "At least think about the possibility of this place. The owner is motivated to sell. Adding in the renovations, the purchase price is around a third of the cost to build. You could save millions."

Yes, she could. The savings could be rolled forward into operating costs, and it would be years and years before she needed to worry about additional funds beyond the trust money. The idea had merit. She could run the shelter without donations, a huge plus in her mind.

Maybe Lucas could talk the owner into waiting to sell until the divorce came through and she had access to the trust.

She surveyed the site again. The hotel was tucked away in a heavily treed area, off the beaten path. Bad for a hotel and good for a shelter the victims didn't want their abusers to find. "I do like the location. It's important for women who've taken the step to leave their abusers to feel safe. An out-of-the-way place is ideal. Tell me more about your thoughts."

Lucas started talking, his voice wandering along her spine, the same way his hands did when he reached for her at night. He threw around real estate terms and an impressive amount of research. When he was all professional and authoritative about his area of expertise, it pulled at her and bobbled her focus, which wasn't so sharp right now anyway.

Her brain was too busy arguing with her heart about whether she'd actually been stupid enough to fall for her all-too-real husband.

No question about it. She'd put herself in exactly the position she'd sworn never to be in again—reliant on a man to make her complete and happy. All her internal assurances to the contrary and all the pretending had been lies.

This was where brainless had gotten her: harboring impossible feelings for Lucas.

It hardly mattered if Lucas freed her to jump in and enjoy life alongside him. It hardly mattered if she'd accidentally married a man who understood her and everything she was about. It hardly mattered if she wished her soul had room for a mate and that such fairy tales existed.

They didn't.

Life didn't allow for such simplicity. Anything she valued

was subject to being taken away, and the tighter she held on, the greater the hurt when it was gone. The only way to stay whole was to beat fate to the punch by getting rid of it first.

She'd married Lucas Wheeler because he wasn't capable of more than short-term. She could trust him to keep his word and grant her a divorce, the sole outcome she could accept.

They had a deal, not a future.

Midway through an email, Lucas realized it had been four days since he'd spent time with his wife outside of bed. Their time together in bed had been less than leisurely and far from ideal. It was criminal.

He picked up the phone. "Helena. Can you reschedule everything after five today?"

"I can," she said. "But your five-thirty is with Mr. Moore and it's the only day this week he can meet. The counteroffer was a mess, remember?"

He remembered. Once upon a time, he would have passed it off to Matthew and dashed for the door. The deficiency created by his brother's vanishing act multiplied every day, demanding one hundred percent of his energy and motivation, leaving none for Cia.

He missed her. "Reschedule everything else, then. Thanks—you're the best."

If he put aside a potential new client's proposal, skipped lunch and called in a couple of favors, he'd have an infallible amended contract ready to go by five-thirty and a happy Moore out the door by six. Dinner with Cia by seven.

The challenge got his blood pumping. The tightrope grew thinner and the balancing act more delicate, but without his brother to fall back on, new strengths appeared daily.

He was thriving, like Matthew had predicted, because every night Lucas went to bed with the ultimate example of sacrifice and commitment. He and Cia were partners. How could he look in the mirror if he didn't step up?

He texted Cia with the dinner invitation, and her response put a smile on his face for the rest of the day: It's a date.

A date with his wife. The wife he secretly contemplated keeping. *Forever* didn't fill him with dread or have him looking for the exit. Yet. He'd been nursing the idea in the back of his mind, weighing it out. Testing it for feasibility. Working the angles. If he didn't file for divorce, he'd have to give up Manzanares because he hadn't fulfilled his end of the bargain.

There was a lot to consider, especially the effort required to convince Cia to look at their agreement in a different light.

It was time to take the next step and see how difficult Cia would be about staying married. The six months were more than half over, and he had a suspicion it would take a while to bring her around, even with the added incentive of his idea of using the hotel for the shelter.

Moore agreed to the amended contract and walked out the door at five forty-five, giving Lucas plenty of time to cook a spectacular dinner for Cia. The poolside venue beat a restaurant by a country mile, and the summer heat wasn't unbearable yet.

They sat at the patio table and exchanged light stories about their day as a breeze teased Cia's hair. He waited until dessert to broach the main topic on his mind. "Have you thought any further about the hotel site?"

Her eyes lit up. "That's all I've thought about. Courtney and I have been redoing the numbers, and she's excited about it. I'm pretty sure I'm going to buy it. It was a great idea, and I appreciate all the work you put into it." She hesitated for a beat and met his gaze. "Would it be weird to ask you to be my broker if we're in the middle of a divorce?"

Perfect segue. "About that. You can't wait until you get your trust fund to buy. There are other interested parties already. A bank loan is out, I realize, but I can scrape up the money. Would you accept it?"

She stared at him. "The entire purchase price, plus reno

vation costs? Not just the thirty-five percent down? Lucas,
that's millions of dollars. You'd be willing to do that for me?"

Yeah, he knew the offer was substantial. What he hadn't
realized until this moment was that his high level of motivation at work hadn't been solely to prove something to himself
and to Matthew. The more successful he could make WFP
now, the less of a blow it would be to lose Manzanares, which
was a given if he convinced her to forget about the divorce.

"Not as a loan. In trade."

"Trade? I don't have anything worth that much except my
trust fund."

"You do. You."

"We're already married. It's not like you have a shot at
some sort of indecent proposal," she said with a half laugh.

What he had in mind was a thoroughly decent proposal.
"I'm curious. What do you think of this house?"

"Could you veer between subjects any faster?" Her eyes
widened. "Oh, you were seriously asking? I love this house.
It'll be hard to go back home to my tiny Uptown condo after
living here. Why, are we about to be kicked out?"

"Before Matthew left, he sold it to me."

"This is *Matthew's* house? Shocking how that hasn't come
up before." She waved it away before he could formulate a
response. "But I'm not shocked you bought it. It's beautiful,
and I'm sure you'll be happy here for a long time."

It hadn't come up before because it hadn't been important.
When she'd first proposed this deal, the house represented a
place to live, which he had been able to access quickly and
easily, and it had provided a good foundation for their fake
relationship.

Now, as he sat at the patio table with his wife, eating dinner in a house he owned, it represented a potential future. A
real future. One where he could fulfill the expectations that
came with being a Wheeler.

"Actually…" He traced a line across the back of Cia's hand

and then threw every last card and a whole second deck on the table. "I'd like for you to be happy here, too. Married to me. Long-term."

The sip of wine she'd taken sprayed all over the flagstone patio. "That wasn't funny."

"It wasn't a joke. We're partners, and we're amazing together. Why ruin a good thing with a divorce?"

"Why?" Fire shot from her expression and singed the atmosphere. "Why? Because we *agreed.* If you don't file for divorce, I can't access my trust fund and I'll tear up the Manzanares contract. We both have a huge stake in this."

Interesting how her argument summarized the deal instead of listing the evils of marriage. He shrugged. "But the divorce isn't necessary if I give you the money for the shelter."

She sprang to her feet and both palms slammed the table, rattling the dishes. "Are you sure you have a business degree, Wheeler? You're forgetting about a minor detail called operating expenses. Without the trust fund, I won't have a dime once we open the doors. The residents have to eat. There are administrative costs. Utilities."

Like that, they were back to *Wheeler* and insults. And logic. No, he hadn't considered the operating expenses because his involvement in any deal ended the moment papers were signed. Poor excuse, regardless, and a huge miss. It had been much easier to coax her into his bed.

He blew out a frustrated breath. "What if we could get donations for operating expenses? Would you still want a divorce?"

Her eyes flared wide, deepening the blue. "What have you been drinking, Wheeler? Our whole agreement centers on the divorce."

Okay. He'd botched this up. Clearly. He'd opted to go with money as his negotiation instrument and had ignored what he'd learned about Cia over the past few months.

Figure it out, or lose everything.

Pulse tripping with a rush of sudden alarm, he rose and cornered her against the table. The heat between them, the absolute beauty and inexpressible pleasure of making love—that was his best bargaining tool, his best shot at getting her to stay.

Her arms came up and latched into a knot across her chest. She was not budging an inch.

"Darlin'," he said and slid a hand through her curtain of hair to cup the back of her silky neck. "I've been drunk on you since the moment you said I look like a Ken doll. Loosen up a little. We're just talking."

The rigid set of her shoulders and the corded neck muscles under his fingers were the opposite of loose and getting tighter by the moment. "Talking about how you're second-guessing our divorce."

He leaned in and set his lips on her forehead, mouthing his way down to her ear. "Not second-guessing. Presenting a possible alternative. Can you blame me? Honey, the things you do to me are indeed mind-blowing. I'd be a few cows shy of a herd if I was willing to give that up so easily."

His hands found her breasts, and she moaned. "Animal analogies. That's sexy, Wheeler. Talk to me some more like that." Her arms unknotted and fell to her sides, melting into pliancy as he sucked on her throat. She didn't move away.

"You like that? How about this?" He backhanded the dishes to the ground, and amid the crash of breaking pottery, set her on the table, splaying her legs wide to accommodate his hips. Her dress bunched at her thighs and hot pink flashed from the vicinity of her center. "You make me crazier than a monkey on fermented melons. Hotter than a rattler on asphalt. Shall I go on?"

"No. No more animals."

She was laughing, and he captured it in his mouth, then parted her lips and tasted the wine lingering inside with firm strokes of his tongue. She arched against him, rubbing her heat against his blistering erection.

He worked a hand under her bottom and pushed, grinding that heat hard against his length. "You feel that?" he growled. "That's what you do to me. I want to be inside you every minute of every day. I want your gorgeous naked body under me, thrashing with climax, and my name on your lips. I cannot get enough of you."

Her body spasmed, and she moaned again, her chest vibrating against his. He pulled her dress over her head and feasted on the sight of one very sexy hot-pink bra and panty combo.

It needed to come off now. He needed to touch her.

With one finger, he hooked her bra and dragged it down across her taut nipples, popping them free. He took one in his mouth, rolling it across his tongue, nibbling and sucking, and she pushed against his teeth, begging him to take her deeper.

He sucked harder. Her nails bit into the back of his head, urging him on. His erection pulsed, aching to be free of the confines of his clothes.

Not yet.

He dragged his tongue down the length of her abdomen and fingered off her panties, then knelt between her legs to pleasure her there.

"Do you like this?" he asked. "Do you like the way I make you feel?" He treated her to a thorough openmouthed French kiss square in the heart of her wet heat. She bucked against his lips, seeking more.

"Yes. *Yes.*"

She was so responsive, so hot. Fingers deep inside her, he flicked her sweet nub with his tongue. "What do you need?"

She whimpered, writhing as he held back from granting her the release she sought. "You, Lucas," she said on a long sob. "I need you."

The syllables uncurled inside him, settling with heavy warm weight, and only then did he realize how much he'd

burned to hear them. He vaulted to his feet. His clothes hit
the patio, and he had a condom in his hand in record time.

His luscious wife watched him with dark, stormy eyes,
one leg dangling over the edge and one leg bent up, opening her secrets wide. A wanton gift, spread out on the table,
just for him.

He kissed her, covering her mouth and her body simultane-
ously, then entered her with a groan, filling her, and squeezed
his eyes shut to savor the hot, slick pressure.

They were awesome together. How could she deny it? How
could she walk away? No other man could fulfill her like he
could.

She needed him.

She only thought she wasn't in the market for a long-term
marriage, like she'd once insisted she didn't want him like
this. She was wrong, so wrong, about both, and he had to
convince her of it.

Relentlessly, he drove her off the edge and followed her
down a brilliant slide toward the light.

Later, when Cia lay snuggled in his arms in their bed, she
blasted him with the last word. "The divorce is happening, no
matter how hot the sex is. I asked you to marry me because
you're a close-the-deal-and-move-on guy. Stop talking crazy
and do what you're good at."

Yeah, he excelled at moving on. Always on the lookout for
the next deal, the next woman, the next indulgence. Matthew
was the solid, responsible one.

Was. Not anymore.

Lucas pulled Cia tighter into his arms without respond-
ing. Matthew was gone. Lucas had assumed his place at the
helm of Wheeler Family Partners. Lucas owned a house constructed for marriage. With these shifts, life could be whatever he wanted.

He wanted what Matthew had lost. With Cia. For the first
time in his life, Lucas wasn't interested in moving on. But

how did he convince Cia to stick around? Maybe she was
right and he wasn't cut out for long-term. Gray sheep didn'
spontaneously turn white overnight.

But the shifts had already occurred, and he didn't have to
stay on the same path. This was it, right here, right now. I
he wanted to change the future, he had to figure out how to
make it happen.

Eleven

When the doorbell chimed, Fran Wheeler was the very last person Cia expected to view through the peephole. She yanked open the door and summoned a smile for her mother-in-law. "Mrs. Wheeler. Please come in."

"I'm sorry to drop by unexpectedly." Fran stepped into the foyer, murmuring appreciatively at the way Cia had decorated the living room. "And please, call me Fran. Formality makes me feel old, and if I wanted to be reminded of my age, I'd look in a mirror."

"Of course. Fran, then. Lucas isn't home, I'm afraid." Cia waved at the couch. "Would you like a seat? I'd be happy to get you a drink while you wait, if you'd like."

Coolly, as only a pillar of Dallas society could, Fran cocked her head, and the chic style of her blond hair stayed firmly in place. "I'm here to see you. Lucas is with his father at a boring real estate seminar, so I took a chance you'd be home alone."

Uh-oh. Well, she was way overdue for the tongue-lashing Fran likely wanted to give her for refusing the pearls. "Your timing is good, then. I took the day off from work. The offer of a drink still stands."

A squawk cut her off. Fergie couldn't stand it when someone had a conversation without her.

Fran glanced toward the back of the house. "Was that a bird?"

"A parrot." Another squawk, louder and more insistent. "Fergie. She was a wedding present from Lucas."

"Oh." Fran's raised brows indicated her clear interest, but she appeared reluctant to ask any further questions.

Cia's fault, no doubt, as she had no idea how to break the awkward tension. The divorce loomed on the horizon. She was sleeping with this woman's son. The mechanics of a relationship with a mother figure escaped her. The odds of successfully navigating this surprise visit were about the same as winning the lottery without buying a ticket.

Squawk.

"Fergie probably wants to meet you." Cia shook her head "I mean, she's a little temperamental and likes people around If you're not opposed to it, we can sit in the kitchen. She'l quiet down if we do."

"That's fine." Fran followed Cia into the kitchen and immediately crossed to Fergie's cage. "Oh, she's precious. Doe: she talk?"

"When she feels like it. Say hello to her. Sometimes tha works."

Cia poured two glasses of iced tea.

Fran and Fergie exchanged hellos several times, and Fergi went off on a tangent, first singing the national anthem and then squawking, "Play ball!" to the older woman's delight Fran laughed and praised the bird for a good five minutes Cia wasn't about to interrupt.

Finally, Fran joined Cia at the breakfast table and sippe her tea. "The last few weeks have been difficult, and I wante to thank you for the shoulder. It meant a lot to me that yo stayed with us the afternoon Andy's father died and then all through the funeral and…" She took a deep breath. "Well, you know, you were there. So thanks."

"Oh, um, you're welcome." Cia's tongue felt too big for her mouth, swollen by the sincerity of Fran's tremulous smile. "I know how it feels to lose a parent. I was glad to do what I could."

"You're very good for Lucas—did you know that? Andy says you're all he talks about at work. My boys are everything to me, and I'm grateful Lucas has found someone who makes him happy." The older woman reached out and clasped Cia's hand. "We got off on the wrong foot when I pushed too soon for a relationship with you, but I'm hopeful we can start over now."

Cia shut her eyes for a blink. What was she supposed to do? She wasn't just sleeping with Lucas; they were married. And it wasn't over yet. Abuelo could still get suspicious if Fran happened to mention Cia's aloof brush-offs. Dallas was a small town in all the worst ways.

"Fran, you aren't to blame. It's me." Might as well lay it all out there. "I just don't know how to be around a mother-in-law. Or a mother, for that matter."

Okay, she hadn't meant to lay it *all* out there. Tears stabbed at her eyelids, and Fran's expression softened.

"There aren't any rules, honey. Let's just sit here, drink tea and talk. That's all I want."

Yeah, she could pretend all day long this was about keeping the heat off and guarding against her grandfather's suspicions. It wasn't. Fran was offering something she couldn't refuse—friendship.

Cia nodded and cleared her throat. "That sounds nice. What would you like to talk about?"

"Tell me about the shelter. I've been looking for a volunteer opportunity. Can I help?"

And for the second time in less than a week, Cia's heart

splattered into a big, mushy mess. A man she could get over in time. A mother? Not so much. And now it was too late to back away.

With her nerves screaming in protest, Cia told Fran every detail about the shelter and how she'd picked up where her mother left off. Silently, she bargained with herself, insisting the cause could use a good champion like Fran Wheeler and evaluating the possibility of still working with her after the divorce.

But she knew Fran wouldn't speak to her again after Lucas divorced her. That was better anyway. A clean break from both mother and son would be easier.

Way back in the far corner of Cia's mind, a worm of suspicion gained some teeth. What if Lucas had put his mother up to coming by in some weird, twisted ploy to get her to reconsider the divorce?

No, he wouldn't do that. She pushed the doubt away.

Lucas was honest about everything, and he hadn't mentioned staying married again anyway, thank goodness. For a second after he'd casually thrown out *long-term,* her pulse had shuddered to a halt and her suddenly active imagination had come up with all sorts of reasons why it could work. All pure fiction.

His suggestion had been nothing but an off-the-cuff idea which he hadn't been serious about in the first place. Exactly why she was ignoring all the feelings Lucas had churned up when they'd stood outside the old hotel—she'd be gutted if she gave him the slightest opening.

Besides, there was no *alternative* to divorce. The trust clause stated she couldn't file for divorce. He had to.

As she ushered Fran to the door with the promise of meeting her for lunch next Monday, Cia had herself convinced she and Lucas were on the same page about the divorce.

* * *

The green dress Lucas bought Cia for the Friends of the Dallas Museum of Art benefit gala was her favorite. Sheer silk brushed her skin like a cloud, and the neckline transformed her small breasts, giving her a bit of cleavage. She'd twisted her hair into an updo and a few rebel tendrils fell around her face. Sexy, if she did say so herself.

Lucas, criminally stunning in an Armani tux, came into the bathroom as she stepped into her black sandals. He swept her hand to his lips and zapped heat straight through her tummy.

The man had touched her as intimately as possible, in more ways than she'd imagined existed. Yet a simple kiss on the back of her hand turned her knees to jelly.

"Mrs. Wheeler, you are indeed ravishing." He pulled a flat box from the pocket of his jacket. Without taking his eyes off her, he opened the lid and offered her the box.

Cia glanced inside and her already weak knees almost pitched her to the travertine tile.

"Lucas," she squeaked, and that was the extent of her throat's ability to make sound.

He extracted the necklace and guided her to the mirror, then stood behind her to clasp the choker around her neck. Emeralds set in delicate filigreed platinum spilled over her collarbone, flashing fire and ice against her skin. Every eye would be drawn to the dazzling piece of art around her neck, and no one would even notice her cleavage.

"It reminds me of you," he murmured in her ear, not touching her at all, but his heat, a signature she recognized the moment he walked into a room, raced up her bare back. "An inferno captured inside a beautiful shell. All those hard edges polished away to reveal a treasure. Do you like it?"

Did she *like* it? That was akin to asking if she liked the sun or breathing. The necklace wasn't jewelry, the way every

other man on earth gave women jewelry. It was a metaphor
for how well he understood her.

Lucas had an uncanny ability to peer into her soul and
pluck out her essential desires, then present them to her.

Similar to his mother's pearls, this necklace represented
all the frightening, unexamined things in her heart, which
Lucas never let her forget. Neither could she forget he'd very
pointedly failed to mention the things in *his* heart.

"I can't keep it." Her hand flew to the clasp, only to be
stilled by his.

"Yes. You can. I insist."

"It's too…" Personal. Meaningful. Complicated. "Expensive. I'm sure you still have the receipt. Take it back."

"The artist custom-made it for you. All sales are final."

She shut her eyes for a beat. "That's not the kind of thing
you do for a woman you're about to divorce. How are we
going to make it look like we're on the outs if you're buying
me custom-made jewelry?"

They had time, but they'd done such a bang-up job of making a fake marriage look real, reversing it presented a whole
new set of difficulties. She wished she'd considered that before hopping into Lucas's bed.

"Maybe I'm trying to earn your forgiveness," he suggested
and in the mirror, his gaze locked on hers, a blue firestorm
winding around her, daring her to ask what he'd done that
required forgiveness.

Was this an apology for bringing up an *alternative* to di
vorce? "Forgiveness for an affair, maybe? You wouldn't do
that."

His forehead tightened. "How do you know what I'm ca
pable of?"

She spun away from the mirror, about to remind him that
he'd been the one to convince her he'd never cheat. His black
expression changed her mind. "Because I do. Only someone

with a huge ego and a heaping spoonful of selfish has an affair. You don't have the qualifications."

They stared at each other for the longest time, and, finally, Lucas blinked, clearing his expression, and gave her a slow smile. "So maybe I'm trying to earn your forgiveness or slaving away at the office. Leaving you alone for days on end, crying into your pillow about how your husband never pays attention to you anymore."

"That could work," she said, then squealed as he backed her up against the vanity and slid magic fingertips up her leg, gathering green silk against his wrist.

"It's been so long, hasn't it, darlin'? Are you desperate for my hands on you? Like this?" His palm flattened against her bottom and inched under her panties, stealing her breath as he dipped into her instantly wet center.

Yes, exactly like that.

"We have to leave or we'll be late," she choked out and squirmed against his wicked fingers. "Rain check. You and me and a coat closet. Nine o'clock. We'll pretend it's the first time we've been able to connect in weeks."

With his eyes blazing, he hooked the edge of her panties and drew them off to puddle on the floor. "How about we connect right now *and* I meet you in the coat closet? But only if you make it eight-thirty and leave your underwear at home."

As if she could resist him. Within moments, he'd sheathed himself and they joined, beautifully and completely.

She clung to him, wrapped her legs around him and plunged into pleasure. Pleasure with an edge because her brain had left the building, and he'd ended up with a piece of her heart after all. She couldn't find the courage to shut off what she was feeling.

When Lucas made love to her, she forgot all the reasons why the *alternative* wasn't plausible. Lucas glided home slowly, watching her with a searing, heavy expression, and her heart asked, "What if it could be?"

The question echoed with no answer.

No answer, because Lucas was *not* presenting an alternative to divorce so they could continue having spectacular sex no matter what he claimed.

Sex wasn't the basis for a relationship. Sex wasn't guaranteed to stay good, let alone spectacular. He hadn't miraculously fallen in love with her. So why had he really brought up long-term?

And why was she so sad? Because his alternative hadn't included a declaration from his heart or because it felt as though she didn't know the whole truth?

It didn't matter. This time she wouldn't end up broken hearted and disillusioned because she wasn't giving Lucas the chance to do either.

They arrived at the benefit twenty minutes late, and it would have been thirty if Lucas hadn't tipped the driver to speed. Regardless, heads swiveled as they entered the ballroom, and Cia struggled not to duck behind Lucas.

"What are they looking at?" she whispered. "I told you there was no such thing as fashionably late."

"Maybe they know you're not wearing any panties," he said, a lot more loudly than she would have liked, and made her skin sizzle with a sinful leer.

She smacked his arm with her clutch. "Maybe they know you stuffed them in your pocket."

The swish of fabric alerted her to someone else's presence. Lucas's mother. She stood right in front of them, and as far as Cia knew, still possessed working ears. Cia's smile died as heat climbed across her face.

"Lovely to see you, Mrs. Wheeler," Cia croaked. The fire in her face sparked higher. "I'm sorry, I mean Fran. You'd think it would be easy to remember. I don't like being called Mrs. Wheeler, either. Makes me feel like an impostor."

Where had that come from? She sealed her lips together before more stupid comments fell out, though dragging her on's sex life into public had probably already killed any warm feelings her mother-in-law might have developed over afternoon tea.

The older woman's cheeks were a little pink, but she cleared her throat and said, "No problem. I couldn't answer to it for at least a year after Andy and I married. Such a big change in identity. Wait until you have kids and they start calling you 'Mama.' That one's worse, yet so much more wonderful."

Another couple joined them, and Cia was caught up in introductions instead of being forced to come up with a neutral response to Fran's casually thrown out comment. It didn't stop the notion from ricocheting through her head.

Kids. No, thank you.

Lucas's warm hand settled at the small of her back as he talked shop to the couple who had asked Fran for an introduction. The wife needed larger office space for her CPA business. Cia smiled and nodded and pretended as though she wasn't imagining how Lucas would approach fatherhood.

But she was.

He'd kiss her pregnant belly while peering up at her through those clear blue eyes. He'd treat her reverently, fetching her drinks and rubbing her feet.

When the baby cried at night, he'd smooth Cia's hair back and tell her to stay in bed while he handled it. Later, he'd throw a ball for hours with a little dark-haired toddler. Lucas would label it fun and insist work could wait, even if it couldn't.

As quickly as those wispy images materialized, they vanished in favor of much clearer images of flashing lights atop black-and-white squad cars and grim-faced policemen who knocked on the door in the middle of the night to utter the words, "I'm sorry. The accident was fatal. Your parents are gone."

The only way she could guarantee that no child of hers

would ever go through that was not to have any children
She tucked away the sudden, jagged longing for a life tha
would never be.

Fran's friends wandered toward the dance floor, the wife
clutching the business card Lucas had retrieved from a hard
silver case, and another well-dressed couple looking for a rea
estate broker promptly replaced them.

"This is my wife, Cia Wheeler," Lucas said.

"Robert Graves," the male half of the couple said an
shook Cia's hand. "Formerly Allende, right?"

"Right. Benicio Allende is my grandfather."

Robert's eyes grew a touch warmer. "I thought so. M
company does the advertising for Manzanares. It keeps u
hopping."

"Oh?" Cia asked politely.

It never ceased to amaze her how people loved to name
drop and rub elbows because of her last name. *Former* las
name. Robert Graves was no exception, prattling on abou
Abuelo's shrewd negotiations and then switching gears to an
nounce right then and there that he'd like to do business wit
Lucas. It wasn't said, but it was clearly implied that he'd de
cided because of her.

She made Lucas stable. Connected. Exactly as they
hoped this marriage would do.

The room spun. Was that why Lucas wanted to blow o
the divorce? Because he didn't need the Manzanares contrac
to save his business anymore but he did need her?

Not possible. A few paltry clients couldn't compare to th
coup of Manzanares. She'd done exhaustive research. She
considered all the angles.

Except for the one where she worked hard to be an ass
to her husband and succeeded.

No. He'd keep his word. He had a high ethical standar
Surely he'd return to form before too long. Lucas excelled

acing off to the next woman—his brother had even warned er of it.

Lucas didn't want to give up sex. Fine. Neither did she, and *ompromise* wasn't a foreign word in her vocabulary. They ould keep seeing each other on the sly after the divorce.

The idea loosened the clench of her stomach. She didn't ave to quit Lucas cold turkey, and, as a bonus, she would ain a little extra time to shut off all these unwelcome feel-igs she'd been fighting.

As soon as the Graves couple coasted out of earshot, Fran ignaled a waiter, and Andy Wheeler joined the group in time) take a champagne flute from the gilded tray.

"A toast," Lucas's dad suggested with a raised glass. "To ll the new developments and those yet to be born."

Cia raised her glass and took a healthy swallow.

"Oh, you're drinking," Fran said with obvious disappoint-ient. "I guess there's no news yet."

Lucas flashed a wolfish smile in Cia's direction. "You'll c the second to know, Mama."

"Why do I feel like you're talking in code?" Cia whis-ered to Lucas.

"I might have casually mentioned we're trying to get preg-ant," Lucas whispered back. "Don't worry. It's just window ressing."

"Window dressing?" Cia said at normal volume, too star-ed to rein in her voice. "What kind of window dressing is aat?"

"Excuse us for a moment, please." Lucas nodded at his arents and dragged Cia away by the waist to an unpopu-ted corner of the room.

"Pregnant? Really?" she hissed and blinked against the carlet haze over her vision. "No wonder your mom stopped y for tea and chatted me up about identity and being called Mama.'"

"Well, now. I guess I don't have to ask you how you feel

about the idea." Lucas tucked a tendril of hair behind her ear and it took supreme will not to slap his hand away.

"It doesn't matter. We don't have a 'trying to get pregnant' marriage and never will. Should I say it again? In Spanish maybe?" She stuck a finger deep into his ribs. "Why did you tell your parents something so ridiculous? We don't need any more window dressing. In fact, we should be taking the dressing *off* the window."

"Since several people are at this very moment watching us argue, I believe dressing is peeling away rapidly with every finger jab," Lucas responded. "Simmer down, darlin'. Matthew's gone. I'm the only Wheeler who has a reasonable shot at producing the next generation. It's Wheeler Family Partners. Remember?"

She swallowed, hard, and it scraped down her throat as if she'd gargled with razor blades. "So I'm supposed to be the factory for the Wheeler baby production? Is that the idea?"

"Shocking how people leap to cast my wife in that role. One might wonder why you're having a meltdown about the mere contemplation of bearing my children, when you've been so clear about how our marriage is fake and we're divorcing, period, end of story." He stared her down with raised eyebrows. "Mama was upset when Matthew left, and I told her we were trying for a baby to soften the blow. Not because I have some evil scheme to start poking holes in the condoms. Okay?"

Oh, God. All part of the show.

She filled her lungs for what felt like the first time in an hour and let the breath out slowly, along with all the blistering anger at Lucas for…whatever offenses she'd imagined. It was a lot to balance, with the sudden presentation of *alternatives* and being an asset and baby talk.

Evil scheme aside, Lucas still had a serious obligation to start a family, and he'd never shun it. Her lungs constricted

again. They'd have to be extremely careful about birth con-
rol going forward.

Going forward? There wasn't much forward left in their
relationship, and she stood in the way of his obligations. It
vould be selfish to keep seeing him after the divorce.

She grimaced at the thought of another woman falling all
over herself to be the new Mrs. Wheeler. Cooing over his babies. Sleeping in his bed. Wearing his ring.

Soon, she'd be Señorita Allende again. That should have
cheered her up. It didn't. "We could have easily coordinated
torics. Why didn't you tell me earlier?"

Lucas lifted one shoulder and glanced at his Rolex.
"Slipped my mind. It's almost eight-thirty. I'll race you to
the coat closet."

She crossed her arms over another pang in her chest. "It's
even-fifteen, Wheeler. What is going on with you? As slip-
pery as your mind is, you did not forget casually mentioning
ve're trying to get pregnant. You wanted to see my reaction
in a place where I couldn't claw your skin off. Didn't you?"

A smear of guilt flashed through his eyes. He covered
it, but not quickly enough to keep her stomach from turn-
ng over.

She was right. Oh, God, she was *right*.

Long-term marriage suddenly didn't seem like an off-the-
uff, not-really-serious suggestion. The anger she'd worked
o hard to dismiss swept through her cheeks again, enflam-
ng them.

"Not at all," he said smoothly. "I have a lot of balls in the
ir. Bound to drop one occasionally."

"Learn to juggle better or a couple of those balls will hit
he ground so hard, I guarantee you'll never have children
with anyone." She whirled to put some distance between them
efore she got started on that guarantee right this minute.

Lucas followed her back into the mix of people, wisely opt-
ng to let her stew instead of trying to offer some lame apol-

ogy or, worse, throwing out an additional denial. Matthew's exodus had triggered more changes than the obvious ones.

Lucas's commitment phobia had withered up and died and now he'd started hacking away at hers with a dull machete. How could this night be any more of a disaster?

Fifteen minutes later, she found out exactly how much more of a disaster it could become when she overheard a conversation between four middle-aged men with the distinct smell of money wafting off them. They were blithely discussing her shelter.

She listened in horror, frozen in place behind them, as they loaded up plates at the buffet with shrimp and caviar, oblivious to the fact that they were discussing *her shelter*.

"Excellent visibility for the donors," one said, and another nodded.

Donors? Maybe she'd misheard the first part of the conversation. Maybe they weren't talking about the hotel site of her new shelter. They couldn't be. She'd made it very clear to Lucas she didn't want to depend on donations to run the shelter. Hadn't she?

"Any venture tied to Allende is a gold mine," the third declared. "How could you not be in after Wheeler's fantastic sales pitch? The property's in great shape. Most of the updating will be cosmetic, and the renovation contract is already on my lawyer's desk."

The property? Lucas had taken people to the site? How many people?

"Domestic violence is a little, shall we say, uncouth?" the fourth one suggested with a laugh. "But the Hispanic community is a worthwhile demographic to tap from a charitable perspective. It'll cinch my bid for mayor. That's the kind of thing voters want on your résumé."

Acid scalded her stomach. No. She hadn't misheard. Lucas had charged ahead without her—without her permission or ven her knowledge. He'd made the proposed shelter site public, rendering it useless.

What more had Lucas done? Had he been presenting an *alternative* to divorce or a done deal?

What exactly had the necklace been an apology for?

Twelve

Lucas and Cia had been home a good twenty minutes and she hadn't spoken yet. In the car, she'd blasted him with tirade about an overheard conversation, which she'd taken out of context, and then went mute. That alone chilled his skin, but coupled with the frosty set of her expression, even a stiff drink didn't melt the ice forming along his spine. So he had another.

Then he went looking for her.

The little ball in the center of the mattress was quiet, so he eased onto the edge of the bed. "I didn't know they were going to make such a big deal out of it."

Nothing.

He tried again. "Talk to me, honey. Scream at me. I don't care, as long as you don't keep up this deep freeze. This is all a big misunderstanding. I can fix it."

"Fix it?" The lethal whip of her tone sank into his skull which was already sloshy with alcohol and the beginning of a headache. She sat up, and the light from the bedside amp cast half of her scrubbed face in shadow. "You've done nough fixing for today, Machiavelli. I'm tired. Go away and leep somewhere else."

"Ouch. I'm in that much trouble?" He grinned, and she idn't return it. So, jokes weren't the way to go. Noted. "Come n, darlin'. I messed up. I shouldn't have taken people to the te. I'll find another hotel for your shelter if that site's com-romised. It's not worth getting so upset over."

"Do I seem upset?" She stared at him, and her dry eyes othered him more than the silent treatment. Unease snaked through his gut.

"No." He'd wandered into the middle of uncharted terri-ry full of quicksand. This had all the trappings of their first fficial fight as a couple. Except they weren't really a cou-le—yet—and, technically, they argued all the time. "Does at mean you've already forgiven me?"

She palmed her forehead and squeezed. "You really don't et any of this, do you?"

"Yeah, I get it." Somehow, his plan to come up with the perating expenses for the shelter hadn't happened as envi-oned. "You're ticked because I tried to tap sponsors for the elter site, and now the location is compromised. I'm in real tate, darlin'. I'll find another one. A better one."

"I'm sure you will. Eventually." She lay back down and overed her head with an arm, blocking his view of her face. is firecracker's fuse was noticeably fizzled. How could they et past this if she wouldn't yell at him?

"Cia." He waited until she peeked out from below the crook her elbow. "I should have talked to you before talking to e money. I'm sorry. Let's kiss and make up now, okay?"

"No. No more kissing. This isn't only about the shelter." er voice was steady, a monotone with no hint of the fire or ssion she normally directed at him. "It's about you running e show. You say I have a choice, but only if it's a choice you

agree with. I'm not doing this anymore. In the morning, I'm
moving back into my condo."

"What? You can't." This situation was unraveling faster
than he could put it back together. But whatever happened,
he couldn't let her leave. He wiped damp palms on the com
forter and went with reason. "We have a deal. Six months."

The arm came off her face, and bitter laughter cut throug
the quiet bedroom. "A deal, Wheeler? We have a *deal*? Of
that's rich. We have a deal when it's convenient for you to re
member it. Every other waking moment, you're trying to alte
the deal. Presenting alternatives. Trying to give me money
Talking about babies with your mother and seducing me int
believing you really understand me. It's all about the dea
isn't it? As long as it's the best deal for *you*. What about wha
I want?"

He swore. Some of her points could be considered vali
when viewed from a slightly different perspective. But he
perspective was wrong—the tweaks to the deal were goo
for everyone. "What do you want?"

"A divorce! The same thing I've wanted since day one.
fail to understand how or when that fact became confusin
to you."

"It's not confusing." He refused to lose control of the cor
versation. She needed him, and his job was to help her rea
ize it. "I know that's what you think you want. But it's not

"Oh, well, everything is so clear now. Are you aware
the fact that you talk in circles most of the time? Or is it d
liberate, to bewilder your opponent into giving up?"

"Here's some straight talk for you. We're good togethe
We have fun, and I like being with you. You're fascinating
compelling, inspiring and all of that is out of bed. In bed..
He whistled. "Amazing. Beyond compare. I've told you thi
No circles then. No circles now. Why can't you see a divord
is not what you need?"

"Do you hear yourself?" she asked so softly he straine

o pick up the words. "Your whole argument was about why divorce is not what *you* need. My needs are foreign to you. And you've spent the last few months fooling me into believing the opposite, with the dresses and taking care of me and pretending you were interested in the shelter because you wanted to help me."

"I *do* want to help you," he snapped. God Almighty, she pushed his limits. Stubborn as a stripped screw. He forced his tone back into the realm of agreeable before he gave away the fact that she'd gotten to him. "You're mad because it was mutually beneficial? That's what made the original deal so attractive. We both got value out of it. Why is it so bad to continue the tradition?"

"All lies! Matthew left and now you're hot for a wife who'll give you a baby. You're too lazy to go find one, so you thought, 'Hey, I already have a wife. I'll hang on to her.'"

Lazy? She was more work than a roomful of spoiled debutantes and jaded supermodels. Yet there was not one woman he'd want long-term besides Cia. They were compatible on every level, and the thought of living his life without her— well, it wasn't a picture he liked. Why else would he be talking about it? "I get the feeling anything I say at this point would be wrong."

"Now you're onto something. There's no defense for any of it, least of all compromising the shelter site. If a woman's abuser finds the shelter, he might kill her. Do you understand how horrible your cavalier attitude is? Do you have any clue how it made me feel when I realized what those men were talking about?"

"I'm sorry. I do understand how important discretion is. It was a mistake. But I stand by my offer to find another site."

"How magnanimous of you," she said with a sneer. "I'm not stupid, Wheeler. You got me all excited about it, then oh, no. Bring in the entire upper crust of Dallas, so everyone knows where the shelter is. Oops. You sabotaged that site, hoping to buy time to talk me out of the divorce. Maybe *ac cidentally* get pregnant in the meantime."

Was she listening to anything he had said? He'd apologized twice already. "Compromising the site might have been the result but that was not my inten—"

"Betrayed. That's how I felt when I stood there listening to my entire world crumble around me."

Everything with Cia was a hundred times more effort than it needed to be, which he knew good and well she did on purpose to keep everyone at bay. But why was she still doing it with him? Hadn't they gotten past this point already? "That's a little melodramatic, don't you think?"

There came a tear, finally, sliding down her cheek. "Melodramatic? You broke my heart, Lucas!"

"What?" Every organ in his chest ground to a halt, and he couldn't tear his eyes away from the lone tear laden with despair and hurt.

No. No way. This marriage was about the benefits, both physically and business-wise. She needed his unique contribution to the relationship. Period.

He'd been one hundred percent certain she was on board with that. Hurt and feelings and messiness weren't part of the deal. And when the deal fell apart, he walked away. Usually.

But he was still here.

She dashed away the teardrop, but several more replaced it. "Surprised me, too."

All of this was too fast. Too much to process. "Whoa. What are you saying?"

"Same thing I've been saying. Since you have to file for the divorce, I have no power here. Therefore, I'm leaving, and have to trust you'll eventually find another potential mother for your next generation, at which point I'll get my divorce. Clear enough for you?"

"No." He shook his head. "Back up, honey. Now *you're*

alking in circles. I didn't make you mad—I hurt you. How
did that happen?"

"Because I'm an idiot." Her eyes shone with more unshed
ears. "I had expectations of you that you couldn't fulfill.
You're not the man I thought you were."

"Wait a minute. What did you expect?" He was still reel-
ng from the discovery she'd developed *feelings* for him and
adn't bothered to say anything.

What would he have done with such information? Run in
he other direction? Run faster toward her?

Actually, he didn't know what to do with it now.

"I expected you to be honest, not hide your real agenda."
he snorted. "*Dios,* how naive am I? I walked right into it,
yes wide open, certain I could hang on to my soul since you
eren't asking for it. You gave and gave, and I never saw it
or what it was. An exchange. You slipped under my guard,
nd the whole time, you were planning to exact payment. You
etrayed me, not once but twice, with alternatives and then
ith sponsors. You don't get a third chance to screw me over."

When thunderclouds gathered across Lucas's face, Cia was
o tired to care that she'd finally cracked his composure.

"That's enough," Lucas declared. "I listened to your men-
al origami, and let me tell you, I am impressed with your
bility to fold facts into a brand-new shape. But it's my turn
o talk. Are you in love with me?"

She almost groaned. Why did he have to go there? "That's
relevant."

He tipped her chin up and pierced her with those blue laser
eams. Scared of what he'd see, she jerked away and buried
er face in the pillow.

Great. The entire bed smelled of pine trees mixed with
er lotion.

"It's not irrelevant to me," he countered quietly. "I'd like
 know what's going on inside you."

So would she. Thoughts of babies and long-term should not be so hard to shove away. The hurt shouldn't be so sharp.

"Why?" she mumbled, her face still in the pillow.

He growled in obvious frustration, "Because I care about you."

She rolled over and said, "You have a funny way of showing it."

"Really? I'd argue the exact opposite."

"You can argue about it all day long. But you'd be wrong. You like to take care of me. That's different than caring about me."

He snapped out a derisive laugh. "Maybe we should start this whole conversation over. We suck at communicating unless it's 'more,' 'faster' or 'again,' don't we?"

No, they didn't have any communication problems when they were naked, which was exactly what had gotten her into this mess. Intimacy with Lucas could never be divorced from emotion. Why had she pretended it could be? "Which is why we're done with that part of our relationship."

He sighed. "Look, honey. I messed up. But I'm here, talking to you, trying to fix it. And you still never answered the question. Are you in love with me?"

"Stop asking me!" she burst out, determined to cut off his earnestness and dogged determination to uncover the secret longings of her heart that she didn't understand and did not want to share. He had enough power over her already. "It's just warm feelings for the man I'm sleeping with because he's superawesome in bed, okay? It doesn't change anything. You're not in love with me. You're still on the lookout for a baby factory. And I need a divorce, not all of these complications."

"Complications are challenges you haven't conquered yet," he said, and the tension in his face and shoulders visibly eased.

Her tension went through the roof.

Of course he hadn't fallen all over himself to declare his undying love. Not that she had expected him to after she'd backtracked about her broken heart.

In matters of the heart, they were cut from the same cloth—excellent at emotional distance and not much else. The divorce deal was perfect for them both.

"I'm not up for any more complications *or* challenges, thanks. Can we cut to the chase?" She sat up and faced him. "Are you going to file for divorce or not?"

He held her gaze without blinking, without giving away his thoughts. "No."

Her eyelids snapped closed. He'd finally made his move. *Checkmate.* "You can't do this to me, Lucas. Please."

"I can't do what? Give you what you really need instead of a divorce you'll regret? You're a vibrant, beautiful woman, yet you aim to shrivel up alone for the rest of your life. That's not right."

He ran a hand through her hair, letting it waterfall off his fingers, and his touch, so familiar, nearly caved in her stomach.

Being alone had never been her goal. Avoidance of suffering had been the intent, but she'd done a shoddy job of it, hadn't she? The tsunami of agony hadn't just drowned her; it had broken through every solid barrier inside, allowing sharp-edged secret dreams to flow out, drawing blood as they went.

"Cia, I'm offering a long-term partnership, with advantages for both of us. We already know we like each other. The sex is great. We'll figure out how to do your shelter without the trust fund. Together, we're unstoppable. Why can't you consider it?"

"Because it's not enough. There's a reason why I'll be alone for the rest of my life. I don't know how to do long-term." He started to respond, but she cut him off. "And neither do you. Sex isn't enough. Liking each other isn't enough."

He hurled out a curse. "What is enough?"

Love.

Oh, God. She wanted something he couldn't give her Something she didn't know how to give him. No wonder sh couldn't answer his questions.

She shied away from relationships because she had no ide how to love a man when living in constant fear of the pai and loss sure to follow. She had no idea how to love withou becoming dangerously dependent on it.

Her parents had been in love. Until Lucas, she hadn't re membered all the long glances and hand-holding. The acci dent had overshadowed the history of their lives before tha one shattering, defining moment. If they had lived, would sh be having an entirely different conversation about the magi ingredients of a long-term relationship?

Would she better understand her own heart and deman Lucas know his?

"I can't tell you," she said. "You have to figure it out o your own."

He pressed the back of his neck with stiff fingers. "Fan tastic. An impossible puzzle with no correct answer. Wh can't this be about what looks good on paper?"

Sacar los ojos a uno. He was bleeding her white.

"It's all about how things look with you." She should hav seen that before. Appearances were everything because skir deep was all he permitted. Nothing could penetrate the armo he kept over his heart. "As long as it looks like fun, you'r on board, right?"

"That's not fair. I never said a long-term marriage woul be a big party. I don't know what it'll look like, but I do kno I don't want what we have to be over." Gently he gripped he shoulders, and for a moment raw tenderness welled in hi eyes. It made her pulse stutter and wrenched a tendril of hop from inside her. But then he said, "And I know you need wh; I bring to this relationship. You need me."

"No." She looked straight at him as her heart broke anev

His entire offer hinged on dependency, the certainty that she was willing to be dependent. Not because he wanted to be with her. "Need is dangerous. It creates reliance. Addiction. Suddenly, you can't survive without the thing you crave. What happens when it's gone? I don't need selfishness disguised as partnership. I don't need someone who doesn't understand me. I don't need you, Lucas. Let me go."

Pain flashed across his face. Finally. This conversation had gone on for far too long. She'd run out of arguments, ways to get him out of the room before she went completely insane and begged him to figure out how to give her what she wanted.

"Yeah," he said and cleared his throat. "Okay. It's for the best."

As he slid off the bed and gathered some clothes from the dresser, she twisted off her rings and set them on the bedside table. The light scorched her eyes. She reached out and snapped it off, staring at the now-invisible rings until she had to blink.

At the door of their bedroom, he stopped. Without turning around, he said, "I'll help you pack in the morning. It'll work in our favor to separate now so it won't be such a surprise when I file for divorce."

Then he did turn, and his gaze sought hers. The hall light created a shadow of his broad shoulders against the carpet and obscured his face. "Is there anything I could have offered you that would have been worth reconsidering the divorce?"

Her throat cramped with grief. If she tried to talk, she'd break down, and every time she cried, he held her and made her feel things she shouldn't. Feelings he couldn't return.

When she didn't answer, he nodded and left.

In the darkness, she whispered, "You could have offered to love me."

Thirteen

The divorce papers sat on the edge of Lucas's desk, where they'd sat for a week now, without moving. Cia's loopy script was buried on the last page, where he couldn't see it. The papers lacked only his signature, but he couldn't sign. It didn't feel right. Nothing did. Certainly not his big, empty house where he'd aimed to remove all traces of the previous couple who'd lived there and had succeeded beyond his wildest dreams.

Cia was everywhere. Sitting on the counter in the kitchen, eyes black with passion as he drove her to a brilliant climax. Walking down the stairs with careful steps, wearing a dress that had taken him an hour to find because none of the others would put appreciation on her face the way this exact one would.

Cia sleeping in his bed, hair tousled and flung across two pillows as she nestled right at the mattress's halfway mark, ripe for him to join her, to fold her against his body and sink in.

He groaned and slammed his head into his hands, ignoring the document filling the laptop screen before him.

That was the worst, trying to sleep alone after having Cia here, night after night. A blink in time, compared to how long he'd slept without her. But no matter how many times the maid washed the sheets, lime and coconut lingered in the creases, lying in wait to spring from hiding and invade his nose with the memory of what he'd lost.

No, not lost—what he'd never had in the first place.

He'd been wrong. Cia didn't need him. What could he say, what could he do, to counter that? If she didn't need him, he had no place in her life, as hard as that was to accept. She'd probably already whisked away whatever feelings she'd had for him, warm or otherwise.

At least he could bury himself in eighteen-hour days with no distractions and no one waiting at home.

All those closed-door sessions with Matthew had taken root. New clients vied for his attention. Contracts spilled from his workbag. Wheeler Family Partners for-sale signs dotted properties all across the city. The National Commercial Development Association had nominated WFP for an award—the highest percentage increase in listings for the year. Manzanares was icing on the cake.

Success and acknowledgment of his efforts. That's what he should be focusing on. Not on how every contract reminded him he should be closing the deal on his divorce and moving on. Every contract mocked him, silently asking why he couldn't just pick up a pen, for crying out loud.

He had to get out of here. Take a walk or a drive to clear his head. When he got back, he'd sign the papers and send them to his lawyer to be filed with the court. In no time, he'd be rid of this ache behind his ribs and free to pursue...something. Anything. The world was his for the taking.

But nothing interested him. At all.

He fingered the box in his pocket, which held Cia's rings.

It was time—past time—to stop carrying them around, bu
whenever he dug out the box and held it on his palm, hi
lungs cramped. The same cramp happened when he tried to
remove his ring.

Maybe he should see a doctor. His throat hurt all the time
Some bug had probably wormed its way into his system.

When he rounded the corner to the reception area, Helen
gave him her you-have-company-and-it's-not-a-client smil
and said, "I was about to buzz you. You have a visitor."

Cia. His stomach flipped and a cold sweat broke out acros
his forehead. Maybe she'd thought it through and had recog
nized the excellent logic he'd so clearly laid out for why the
belonged together.

Maybe she was pregnant. The image of her belly rounde
with his child materialized in his head and pricked the back
of his eyes.

Or—he dragged his imagination back to the real world—
she intended to flay him alive for not filing the papers ye
He pasted a smile on his face and pivoted to face the wrat
of Hurricane Cia in full category-five mode.

He could never have prepared enough to greet the woma
seated on the leather couch.

"Lana." *Not Cia.* Of course not. She'd never concede. H
swallowed his disappointment. "This is a surprise."

"As it was meant to be. Hello, Lucas." Lana stood, balan
ing on delicate stilettos and clad in an expensive designer su
Cia would have sniffed at righteously.

Funny. He'd never noticed what Lana wore, other than t
figure out the best way to get it off without ruining it, as sh
was ridiculously fussy about her clothes. Again, hindsigh
Couldn't go home to her husband with buttons missing. "
something wrong?"

With a glance at Helena, she said, "Can I buy you a cu
of coffee?"

Yeah. Go out in public with Lana while still married t

ia. Exactly what he needed. Actually, even a private con-
ersation with Lana sounded less than fun, but as he took in
e classy blonde who'd thanked him for his time and effort
ith lies, he realized he was over it.

And he was curious what she wanted. "Helena's coffee is
etter than any coffeehouse's. I have a few minutes. Let's sit
the conference room."

Lana followed him to the conference room across from the
ceptionist's desk, which he'd chosen due to the glass walls
case she thought there was a chance in hell he'd pick up
here they'd left off.

He had a strong sense of propriety, not a shallow love for
pearances as Cia liked to accuse him of.

Helena entered with two cups of coffee and left them on
e table, along with an array of creamers and sugars. Lucas
aited for Lana to take a seat and then chose a perpendicu-
r chair.

"What can I do for you?" he asked politely.

Two artificial sweeteners and four creamers. Lana hadn't
anged the way she drank coffee and likely nothing else,
her. She took her time stirring, then looked up. "I came
apologize."

Lucas raised an eyebrow. "For which part?"

"All of it. I was lonely. Bored. Feeling adventurous. Take
ur pick. My shrink would agree with all of them. I'm not
king you to understand why I did it. Just to believe I'm
rry I hurt you."

"You didn't hurt me." He laughed and hated that it sounded
rced. "You lied to me. You used me. Then you unleashed
ur husband on me to finish the evisceration job you started.
at was the most unforgivable part."

He took a deep breath. Maybe he wasn't as over it as he'd
agined.

She sipped her coffee, as if for fortification, and blinked
r baby blues. "I'm here to apologize for that, too," she said.

"And to tell you the truth. I didn't unleash my husband o
you. All the rumors and hits to your business, I did that. Nc
Henry."

"What?" Shock froze his tongue, preventing him fror
voicing anything else. No. Not over it *at all*.

"Henry will be fifty-eight in December. I had no illusior
about being in love when I married him and neither did h∢
When I told him about you, he patted my hand and said
was cheaper than a divorce, then went back to work. I playe
him up as the jealous husband because, well, I wanted you ♠
believe I had worth to him."

"Why?" he prompted when she paused.

"Because you're so hard to faze, Lucas. Emotionally. D
you feel anything at all? I wanted you to love me and yc
didn't. I thought…maybe if you believed he loved me, you
see something desirable in me, too. Only it didn't work. I w∢
heartbroken. Devastated that it was just all fun and gam∢
to you."

"It was fun," he reminded her harshly. She had a lot ∢
nerve, talking about love when they'd been nowhere near s∢
rious. "It could have been more, maybe. Eventually. At lea≀
I thought it could."

Genuine sadness laced her small smile. "Could have bee
Maybe. Eventually. That's how it is with you. No comm
ment. So I lashed out. Tried to ruin you. Instead, you fell
love with someone else, blew past all my efforts to destr∢
you and went on to be happy without me."

A catch in her throat cut off the sentence and a catch in h
gut kept his resounding "No" from being voiced.

He wasn't happy.

The rest of it was true. He was in love with Cia, and ▮
needed her, like a tree needed water. She brought out all t▮
best parts of him and kept him on his toes. She challeng∢
him and made him feel alive.

He'd given her up, so sure that if she didn't need him, they had no reason to be together.

Ironic how Lana hadn't accused him of marrying Cia on the rebound after all. Instead, she'd put a microscope on his marriage, and the view shook his spine something fierce.

She coughed and touched a finger to the corner of her eye. I'm sorry, and I'm not going to bother you anymore. I'm in place now where I can be happy for you."

And he was in a place where he could accept Lana had cut him deeper than he'd been willing to admit, spilling over into his relationship with Cia and causing missteps visible only in hindsight. *Hindsight.* The word of the day.

"Okay." He stood so fast the rolling chair shot away from the backs of his legs. "Thanks for coming by. You didn't have to, and I appreciate it."

Surprised, she glanced up. "Rushing me out? I guess I don't blame you. Good luck, Lucas. You deserve a much better life than what I could have given you."

In his head, the word *life* became *wife*. He agreed. He deserved a better wife than one who betrayed him the way Lana had. But his wife deserved a better husband than one who had betrayed her. Like he'd done to Cia. He'd done all he'd accused him of, and more, and probably not as subconsciously as he'd insisted.

He'd refused to see the truth. He'd been so busy trying to save what Matthew had had that he'd missed the most critical element. It was clear now why his brother hadn't been able to live in the house he'd built with Amber, why he'd taken off despite being a Wheeler.

Love made a person do crazy, irrational things. Things he'd never do under normal circumstances, like offer a short-term wife millions of dollars to make it long-term. Instead of blowing off Cia's broken heart like a complete moron, he should have just opened his mouth and admitted he wanted to alter the deal because he loved her and couldn't live without her.

It might not have changed the outcome. But it might have

Love. That was the reason he couldn't move on this time
He'd been too afraid of it, too much a coward to examine wha
he was feeling, and it would serve him right to have lost Cia
forever. But he wasn't going down without a fight.

He hurried to his office to start on the Lucas Wheele
Philosophy of Cia Wheeler. He had to get it right this time.

Something was wrong with Fergie. Cia had tried every
thing, but the bird wouldn't eat. The blob of gray feather
sat in the bottom of the cage and refused to acknowledg
the presence of her owner. It had been like this since the da
she'd moved back into her condo.

Every morning, she rushed to Fergie's cage, convince
she'd find the bird claws up and stiff with rigor mortis, whicl
would be about right for a companion she'd anticipated hav
ing for fifty years.

One more thing ripped from her fingers.

"You have to eat sometime," she told Fergie. Not that sh
blamed her. Cia had no appetite, either, and after cooking i
Amber's gourmet kitchen, the one in her condo, which she'
been using for years, wasn't the same. "We'll try again to
morrow."

At quarter till nine, she went to bed, where she woul
likely not sleep because she refused to turn on the TV an
refused to acknowledge she'd grown used to it.

She didn't need the TV, and she didn't need Lucas Wheele
For anything, least of all to "help" her find another shelter sit
She had an internet connection and lots of patience. Oka
maybe not so much patience. Tomorrow she'd investigat
using another real estate professional. A female.

Cia stared at the dark ceiling and shifted for the hundredt
time into yet another uncomfortable spot on the hard ma
tress. It was just so quiet without the TV. Without the rustl

f sheets and the deep breathing of a warm, male body scant
iches away.

Not a night went by without a stern internal reminder of
ow much better it was to be alone, instead of constantly
ooking over her shoulder for the guillotine that would sever
er happiness.

A knock at the front door interrupted her misery. Grum-
ing, she threw on a robe and flipped on a light as she crossed
ie small condo. A peek through the peephole shot her pulse
ito the stratosphere.

Lucas.

With a sheaf of papers in his hand. The divorce papers. He
as dropping them off—personally—this late?

Hands shaking, she unlatched the door and swung it open.
Vhat are you doing here?"

"Hello to you, too." He captured her gaze, flooding her
ith a blue tidal wave of things unsaid. Unresolved.

The porch light shone down, highlighting his casual dress.
argoes and a T-shirt, which meant he hadn't come straight
om work. Was he not working all hours of the night any-
ore? Dark splotches under his eyes and lines of fatigue in
s forehead told a different tale.

She set her back teeth together. She had to get out of the
bit of caring.

"Come in, before I let in all the mosquitoes in Uptown."
ie stepped back and allowed him to brush past her, to prove
s raw Lucas-ness didn't have any power here. His heat
armed her suddenly chilled skin, and the quick tug in her
domen made a liar out of her.

A squawk stopped his progress midstride. Fergie flapped
r wings and ran back and forth along one of the wooden
wels anchored across the top of her cage. "Lucas, Lucas,
icas," she singsonged.

Cia glared at her miraculously revived bird. "I didn't know
e could say that."

"Took her long enough." He grinned, and his eyes lit up. All the butterflies in her stomach took flight. "We've been working on it."

So. Fergie and Lucas had been buddy-buddy behind her back. She sighed. Maybe Fergie would eat, now that her precious Lucas was here. Traitor.

She waved at the couch. "Sit down."

He sank into the giant white sectional, and it shrank as his frame dominated the space. Then he spilled his masculinity into the rest of the room, overwhelming her.

Why had he come here, invading her refuge?

Luckily, he'd had the wisdom to move them into Matthew's house—his house now—instead of moving in here for the duration. The separation would have been a hundred times more difficult if she'd had to wash his presence from the condo. No way she could have. She would've had to move.

Might still have to, just from this visit.

"Will you sit with me?" He nodded to the couch.

"I prefer to stand, thanks. Besides, you're not staying long. Are you dropping off the papers?"

"In a way," he said. "But first, I'd like to tell you something. You know my great-great-grandfather founded Wheel Family Partners back in the eighteen hundreds, right?"

When she nodded, he went on, "Back then, there weren't many buildings. Mostly land. That's true real estate, and it's in my blood. I used to think real estate was about deals. A piece of paper, signed and filed. Then I was done, ready to move on to the next deal. But that's not who I am anymore. I'm in the business of partnering with people to build something real. Something permanent. That's why I grew WFP without Matthew. Not because I got lucky or worked hard. I fell in love with someone who challenges me to be more. Who taught me the value of wholehearted commitment."

¡Dios mío!

"Is *that* where you were going?" She laughed, and it came

t more like a sob. So now he was in love with her. Conve-
ently. "You came to deliver divorce papers and tell me you
·cided you're in love with me. Anything else?"

He came off the couch in a rush, feet planted and eyes
azing. Involuntarily, she backed up from the heat of his
.ger. *This* was Lucas mad. Before, by the pool, was noth-
з in comparison.

"I'm not here to deliver divorce papers." He held them up
d flicked his other hand. A lighter appeared between his
.gers, flame extended.

Before she could blink, he set the papers on fire.

Smoke curled away from the burning pages, and her di-
rce deal turned to ash. He blew out the fire before it reached
s fingers and threw the charred corners on her pristine cof-
e table, metal glinting from his third finger with the mo-
n. He was still wearing his wedding ring.

"What did you do that for?" she demanded, pulse pound-
з. "I have a copy in the other room, and you're not leaving
re until you sign it."

His taut frame still bristled as he dismissed the demand
th a curt slice of his hand. "I am not divorcing you. Period."
took a deep, steadying breath. "Cia, listen for a minute. I
.ndled it all wrong. I'm sorry. I cut down what mattered most
you and undermined your goals with the shelter, trying to
ce you to need me. I was too much of a dingbat to realize
done everything except the one thing you really wanted."

"Oh, what's that?" she asked. Tears stabbed at her eyes,
rned down her throat.

"You stuck your heart out and then yanked it right back so
·ickly, I almost didn't see it. You don't give a guy a chance
think about what to do with such a gift, and I'm sorry it
k me so long to figure out what would be enough." He
hed toward her slowly, giving her time to move. Or to stay.
ɔu want someone to love you. You want *me* to love you."
Her lungs contracted as his heart splashed onto his face.

This was definitely not some conveniently discovered feeli[ng] calculated to get his way. He'd never looked at her with su[ch] fierce longing coupled with aching tenderness.

And yet, he'd always looked at her like that. She'd nev[er] dared examine it. Never dared hope it meant more than war[m] feelings for the woman he was sleeping with.

When he'd taken all the steps he could, she hadn't move[d.] He swept her up in his arms.

"Darlin'," he whispered into her hair. "Let me love you[."]

She shut her eyes and breathed in Lucas. Breathed in t[he] acrid, charred scent of burned paper as his body cleaved [to] hers and he held her. It would be so easy to plunge into t[he] new Lucas, the one who opened up and poured out poet[ry] and promises like sap from a felled tree.

With her stomach and heart twisting, she broke his e[m]brace. "That's not what I want."

"Stop pretending." Ferocity leaped back into his expre[s]sion. "You're so afraid, you either fake everything or y[ou] fight it, as if that will insulate you from hurt. Nothing wi[ll.] But being alone hurts in a different way."

His blue laser beams punched right through her, past t[he] flesh and bone. She'd struggled so hard to be whole, to he[al] from losing pieces of her soul. First, when her parents di[ed] and after, when she tried to replace the loss with disastro[us] relationships.

And here she was, with no empty space. No room for a[ny]one, not even this surprising, layered man who stood bef[ore] her, asking for something she couldn't give.

"I am afraid." Had she said that out loud?

"I know, honey. I know all about fear. Do you think it w[as] easy for me to come here with nothing to give except m[y]self? Jewelry and spectacular sex are much easier to of[fer] than risking you'll accept plain old me. But I'm hoping [I'm] enough, because I can't live my life without you."

He was saying all the right things. Except he was first a[nd]

foremost a salesman, and she'd experienced his stellar abil-
ty to sell himself firsthand. "You wanted me to be needy.
But not anymore?"

"Yeah. I wanted you to need me and told myself fulfilling
your needs was my half of the partnership. A total lie. It was
so I didn't have to do the work. So I could keep from invest-
ing emotionally. The worst part is, I was already in deep and
couldn't tell you how much I need *you*. You're right. Need is
dangerous." He inclined his head in deference. "I can't survive without you. I'm completely addicted to you. And I love
you too much to let you go."

The sentiment darted right through her flimsy barriers
and spread with warmth into the emptiness she would have
sworn wasn't there.

Lucas had known, though, and burrowed right past the
pretense, past all the lies she told herself. It was frightening
to consider just being real for once and more frightening still
to consider giving up her defenses. "How can I know for sure
this isn't all going to evaporate one day?"

"I don't have a crystal ball. All I have is right here." He
held his hands wide, palms up. "Can you forgive me?"

She shut her eyes against the raw emotion spilling from
the sea of blue trained on her face. No sales pitch there. Just
a whole lot of Lucas, showing her the inner reaches of his
heart. "This is a lot to take in. Without the divorce, I don't
get my money. How can I live with that?"

His expression grew cunning. "How can you live with
yourself if you do get your money? You don't want to be a
slave to need, yet you're willing to be one to your grandfather."

She flinched. "What are you talking about?"

"You're dependent on your grandfather and his money
to grant you a measure of control over a life that can't be
controlled." He advanced on her, backing her up until she
hit the wall. "I'm not above stacking the deck to get what

I want, and I want you, Cia Wheeler. I dare you to take a risk on us. I dare you to stare your grandfather in the eye and tell him to keep his money, because you're keeping your marriage."

Vocalized in Lucas's whiskey-smooth voice, her name sounded beautiful. Exactly right. It was too much. He saw too much, wanted too much. He made her want too much.

"How can I?" she whispered.

"Simple. You have needs, whether you like it or not. They're part of being human, so you have to make a choice. Do you need your grandfather to take care of you financially? Or do you need to take a chance on a new deal with me? A mutually beneficial deal, because, honey, you need me as much as I need you. The question is, can you admit it?"

There it was. He'd drawn the line, given her a choice. Maybe it was that easy to just say *yes*. But it couldn't be. "What if I don't want kids?"

He flashed a grin. "What if I do? What if I don't want you to keep a single stitch of your wardrobe? What if I want to put on clown makeup and join the circus? What if—"

"Okay. I get it." And he got her. Not so difficult to believe after all, not when it was Lucas. That's why the betrayal had hurt so much, because he'd twisted the knife with expert knowledge. "You're saying we'll figure it out."

"Together. I love you and that will never change. It's the only guarantee I've got. Well, I can also guarantee we'll fight over the radio station. But I'm willing to overlook your terrible taste in music if it means I get a real wife out of the deal. Do I?"

Real. Everything she'd been afraid to want until Lucas. The divorce deal was a flawed shield against a real relationship, but fear of losing something meaningful had squelched all her courage to reach for that dream.

She'd done her best to get rid of Lucas before he could hurt er, but he kept coming back. Maybe it was finally time to top fighting it. Time to admit she loved him fiercely.

Could she take a chance on a marriage deal? Could she isk the possibilities, bad or good?

"No." Mind made up, she inspected him through narrowed yes and crossed her arms. "How is that fair? You get a real wife in exchange for exposure to my excellent taste in music. et I'll be forced to listen to songs about cheating, honky-onks and cheap beer? No deal. Find a pen and sign the copy f the papers right now unless you can agree to find a type f music we both like."

His gaze played over her face, and when he smiled, the un rose. No point in denying it. She'd given a huge piece of er heart to Lucas a long time ago, and he was offering to ill that hole with himself. Love had healed her, and now, she ould let him do that.

"Opera?" he suggested and yanked her into his arms, en-ulfing her in the scent of clean pine. The scent of her real usband.

His mouth captured hers before she could argue opera was ore a type of theater than a type of music. Lucas kissed er, and her heart became whole, then swelled, too big for er chest.

She pulled back a tiny bit, unwilling to be too far from im. "I really, really hope you meant it when you said you ve me, because if you want a real wife, you're going to have suffer through a big, formal wedding. And I'm asking your other to help plan it."

He groaned. "I meant it. You know you'll have to suffer rough a real honeymoon in exchange, right?"

"With lots of real sex? *Dios,* the things I do for you." With tsk, she smiled. "I must love you a lot."

"Well, then. Since we're already married, the big, formal edding is merely symbolic. So the honeymoon comes first." e peeled back her robe and rolled his eyes at the tank top underneath. "Please. I'm begging you. Let me buy you some nice, tasteful sleepwear not made from cotton."

"Not unless you let me teach you to dance." His hand slid under the tank top and claimed her body, just like he'd claimed her heart. "Lucas," she breathed.

Fergie squawked, "Lucas, Lucas, Lucas."

Lucas laughed against Cia's mouth. "That's a deal."

Even with Fran's help, the wedding plans stretched over the course of two months. The real story was far too incredible, so Lucas smoothed over everyone's questions with the partial truth—Cia'd had a change of heart about including everyone in their marriage celebration, and she wanted a lavish second ceremony.

Finally, after endless rounds of making decisions and sampling cake and addressing invitations, Cia clutched Abuelo's arm and walked down the aisle to her husband. Then, nearly five hundred guests accompanied them to an extravagant reception, where the bride and groom danced to every song, be it fast or slow.

Lucas twirled Cia to one of his favorite country numbers and she sang along, not ashamed to admit she kind of liked it, twangy guitars and all. He gathered her close and smiled. "Was it worth it? The big wedding?"

"It's everything I dreamed it would be. Exhausting but so wonderful."

That morning, she'd begun to suspect the exhaustion wasn't due to frantic wedding plans but another reason entirely. But she'd had no time to slip away and buy a pregnancy test. Tomorrow was soon enough to confirm it.

She couldn't wait to find out for sure. A whole, intact heart allowed for plenty of possibilities, and, finally, she was in a place where the thought of a baby didn't scare her blind. And if the test came back negative, they'd try some

ore. It was all in the journey and the pleasures to be had
long the way.

When the music ended, Lucas escorted her to the table,
nd Fran flashed yet another proud smile. Cia touched the
earls around her neck and grinned at Fran and Andy in turn.
he'd gained a family along with a husband.

Well, most of a family—Matthew hadn't come back for the
edding and it weighed on Lucas. Hopefully she could cheer
im up tomorrow with the news he'd started on the next gen-
ation of Wheelers a little earlier than expected.

Abuelo approached the table and took Cia's hand. "I'm
raid this old man must retire for the evening, my dear.
ucas, I'll be in your office a week from Monday to sign
e papers. I'm a little sad to see the Manzanares complex
ange hands, but I couldn't be happier with the deal you
gotiated."

"Anything for family. I'm glad to be of service." Lucas
asped Abuelo's outstretched hand and wished him a good
ening.

Only after a knockdown, drag-out fight, which Cia refused
lose, had Lucas agreed to still represent Abuelo in the sale
Manzanares, even though he hadn't followed through with
e divorce. Seriously, her husband took integrity to a whole
w level. When Cia pointed out she couldn't trust any other
al estate broker with Abuelo's business except Lucas, he
nceded.

Abuelo hadn't budged on changing the terms of the trust,
spite Cia's zealous pleas, but she was okay with that. In lieu
wedding gifts, Cia and Lucas had asked for donations to
e newly formed Wheeler Family Foundation, helmed quite
pertly by Fran Wheeler, and the balance grew by leaps and
unds daily.

Every time Cia launched into an impassioned explana-
n about the work she and Fran were doing, and every time
meone handed her another check, she could feel her mother

smiling down in approval. Nothing could bring back her par
ents, but trusting Lucas with her heart had finally allowe
Cia to close that chapter and embrace the next one.

She dreamed of forever, and Lucas Wheeler was exactl
the man to give it to her.

* * * * *

A sneaky peek at next month...

Desire

PASSIONATE AND DRAMATIC LOVE STORIES

My wish list for next month's titles...

In stores from 19th April 2013:

☐ A Wedding She'll Never Forget — Robyn Grady

& Millionaire in a Stetson — Barbara Dunlop

☐ Beguiling the Boss — Joan Hohl

& A Trap So Tender — Jennifer Lewis

2 stories in each book - only £5.49!

☐ One Secret Night — Yvonne Lindsay

& Project: Runaway Heiress — Heidi Betts

Available at WHSmith, Tesco, Asda, Eason, Amazon and Apple

Just can't wait?

Special Offers

Every month we put together collections and longer reads written by your favourite authors.

Here are some of next month's highlights— and don't miss our fabulous discount online!

Australia
OUTBACK FANTASIES

Margaret WAY   Barbara HANNAY   Leah MARTYN

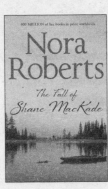

Nora Roberts
The Fall of Shane MacKade

THE CORRETTIS
Sins

CAROL MARINELLI
SARAH MORGAN

On sale 19th April   On sale 3rd May   On sale 3rd May

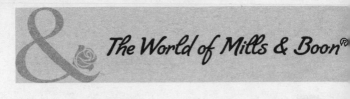
The World of Mills & Boon®

There's a Mills & Boon® series that's perfec
for you. We publish ten series and, with ne
titles every month, you never have to wait
long for your favourite to come along.

Blaze®

Scorching hot, sexy reads
4 new stories every month

By Request

*Relive the romance with
the best of the best*
9 new stories every month

Cherish™

*Romance to melt the
heart every time*
12 new stories every month

Desire™

*Passionate and dramatic
love stories*
8 new stories every month